Cover design and interior layout:
Angela K. Durden
Editor: Tom Whitfield

ISBN: 978-1-950729-12-8

THE CASE OF THE
SNUFF TAPE KILLERS
DURDEN KELL

978-1-950729-12-8
BLUEROOMBOOKS.COM
DECATUR, GEORGIA

DURDEN KELL

a SMITH & JONES
mystery

The Case of the
Snuff Tape Killers

Week One

Monday PM: Torture and death

"Only a bitch," the first male voice dripped contempt.

"Yeah. Aaahhh, man," said the second male voice. "That was great. Let's listen to the tape and see if we got it all."

"You better got it all," the first threatened. "The whole thing was perfect. We'll never find anyone as good again."

"Yeah, she was sweet."

Carmelita Oliveira pulled her car into the nearest parking lot and let it play from the beginning again. The second hearing was more horrifying than the first. Begging for her life was not the last indignity the woman suffered, but dying was her final pain and her sweet release.

Carmelita's stomach churned. She fought her way out of her seatbelt, braced herself on the rear bumper, and gulped cold air. When she knew she'd no longer throw up, she returned to her car, secured the discs in a zippered pocket inside her purse, and continued to the grocery store.

Who can tell from this when the woman died? After the kids left for school tomorrow she would call the Georgia Bureau of Investigation. She'll tell no one, not even her husband, Martin, who always freaked about the smallest things and only God knew what he would think or say or do if she told him about this. It was a safe bet he would forbid her to get involved. She would ignore him. They would argue. Yes, telling him would bring nothing but trouble and this dead woman depended on her.

Sickened and horrified, Carmelita operated on autopilot. She didn't remember shopping — but when she unloaded the groceries she had everything she needed on her kitchen island. Her kids got home — but she didn't ask about school.

Her husband arrived from work — but she didn't ask about his day. She served dinner — but heard no conversation. She watched television — but saw no images. She brushed her teeth, put on her pajamas, said goodnight to her children, and laid herself in bed — but she could not go to sleep.

The torture of this woman became her torture and the woman's death her death. Until she did her part in finding these men who thought they had the right to do these things, until she took action for this woman, she could not focus nor could she feel or live or breathe. Yes, she would handle this in the morning.

Tuesday AM: Hopeful Carmelita calls The Law

Frank Smith and Al Jones had heard all the jokes involving the words *alias* and *men in black*. It certainly didn't help matters any that Frank was white and wore cowboy boots and Al was black and wore dark sunglasses. The partners often used the resemblance to their advantage.

Unlike the movies, though, where the bad guy is usually some sort of genius who outsmarts The Law for a time, in real life bad guys are stupid and gullible. Often the only advantage The Law has is they're just watchful dogs who won't leave the bone of injustice alone until they get every last morsel of marrow out of it.

Ask enough broad, open-ended questions with just the right amount of slack-jawed, wide-eyed awe at the genius of the suspects sitting before them, and the bad guys feel as if they're in a movie script. Suspects always take opportunity to fill in the blanks of a script they believe they can control. Fake explanations, often clever, always include a kernel of truth. Frank and Al listen closely because in that kernel criminals never fail to seal their fate. Bad guys need to have their fates sealed — and Frank Smith and Al Jones very much want them to get what's due.

But things had been real quiet for some time. It was as if all the criminals were taking a vacation. Not that Frank wanted anyone to get hurt; he didn't. But he was trained to find bad guys; his frustration level was high when there wasn't one to chase. Frank hoped for a complicated case to come across his desk. So when Frank's phone rang this morning, he hoped this call wasn't another crank, but a sure-enough real case in the making.

"Agent Smith."

"Yes, sir. I'm not sure who I need to talk to," said a female, the very slight trace of a Southern accent coming through. "The receptionist said you could probably help. I've found something weird; don't think the local police can handle. Do I need to explain this to you?"

"What does it involve?" Frank asked.

"Hmmm…I believe it is what could rightly be called a snuff film only…" She paused to wait for his question.

"You mean a movie where it looks like someone gets killed for real?"

He did not try to keep the sarcasm out of his voice. He usually received at least one of these calls every month. This would make the second in two weeks. He always followed up, but each time the film was a badly written, cheaply staged cinematic effort by a budding filmmaker who couldn't keep up with his own footage.

"No, sir. Not a film. But audio. You see, on Monday, yesterday, I was shopping at Tuesday Morning when —"

He interrupted. "Wait. You were doing what, when, and where?"

"Shopping." She paused to let that sink in. "Monday, yesterday." She paused again. "At Tuesday Morning." Pause. "It's this great store where you can get things for the house and other neat stuff at a bargain."

He was impressed. She'd understood his sarcasm-heavy, three-part question, answered lucidly, and wasn't mad.

"Okay. Gotcha. Neat stuff. Go on."

"Okay. So, I saw this audiobook by John le Carré. A novelist, great stories. One of the discs has something on it. Very disturbing. I would like to bring it to you."

"Ya sure whatcha heard wasn't part of the story?"

"Yes, sir. More than sure," she replied.

Frank believed her. Maybe it was calling him sir. Maybe it was her respectful tone of voice. "Okay. Well. Let me get some information. What's your name?"

"Carmelita Oliveira." She spelled it.

"Where are you located?"

"Ellenwood. Why?"

"My partner and I could come get them tomorrow morning and make a report. Would that be convenient?" Frank usually offered to pick these things up. If the call was truly a crank, the person hung up and never told them where he lived. Like he couldn't trace the call, but problem solved, nonetheless. This respectful crank had a better idea.

"Agent Smith, I appreciate your willingness to come out here, I really do. But I don't want to be responsible for this stuff anymore. Can't I bring it to you, like…now? I can be there in an hour…that is, barring any accidents on 285."

Traffic on Atlanta's ring highway is legendary. Every day there is at least one auto flambé at morning rush hour and two in the evening's rush, two or three king-sized mattresses in the middle lane looking for love in all the wrong places, and three extension ladders straddling the two middle lanes — and those are just for starters. He had never had a civilian offer to bring him evidence.

"Uh. Sure. You need directions?"

She confirmed the GBI headquarters address. "I'll MapQuest the address. Besides, I think I know where it is. See you shortly." She hung up.

* * * * *

Traffic must have been good. True to her word, one hour later he received the call. When the elevator opened, Frank noticed a woman, medium height and build, late thirties to early forties, holding a paper sack as if it contained explosives, carrying an expensive black leather bag slung over one shoulder.

"Agent Smith?"

He held out his hand. "Yes. Mrs. Oliveira?"

"Yes, you're right, it is Mrs. Oliveira," she said, emphasizing the Mrs. "You can call me Carmelita. Do I give this to you here?"

Normally he would have said yes, taken the bag, and said goodbye. But when he saw her, he knew he wanted to know this woman, and he wanted her in his office.

You old dog, where did that thought come from, Frank? He shook his head and answered, "Not here. Let's go upstairs to my office." He led her to the elevators.

He covertly studied her stance in the highly polished elevator walls. He had never given any thought to the reflective nature of the inside of those boxes. But today, he wanted to thank the designer. She was taller than he had thought at first glance, but had a way of standing so her height was minimized, as if she was ashamed of it. Yet she seemed perfectly at ease, as if he was the visitor and she who belonged. The too-short ride ended and they were at the fourth floor.

"Here we are." Smith gestured *ladies first* and enjoyed the view as she stepped out and waited for him to lead the way down the hall. She followed to his office, sat the bag on the desk, but did not remove her hands from the top of it.

Here we go. Here comes the weird stuff. She won't let me see it. Shit. She seemed so normal. Frank waited for the weird stuff to begin. You never knew what shell a nut would come in and this was one hot shell.

"Okay, before I open the bag, let me tell you what's in it. The entire packaging, including the one with Genesis, the band not the Bible book. Also..." Carmelita opened her handbag and pulled out one typewritten sheet of paper, handing it to Frank as she finished. "I wrote down the information I thought you might need."

A quick glance showed him a concise report with every bit of information spelled out and perfectly organized. Where the purchase was made. A copy of the receipt. The order in which she listened to the recordings. Her contact information, cellphone number only, no landline.

He was impressed. She lifted the bag and placed it in front of him. *Okay, so maybe not a nut after all.* As he opened the bag to reach in, she grabbed his hands to stop him.

"What?"

Surprise at her action was followed immediately by a mental kick to his butt. He knew what she was going to say about such a newbie move. Even while kicking himself for that bit of idiocy, he was glad he did it because she touched him. He liked her touch and had a difficult time concentrating on her next words.

"Aren't you gonna wear gloves?"

She held his hands. He could feel her heat. He blinked twice, cleared his throat, and finally managed, "Uh, yeah. Sorry about that."

Frank felt like a silly little schoolboy who forgot to put on his rubber boots and raincoat before he went out in the rain. *Am I blushing? I am blushing.*

He pulled a pair of gloves from his briefcase. She nodded in approval. He felt proud of her approval.

What the hell?

He shook his head to clear his mind and refocus on the task at hand. He put on his gloves. As he reached in, Frank said with his best disarmingly contrite smile, "You know, I feel pretty stupid right about now."

Frank might be able to smile at such a time because he was used to dealing with crime, but Carmelita wasn't. She smiled distractedly as she pointed, indicating the disc in question. Frank wasn't about to put it into his computer in case there was a virus on it she didn't know about, so he pushed it into a portable player and hit play. For a full minute they listened to bits and pieces of words.

He raised his eyes to her. Without taking her eyes off the machine all she said was, "Be patient."

She had not looked at him but knew what he was thinking. Again he felt childish but didn't know why. Get it together, man, he silently chastised, then listened closely.

His patience was rewarded when he heard voices of two men and one woman, all of whom sounded young, though voices are not always indicators of age. Carmelita said she'd listened to it all and would know what was coming.

He saw tears fill her eyes, then her face harden as she steeled herself for hearing it again. Along with the tears and steel, though, there was hope. Hope that somehow this was all a big joke and that he, Agent Frank Smith, expert in all things bad, would pretty please prove her wrong.

A full fifteen minutes later he turned it off. Experience told him this wasn't a joke. It was real. Even he was sick.

He, an experienced field agent who had seen plenty of murdered and mangled bodies. A battle-hardened combat vet who had seen and heard death, and hell, had killed other men in battle up close and personal. Who knew violent death was never the neat, quiet, or quick process people thought it was as they watched movies. Who knew there was no glory in killing, had hated doing it even if it was the enemy he had to kill in the time-honored game of war.

But this?

This was not an honorable death. He had never heard the murder and torture of a true and innocent victim. He wondered how this woman in front of him had been able to handle this knowledge.

His admiration for her grew as he saw her deal with what most people would have run from. He ejected the disc.

Carmelita knew from Frank's expression her hope for a happy ending would go unfulfilled. Out of respect for the victim, for the full fifteen minutes she stood in place, ramrod straight, at attention as a man would when a fellow soldier's body bag passed by.

Hope was no longer in her eyes. Her tissue wiped at the tear tracks on her face. "It's real, isn't it?"

"Look. Uh. Look, I don't wanna say conclusively," he said. "I'll see if I can get the sound techs involved and some other agents to listen, too. See if they come to the same conclusion. Thank you for bringing this to me."

With his answer, she blew out a long breath, reached behind her and felt for a chair. She welcomed the reprieve. "You're welcome. I...I did not listen to the other discs, so, you know, I can't say whether or not anything is on them. I guess you'll have to listen. Except the first one I listened to. I thought it was an added bonus to the audiobook package. That was Genesis."

Frank raised his eyebrows. She explained. "You know, the band? I listened to it. All the way through. Didn't hear anything except their music but I'm sure you will want to check and make sure." She stood up, relieved this dead woman was now in good hands. "Well. Okay. I guess that's it. Thank you for seeing me. If you need anything else, you have my cell number." She drew a deep breath, straightened tensed shoulders, leaned toward him, put out her hand. He held out his, she shook it — one pump, a pause, release — and walked out.

He watched from his door as she walked the long hall toward the bank of elevators. *Damn.* This was one time he was happy his office was at the far end. Still watching, leaning against the doorjamb, he stepped over to his partner's office.

Damn, damn. Just damn.

Al looked up. Frank said, "My office." He looked back down the hall and watched as the elevator doors opened. Watched as she stepped in. He never blinked as she faced the opening. He stared at her as she punched the button. He held up his phone in a solemn goodbye after she gave a little wave and flashed him a slight smile. The doors slid shut. He didn't move. He didn't move because he couldn't. He could barely breathe. He simply stared at the elevator.

Damn.

"Hey, Smith," said Jones, staring at Frank. "Whatcha doing, bro? Hey!"

Jones snapped his fingers in front of his partner's face. That got Frank's attention. "What's up?"

Smith turned his attention to the other woman — the dead one. "We gotta case."

* * * * *

As soon as the elevator doors slid shut, Carmelita's knees almost buckled. She tried to convince herself her imminent collapse was the result of emotion from hearing the murder again. But she had to be truthful with herself — it wasn't the murder.

She knew she was having a purely physical reaction to Frank Smith. She could barely remember the last time her body had been that fired up. She knew nothing about him except his title and name, but if he asked her to run away with him, she would scream yes and jump in the car. This was not like her level-headed, calm, unromantic self at all.

Fighting the weakness in her knees and attempting, unsuccessfully, to ignore the tingling in her thighs, Carmelita eventually made it to her car. The short trip to the parking lot seemed to take forever, but the cold air cleared her brain.

She remembered his blush and smiled.

What the heck? What's going on with me? What was his blush about? Aww. So sweet.

Her phone vibrated when she turned the key. "Hello?" Martin's voice, a bucket of ice water on her heated thoughts, quickly doused the raging fire in her thighs.

"Where are you?" he whined. "I've been trying to reach you for an hour."

"Really? The phone hasn't rung once until just now," she told him. "Sorry. What's up?"

"Nothing. I couldn't find you, that's all," he said sullenly. "Where are you?"

"Running errands. You need anything while I am out?" Carmelita asked.

"I'm almost out of antacid."

"I'll pick some up. Okay? Okay. Bye. See you this evening," she said, gratefully hanging up.

She checked her phone. Her husband had called several times, yet she had never thought to check her phone. Well, how could she? Her attention had been on the murder. Until she did her duty to this dead woman, everything else was insignificant.

Tuesday PM: "Give me some men who are stouthearted men..."

For the third time Tuesday afternoon, Frank Smith and Al Jones listened to all the recordings. It didn't get any easier, yet nothing they heard did anything to dissuade them from believing this was a genuine murder. The other discs contained bits and pieces of voices. The two males were the same throughout, at least they thought so. Sound techs would attempt to confirm that.

Females' voices changed, though. This case was not going to be pretty and it would take a lot of time and effort to solve, even if it could be solved.

Already their notepads were filling with questions and comments. Two kills could be confirmed if what they heard was real. The sound techs would earn their pay on this one, for sure. The egos of the murderers would be their undoing.

"Whaddaya think?" said Alfred George Jones the Fourth. He didn't look like an Alfred. He didn't act like an Alfred. But he was the fourth to carry this name and his forebears were people he was proud to lay claim to. Still, Al suited his persona better. At thirty six, he was still unmarried, and his mama despaired there would never be an Alfred the Fifth.

"We're gonna have a helluva time tracking this down, that's what I think," Frank C. Smith the Third sighed. He wasn't proud of his ancestors though their antics provided myriads of tales many thought he made up and embellished with each telling. If they only knew the best stuff — which he kept to himself — they would think he was lying. "If she found the discs like she said she did —"

"You don't believe her?" Al asked.

Frank raised a hand. "Let me finish. So, if she found them like she said she did, then how did they get there?"

"Yeah. I can see the problem. That was one of my first thoughts, too," Al said, slapping his pen on the notepad.

"Let's get it down to The Lab and let 'em have a go at it." Smith placed everything back in the bag. "Wanna come?"

"No. I'm gonna call the store — Tuesday Morning, right? — and start asking some questions," Jones said as he walked out the door and down the hall.

He hollered back, "Hey, you know what we need, doncha? We need that lady's fingerprints so we can eliminate her. You wanna call her and get her back in here or you want me to?"

Frank hollered in his mind: Hell, no, you better not call her, I'll do it. But out loud he said in his best underling's voice, "I'll get right on it, bozz."

"Good man. I'll see if I can gitcha that raise you been a-wantin'," Al laughed as he turned the corner for the stairs.

Smith and Jones, for all the jokes, made a good team. While it is true they got the nut-job cases most of the time, they had a good record of solving those. Maybe it took a couple of nuts to understand nuts. Who knew? In any case, their records were good and their reputations excellent with every agency they worked with.

Smith went to his office dialing nine digits of Carmelita's number, but hung up before he pushed the tenth. He didn't want to call her quite yet. She was married and probably had kids. They'd be getting home from school right about now and she'd be preparing supper for her family. He'd wait until the morning and call her. Why didn't he want to call her now? He told himself he was being noble for not disturbing her family time.

Noble? What's noble got to do with solving a case? Nothing, that's what. You ain't never been noble with anybody ever before. What's the matter with you, boy? Face it — you got the hots for her, that's what.

A married women with kids, for God's sake. Okay. Maybe there weren't any kids. He would know tomorrow for sure. More than likely she had kids because she talked with authority in her voice only a mother can have. He heard that authority when she told him *be patient*. She said it the same way his mother had when he was a kid.

He was hot for a mom. Would wonders never cease?

When Al found out, and Al was going to find out, Frank knew he was going to be in for a bad case of kidding. But, yeah, it was worth it. Very much worth it. He couldn't figure out why he knew it — after all, what did he really know about this woman other than her title of Mrs. and her name? — but he was convinced she was worth whatever effort he had to put forth and whatever time he had to wait. Frank left his office a happy man. Two women now in his life, both of whom counted on him. He would and could spend time on them and be there for them. His smiled all the way home.

* * * * *

Carmelita arrived home five minutes before the kids' school bus pulled up at the corner. Today was the day they'd both have all homework assignments for the week.

Anne, her perfectionist, obsessive-compulsive daughter, would be freaking about getting it all done, completely convinced she would fail to complete her assignments within such a short period of time. To hear her tell it, the world would stop spinning if she was less than perfect. Anne was like her father.

Will, her son, was his sister's complete opposite. He would laugh at Anne then complete his week's homework in one evening so he could have his other evenings free. Will was like his mother — intense and organized, but in a laid-back kind of way. They knew the world would keep spinning no matter what.

Carmelita had five minutes to get her mind back on domestic matters, but she was having a tough time doing it. With a great act of will, she successfully faked interest in the kids and their day, and her husband and his day when he finally did arrive — late, and without calling.

When she put herself to bed that night, though, she couldn't sleep. Martin, upset at her tossing, said, "Good grief. I have work tomorrow. Can't you go somewhere else?"

She wasn't about to turn down that invitation. Making herself a cup of hot tea, she quietly made her way to the back porch swing, hugging a heavy blanket tight against the cold. She wrapped her hands around the hot mug and slowly sipped. She let the rhythm of the night songs steep into her soul. When she gasped, the night songs stopped filling the night with a momentary silence before they began again.

My fingerprints are all over it.

They would need to take her finger-prints so they could eliminate her. She finished her tea, returned to bed, and fell asleep a happy woman.

Wednesday AM: Fingerprints and the call of *Lurrrvvv*

When morning came and everyone left for work or school, Carmelita called Frank — Agent Smith, she reminded herself — but he was on the phone. She was leaving a message for him when her phone vibrated with an incoming call. She didn't recognize the number and finished leaving her voice message. When she hung up, she listened to the message.

"Mrs. Oliveira, this is Agent Smith. I failed to do two things yesterday and was wondering if you could come down and handle them. One: We need to get your fingerprints so we can eliminate them from the search. And two: I failed to do some paperwork on my end. I'll need your help with it. If you could please call me so we can set up a time to get these things done, I would...well, *we* would appreciate it. You have my number. Thank you."

His voice is very nice.

She saved the message.

Frank heard her voicemail greeting. As he left his message, his phone showed an incoming call, but he couldn't check who it was because he was leaving his message for Carmelita. He let it go to voicemail. After he hung up he checked his messages. There was a message from her.

"Agent Smith, this is Carmelita Oliveira. Late last night it dawned on me you may need my fingerprints for comparison purposes. If that's the case, please let me know. If I don't hear otherwise from you, I'll know these weren't needed. You have my number. Thank you."

He laughed out loud. *Damn.* He dialed her number again. This time she answered; she was laughing. He enjoyed the sound.

"Too funny. We were leaving each other messages at the same time about the same thing," she laughed out loud. "What a hoot! Well, I take it you need me to do this fingerprint thing. I assume time sensitive?"

"Yes, Mrs. Oliveira, it's time sensitive," he said through his laughter. "Would today be alright with you? Say, around ten-thirty this morning?"

"Absolutely. Of course. Same place?"

"Yes, ma'am. Same place. I'll meet you in the lobby, same time. No need to call up," he said.

"Alright. See you soon," she replied matter-of-factly.

"Yes," he said simply, and hung up. He hoped traffic was light today. Frank had not realized how long ninety minutes could be as they dragged on and on. He used his time wisely, but every other minute checked his watch.

Only 9:15! Will 10:30 ever get here?

He called The Lab and told them he was bringing someone in for fingerprinting around 10:30.

Only 9:20! Is this watch working properly?

He got the paperwork ready for her. When they returned to his office he would look like the prepared and professional field agent he was.

Only 9:30! Watch, wall clock, and computer all agree. One more hour.

He double-checked everything he would need for the interview so he wasn't rooting around his desk like a puppy looking for a long-lost buried bone. *Only 9:35! Shit.*

"Frank?" Jones said when his partner answered.

"Yeah," Frank drawled lazily in reply. He hid his eagerness from his partner.

"I have an appointment today with the people at Tuesday Morning to find out about their distribution and such. You want to go?" Al had plans for lunch at a tapas restaurant on that side of town. "Lunch at Noche afterwards. Yeah? Good for you?"

"No. Mrs. Oliveira is coming in for fingerprinting and then I have to do my interview paperwork with her I forgot yesterday, so...sorry," Frank said, though he would have liked the lunch. Al knew all the really great places.

"Okay. Too bad. I'll think about you when I'm having lunch. Not! Hey, you forgot to do the intake yesterday when she was here? My God, man, what were you thinking? Don't know if I'll be able to get you that raise after all," Al laughed and slammed the phone without a goodbye.

Only 9:40!

Frank rooted around his office for something else to take his mind off the clock. He thought of Al's phone habits. Al's slamming of the phone and not saying goodbye didn't mean he was mad. Al just slammed the phone. His phone manners were atrocious, just like his daddy, and granddaddy, and great-granddaddy before him who was the first to have a phone in his town. Al said it was genetic. Frank said it was learned behavior. They argued that fine point often. Frank threatened to call in the profilers. Al said he could do it, as long as he could ask the profilers some questions about some of Frank's habits. Frank never got around to making the call.

He found enough to do and kept busy until 10:15. Finally it was time to go to the lobby. As he walked to the elevator from his office, he was remembering watching her walk toward it yesterday. *Damn.* He arrived in the lobby at ten-twenty.

He was not going to make her wait. Not for him being late. No sir. He was a timely and helpful fellow. He wanted her to be proud of him.

Whoa. Where did that come from? My God, I have it bad.

The receptionist in the lobby interrupted his very private thoughts. "Hey, Frank. Whatcha doin'?"

"Aahhh, I'm waiting on somebody to take them to The Lab for fingerprinting," he drawled in what he hoped was an offhand manner, not the eager, young boy he felt like.

"Oh. A suspect?" she said.

"No. Someone we're eliminating, but not a suspect. Not at all!"

Now he did sound like an eager, young whipper-snapper. Sheesh.

"Okay. Whut…everrrr," she said in her best Valley Girl drone as she reached for the phone. "Didn't mean to pry." Switching to her professional law enforcement receptionist voice, she said, "Georgia Bureau of Investigation. How may I direct your call?"

The receptionist was on the phone; he didn't owe her an explanation. Besides, Carmelita had arrived. Not a particularly religious man, Frank felt a powerful need to give thanks to the Maker he had never acknowledged but now knew existed.

Lord God Almighty, I don't know your name, but please, allow me to thank you, Lord, for such attention to detail when you created such an exquisite creature. Amen and Amen!

Carmelita reminded Frank of a giraffe walking across the Serengeti, all grace, long legs, and fluid movement. Long hair blew across her face. He was rooted in place, right there, in the middle of the lobby, unable to move. She dragged the door open against the force of the strong wind. She jumped through before it could hit her. She straightened her hair, shook herself, checked her shoes, looked up and around. She spied him, smiled, and glided toward him. She held out her hand for shaking.

"Hello, Agent Smith."

"Good grief," he said, shaking his head to wake himself up, then shaking her hand. "I'm sorry. I didn't open the door for you."

Teasing him, she said, "I think I'll live. But if you feel very badly about it, I will allow you to open another door for me some other time. Okay?"

He teased back. "Let me know where and when."

They continued to smile at each other until finally she leaned forward a tiny bit and looked up at him. "Well, I guess we need to get this thing done, huh?"

There was that mama authority and there was that schoolboy feeling again.

"Yes. Follow me." He led the way toward The Lab in the basement. "I hope you don't mind, but we're gonna take the stairs. It's one floor down and is quicker."

"Perfect. More exercise for me."

Within five minutes they reached The Lab. She worried about explaining to Martin the ink stain on her fingers, but she needn't have worried. They had the newest digital scanner and before she could barely take it all in, they were done with her.

Wednesday: Lunch...and learn

Fingerprinting behind them, they took the elevator to the fourth floor to finalize the paperwork. The elevator did not stop at any other floor and no one else joined them. As they rose through the center of the building, they leaned against opposing walls and faced each other. They simply watched each other's eyes but did not speak. The silence was not uncomfortable. He didn't have to chat her up to fill an awkward silence. At the lighting of the second floor indicator, she smiled.

At the lighting of the third, he smiled.

At the fourth floor, they exited the elevator together and, stride matching stride, walked down the hall. Frank opened his office door for Carmelita. Her shoulder brushed his arm as she passed. Her vision clouded and she felt faint. He left the door open though what he really wanted to do was slam it, lock it, throw her up against it, kiss her slowly and thoroughly, and more, so much more.

She managed to lower herself into a seat across the desk from him, her back to the window. She carefully placed her purse on the floor beside her, each action designed to get herself under control. He methodically lowered himself into his seat, and just as methodically programmed his phone to go directly to voicemail so they wouldn't be disturbed. He pulled out his perfectly organized intake packet.

A half-hour later, his business voice intact, he straightened the papers and put them into the case file. "Well, that just about does it. I thank you very much for taking the time to do this."

"It was my pleasure. Of course, I wish I didn't have to do it. But since I had to, it was my pleasure to help The Law," she said, her emotions and physical responses now under control. She smiled at him again. She enjoyed teasing him. She knew he knew it, and he knew she knew he knew. They smiled more, enjoying the moment.

"Let me walk you down to the lobby," he offered. She did not decline.

This time the elevator was crowded and they happily squeezed into a corner. It was a tight fit, but they did not mind the lack of personal space one little bit as their shoulders touched in time to the rocking movements of the elevator. When the doors opened onto the lobby, they hung back and waited for the hungry lunch crowd to press past them and spill out. They were the last to walk off and again they exited together.

They walked slowly then stopped in the middle of the lobby. Frank rocked on his feet and crossed his arms. "Well. Thank you again, Mrs. Oliveira. I'm sorry you have to be involved in this sordid mess. But thanks for your cooperation and courage."

"What courage? All I did was turn in a package."

"Maybe not courage, then; thank you for caring enough for someone you didn't even know."

"Well, I will take that," she agreed.

They fell quiet and neither moved. With a slow smile and his best Gary Cooper drawl, he said, "Hey, listen. I don't normally do this, but since you are a good citizen and all and this has taken some time out of two of your days, why don't you let me take you to lunch as a way of saying thank you?"

He made the offer as if it was a last-minute thought when — truth be told, he wasn't a good liar even to himself

— he had practiced that line since last night. It took him a while to get the right offhand tone.

Her right hand flew to her mouth and her eyes widened in shock. "Oh!"

He backpedaled. "Listen, just a thought. Didn't mean to shock you or anything. Hope you don't think I was implying anything. Look, just forget I said anything."

"No. No. I'm not shocked. I...well, I... it's...well. I want lunch, yes, *please!* But I have to get home in time for the school bus. Need to leave by two. Will that work?"

Unable to speak, his nod declared that yes indeed it would work.

"Shall I follow you?" she asked.

Again he nodded. He finally managed, "Mexican? Sushi?"

"Sushi? You like sushi?" She almost drooled the words. Martin hated sushi.

"Love it. You?" he asked. She nodded happily in the affirmative. "Then sushi it is. Let's go."

Good sushi in Atlanta isn't hard to find, but in Decatur it isn't easy. Frank, though, knew the spot and had known it before Al did. A little place off the downtown square in Decatur called, oddly enough, Eddie's Money Pit. If you didn't know it was there, you would never find it, tucked as it was into an alley behind the old courthouse. Eddie was a Chinese dude raised in Reno, Nevada. His parents spoke Swedish and German. Neither had ever lived in China and did not speak Chinese, and only learned English when they finally came to America with Eddie when he was four.

Eddie had followed a girlfriend to Atlanta almost fifteen years ago. When she split, he decided to drown his sorrows in a huge plate of sashimi. The restaurant was for sale.

Naturally, he bought it, renamed it after himself and the bad financial decision he was now making with abandon, and the rest was history. The place was successful despite the name. Now pushing forty, married with four kids, he happily supplied his elite clientele — and by elite he meant those who could find him and then kept coming back — with the best in Atlanta.

"Hey, Smith. Where's Jones?" Eddie called out to Frank when they entered. Eddie cocked an eyebrow at Frank while extending a hand in greeting. "Hey. You ain't never brought a girl here before. Who's this?"

"I've brought girls here before," Frank objected, face reddened in embarrassment.

"Yeah. But all wear guns. They don't count," Eddie said. "Introductions, man!"

"Carmelita Oliveira, I'd like you to meet the sushi master, Eddie Clark. Eddie, meet Carmelita." Frank smiled at both as he said their names.

"Well. Finally. A girl. Where ya been hiding her, Frank?" Eddie asked, taking Carmelita's hand and leading her to a booth at the very back of the restaurant. Eddie didn't miss the wedding band and giant rock on her left hand.

"Get your mind out of the gutter, dude," Frank told him. "She's been helping with a case. I thought I would thank her with lunch."

"Okay, Frank. Whatever you say." Eddie winked at Carmelita. "So. What'll it be for you today? I assume you like sushi?"

"Well, actually, do you do sashimi instead? I don't like all the rice," Carmelita asked.

"Certainly. What is your pleasure?"

"Ahi tuna. Umm...let's see. Salmon. And...more Ahi, as a matter of fact. I love Ahi." Carmelita's eyes lit up in anticipation. "And water. With lemon."

"Same for me, Eddie," Frank said and sat in the booth across from her.

"Coming right up. May take a little while. Busy today with to-go orders. Some big embezzlement case at the courthouse. Love those days when the rich guys are on trial. Attorneys always spend lots of money on lunches," Eddie laughed, rubbing his hands together as he left the table.

"Sure. Hey, Eddie, she has to leave here by two o'clock, so don't drag your feet," Frank yelled at Eddie's back.

Eddie waved to let him know he heard.

"This place." Carmelita waved a hand around. "I never would've known it's here. It isn't on any online eatery lists."

"They don't even have a website. Eddie always knew the place would fail and he would lose his shirt so he never spent any money on advertising or marketing or none of that sh-- stuff," Frank said as he caught himself from being rude in front of her. "Now he has four kids and four college funds, and more business than he can take care of. Sooo —"

"If it's working, why mess with a good thing, right?" she finished his sentence.

"Exactly," he agreed. "So. Tell me. Where you from?"

"Born and raised right here in Georgia," she told him.

"Un. Be. Leave. Able. A native," he said. "Not many of you in Atlanta. Everyone I know came from somewhere else." Then he thought of Al. "Well, almost."

"Not me. Raised in South Georgia in a little town called Adrian. My grandfather was valedictorian of his high school class there in nineteen forty nine. His class had twelve people in it. My graduating class had forty. Not much more than his," she said. "And, no, I wasn't valedictorian."

"Me neither. How did you end up in Atlanta?" he asked.

"Well, same old story, I guess. Married and went where he went," she said with a small tight shrug. "You know. Nothing better to do…at the time? Seemed like a good idea…*at the time?*"

"Not really. I mean, yeah, I get the concept, but never been married," he said, pointing to his chest.

"Oh. Kids?" she asked. "Nowadays you never know."

"Nope. No kids either. Thank God," he said as he raised his eyes to heaven. Then he realized what he said, and tried to correct it. "What I mean is…it isn't that I don't —"

"I know what you meant. It isn't that you don't like kids, but you're glad you don't have them if you don't have the right woman with them, yes?" she asked.

"Exactly. I'm not looking to add to the gene pool just to say I've done so," Frank said, all the while not believing he was having this conversation. "I'm not that egotistical. Which isn't to say that, you know…one day…if…you know." Now it was his turn to shrug his shoulders.

"I know," she said. "I'm glad I had my kids early."

Oh, shit. She thinks I'm old.

"I guess it is getting a little late for me to have kids —"

"Frank, I wasn't implying —"

"Yeah, sure. I know. I'm just saying. One of the guys I work with is on his second marriage. She's a lot younger and wants kids. He has three in college now, but guess who's expecting any day now? He'll be seventy when that kid goes to college."

Thankfully, Eddie arrived with their plates and drinks. "Fast, huh? Just for you. Take your time eating and enjoy," he said, then chided Frank. "Don't wolf your lunch like you always do. Sake's on the house."

"Yessir. I'll go slow today. Thank you for looking after my health," Frank said as he looked at his plate, then hers. "Looks good, huh?"

"Yeah. I don't get this very often. This is a treat for me," she said, sliding the first bite into her mouth. He watched as she closed her eyes, cocked her head as if listening to the symphony of the tastes upon her tongue. She savored the flavors and as soon as she swallowed she opened her eyes. The expression on his face was not one a brother would give a sister, that's for sure.

Enjoying his gaze, she sighed softly, "Mmm...yummy. How's yours?"

"What?" Frank said.

"How's your lunch?" she repeated.

"Oh." He looked at his plate as if seeing it for the first time. "Ummm...I don't know. Better find out, huh?"

Frank took his time over lunch; Eddie was proud of him. But before they knew it, their time was up.

"Darn," she said, checking her watch. "I have to go."

They sat. He said nothing. She intensely searched for car keys and had a difficult time finding them in her large purse.

He finally heard the jangle and this time, with keys in hand, she said again, "I have to go."

His gaze was intent. "Yes. I know."

She nodded her head toward the door. "I have to...you know...go."

"Yeah." He dragged out the word.

"Well. Here I go. I'm going." But she didn't move. "Okay. I'm going now," she said, finally rising from the table. Frank rose with her...with obvious effort.

"Listen. Frank, this...lunch...this place... *this lunch* —"
Her breathing was shallow and quick as they stood a few
inches apart.

Eddie closely watched the scene from behind the bar. He
reached under the counter and pulled out two sheets of
paper and waited for the right moment.

She seemed at a loss. For a certainty, Frank was. Her
expression changed and when it did Frank's knees went
weak. He put a hand on the back of the booth for support.

She leaned toward him.

"You will never, ever know how much I enjoyed this
lunch." She spoke each word distinctly. "Never. Thank you,
Agent. Frank. Smith."

Eddie knew the time was right. "Carmelita," he called as
he sped toward her. "Come back as my guest. Here are two
coupons. I only give these to people I like and I like you. So
you come back, yes?"

Frank could have killed Eddie. Eddie could have been a
fly buzzing around her head for all Carmelita knew, but
then her eyes cleared and he came into focus. She smiled at
Eddie. She would be back.

Turning back to Frank and now under control, she held
out her hand. "Agent Smith. It's been a pleasure."

"Mrs. Oliveira." He slowly took her hand. "The pleasure
was all mine, Carmelita." As he released her hand he could
swear she pushed her middle finger into his palm and slid it
the length of his hand. He blinked to regain his focus so he
could watch her walk out.

When the door closed, he sat heavily into the booth. His
body was on fire and his brain almost shut down. He
reminded himself to breathe.

Eddie sat across from him in the booth. "You got it bad, dude." It wasn't a question. It was a bald statement of fact.

"Whatcha gonna do now?" Eddie asked.

Frank managed to focus on Eddie and shook his head. He had no fully formed ideas except one. He was going to solve this damn case if it was the very last thing he ever did. He paid the bill and called Jones on his way to his car.

Wednesday Late PM: Carmelita can't stop smiling

Carmelita was dumbfounded. All the way home she thought about their lunch. *I don't feel shameful. I feel...*

What did she feel? She arrived home ten minutes before the school bus arrived. She was in a very good mood. She remained in a good mood all evening. Martin frowned at her later when she walked through the living room.

"Why are you smiling?" he demanded.

She stopped mid-stride and turned to him. "I'm sorry. What?"

"Why are you smiling?" he asked again.

"I had a good day. Is that all right with you?" She stared in disbelief at his question. He didn't like her answer and didn't know what to say, so he turned to the television.

Carmelita continued on to the laundry room to do another load. Her smile returned in all its glory as she turned the corner out of his line of sight. She asked herself what was so good about her day that she couldn't stop smiling? She knew the answer, but pretended she didn't. Today, in the presence of Frank, she felt more alive — more like a woman — than at any time in her marriage. That thought, that reality, scared her. Still, with the specter of a changing life staring her in the face, she couldn't stop smiling. But she stopped thinking about it and threw all her energy into loading the washing machine.

Friday AM: Tweeter, Twitless, and word from The Lab

Friday morning Frank asked about Al's Tuesday Morning inquiries. "Okay, Jones. Whaddya find out?"

"First let me tell you what The Lab said," Al began. The Lab, the mysterious place where potions and fumes and microscopes and a hundred other things neither Frank nor Al could name, identify, or otherwise say what they were used for, was headed by Tweeter, not his given name. Tweeter — one of the few Georgia natives Frank knew besides Al and Carmelita — was a good ol' boy from the northwest part of the state, around the Calhoun area, where they tended to nickname their boys Tater, Gumlog, Snake, and Bubba, and tough professional football players were grown and tested on the hard, rocky soil. Tweeter was one of the more colorful names in his area, though he didn't play football.

When asked how he got his name, Tweeter laughed. When he was three he had his first little hard-on. His daddy and mama loved telling about how he ran into the living room bare naked and as proud as a coon dog treeing his oldest nemesis. "My tweeter got big! Ooooo!"

Yes, these are the stories from those parts upon which legends are built. Supposedly, his legend was worth that story, and that wasn't bar talk.

"Tweeter said the packaging had a price tag. I asked the store if those particular price tags are generated at their warehouse facility or further up the food chain. It is generated at the warehouse. That's where they sort through the remainders as they come in from various vendors and price them out," Al continued.

"I know what you're gonna ask. Hang tight." Al read his notes. "Tweeter also said the packaging was carefully disassembled so that it could be put back together. He also identified the glue used to reseal it. Whoever put it back together is committed to detail," Al explained. "The glue is unvulcanized rubber in a solvent. Readily available anywhere, what you would call rubber cement. Interesting point, the glue had some sort of, well, for lack of a better word, microscopic fiber things in it."

"Fiber things? I don't think 'fiber things' is listed anywhere in a forensic manual. Can you be more specific?" Frank asked.

"Yeah. But it's gonna to take some time. Depending, it could be a couple of weeks or so. They're kinda backed up down there and, besides, he may need to send it off for some sub-cellular investigation if he can't find it in his database. He'll let us know. Whatcha been working on?"

Frank had been busy building a fire under the sound tech's butt. He needed a transcript of the recordings and he needed it fast. He wanted to study the language used by each of the bad guys.

He also wanted to get a copy of the transcript and cleaned-up audio to the profilers so he could begin to understand who these guys were.

"Twitless has a new girlfriend and he seems to be spending his time texting her dirty messages instead doing what I needed, so I have been motivating his butt," Frank said as he stretched his back and rolled his neck. "He is driving me crazy. The boy is stone-cold horny and can't seem to get his mind on business."

Al shook his head slowly. "This younger generation. Can't understand them and their obsession with sex. You don't know what that's like, do you, Frank?"

"What's that supposed to mean?" Frank demanded.

"Hey. I ain't saying nothing, but —" Al jumped out of his chair and took off out the door, yelling back, "Eleanor!"

"Don't you say that name ever again. You hear me, you sumbitch?" Frank yelled back, laughing but scared, nonetheless.

Yeah. Eleanor. She may have been a natural blonde hottie who knew her way around a bed, God Almighty did she ever, but she was more than just a little bit touched. You knew somehow it would not be a good relationship when the woman stalks and terrorizes a GBI agent and the FBI gets involved because the GBI agent was only the last in a series of men across the nation who got her cruel attentions.

Frank only hoped by the time she got out of the "home" she was in and then did her Federal time, she would have forgotten why she was there in the first place. He knew he was doing his level best to forget his first — and he hoped last — stalker.

It was time to check on Twitless' progress on the transcript and cleaned-up audio. It seemed Frank's continued presence was not something the boy wanted to have anymore. By the time Frank reached the floor on which Sound was housed, the boy was coming down the hall with four packets in his hand.

"Agent Smith, I have what you need. These are identical packets. One for you. One for Agent Jones. One for your profilers. And one to keep in case somebody loses theirs," Twitless said, anxious to keep his free sexting time at a maximum. He really didn't want Frank back in his domain.

"Each packet has as clean a version of the audio as is technologically possible. There are CDs in each packet that include all the relevant sound from all five discs so that everyone can hear everything real-time as it was. There is also a transcript of the audio with indications and time markings. If anyone wants to listen to a particular portion, all they have to do is queue it to that segment and listen without running through everything. I also emailed all of this to you. They should be in your inbox. Save them to your hard drive."

With his last command and a roll of his eyes, Twitless turned around, his thumbs already thumping out his next masterpiece of porn to his girlfriend who by now, he was sure, was feeling thoroughly ignored, underappreciated, and ready to dump him. He had to salvage his relationship.

Frank thanked the retreating back and made his way to Jones' office.

"Here," he said as he dropped the packet on his desk, "this is for you. Don't say I never gave you nothing."

"Okay. What do we do now, bozz?"

"Already in touch with profilers at Quantico. I'll get this packet sent. Digital files, too," Frank said, staring at the floor. "Then we wait. Unless you got a better idea?"

"Nope. Can't think of anything," Al said. "Fingerprints aren't back yet, either."

"Alrighty, then," he said and returned to his office. After posting the packet and forwarding the files, Frank left for the weekend.

Saturday AM: Frank gets some advice. Al goes to Stone Mountain.

Al's plans for his weekend, Saturday at least, included a new girlfriend. She wanted to hike up Stone Mountain. He couldn't understand why anyone would want to walk up and down the world's largest piece of exposed granite, but he couldn't figure a way to get out of it. Friday evening he went to an urban outfitter and bought shoes and other clothes suitable for hiking.

Saturday morning, when his girlfriend saw his shoes and outfit, she smiled indulgently. She was wearing old sneakers and jeans and a windbreaker over a sweatshirt. No hiking gear for her.

"You've never been to Stone Mountain before, have you?" LaVonne teased him.

"I've driven by it. Why do you ask?" Al couldn't understand why what he had done   deserved any teasing.

"It's not that much of a hike. You look like you're dressed for the Himalayas." She shook her head.

Al didn't think this relationship was going to last. "Shall we get started?" he asked with polite terseness.

LaVonne seemed to float over the smooth boulders. She never got out of breath and was getting impatient with his progress, or rather lack of it. He couldn't catch his breath, his head felt light, and his muscles were twitching. The new hiking shoes seemed to weigh a ton. They finally made it to a small shelter halfway to the summit. He sat, legs and lungs grateful for the break, and wondered if he was ever going to be able to move again.

"I thought you GBI agent types had to be in good shape," she teased.

Al didn't have the energy to give her a dirty look or crack a joke. His breathing was still ragged.

"What will you do if you have to chase a bad guy?" LaVonne asked.

Al seriously considered going back down without saying another word.

"Are you ready to get started?"

Hell, Al thought, she's impatient. He was dying here and all she wanted was to get to the stinking top of this stinking rock. Living in Atlanta since he was five, he had never come to the landmark except once, and that was when he helped with a murder investigation when he was with the DeKalb County Sheriff's Department.

The victim had the forethought and courtesy to get done in at the bottom of the mountain. Al was never coming back here and if anyone suggested this type of fun again, he would murder them himself.

"Are you ready?" LaVonne stood.

He could take a hint. Al pushed himself up. This was as good a time as any to leave his body and go somewhere in his mind. Somewhere more fun than this. He thought about the Snuff Tape case.

For every step he took, he saw each piece of evidence anew and from every angle. For every breath he fought for, he heard each woman's battle for her life.

Before he knew it, they were at the top and LaVonne was impressed he made it so quickly. She looked at him like he was a hardbody, a stud even. Maybe he was being too hasty in kicking her to the curb. They bought popcorn and Slushies at outrageous park pricing, found a place to sit for a good view, refueled, and rested.

To his right, Al saw the Atlanta skyline. To his left, buzzards riding the currents. Straight ahead was the best sight of all: the cable car.

Stud or not, he was taking that down.

* * * * *

Frank didn't quite know what to do with himself when he woke up late Saturday morning. He walked to his favorite coffee shop, ChocoLaté, three blocks from his house. There he could easily put off having to make a to-do list. While enjoying the paper, his coffee, and a toasted bagel with a schmear, he heard, "Frank?"

"Oh, my goodness! It's you!" Frank was overjoyed to see Ruby. Ruby was now seventy five.

The last time he saw her was at the trial of her only living kidnapper, a kidnapper who was sorry he ever laid eyes on Ruby. She was sixty eight when she was kidnapped, seventy when the trial began, and seventy one when the sentencing was finalized. Each time the kidnapper saw her, he flinched and paled whiter than white. He couldn't wait to get to prison where he would be safer.

You wouldn't know she would be capable of killing anyone, but the woman was practical and did what she had to do when she had to do it. As she told Frank at the time, "It isn't my fault they were stupid and underesti-mated an old woman and left their guns where I could get at them. Stupid is as stupid does, right?"

Her children and grandchildren stood beside her in the court as proud as they could be when she gave her victim impact statement. They laughed about it later, because it was the kidnapper who had been the most impacted by Ruby.

This was a story which never made it to the papers or was even mentioned on the evening news, local or national, though a radio talk show host based in Atlanta with a national audience gave her props on his show. Little old ladies blowing away bad guys and not apologizing for it didn't play well with the gun control crowd, quite a few of whom worked for news outlets.

But, as Ruby said to Frank during a break in the trial, "I'm too old to feel guilty about what's not my fault."

"How are you?" Frank said. He stood to give this wonderful woman a bear hug.

"I'm good. Getting older and all that, but doing okay." She smiled and hugged him. "How about you?"

"Life is good," Frank began.

"Married yet?" Ruby's eyes twinkled the question.

"No. Not yet." Frank smiled.

"Hmmm. You say that like there's hope. Anybody special?"

A couple of months before her kidnapping, Ruby read in the newspaper about a GBI agent being stalked by a psychotic woman. For some reason she remembered his face from the article. When it was Frank who was the first on the scene, she formed an instant bond with him. She felt as if he understood her dilemma and her choices and the actions she had to take.

Ruby often said she wished for Frank to have a happiness like she had with her Charles. Frank thought of Carmelita. It had been only been two days since he last saw her, yet he felt as if torturous years had gone by. His mind — and his body, he had to admit — yearned for her. Could he tell Ruby? He concluded he could.

"Funny you should ask," Frank said as they sat.

"Really?" Ruby leaned in. "I want to know everything."

"Tall cappuccino with low-fat and two Splendas," the barista called out.

"Oh, that's mine," said Ruby as she went to rise.

Frank told her to sit. He got her coffee and set it down on the small table beside her. "Okay. Details," she said.

Frank told her everything. From the first phone call all the way to that wonderful, unforgettable lunch at Eddie's Money Pit. The fact that she was married and had kids. Everything he thought about the situation and everything he wished for it to be.

Ruby listened and didn't interrupt. Instead, she watched him. She saw his eyes light up. She saw the animation in his face. She saw the relaxed and happy set of his shoulders. She saw a man in love even if he did have a bit of a situation.

"Frank, she's married," Ruby said.

"Tell me something I don't know, Ruby." Frank slumped against his cushions.

"You've only met her those two times?"

"Yes, ma'am."

"And you have all these conclusions?"

"Yes, ma'am."

"Listen to me, dear. Are you listening?" Ruby said.

"Yes, ma'am."

"If she's the one, you must be honorable about everything you do with her. Are you sure she's a keeper?" Ruby asked.

"Yeah. She's a keeper."

"Then treat her like one. If her marriage is on the rocks, let it die when it needs to. Don't force it. Don't rush it. Your presence may give her hope and may spur her to do something more quickly than she would normally have done. But don't *you* dare force it. And, for goodness' sake, boy, don't give her husband any ammunition to use against her. Especially with custody issues at stake, though the kids are probably old enough that may not be a huge problem," she said, and wagged a finger. "You prepared for kids?"

"Last week I would have said no," Frank said, bemused at his change of mind.

"I see you have given it some thought," Ruby said.

"Yes. As a matter of fact, I have. I'm good with it," Frank assured her.

"Well, then. If it is to be, it will be. You may not know this but my Charlie is my second husband," Ruby told him.

"Really?" Frank never knew that.

"It's true. The same sort of thing happened with me and my first husband. My kids were teenagers. Things were bad but what could I do? Especially back then. Divorce was not a common thing. Especially if instigated by the wife. I had kids and no job and no prospects for one." Ruby's face showed the pain of looking back on that sad part of her life.

"I never entertained the idea of leaving my husband. Never! I never gave any thought to what was missing in my marriage and I wasn't looking for a replacement husband. But then...there was Charles," Ruby said simply, and smiled.

She continued, "Immediately, and I mean immediately upon meeting him, the full weight of what was missing in my marriage and what would never be hit me like a ton of cow manure and stank as bad. There was some drama with the divorce and all. But Charlie was a gentleman throughout the ordeal. Even with all the drama, the time it took to finalize everything, and other stuff, we were happy just knowing we would eventually be able to make happy lives for ourselves."

"What about the kids?" Frank asked.

"Ah. That's the surprising part. I am very fortunate to have children who are observant," she said. "As the years have gone on and they have seen how happy Charles and I are together, they love him dearly because he treats their mother quite well. Look, if you decide this is what you want to do, you better do the same for her, my boy; don't be stupid. Make those children love you because you adore their mother. Do you hear me?"

Ruby's stern look made Frank promise he wouldn't be stupid. They visited for another half-hour, Ruby hugged Frank and left, and he ordered another coffee. He contemplated how he was going to make Carmelita a happy woman. By the time he finished his coffee, his subtle, but hopefully effective, plan of action was in place.

Week Two

Monday AM: A few cotton fibers equal one big lead

On Monday morning, Smith and Jones rolled into the parking lot at the exact same time. Al had finished his weekend with another physical activity; he and LaVonne took a boat onto the Chattahoochee River and spent the day paddling and enjoying a picnic. Several of her friends joined them as their happy little procession explored the river. A couple of her friends were photographers and shutters snapped all day. All in all, it was good and Al very much enjoyed himself.

Frank had cleaned his house, bought a few groceries though snacks could hardly be described as groceries, had the oil changed in his car, and bought a few new ties, shirts, and two new suits. He even upgraded his shoes. Wingtips. Black. Very expensive.

Frank heard the wolf whistle from across the parking lot.

"What have you done with Frank?" Al asked Frank's doppelganger.

"Shut up. I just got a few new clothes. The others were wearing out."

"Yeah. What's her name?" Al asked. He knew his partner well.

"What are you talking about?"

"Don't give me that load of bullshit. What's. Her. Name?" Al asked pointedly.

"I don't want to talk about it," Frank said, hurrying across the parking lot though not denying anything.

"Aaghh, geez, Edith," Al crowed. "That means it's serious."

Frank always liked it when Al did his Archie Bunker imitation. But this morning it fell on deaf ears. Frank shot him a dirty look and Al's smile disappeared.

"It's really serious? Who is it?"

"I told you. I don't want to talk about it. Drop the subject," Frank warned with a hard stare.

"Okay."

Al had been around Frank plenty of times when a new girlfriend was on deck, and he never hesitated to talk about them immediately. Frank's unwillingness to talk about this one meant it was serious indeed. Al would find out when Frank was ready. He dropped the subject and they joined the elevator queue. They went to their offices without another word spoken.

The staff meeting ran long but finally they could get back to their desks to check emails and the status of ongoing cases. Later that morning, Frank saw Al.

"Hey, guess who I saw Saturday?"

"Who?"

"Ruby." Frank smiled at the name.

"Ruby! How is she?" Al loved Ruby, too. What wasn't to love? A woman who wasn't afraid to use a gun, who could blow away the bad guys, and then go home to bake the best red velvet cake and apple crumb pie in the whole state. Frank filled him in on Ruby's activities of late. It was nice to have a victim who was still alive and doing well after such gruesome events. They both smiled at her memory.

Frank's cell rang at 11:45. "Hello?... Okay. Be right down," he said and hung up. Then to Al, "It's Tweeter. He's got something for us."

Tweeter bounced around The Lab like a kid in a candy store. "What took ya so long?" he hollered but didn't wait for an answer. "You're gonna love this."

"Whatcha got there, Tweeter?" Al asked the bouncing back of the lab coat.

"Remember those fibers in the rubber cement?" Tweeter's eyebrows raised.

"Yeah. You were gonna do a search on it," Frank stated.

"Yep. Well, the fibers are in my database so I didn't have to send it off for analysis."

"Okay. What'd you find?" Al asked.

"Cotton fibers."

"From clothes?"

"No, from before they became clothes. These fibers only exist while the cotton is being carded, spun, and woven. These fibers only exist in a cotton mill and got out by being attached to someone who works in a cotton mill. They're so small, you wouldn't even notice they're there. They can burrow into crooks and nannies."

Tweeter laughed at the borrowed joke then went on, "I mean nooks and crannies in clothes, hair, nostrils, lungs, shoes, under fingernails. Either one of the victims or the perp who put this package together worked or works at or has access to a cotton mill or someone who works at a cotton mill. There are only seven of these in the state anymore that would have this level of microscopic cotton activity."

Al turned to Frank. "I call that a lead."

Frank nodded. "Anything else?"

"Yep," Tweeter said, "I got a hit on a fingerprint. Well, a partial, actually. Want the details?"

Frank cocked his head sideways and gave him a *what-do-you-think*.

"Thought so," said Tweeter. "I sent the report to both of you via email. You're gonna love it."

Smith and Jones knew that if Tweeter said something was good, then it was going to be good. They went to Frank's office. He logged on, printed out the PDF file, one for him and one for Al. When they got to the end of it, they each whistled long and low.

"Would you look at that," Al said.

"What are the odds?"

"A gabillion to one, that's what."

"Okay. Well, make your phone calls. Find out if he's in jail or prison or dead or missing. Once we know that, we'll have our next plan of action," Frank said.

"Okay. What are you gonna do?"

"I have some paperwork that's been dogging me, better get it done."

Al left, giving Frank opportunity to put his subtle plan in place.

With a few strokes he brought her name up on screen, hit call, and heard it ring. He knew it was a good time, kids not home yet, husband still at work. He only hoped she —

"Hello," Carmelita answered.

"Yes, Carmelita, this is ummmm...uh." Frank forgot his own name. "Uh, this is, ummm…GBI man...uhhh..."

There was a deafening silence following his stammer. His subtle plan bit the dust. He dropped his head into his free hand, pushing the phone ever more tightly to his ear, hoping to make the silence end on a positive note. He heard her giggle and he smiled; his subtle plan was back on track. Then she let loose. He could tell she moved the phone away from her mouth because she was laughing loudly, deep belly laughs, but the sound was far away.

By this time he was laughing loud, too. Eventually, she came back on the phone. "I am *so* sorry for laughing," she said through the tears of laughter. "I am so, so, so very sorry!" She got herself under control and said, "Hello, GBI Man. How are you?"

Frank liked the tone of her voice and it made him feel fine. "I'm fine. You?"

"I'm fine, too." She waited for him to tell her why he called. He didn't say anything. She prodded him. "So..."

"So...what?"

"Why are you calling, GBI Man?"

"Oh! Yeah. Sorry, I got distracted. Well, wanted to let you know we have a couple of leads and we'll be checking them out this week. I just...wanted...you know...t-to tell you. That's all." The stammer was back.

"Wonderful. I am happy to hear it. I assume my fingerprints didn't come back showing I was wanted or anything, right?" she laughed again.

"They were clean. You aren't wanted in any state. And Interpol cleared you, too," he teased.

"Hmmm. Well, it's nice to know I can prove I am an upstanding citizen."

"Yeah. That's very nice to know," he said, his tone now lower.

"Yeah. Right," she replied slowly, matching his tone.

"Okay. Alrighty then. Just wanted to keep you up to speed. Say," Frank said as if it was an afterthought though he knew it was part of his subtle plan, "whenever you come up to Eddie's Money Pit to use those coupons he gave you, let me know and, if it is where I can get away, my partner and I will meet you for lunch."

"Sounds like a plan."

"I mean it. Okay? I mean, I *really* mean it," he repeated.

"Yes. I know you do. I know you really, really do," she confirmed.

"Okay! Well, I'll talk to you another time then," he said. "Until then, okay?"

"Until then," she confirmed again.

With renewed vigor, Frank now turned to his paperwork. Fellow agents walking by his office didn't understand what they saw. When elbow-deep in paperwork, Frank was usually a growling, impatient, fuming bear, irritated with all interruptions.

But on this day they saw a man happily filling out forms, updating files, and in general, making great headway. They saw a smiling man sitting ramrod straight. As each file moved from the needed-to-be-finished to the done pile, he patted it as if to say good puppy, and reached for the next one with no break in between.

Monday AM: An assessment and an action plan

Contrary to what her name suggested, Carmelita Oliveira was not of Spanish or Portuguese descent. Her given name was one her mother read in a story long before she was born. That her married name synced up was simply coincidence. She met Martin when his company sent him to her small town to oversee a pipeline job. Martin was very good at what he did. He was unlike anyone she had ever known in her limited South Georgia experience.

Martin had been married once before, though only briefly, and no children came of it, thank goodness. The first time he walked into City Hall, where she worked answering the phone, he set his eyes upon her and never looked back. Within six months they were married. Within a year the job was finished and they moved to Atlanta. Within another, their Anna was born and Will joined them two years later.

Carmelita loved the big city, even if they were living in a suburb on the south side. Martin's job afforded her opportunity to be a stay-at-home mom, something she was proud she could be. And she did her job very well indeed. Volunteering at their schools and with the PTA, as well as being a room mother during her kids' elementary school days, brought back memories of her mother when she was in school. Home-cooked meals every day as well as freshly made, delicious snacks were her forte and her kids loved it.

Martin, though, was another matter; she wasn't quite sure what was wrong with him. Nothing she did ever pleased him, nor was anything ever good enough. His charm quickly turned to acid not long after they married. At first, Carmelita assumed she was in the wrong. After all, she was raised in a small town with limited access to the world. He was a world traveler who knew everybody and — seemingly — everything. His opinion carried great weight with her.

But now? Now she was tired of hearing it. His acid ate away at her soul until she had nothing else to give him. Respect for a husband had been ingrained in her from early childhood and she did her best to do what God wanted her to do.

"The Lord 'spects the man to be the head of his household and he 'spects the women to respect 'em,"

Reverend Bush said every time he gave his sermon on marriage. Carmelita heard it repeatedly.

When Reverend Bush died, the new pastor, Reverend Price, was a bit more enlightened. "The Lord expects the man to earn the respect of his wife and he expects the wife to be worthy of his efforts at earning it," he intoned every time he gave his sermon on marriage. These words were often heard at marriage ceremonies, too.

Carmelita believed those words. She lived by them. But a lot of good it did her. The more she became what Martin said he wanted, the unhappier with her he became. But doing less brought his anger, too.

Her soul was stripped bare. There was nothing left to give him. She stayed for the children. When Martin wanted sex, she gave him sex. What was a little bit of the giving of her body so her children could have a stable life? But they would soon be in college. A few more years and she could...what?

What skills did she have? None. Martin wanted a stay-at-home wife and Martin always got what Martin wanted. Who would hire her? No one, that's who. The only ones who would hire her wouldn't pay enough to support her. She should get a part-time job and start learning things. Martin would blow a gasket if she did. The question was: Did she care if he blew a gasket or not?

She thought about that as she cooked and cleaned and shopped and volunteered and started the whole process over again. Life threw her one little glimmer of hope and she began to think she could turn that glimmer into full-blown sunshine. Who knew it would take the death of one woman to save the life of another?

It was time for more sashimi.

* * * * *

By afternoon, several agents stopped by Al's office to find out what was going on with Frank. Al wasn't about to tell them he was in love; he played dumb and they went away shaking their heads. His phone rang. They had a case. He went by Frank's office and, sure enough, there was his friend with a bright smile and a finished pile.

"Guess you got the call, huh?" Al asked.

"Yep. You driving?" was all Frank said.

"Sure."

When they arrived at Al's car, Al couldn't hold back any longer. He said, "Hey, Frank, you know you may want to change out of your fancy clothes before we get to the scene or at least borrow some coveralls. Don't wanna get your new GQ clothes messed up."

"Ha. Ha," Frank said, climbing in. "Shut up and drive."

Monday PM: Another victim

The body was not fresh; decomp was extensive, but was fairly well preserved for forensic purposes. It was wrapped very well in plastic before it was buried next to the river in a deep grave that looked as if it may have been dug by a small backhoe. Criminals are lazy, but this was a new twist.

A small, private dam on a feeder stream gave way after one too many heavy winter rains. The flood of water washed hard and fast over the gravesite, effecting the woman's partial resurrection. The big hole in the side of the skull gave a good starting point for cause of death. Forensics would weigh in on this, then they would have something to work with. In the meantime, the area was scoured and every little bit of possible evidence was bagged and tagged by the Butts County Sheriff's Department. Frank and Al did not leave the crime scene until late into the night.

Someone stopped by a Krispy Kreme and brought several dozen assorted doughnuts and an equal amount of coffee. Frank picked out a sour cream doughnut and poured himself a cup. He and Al sat in the car taking a break and getting warm. Frank mumbled, "I guess I should be careful what I wish for."

"What do you mean by that?" Al said.

"A week ago I was feeling sorry for myself, bored, because I didn't have any cases. Now look. Two interesting ones have fallen in my lap. Not that I'm complaining."

He blew on his coffee to cool his next sip, and continued, "It could be a couple of weeks or more before we get anything back on this one. In the meantime, we really should be focusing on the Snuff Tape case."

"Hey, I like that name. Snuff Tape case. Yep, sums it up nicely." Al enjoyed the feel of the name of their case as it rolled off the tip of his tongue. He said it again, slowly, in between chews of jelly doughnut. "Snuff Tape case. STC."

"Please, no acronyms. I hate acronyms. I work for an acronym and I still hate them."

Frank was weary. He was looking forward to a long, hot shower much earlier in the evening. His shower head had the pulsating water blasts and at the end of a day like today, it did his body good to simply stand under it while the heat and pulsing rhythm of the water removed the stress.

The Case of the Snuff Tape Killers

By midnight they were on their way back to the office. Bone tired, they didn't talk much. But when Al dropped Frank at his car, he couldn't stand the suspense any longer.

"Hey, uh, Frank. Before you go, I really need to know. All the guys kept asking me what was up with you. You were doing paperwork and smiling and humming…"

Frank didn't believe it. "I was not humming."

"Jerry said you were humming. I told them I didn't know what they were talking about. But, man, you can't leave me out in the dark here. We're partners. You should tell me these things."

"None of your damn business."

"Ah, geez, Edith," Al said. "Don't leave a dude wondering. Come on."

"Nope. See you tomorrow." And with that Frank unlocked his vehicle, climbed in, and drove home to his shower and thoughts of his future.

Tuesday AM: Seafood and a tip from Boggle's mama

The fingerprint lead Tweeter gave Al and Frank was of a man they both knew well even though they never met him. His street name was Boggle, after the popular word game where adjacent letters joined to form words. He spelled out words when he was nervous. It was a compulsion and he couldn't help it. His legal name, however, was more mundane — Chip Jason Johnson, hometown Lavonia, Georgia, a little town in the northeastern part of the state. His name was always coming up as a known associate of bad guys. Every time things got hot for him in the big city, he would crawl home to Mama, crying about how the big, bad po-po was a-picking on him again.

Mama knew better, but he was her only son and she didn't want to lose him, even if he did take after that no-good dead daddy of his. Besides, when he came home, he was ready to do something good for her and by the time he left, her roof would be patched, the leaky plumbing secured, and the grass mowed, sometimes twice if he needed to go to ground long enough.

Mama never asked Chip for any details of his life or what brought him home. She didn't want to know.

By now, though, Al and Frank were ready to ask him for some of those details.

"I think it is time we went to see Chip's mama. You ready for a road trip, Al?" Frank said.

"You know I am. I figure we can have lunch at Stringers on the way up. Sound good to you?" Al asked.

Stringers was an all-you-can-eat seafood restaurant on I-85 North, barely off the highway at the Commerce exit. It was stuck between a Pottery Barn and three outlet malls but the seafood couldn't have been any better if they were sitting on the dock of the bay eating fresh off the boat. The owner, William, was a genteel Southern white boy whose daddy let him play with the family money all he wanted. And Bill had the touch. "Deddy" was smart in giving him a free hand with it and the family pot grew exponentially. This was not his only successful business, but it was the one he liked best.

But Deddy wouldn't let William marry his soulmate because "she isn't our kind, son". There was always a level of sadness in his eyes even as he smiled and joked and otherwise took care of his loyal diners.

Al learned all this one day when he happened to show up right at closing time. William pulled up a chair and a beer and Al was there for another three hours slowly eating boiled shrimp, drinking wine, and listening to tales about Deddy. They remained friends ever since.

"Hell, yeah. Stringers. Let's go," Frank said. "I'm driving."

The trip to Lavonia was a little more than two hours. Stringers was only an hour and fifteen away; they timed their arrival at the restaurant before the huge lunch crowds, hungry from shopping at the outlet malls, came pouring in off the tour buses.

"Hello, Al. I'll be with you in a sec. Pick a spot," William called as they entered.

They left an hour later, stuffed to the gills as usual. William never failed to load them up with extra portions of everything including the tangiest slaw in the whole of the Southeast and hush puppies so moist they melted in your mouth. Before they got two miles down the road, Frank and Al loosened their belts to ease the pain.

They finally made it to Lavonia. When they arrived at Mama's house, they could see it had been a while since Boggle had been around. The grass was as high as the nose on a lead bird dog sniffing the wind. They knew that because Mama's bird dog came running through the grass, nose in the air toward them, and other than his nose and tail, that's all they saw of him until he got to the car. After buckling their belts with difficulty and opening their doors, they heard Mama's screen door opening and there she stood.

Mama had once been beautiful and could still be if she ever cared to do something about her hair and nails and clothes and skin and attitude. But she wasn't very motivated to do anything about how she looked. What was the point? The only thing she ever got for her efforts at looking nice and being vivacious was her only child and trouble with a capital T. She knew Chip was his daddy's son through and through. She had no hope he would ever turn out right, so she never tried to steer the boy in any direction. As far as she was concerned, his die had been cast.

She had not been proven wrong — even if it did pain her to have to admit it. And here was more proof at her door.

She watched as they slowly climbed out of their car. They seemed to be in pain, like all the lawmen who came around. As they walked to her door she watched them adjusting their belts. They stepped up on the porch. Before they could say a word, she mumbled for them to come in and led the way into a dark living room so devoid of color a picture of it would lead you to believe the photographer had taken a black-and-white.

"Whuzzeedun now?" Mama asked, resigned to hearing bad news.

"How you doing, Mrs. Johnson?" Frank asked.

"Whuddaya care?" she asked, not unkindly, as she sat back and sipped her coffee. She did not offer them any. Not that they minded. Neither of them had room for another bit of food or drink.

"Do you know where Chip is?" Al asked, looking around the room.

"No. Whuzzeedun?"

"Nothing we know of. His name came up as maybe being a witness in a case. That's all," Frank assured her.

Mama snorted her disbelief. "Ri-i-ight. Whuzzeedun?"

"Nothing. Just like Agent Smith told ya, maybe he can help catch a really bad guy. Could go a long way for him the next time he gets caught doing something stupid, you know what I mean?" Al hinted.

Mama studied their faces intently.

"You lyin' to me?" she said.

"No, ma'am," Frank assured her with a straight face. Al nodded in the affirmative with a face to equal his partner's.

"He's not a bad boy. Not really," she tried to convince them. After all, hope springs eternal in the heart of a mother. "He could use a break."

She contemplated her options. With a nod to indicate she made up her mind, she lifted her head. "He's staying with a friend in Athens, near the college."

"Do you know the friend's name?"

"Nope. But I have a phone number for where he's at," she said as she reached for her phone. She scrolled through the Caller ID listings and found it. Didn't take long — she didn't receive too many phone calls.

"Here it is," she said and handed them the phone so they could see for themselves. Al wrote it down.

"Thank you very much, Mrs. Johnson," Frank said.

They rose and left the faded house, leaving the faded woman sitting on the faded sofa. She knew they were lying to her. She always suspected her son was in deep.

She knew he needed catching — it was for his own good and wouldn't call her boy to say they were coming. Once in the car, belts loosened again to ease full stomachs, tires kicked up dried mud clods from the dirt road.

"I wonder if Mama'll warn Boggle about our visit?" Frank asked.

"I don't think so. I gotta feelin' she knew we were lyin' to her. She'd rather see him caught, for his own good."

"Let's hope so. See if you can get an address to go with the number."

Their road trip just got longer.

Tuesday PM: Frank 0, *Lurrrrv* 1.

Athens, Georgia, a well-known college town, is still a small town with small town sensibilities. They don't take kindly to criminals of any sort. It's home to the University of Georgia and their bulldog mascot Uga, played through the years by a series of some of the ugliest but most beloved mascots a college team ever had. By the time they reached the Georgia Guidestones near Elberton, Al had an address and directions. Driving the back roads between Lavonia and Athens, it didn't take but an hour — by cop time, that is — to reach the outskirts, and another fifteen to find Boggle's place, a rundown house that, in a previous life, had been the chic residence of a long-past nabob of the university but was now a legal squat for those living on the fringe.

No one was home. "Now what?" Al said. "Hey, I know a great little place…"

"How can you eat again?" Frank was astonished at how Al could pack it away.

"It's not hard," Al said. "You know my metabolism's fast. I'm hungry."

"Good grief." Frank rolled his eyes as he climbed in the car. "Where do I go?"

It didn't take them long to make their way to Backwoods, a bar and restaurant-slash-grill. After Stringers, it had the best boiled shrimp anywhere in the Southeast.

Even though he recently stuffed his face with shrimp, Al enjoyed a bucket of peel-and-eat — each piece dipped in clarified butter kept perfectly liquid on its own warmer — while Frank nursed a coffee.

Al couldn't talk with his mouth full, but Frank didn't mind. He wasn't in much of a talkative mood anyway. Every time he concentrated on this case, Carmelita's smiling face at lunch — or rather the memory of her walking away from him — intruded and took precedence.

Al interrupted. "Frank. I've been thinking about the snuff tape. Have you heard back from the profilers yet?"

Frank shook his head.

"Do you think we should have someone look at the transcript to see if there are any hints in the word choice indicating where these guys are from?"

"I think that Southern drawl of theirs gives it away."

"Well...there is that," Al conceded.

"Besides, the profilers will be doing all that. It is obvious we have a serial killer team going on here. I wouldn't be surprised if this case isn't taken away from us. These guys have probably crossed state lines."

Al dipped another shrimp, licking the butter from his fingers. "What's her name, Smith?" Al asked, popping it in his mouth and peeling another jumbo.

"None of your damn business, Jones," Frank growled.

"We're partners. We don't have any secrets..." Al began.

"Jones..." Frank warned.

"Okay. I'm just saying I should know what is going on with you, that's all. It seems to me..."

"I don't care what it seems to you. I'm not saying." Frank finished the conversation for him, or tried to.

"Okay. Then would you care to share some thoughts on the case?" Sucking butter from his fingers, Al asked as sweetly as a church choir matron.

Frank ignored him, studiously sipping his coffee.

To anyone watching, it may have seemed as if Al was a shrimp-scarfing machine with no other thought in the world except dipping the next jumbo. But Al was hiding his worry. He had never seen Frank unwilling to share details about a woman. It could only mean Frank was more than serious. Aha! There was a huge problem involved with her. But what was it? What it was hit him square between the eyes — she was married.

Al couldn't let it go. He must know the details. "She's married, ain't she?"

"I said *let it go*."

But Al knew his partner and Al had hit the nail on the head. What was Frank letting himself in for? Grief. Nothing but grief. The next statement flew out of Al's mouth before he could stop it.

"She has kids, too, huh?"

Frank didn't answer but avoided his partner's gaze.

One by one, the bucket emptied as Al methodically peeled. Just as methodically, his mind — razor sharp as ever when confronted with a mystery — mulled the facts. Yet again his intuition, coupled with his keen ability to put together disjointed facts to form a clear picture, did not fail.

His partner's mystery was now clear. "It's that lady who brought in the snuff tape, isn't it?"

Yet again, Frank did not answer Al; he didn't need to. Sagging shoulders told him everything he needed to know.

"Man. I'm sorry." Al peeled another shrimp and stuffed his mouth to keep from talking about Frank's situation.

Al changed the subject. "Hey, you know that body down in Butts County? I'm wondering if our serial killer team might be involved. It wouldn't hurt to find out if there are any cotton fibers on it."

Frank nodded.

"And I'm also thinking we should listen to those recordings again, but this time let's see if we can figure out what sort of injuries they are and in what order they're made. We don't have a body; we've got pretty good audio. It should give us some clues. Then we can compare it to the body in Butts County."

Frank nodded.

"We can start tomorrow morning?"

Frank nodded again.

Wednesday AM: Connecting cotton fibers

The next morning, before Al and he listened to the recordings again, Frank contacted GCC, the Georgia Cotton Commission, and made an appointment. He told Charles Butts, president, about the cotton fiber connection to a murder case. Charles promised to have a list of textile mills in the state and his research team available the next day to answer any questions or provide any help needed.

A murder mystery. Charles couldn't wait to tell his Stella. The next day couldn't come soon enough.

* * * * *

The appointment made with GCC for the following day, Frank and Al spent the next three hours behind closed doors listening to the audio on the computer.

"Man, these are sick dudes," Al said.

Frank stopped the audio. "I need a break." He went to the bathroom, washed his hands, and splashed cold water on his face, stared at himself in the mirror, and thought of Carmelita.

What are you thinking of doing, Frank? You are acting like a teenage boy in love, making plans for forever. You've never made plans for forever. You are obsessing about someone you have no idea is willing to change her life, leave her husband, or marry you. Marry? Stop obsessing. Marry.

He smiled. Couldn't stop thinking of her. Maybe a cup of coffee would help. He got one and took a leisurely stroll outside to clear his head. On his way back in, he called Al from his cellphone. "You ready to get back at it?"

Al was already in Frank's office when he arrived. They finished their list, sent it to the Butts County coroner asking him to compare their list to the nature of the wounds and the order in which they happened on the body from the river.

Thursday AM: Cotton research and Mary Mac's for lunch

Thursday morning, Frank and Al took surface streets to the downtown Atlanta office of the Georgia Cotton Commission to meet with the president and research staff. Per his usual, Al identified a lunch spot for on the way back. Mary Mac's Tea Room would be graced with the GBI's presence.

Frank hated parking decks, and always chose surface street parking lots. He did so again this day even when it meant they had to walk farther to get to the GCC's offices. Three urban outdoorsmen smelled cop and scooted out of sight, but one was bold — or too weak or too high — and never moved from his spot. They took the elevator to the seventeenth floor. Charles himself greeted them as they arrived.

"Right on time, gentlemen. I'm Charles Butts. We're very excited to have you here. Everyone is waiting," he said, as hands were shaken all around.

Although he tried, his excitement could not be hidden. Charles' bouncing steps belied his professional exterior. There was no disguising the timbre of his voice, either, as he addressed his waiting staff. "These are Agents Frank Smith and Al Jones."

"Hey, Smith and Jones. Cool," said a young man from the back of the room who then added, "Where's the boots and shades?" Everyone laughed, including Frank and Al right along with them.

"Have a seat, gentlemen. Here you go. Yes, this one's for you, Agent Smith. And Agent Jones, right here. Okay, staff, I'm going to let the agents tell you the facts and let's see if we can't help them solve this murder mystery."

As Charles moved to a seat at the back of the room, all eyes turned to Frank.

"Evidence of a crime was included in a retail item," said Frank. "It was rewrapped in the original packaging. It was resealed using rubber cement. When we looked at the rubber cement, we found embedded in it small fibers. Our lab identified those as cotton fibers — not from clothes but raw, before it was processed with any chemicals. What can you tell us about where these fibers could be found?"

Frank sat back in his chair.

Al's pen was poised to take notes.

The room was silent. Not because no one understood his question, but because each was thinking of the life cycle of a cotton fiber.

"Is there any way we could get a few samples of the fibers and run our own tests?" The questioner was an older gentleman who looked as if he had once been a cotton boll.

"Why do you ask?"

"In a textile mill, fibers are released at every stage, yet they change based upon the stage they're released. For instance, a fiber is different in the spinning stage than in the carding or weaving stages. If we could see them, we might be able to definitively answer the question. We've been giving it some thought since yesterday. If your killers work in the plant, for the most part they're gonna stay in their area. That information may help identify the department your killer is in."

The Case of the Snuff Tape Killers

Then a young woman said, "But you have management types who move from department to department and there are those whose duties overlap and are in various departments."

The agents had not thought of that.

"I'll send over a sample by tomorrow," Al said. "How long before you will have an answer, do you think?"

"Ah, it shouldn't be too long," said the older gentleman. "Maybe a day or so. Work for you?"

"Perfect."

"Okay. Don't send one little sample. Send as much as you can. If there are differences in them we can also tell you if this person stays in one department or moves around from department to department."

"We'll get with The Lab and see how much we can send to you. May not be much."

Frank took up the questioning. "Can you identify the individual processing plant the fiber came from?"

Excited discussion ensued. Frank and Al could tell this was a ongoing conversation from the previous day. Fifteen minutes passed during which Frank and Al simply listened, not understanding anything they heard. The debate finally ended, the group turned toward the agents. The older gentlemen spoke.

"Some say yes. Some no. We're willing to give it a try. Can't promise anything. Gonna take much longer to answer."

"How long?" Frank asked.

Heads swiveled, eyebrows raised, and fingers were held up. "Three weeks minimum. Is that a problem?"

"Absolutely not," Al said. "Is there anything we can do to help you get what you need to conduct those tests?"

"Yes," Charles spoke for the second time in the meeting. "We have to be at the plants anyway during the next week, so we can get what we need. But if it's gonna be used as evidence, we may not know the best way to collect it. What should we do?"

Six sets of eager eyes turned.

"Excellent question," Al said as Frank pulled out his cell and called The Lab. "We'll have a technician meet each of you at the plants you'll be going to. The tech can do the collecting."

Within two hours, each possible fiber-source manufacturing plant was identified, and collection dates set for GBI techs to meet the research staff were assigned.

Their work completed, Frank and Al shook hands all around and left for Mary Mac's Tea Room, a short mile-and-a-half away. The tea room's name came about in 1945, the offshoot of Georgia women being forbidden by law to open a restaurant. But they could open a tea room. When Mary McKinsey needed to earn money in post-war Atlanta, she didn't argue with semantics. She did what she wanted to do — and let the men call it what they wanted.

At that time, trolley cars clanked up and down Ponce de Leon Avenue in front of her establishment. Down the street, the Fox Theatre was one of many now-forgotten ornate movie theaters. Margaret Lupo bought Mary Mac's in 1964, and sold it to John Ferrell in 1994.

She retired in confidence, for her beloved restaurant was now in good, strong, caring hands.

The Atlanta icon was still going strong and lunch was, as usual, delicious. No one could cook comfort food like Mary Mac's, and Frank needed comfort today. He dove right into his macaroni and cheese, mashed potatoes, and fried green tomatoes served alongside country-fried steak with gravy. If he couldn't talk to or hold the woman he wanted, at least he could soothe his soul with this glorious combination of tastes and textures he never knew existed until he moved to the South.

They made it back to the office around four — in time to check voicemail and return a couple of priority calls before calling it a day. Frank's heart almost stopped when he heard the fifth message.

"Good morning, Agent. Frank. Smith. Or is it GBI Man?"

He smiled when he heard what he now knew was Carmelita's nickname for him. He heard the smile in her voice as well as the flirty teasing. He liked it — a lot.

"This is Carmelita Oliveira. I am ready for Eddie's sashimi and will be going one day. You did say to call to see if you and your partner might be able to join me. So…I haven't picked a day yet. We might could confer by phone? You know my number."

There was a long pause during which Frank held his breath. He didn't want to miss her voice as it became softer.

"Well…um…goodbye," she whispered.

He saved the message. He replayed it twice. He didn't understand what was happening. What was it about *this* woman that got his attention? She was beautiful, but he had known many beautiful women, none of whom had him thinking marriage. Why was he already thinking marriage about this one? She would not settle for less, that's for sure, though she said nothing to force his hand.

How could he win her? She deserved the honor of a true commitment. When had he changed his mind? He didn't know, but his commitment to her was already made.

Who am I?

The Case of the Snuff Tape Killers

He thought long and hard. Maybe she was the one who would help define him. Where would they go from here? Only time would tell — and she was the timekeeper.

* * * * *

Carmelita called hoping to talk to Frank. There was no return call that entire day. She kept her cell on her, turned to vibrate for incoming calls. But other than a friend inviting her to a luncheon in a couple of weeks, she felt nothing. He was busy. There were crimes to solve, after all. She knew these things logically. But after finally screwing up courage to make the call, disappointment grew with each hour.

She often pulled the phone out of her pocket to see if maybe he had called, but somehow missed it as she carried the laundry basket, began preparations for supper, or did any of the other chores that kept her household humming.

The phone's screen showed the same thing each and every time — her children's picture, the date, the time, and her carrier's logo. She was torturing herself and she knew it. But it felt good to feel, even if it was a hurt to her heart.

The evening ended and still no connection made. She slept fitfully.

When Martin complained he couldn't sleep because she couldn't be still, she moved to the sofa. Wrapped in her grandmother's afghan, her head propped on the sofa's low armrest, sleep finally came, but it was a hard-fought battle because her mind would not shut down.

One thought kept her awake: She was pursuing this man, yet felt no guilt. Some might call it betrayal of marriage vows. She took those vows before God and her congregation and she meant every word when she made them. So why did it seem easy for her to give thought to another man in her life now?

Martin made vows, too. He vowed to love and honor her and yet did he ever do those things? He had not. And then there were all those other things she wondered about him. Who broke whose vows first?

It didn't make her feel any better about her actions even if there was no guilt.

It was that lack of guilt which bothered her more than anything else. That lack baffled her and because she couldn't figure it out, she was annoyed. And because she hated to be annoyed, she stopped thinking about it, convincing herself time would tell what was best. She went to sleep.

Thursday PM: Frank reviews Frank's situation frankly

Frank didn't want to call her that late in the day. Her children would be home and maybe her husband. Frank had already formed his opinion about that man. He didn't believe her husband was worthy of being called husband. Though Carmelita said nothing about it, Frank could tell her husband obviously missed the essence of the woman to whom he was married. He also guessed he probably took her for granted and did not view her as a partner. It pained him to see her eyes sad, even if she was smiling.

Frank also knew the ways of the world. He had seen it before. During the years he had known three married women. As he got to know their situations, he found out each of the three husbands not only treated their wives badly, they were cheating on them, too. The men drove them into his arms.

Frank treated them well even as he told them he wouldn't marry them. But they didn't care. They only needed a warm body to hold to get them through their current darkness. They only needed someone to smile as if they were missed. And they only needed someone to look at them with eyes showing some — hell, any — interest.

He was interested in them, for a while, and looked at them with interest, and he did it well. They were sadly happy — or was it happily sad, he never did figure that out — about his attentions. But there came a time when he could no longer do that for a married woman. He didn't feel good about it and couldn't explain why. No more married women was his vow, and he kept that vow for years.

Until this one.

This one was different from all the others. For this one he would change his life. At their first lunch, he removed some sadness from Carmelita's eyes for a short time. He knew it would return later, but he promised himself he would take it out each time he saw her until such time as her sadness never reappeared.

He texted:

Been gone all day. Just got your message. Will call in the morning.

Friday AM: Following destiny's lead to GBI Man

The next morning Carmelita woke well before the alarm sounded. She felt drugged, but knew the hangover was the drug of love lost. The coffee grinder screamed in the early morning light.

"Damn." Martin walked into the kitchen. "Isn't it a little early for all that noise?"

"Oh, I'm sorry. What time is it?" she said, smiling innocently and talking above the noise. "It's almost finished. There." She pulled the tray out of the grinder and held the coffee to her husband's nose. "Smells nice, huh?"

Martin turned on his heel and stomped back down the hall to the bedroom. *What is going on with that woman?*

His usually quiet, calm, obedient wife lately wasn't quiet, wasn't calm, and certainly wasn't as quickly obedient. He couldn't put his finger on it, but chalked it up to hormones, and climbed back in the bed for thirty more minutes of sleep — uninterrupted, he hoped. He would have to have a talk with her if this kept up.

In the meantime, Carmelita felt only a little bit ashamed of her little game, yet was still delighted she injected some commotion into her husband's well-ordered day. While cooking breakfast, she remembered her phone. Why get it when all it would show was nothing? But she walked to her purse anyway. What better way to start the day than with a little self-torture?

Her screen showed a text message arrived. Was it from Frank? She waited to check it, but surely it was from him. Yes? Maybe? Still, she hummed as she woke the kids and called everyone to breakfast. She continued to hum while waving goodbye to each member of her household.

Finally, privacy. She read the text.

Been gone all day. Just got your message. Will call in the morning.

The state of her heart, a few short minutes ago dark and despairing, turned one hundred and eighty degrees, and was now happiness and light.

Excellent, she replied and waited in anticipation for her phone to ring. She was not to be disappointed.

"Good morning," Frank said without identifying himself.

"Good morning to you, too, GBI Man," she replied.

"I understand it's time for Eddie's again."

"Yes. It is definitely time for Eddie's. Sooo —"

"How about today? Al and I are waiting for information on another case. My paperwork's caught up. As good a time as any for me. Say twelve?"

"Perfect. See you then." She hung up, then immediately worried. *What should I wear?*

Her frenzied search for the perfect date outfit began immediately. *Date?*

She shocked herself by calling this lunch a date, but that was the truth and she knew it. She didn't feel any guilt about what she was doing, so she might as well call it what it was. She was not going to fib to herself.

Her closet and all drawers emptied as she pulled and rejected, put together and flung apart.

Would she ever get an outfit together?

Damn.

Damn.

Then *crap-damn* rang through the house as the reject pile grew. She hadn't realized how many mommy outfits she owned. Well, mommy has its place, but today wasn't it. Today definitely was not a mommy day at all.

* * * * *

Frank hung up from Carmelita and immediately dialed Al. He got voicemail.

"Al. Lunch. Today. Twelve. Eddie's. You and me," Frank droned as if it was only another lunch, then turned his attention to the two cases on his desk.

He had sent the snuff tape transcriptions and copies of the cleaned audio discs to Quantico. There was a backlog — as always — but he called to find out where in their backlog his case was. Thirty minutes later, someone on the other end of the line was willing to drag the packet out and move it forward a bit.

But when he attempted to pin down what *a bit* meant, he got nowhere.

It was a sure bet he couldn't wait on the FBI for the solution. He spent the next ninety minutes rereading the transcript. From the accent on the recordings and the matching words and phrases he read in the transcript, it was obvious these were home-grown Southern boys and more than likely from Georgia.

What did he know about them?

The verbal clues were interesting. Other agents who dealt with Boggle noted he always spelled words when he got nervous or excited. He was compulsive about it — and nowhere on the excited utterances in the recordings was there any spelling bee.

How did his fingerprints get on the package? How did it get into Tuesday Morning where Carmelita bought it?

Al slid into Frank's office. It was eleven-thirty. "Dude," he said, and fell into a chair.

"Hey. Ready to go in a minute. Let me finish this email." Frank typed the final words, grabbed the mouse, and clicked send. Al's eyes were closed, signaling one of his legendary catnaps. But Frank was wrong.

With his eyes still closed, Al said, "What's so important we gotta have lunch today at Eddie's?"

Frank played stupid. "Whaddaya mean?"

"Don't give me that crap. You never suggest a place for lunch. All of a sudden you're hot and heavy wanting me at Eddie's for lunch."

Frank's expression was noncommittal. His mouth said even less.

Al continued, "Whazzup?"

Frank couldn't keep up the suspense and smiled. "*She's* gonna be there."

"She?"

"Yes. Don't play dumb, asshole. *Her*. The woman who brought in the snuff tape. Carmelita."

Al knew damn well who Frank was talking about. He dragged the name out in his best Ricky Ricardo imitation. "Carrr-mah-*leeee*-tahhh. Dat 'splains it, Frankie."

Frank ticked off on his fingers the three things required of Al at this lunch. Finger one went up. "Here is what is required of you today. Shut up."

Finger two. "Mind your manners."

Finger three. "Be good."

Al shot him a friendly bird then smiled as he rubbed his hands in anticipation. "Is this my *official* introduction?"

"Listen to me, you sonovabitch," Frank said, smiling viciously. "You would be ill-advised to say anything out of place. You understand me? None of your smartass comments. No mention of any girlfriends or stalkers or nothing. Are we clear?"

Al smiled. "Ten-fer gudbuddy." He stood, smartly saluted his partner, and in his best Marine-recruit voice complied with the order. "Sir, yes, sir. Best behavior, sir. No ill-timed comments, siryessir."

Frank laughed out loud, slapped him on the back, and they left for what Al privately called *Frank's Destiny*.

Friday: Al meets Carmelita

For this important occasion, Carmelita's outfit was classy but understated. Clad in the only pair of jeans she owned that made her butt look good and her legs long, she topped them with a long-sleeved, deep coral pink pullover sweater which made her complexion — already aglow with love — light up even more. She added a long woolen coat and a scarf around her throat to protect from the wind — and out the door.

She was always early for everything. Today, though, it simply wouldn't do for her to be early. She drove around Decatur until eleven-forty-five. To kill a few more minutes, and be fashionably late, she stopped in at Eagle Eye, a secondhand bookstore three miles from Eddie's Money Pit, and picked out a few editions to add to her shelves at home.

She got lost in the stacks and was later than she intended. She stood at checkout and tried to move the process along efficiently, though Bob — she knew his name from his tag — wouldn't let her rush him. She looked at her watch.

"I'm late, Bob," Carmelita said.

"Uh-huh. Only take a minute. Do you want to get on our mailing list?"

"Not today. What's my total?"

"Uh-huh." Bob hit a few keys, scanned the barcodes on her five books, hit some more keys. He stopped and read the screen. "Uh, looks like this book is discounted, I think. Let me check with…"

He didn't finish the sentence. Carmelita tapped her toe as he meandered to the back of the store and checked with someone and had a long discussion and very slow walk back to where she waited while a third person tapped keys and scanned another barcode. Finally, finally, Bob and his helper looked up at her and smiled, but they didn't move.

Carmelita encouraged him to speak. "Discounted?"

"You get this book today for one dollar instead of two."

"Great. Thank you, Bob. How much do I owe you now?"

Bob finished the tally, took her money, and without waiting for her thirty five cents in change, she swept out the door toward her car.

She caught every red light there was between Eagle Eye and Eddie's Money Pit. She gave up worrying about how late she was after the fourth one. It wasn't a bad thing to keep a man waiting every now and then. She pulled into the parking lot, took a deep breath, and smiled.

"Hey, Carmelita. Nice to see you again," Eddie called when she walked through the door. "Follow me. Frank's already here."

How did he know I was here to see Frank? She didn't care how he knew — it felt good to be expected. She smiled. "Good to see you, too, Eddie. Lead the way."

Frank's back was to the door but Al, sitting across from him, saw her coming and notified his partner. Frank slid out of the seat and stood as easily as if they had lunch every day. She slid in, closely followed by Frank.

"Hi. I'm Al. Frank's partner. You're Carmelita. I remember you from when you were in the office. Mind like a freakin' vault." Al tapped his forehead, more nervous than he ever felt when meeting one of Frank's new girlfriends. "I never forget anything. You're Carmelita."

"Hello, Al. Yes."

Al laughed too loud, gulped his Coke, and choked.

Frank leaned toward him. "You okay?"

"Huh? Yeah, yeah. I'm fine. Must be hungry. Blood sugar dropping or something. Hey, where's Eddie?" he hollered toward the general vicinity of the kitchen, then sat back and shut up.

Why are they smiling at me? I must be acting like a fool.

Al got busy checking voicemail. When he next looked up, Frank and Carmelita were busy smiling at each other.

Eddie soon came, orders were given, and food quickly arrived. Carmelita and Frank made an effort at small talk and tried to include Al, but Al simply felt like a flat, third wheel on a high-performance Harley; in other words, totally useless. As he gulped his last bite, Al slid out of his seat and stood, furiously jabbing at his smartphone, then threw down a twenty.

"Hey. Gotta get back to the office. Message just came in. Gotta go. Ya don't have to leave with me, Frank. Hey, hey, Carmelita, ya think ya can bring him back to the office?"

Her eyes never left Frank's face. "Sure. Happy to."

"Great. Well, see you two later. Bye." Al disappeared, but they hardly noticed.

Carmelita folded her napkin, laid it beside her now-empty plate, and said teasingly, "So…you think Al really got an urgent message requiring his presence somewhere else?"

"Nope."

"Me neither."

She turned in the booth and pushed her back against the wall. She kicked off one shoe and drew up that leg into her seat, letting her foot come to rest against his leg. The other she stretched toward his feet, her shoe brushing against his ankle. She couldn't believe she was being so forward. She felt as if she was watching someone else. It felt very nice to be in the presence of a man who was happy she was there.

Frank turned toward her, balanced on one hip and pulled his leg under his knee. His fingers wrapped around her foot and repositioned it against his hip, then he slowly slid his other leg under the table until it was snug against her leg.

She asked, "How ya been?"

Frank replied, "Not good at all."

"I'm sorry."

Audible conversation stopped; breathing was difficult. Their eyes, though, had a conversation of their own going — a conversation where words would have been insufferable intruders. A full five minutes passed, then Frank smiled. Slowly. Thoughtfully. And full of specific intent a girl couldn't miss.

Carmelita returned the smile. But it was she who broke the silence. "What's wrong?"

"What?"

"You said you haven't been good."

"You want the truth?"

"Yes."

"Can you handle the truth?" he teased.

"I believe I can. Tell me."

His smile disappeared and his teasing tone vanished. "I'm miserable without you."

Carmelita's shoulders shook with silent laughter, her smile bigger than he had ever seen. Just as quickly as she began laughing, she stopped. Her eyes and face, a moment ago full of joy, now were solemn.

"I'm miserable without you, Carmelita. Plain and simple. No two ways about it. I want you."

She remained unsmiling.

"I know you're married. I know that!"

He waited for her to say something, anything to stop his misery. Nothing.

He leaned toward her as if doing so would confirm the honesty of his words.

"I know you have kids. I know that!"

Still she sat mute.

Couldn't she see his misery? He wanted to touch her skin. He wanted more than anything to make love to her as he knew she needed to have love made to her. Sex was always sport for him — never seriously taken, everyone knowing the rules, having their fun and moving on.

Yet, here was this woman who completely blindsided him. Sex may have once been sport, but no more. He would never dishonor this woman by having such thoughts. Sitting next to her was the closest thing he ever felt to adoration.

He couldn't hold back any longer. His left hand moved to her right. Slowly he intertwined his fingers into hers. She did not stop him, watching it happen. His fingers tightened around hers and he waited, eyes never leaving her face.

Her breath was shallow and her eyes blinked rapidly several times. She lifted her eyes to his.

Then he felt it — her fingers tightened against his. His chest felt close to bursting and his mind exploded from the happiness which now attempted to kill him. A smile came to her slowly. Their fingers and palms caressed and another few minutes passed. Again it was she who broke the silence. "What are we doing, Frank?"

Now it was Frank's turn to be mute. What could he say? *Divorce the jerk and marry me.* No, too soon. *I love you.* No, that wouldn't do...yet.

"Frank?" she whispered, removing her hand from his and slowly, gently, placing it on his knee to get his attention.

"I want to make love to you," he said simply.

She smiled sadly.

He reinforced his statement. "I want to make love to you for the rest of my life."

"Frank..." Speaking was tough. Pure hunger and desire for this man rolled from each pore. Her fingers gripped his knee even tighter. Finally she said, "Frank, I'm married."

"I know that! Goddamn," he almost shouted but managed to contain the sound though his intensity was undeniable. He leaned into her. "Don't you think that fact tortures me? God. Damn. Goddamn it."

His hand slid over his face as he spoke, then covered his closed eyes. He felt her hand pull his away from his face.

She leaned into him, smiling.

"You are a lovely man, and..."

He opened his eyes. Her description of his manliness did not sound soft or weak at all. He was happy to be lovely.

"I feel the same way about you."

Again he labored for breath.

"Frank." Her whisper was accompanied by a soft finger tracing his mouth. His body shook as if he were cold, yet her words came calm and clear. "I don't have affairs, Frank. I'm the marrying kind."

"I know you are. This is not an affair."

"If this is something real, then we must go very, very slow. Agree?"

"Yes."

"Then slow it will be?"

"Yes."

He took her hand in his, bringing her palm to his mouth. He kissed it in promise and she accepted it.

Eddie waited until he saw they were getting up from the table before he walked over. "Good to see you again, Carmelita. You will be back, yes?"

She smiled and shook his hand. "Yes, Eddie. I will be back. Thank you."

The drive to Frank's office was too short even though she drove leisurely. Where was a red light when you needed one? Two blocks from his office, Frank gently pressed his fingers into her neck one last time before he slid his hand from under her hair. She leaned her head into his caress but kept both hands on the wheel.

By the time they pulled to the front of the building, they each put their game faces on. No one watching would have thought they were anything other than professional colleagues. As his door slammed, they gave little waves without looking at each other. He walked into his building looking every inch the GBI agent focused on the job.

Her phone rang.

"You know what I want to do."

"Yes, I know."

"I'll call you."

"Yes."

"Bye."

"Bye."

Friday PM: It's time for a chat with B-O-G-G-L-E

Al waited in his office for Frank to return from his lunch with destiny. He finally showed up. Never had he seen his good friend in such a state. Happiness seemed to ooze from his pores, his eyes were calm, he walked with an easiness of gait unknown in his hard-driving friend. Al could not explain it except to say that here was a man not only in love, but content with his future.

"How did lunch go? Scratch that. Not my business." Al held his hand, traffic-cop style. "Sorry. Didn't mean to pry."

Frank smiled. In a spirit of openness prompted by love's light, he came right out and told him, "I love her. She feels the same way about me. I'm gonna marry her."

Al dropped his pen in shock. "What? *Marry?* When?"

"The logistics will take some time — she's got the kids, but we're willing to take the time and handle it properly. I know you've been worried. I can't explain it."

Frank searched for the word; Al already knew what it was. "Content?" he asked.

"Exactly. Content, yeah."

Frank enjoyed the thought for a moment and Al contemplated the change in his partner. But introspection and happiness came second to work. Frank turned his mind back to the case at hand.

"Okay. I've been giving this some thought. I think the key here is Boggle. Whether he knows it or not, he knows the killers. They may've tricked him into this little game. Or it could be a total accident he touched the plastic and they didn't even know it. But it's a link in the chain. We need to lay our hands on him."

"Yeah. We have to identify this woman, find out where she's from, how she managed to be targeted, where she was killed. How we gonna find Boggle?"

Frank sighed. "Old-fashioned shoe leather. I say we camp out on his doorstep in more ways than one."

Week
Three

Monday-Thursday: Turning up the H-E-A-T on Boggle

During the next three days, Frank and Al ran down every known associate of Chip Jason "Boggle" Johnson. They let it be known that it was he, Ol' Chippie, who was the cause of bringing undue attention on his lowlife friends because he was not making himself available to the Georgia Bureau of Investigation. They got a car out of the motor pool with GBI written all over it and parked it prominently where every neighbor could easily see.

When they showed up at a house, they took their time talking to his friends on their doorsteps. Frank's business cards flew out of his pocket as all the lowlifes suddenly became law-abiding citizens. Each promised to let Boggle know who to call.

By day three, Boggle was feeling unwanted across all of North Georgia and some metro environs. He sure as hell didn't like that and picked up one of the cards from the stack he accumulated from all his helpful friends.

Frank's cellphone rang Thursday morning. He did not recognize the number.

"This is Agent Smith."

"Yeah, I think you're lookin' l-o-o-k-i-n-g for me?" Boggle was spelling, a sure indicator he was nervous.

Frank put the call on speakerphone so Al could hear. "Well, hello, Boggle. Thank you for calling. Hey, we need to talk, dude. You're in a shitload of trouble and I don't think you even know how much…"

Boggle started protesting. "I ain't done nutten', n-u-t-i-n! What's this about, man?"

"A woman's been killed…"

"Keeuhled! *Keeuhled?* I ain't k-i-l-l-e-d nobody much less a pretty heifer."

"How'd you know she was pretty, Boggle?" Frank asked quietly.

"Aww, man, now ya jus' tryin' to trip me up, man. Why you gotta pick on me? I ain't done nutten', *n-u-t-i-n*," he whined.

"Actually, Chip, I believe you, even if you can't spell it. But my partner, Agent Jones, is totally convinced you did this thing. He's ready to arrest you. Personally, I don't think you're a murderer, much less somebody who'd torture —"

"Torture! Oh, my god. *Torture?* T-o-r-s-h-e-r, sheeeee-it. I love women. I do. I wouldn't hurt no heifer for nuttin', no matter how she looks, man."

Frank calmly suggested a solution. "This is easily handled then. You willing to help me get to the bottom of this thing?"

"Yeah. Sure. 'Course. But, I don't know nuttin' about no murder."

"Somebody wants us to think you do."

"What! I'm being set up? What the —! F-U-K! Who is it? I'll kill him — hey, I didn't mean that."

"Yeah, we get it. Relax. Where are you right now?"

"I'm in the big A-T-L."

"Great. We're not far from there. Hey, I tell you what… I'll buy you lunch and I'm hungry too —"

Frank held the phone at arm's length and hollered, "Shut up, Agent Jones, if I want to buy the boy some lunch I'll buy the boy some lunch."

Al smiled at the good cop/bad cop Frank started.

Frank brought the phone closer to his mouth. "Sorry, Boggle. How about The Varsity at one o'clock today? Good for ya?"

"Yeah. Sure. Anything I can do to help ya. See ya there. I'll be wearing a —"

"We know what you look like. We'll find you."

"Oh. Yeah. Right."

"He's not the sharpest knife in the drawer. I don't see him being our killer."

Al paid Frank no mind. He smacked his lips and rubbed his hands together as he contemplated his next heavenly lunch. "One nekkid dog for you. Two chili dogs with onions and mustard, fresh-cut deep-fried Vidalia onion rings, a Frosted Orange and Fried Peach Pie for me. Let's go!"

Atlanta's landmark restaurant, The Varsity, opened in 1928 across the street from the Georgia Institute of Technology. It took Frank and Al twenty minutes to make the drive. They grabbed a booth at the top of the restaurant, overlooking the carhops in the drive-in area to their right, the Yellow Jackets' stadium behind, and the rest of the Atlanta skyline in front of them. They didn't want to have this conversation in one of the TV rooms. Boggle's attention should be on them, not sports or news.

Eyes closed in appreciation, nose in the air, Al deeply inhaled. Setting his mouth to watering was the sharp scent of fresh Vidalia onions, hand-cut into rings, battered, and cooked in hot oil. He watched a teenage boy devour three chili dogs loaded high with finely chopped onions, and gulp down a Frosted Orange between mouthfuls of hot fries dipped in ketchup.

"Okay, I'm bad cop," Al said as he stared at the food two tables away.

"Yep. You do that so well."

"Yeah. I'll put on my best Angry Black Man snarl for ya. Hey, I think I see him."

"Yep, that's him. Go get him, Shaft."

Al got up from the table and headed straight to him. "Chip Jason Johnson?"

Boggle didn't know Frank and Al by sight and flinched when he saw Angry Black Man walk his way. With some bravado he managed to squeak, "Who wonts to K-N-O-W."

Cupping his badge in his massive hand, Al held it low so Boggle would have to lean over to see it. He growled, "Agent Jones, GBI. I need to read you your rights —"

Leaning over to assess badge authenticity, Boggle heard *read you your rights* and automatically went into the avoid-the-handcuffs foxtrot most career "I'm innocent, who me?" criminals always dance to. His head whipped back and forth as he bounced from one foot to the other, twisting his body while looking for the handcuffs.

"Hey! *Whut?*"

Frank rescued Boggle. In his best superior-agent voice, he sharply reprimanded Al. "Agent Jones! You know as well as I do Boggle is not under arrest. He's gonna be *helping* us with a case."

Frank shook Boggle's hand, man to man, and said, "How are you doing?"

Boggle relaxed, only a little bit, but gave Al his *you-heard-him-boy* look while keeping a safe distance. He turned his head toward the counter. "I'm fine. Lunch?"

"A promise is a promise." Frank was magnanimous. "Come on. Order anything you want."

They walked down the two short flights of stairs into the lobby where all the action was. Ten lines, eight deep with the lunch crunch. Behind the chest-high, stainless steel counter, order takers screamed over the noise of the crowd.

Whaddayahav? Whaddayahav?

You gonna walk that nekkid dog?

NEKKID DOG WALKING!

Boggle was a little bit too slow in giving his order. He was hurried along with a slap of the hand on the steel by the lady behind the counter.

"Whaddayahav?" she shouted at him with a smile.

Already nervous, Boggle jumped. "I wanna, uh, I wanna, chili dog, c-h-i-l-i—"

"I can spell, baby. Just whaddayahav?" She looked over Boggle's shoulder at Frank and Al and mouthed *Bless his little ol' heart.* They grinned with her.

Fifteen minutes later they settled back in their corner booth with loaded trays. Boggle shoveled so fast Frank wondered how long since he'd last eaten. Al, mesmerized by the prospect of digging into his chili dogs and onion rings, had a hard time keeping his Angry Black Man face arranged for best effect. Not that Boggle noticed Al anyway. With Boggle shoveling and Al preoccupied with his meal, Frank thought he was the only one who even remembered why they were here.

Halfway through his naked dog, Frank turned attention back to the crime. He put down his food, propped his elbows on the table, folded his hands together, and said, "Boggle, we have a p-r-o-b-l-e-m."

"What's that?" Boggle slurred through his mouthful.

Monday-Wednesday: Martin misses the wake-up call

While Frank and Al focused on finding Boggle and working their other cases, Carmelita calmly, but thoroughly, reassessed her life. She also reconsidered her insistence to Frank about moving slow and being smart. Now that she knew what she wanted and needed, her hunger for him grew. It didn't help her mind or heart any that he was doing exactly as she asked.

There had only been one text from him during the week and she kept reading it over and over as she parsed its meaning. At the end of three days of obsessing, she laughed when she realized he merely wanted to know how she was — nothing weird, no hidden meaning. She finally replied *I'm fine. Miss you.*

Outwardly, Carmelita spent her time doing what she always did — she took care of her family. But they noticed an obvious change in her. The children found Mama amusing. She was singing and humming yet seemed to be going deaf — their requests went unheeded by her. Martin was not amused.

She heard them just fine, but her reassessment brought home another ugly fact of her life. Her children were somewhat spoiled and it was her fault. It was time each of them — and her husband, too — stopped taking her for granted and learned to take care of themselves. After all, she wouldn't always be at their beck and call. Seven days after her lunch with Frank, Carmelita made up her mind — she was going to get a job.

She made a list of all the chores to be completed, activities the kids had to be at, the meals to be prepared, and the groceries to be bought. She scheduled it all out and assigned the tasks among the four of them.

At dinner the next night she calmly announced, "I'm going to get a job."

Her husband's fork hit his plate, he turned in his chair toward her, and said, "We haven't talked about that."

She began handing out the papers as she said, "No. We haven't. Okay. Here are everyone's assignments. These are all things that must be done to keep the household running. In some circles, these are also called chores." The family missed her little bit of sarcasm.

"You are old enough to be responsible for these things. Get used to it, because you will be doing them when you grow up."

Outraged, Martin asked, "You're giving me a list, too?"

The kids would have laughed at their daddy's predicament except they were too busy taking turns staring from their own list to their mother.

"I'm starting the job hunt tomorrow. The list begins tomorrow." She added graciously, "Enjoy your last evening of leisure. I'll do dishes tonight."

"What the hell is going on, Carmelita?" her husband demanded.

"I told you. I'm getting a job."

"You have a job. In this house. Taking care of us."

Kids nodded their heads in agreement with their daddy's bald statement.

Carmelita turned and slowly said, "So you have said."

For once Martin kept his mouth shut. The kids stared at their daddy, his mouth gawping open and shut like a fish out of water. All three sensed their world was getting ready to change, though what that meant or how it would happen, they had no clue about — much less why.

Thursday: Boggle spills the beans

Boggle licked grease from his fingers, smacking enjoyment of his first full meal in three days. Not because he didn't have the money, but because he spent it on meth. Clearly, his priorities were messed up. Leaning back comfortably in the booth, he noisily sucked the straw in his Frosted Orange. Al pushed his tray away. Boggle avoided Angry Black Man's glare as he stared at Frank, waiting.

Frank began, "We have your fingerprint on the plastic wrapping on some discs —"

"Music discs?" Boggle asked helpfully and sucked noisily again.

"No. A book on disc."

Boggle's uncomprehending stare told Frank and Al he didn't have a clue. "Whut's a book on disc?"

"It's where somebody reads a book out loud and records it. Then others listen. It's called an audiobook."

Boggle didn't understand the concept at all. "Why would they wanna to do that? Why don't they just read it?"

Frank continued to speak calmly, even though he was frustrated with this idiot. "It doesn't matter, Chip. What does matter is we have your fingerprint inside a sealed package containing a recording of some bad stuff, maybe four tortures and murders. How did it get there, Chip?"

Boggle was confused and too stupid to be nervous. "I dunno. I ain't never seen such a book."

Frank added, "And we also have something else."

"Whut?"

"Cotton fibers."

"Huh?"

Al leaned forward quickly, pointing a finger in his face. "Do you work in a cotton mill, Chip?"

"Hell, no, I don't. N-e-v-e-r been 'side one. I cain't take all dat noise."

Al hammered him. "If you've never been in one, how do you know it's noisy in there, C-H-I-P?"

"I heered tell 'bout it, that's whut." Boggle jutted his chin out defiantly. "I h-e-e-r-d, heered tell."

Frank soothed him. "Who do you know works in a cotton mill, Boggle?"

"Sheeeee-it. I know lots of peeople." Boggle's face fell as he realized what they were asking of him. "Whut? You want I should rat out my friends? R-a-t 'em out?" He picked up a remnant of onion ring batter in the paper tray.

Halfway to his mouth, Al reached across and slapped it out of Boggle's hand. "Answer the man, Chip."

"Hey!" Boggle hollered as his fists came up, ready to fight. The glare from Angry Black Man got his anger under control quick. He sat on his fists, stared up at the ceiling, and didn't say a word.

Frank quietly and slowly repeated the question. "Chip. Think. Who do you know that works in a cotton mill?"

Boggle was obviously under duress. Al wanted to laugh, but he didn't. Boggle squirmed his way from one end of the seat to the other as he considered his options. Piss off The Law or piss off a few friends. The friends might forgive him;

The Law wouldn't. His shoulders slumped as he realized the only thing he could do to save his ass was name names. He glared from one to the other and began his recitation.

"My Aunt DeeDee. My Uncle Joe…"

Al said, "Last names."

"Hunt. My cousin, Timmy. Hunt," he quickly added. "Ummm…you want evvabody I know?"

Frank continued to stare patiently. Al made a face: *duh, ya think?* Boggle continued for seven minutes and soon Frank and Al had ten names. Boggle picked up his Peach Pie packet, opened up one end, slid it out, and put his mouth to work, oblivious to the fact the interview was not yet over. They didn't stop looking at him nor did they resume eating.

Popping in his last bite, Boggle stared at them while slowly chewing his Peach Pie crust. He swallowed, then whined, "Man. Now whut?"

"Chip," Al growled as if he was using every bit of strength he had to be patient. "You, uh…you forgot to give us the other two names."

"I suhware to Gawd thas awl I know." He crossed his heart then made the sign of the Boy Scouts' honor code. "I dunno nobuddy else. Not w-u-n…one."

Frank lowered his head, his voice dripping in disappointment. "Chip. Chip. Chip. I thought you were helping us here, man. I thought you would want to help seeing as how, you know, somebody's trying to set you up big time for the murder and torture of several women…"

Boggle sat ramrod straight, his hands on the table pushing him through the back of the seat. "How many? For Gawd's sake, I thought you was talking 'bout just one h-e-f-f-e-r whut got done in."

"What's the names, Chip?" Frank coaxed real friendly.

Boggle rocked in his seat, forward and back. "Aw she-it. Okay. Awright. There's two more good ol' boys I know whut work in the cotton plant. But they ain't no murdering kind, I know. Thays nice and we go h-u-n—"

Al had enough of his quirk. "S-T-O-P that stupid spelling. Just talk."

Boggle hurriedly finished, "Huntin'-an-'fishin'-an-stuff."

Frank smiled as if he was completely interested in Boggle's leisure activities. "Fishing? Hunting? Where's that? I've been wanting a good place to go hunting."

Boggle was eager to be helpful. "Yeah? Like what?"

"Deer. Quail. Wild turkey. What do you hunt?"

"Deer, most times."

Frank was still smiling. "Yeah? Man, last year I bagged a ten-pointer down in SOWEGA, but I could hardly believe it. I think that buck put all his energy into growing his rack because he was puny. Didn't get much meat off him." Almost as an afterthought, Frank asked Boggle's advice. "Say, where do you recommend is a good place for deer?"

"Me and Tommy and Otter go down to Butts County. Thays a place near a river and a bridge, easy to git to. Now thas a nice place, and not just for deer neither. Thays got some girls in Butts County...whooo-eeeee, sho nuff home-grown and ready to show a man whut it is all about iffen you know whutta mean." He winked.

"Butts County. I'll have to look into it. The deer *and* the girls." Frank winked at Boggle, man to man. Al still stared, Angry Black Man act getting better each minute.

"What. Are. Their. Names?" Al growled.

"I tol' ya. Tommy and Otter."

"Last names, you idiot."

Boggle must have been sucking up his Frosted Orange too fast and froze up his brain cells. "Oh. Yeah. Right. Uh, Tommy Higginbotham, thas H-i-g-i-n-b-o-t-a-m, and, uh, Otter…thas not his real name…let me think now…Jimmy Stonecypher. Thas S-t-o-n-s-i-f-e-r. Otter got his name cuz he's real good at gettin' outta girl trouble, if you know whutta mean. Kinda like a weasel. Get it? Slides in and slides on out, and none knows how he does it." Boggle couldn't wink knowingly fast enough to keep Angry Black Man from staring another hole through him.

"Tommy Higginbotham and Jimmy Stonecypher. Where do they live, Chippie?" Al's growl grew deeper. Frank almost laughed out loud at his theatrics.

"Thays up near Elberton, E-l-" Boggle squeaked.

Al cut him off. "I know how to spell Elberton."

"Uh, yeah. I dunno the address."

"They live together, Chippie?"

"I dun't thaink so."

Voice soaked with confidence in Boggle's helpfulness, Frank turned to Al. "Agent Jones, I believe Boggle's been of great help to us today. Do you still believe he could have had a knowing part in these heinous crimes?"

"Heinous. Thas right. Thays h-a-y-n-u-s, but I din't do 'em."

Al stared a couple of seconds longer at Boggle, squinted his eyes. He nodded his head as if giving in to superior logic. "You might be right," he admitted reluctantly.

Boggle began to ramble and his compulsion couldn't be held in check. "Oh, Agent Smith's right, awright. I'm innocent totally. T-o-t—"

Al held up a hand. "Zip it. By the way. You ever been to Tuesday Morning?"

Boggle shut up and swallowed hard. Then he thought some humor was called for and smiled wide. "Uh, no. But I been to a few Saturday nights. Hahaha!"

Neither GBI agent smiled. Frank poured on the Good Cop. "Okay, then. Thank you, Chip. If we find more evidence pointing to you, we'll remember how helpful you've been and we'll know somebody is trying to set you up and Agent Jones and I will have your back. Isn't that right, Agent Jones?"

Never moving a muscle, Al droned, "Absolutely. Helpful. Gotcher back."

Boggle wasn't sure about Al's declaration of helpfulness. They stood; Frank shook Boggle's hand. Boggle boogied on out of The Varsity before Al could get near enough to shake his hand. Boggle might be stupid, but he wasn't an idiot.

"You thinking what I'm thinking, Al?"

"Yeah. Hunting trip to Butts County."

Thursday AM-PM: Carmelita starts her job hunt

Carmelita's job hunting campaign was difficult. She had not been in the workforce since her marriage — technology had passed her by. She had no marketable skills she could think of and by the end of the third day she had filled out multiple employment applications and now knew everything she wasn't.

Several people sarcastically suggested she might want to go back to school and *get her degree*. Which degree and how it would be helpful to her right now, they couldn't seem to tell her. Those suggestions she dismissed — she didn't want to go back to school because she was ready to make some money. What could she do? She took a break at a nearby coffee shop. Strong espresso with hot milk revived her spirits. She went over her options, confirmed she had none, and felt like giving up. A magazine was on the low table in front of her and, to divert her mind from her sorrows, she picked it up.

It was a local magazine. She began at the front and read to the back. Buried in the back, in the middle of the classified listings, was a small ad wanting someone to sell ad space for the publication she held. She thought she might as well twist the knife deeper into her ego, give them a call and let them turn her down because she had no experience. She dialed the number. Someone answered.

"Hello. Yes. I'm calling about the ad for someone to sell ad space."

"Uh-huh. Yeah."

"Is the position still open?"

"I wouldn't call it a position. But, yeah, the job is still available. Why? You want to do it?"

"I would like to, yes."

"Come see us."

"When should I come over?"

"I'm here now."

"Okay. Then I'll be right over. Where are you located?"

Within fifteen minutes she was pulling into the office park and walking into the office. A cat scooted out the door when she opened it.

"I'm sorry. The cat got out."

"Don't worry. She'll be back. How can I help you?"

"Yes, I called a few minutes ago about the job? My name is Carmelita Oliveira."

"Hey. I'm Van Morrison." He held out a hand and they shook. "I've heard all the jokes. You wanna sell for us? Have you ever done any sales before?"

Here it comes, thought Carmelita. She gave them her work history, bluntly with no frills. "No. I have been a stay-at-home mom since the first child came along and basically can do everything for them and nothing for the rest of the world. If it's experience you need, I'm not it."

Van jerked his head up at her description. "Are you stupid?"

There was the knife; surprisingly it made her mad. "No."

He noticed the spitfire in her answer. He liked it and smiled. "Can you learn?"

"Of course."

"Are you willing and eager?"

"Yes."

"Then I think we may have us a match."

Carmelita didn't want to get her hopes up, so she confirmed her conclusion. "What does that mean?"

He smiled. "It means you're hired."

With a little bit of paperwork, the commission schedule explained, and a list of businesses to call on, Carmelita was now in sales. She couldn't wait to tell her family. What would Martin's reaction be? He wouldn't be pleased — but she simply did not care anymore about his pleasure.

Carmelita was correct. Martin was not happy she got a job. Over dinner, he painstakingly explained, in microscopic detail, just how much she didn't know about sales and ad copy and the complicated, complicated world of business.

The Case of the Snuff Tape Killers

She watched her children as they listened to their mother being insulted and having criticisms delivered patiently as if to a stupid child.

She wasn't happy with what she saw. Instead of her usual non-reply, she cut him off. "Martin, do you think I'm so stupid I can't learn?"

He sighed deeply. "That isn't what I said. What I said was, I don't think you gave it much thought as to the difficulties you will encounter."

"I heard that part. So you do think I am smart enough to learn how to do this job?"

He was backed into a corner and he knew it. He decided to be diplomatic.

"Of course I think you're smart."

Carmelita didn't let him get out another word. "Thank you. Now that I know you are confident in my ability to learn, I feel even better about taking this job offer." She emphasized *this* to imply other offers had come but she chose this one. Martin blinked, started to reply, thought better of it, and attacked his food. She turned her head toward her children. They were smiling. That's the look she wanted on their faces and that's the one she got.

Friday AM: A celebration

The next morning Carmelita arrived at the first business on the list, took a deep breath, and walked in. She didn't make the sale. But they were friendly, said budgets were tight, and to check back in a couple of months. She put them on her calendar for follow-up. The day went fast. She made one sale out of the ten businesses she called on; she went home happy.

She wanted to be rewarded. She wanted to share with someone who she knew cared. She sent a text: *Time for sushi?*

He replied *yes*.

Saturday, 0-Dark-30: A morning in the woods

"Which rifle did you bring?" Frank unzipped Al's bag. "Winchester. Nice."

"Yeah. Ain't it though? Full metal jacket. Incredibly accurate."

"When did you get this?"

"Inherited this baby from Granddaddy. He used to hunt with it. I get my crack shot from him. It skipped a generation, though; Daddy…" He shook his head.

Frank zipped the rifle back in the bag, laid it in the trunk with his gear, and slammed the lid. "Let's roll."

After the meeting with Boggle, the agents spent Friday running down every name on the list. Anything that popped made them go deeper. They eliminated Boggle's aunt, uncle, and cousin, along with four other people, leaving five possibilities, remote but possible. They both agreed the two that stood out were Tommy and Otter. Especially since their hunting grounds were right next to the Butts County grave they were called out to last week. Coincidence could only explain so much, and this didn't seem like a coincidence.

"I tell you what other job Otter's got?"

Frank shook his head, eyes on the road.

"He works part time for a construction equipment rental company."

Frank whistled. "Are you kidding me?"

"Nope. How did that grave get dug?"

"Maaaahh-sheen."

"That's right. I made a call. It seems they rent these small backhoe things to anybody. Even will give lessons on how to use them. Doesn't cost much to rent."

"Huh."

"Take the next exit," Al instructed.

"That's not the exit we need."

"Yeah, I know. But there is this great place. Serves a killer breakfast."

"How do you find all these places, Al?"

Frank pulled off the exit and, following Al's instructions, turned left back over the interstate, drove five miles, turned right on a dirt road with no signs, drove another half mile and behind a stand of pine trees was Mama's Breakfast Table. The parking lot was full.

Frank didn't want to have to wait. "Ah, man. Looks like it'll be awhile before we get a table."

"Don't worry. I know Mama." Al let Frank work on that for a minute as they walked across the graveled parking lot. "She's my cousin on Mama's side."

Sure enough, they got in and out quickly — perks of having connections — and soon arrived at the grave.

"Do you think they know this one's been found?"

Al was hunkered down on one side with Frank on the other. They both hunkered slowly, and painfully, because their bellies were still full from Mama's breakfast. Cousin wasn't about to let any stories get back about how she didn't properly feed a relative and his friend; she laid on a breakfast banquet unlike anything Frank had never seen.

Frank slowly shifted his weight from one knee to the other. "I don't know. Possibly. You know those serial killer types. They like to go back and visit and relive the triumph, so who knows what they've seen."

"Yeah. Sick bastards."

They sat quietly listening to the sounds the killers hear when they come back. There was a slight noise of traffic crossing a bridge upriver, though the bridge could not be seen from their position. Wind in the trees and small animals digging through the leaves complemented each other. They heard the noise of a putt-putt engine on a small fishing boat.

It soon came into sight; a man and his son were out for a quiet day on the water. Al jumped up, ran to the riverbank, and flagged them down. Man and boy discussed the waving man before they came to the conclusion that yes, indeed, it was they who were being flagged. Al pulled out his ID and held it high. They turned the boat and putt-putted over to the bank. By this time Frank joined him with his ID showing.

"Good morning," Al hollered as they pulled up. "Don't know if you know about this hole over here." Al emphasized *hole* so as not to scare the boy.

The dad didn't have any problems with calling it what it was, though. "You mean the grave of the dead woman what got washed out a couple months back?"

Al watched the boy to see if he was freaked. He wasn't. "Yeah. You ever seen anybody out here with machinery?"

"What kind of machinery?"

"The big digging kind."

The dad shook his head after giving it a moment's thought. "Nope. Can't sez I have." He turned to his son. "You, boy?"

Boy shook his head no likewise.

"Great. Okay. Thank you. Caught anything yet?"

"A few crappie. Not hardly enough for a meal yet." With that they putt-putted away with a wave.

Frank shrugged. "It was worth a try."

"See, here's what I'm thinking. If I was a serial killer and a lazy one at that — "

"Aren't they all lazy?"

"True dat. But here's the thing, if it worked good the first time and I got away with it, would I change where I buried the bodies of my other victims?"

They spent three hours walking the riverbank looking for any other possible gravesites, old, current, or to be. Then they found an identical hole, machine dug, waiting on a new victim. Frank furiously kicked a clod of dirt into the hole.

"Shit. Shit. Shit! Shit."

Al stared at the hole. "Why don't you tell me how you really feel, Frank?"

Frank kicked another clod. "Fuck!"

"Thank you for that clarification." Al wasn't smiling.

They hunkered down again, though this time the pain was in their hearts. Who would she be? When would she arrive? Could they find out in time?

The hatred of the men gave way to close scrutiny. "Looks new to me."

Frank was still mad, but he agreed. "Yeah. Very new."

Al thought over the situation. "I wonder if they dig it first, then start hunting for a victim. Or if they identify their victim, then dig the grave, then kill. Or do they kill first, store the body, dig the grave, then bring her here?"

Al continued after a minute, "You know what I'm wondering? I'm wondering if they have a hunting trailer near here."

"We gotta catch these sumbitches."

"I think I have an idea that just might work." Now Al was smiling.

Week
Four

Tuesday PM: The long wait

The text read *Hey, baby. Sorry. Gotta break our lunch date for tomorrow. Something came up with work. Will explain later.*

Moments before, Carmelita was flying high. She made three sales and her employer was happy. Her first paycheck was due the next week and she was looking forward to starting her own checking account. Now this. Postponement of sharing her happy news brought her crashing. She chastised herself for being weak. She replied *Hope all is well. I have happy news. Can't wait to share it. Reschedule to when?*

She got busy as she began the wait for the reply.

Thursday PM: Surveillance

Frank kept an eye out for anyone approaching. He didn't want the bad guys to see them hiding the motion-sensitive camera. No matter the light source or lack of it, this unit took high-resolution video.

"I think this is gonna work, Al."

"Hell, yeah, it's gonna work," Al hollered from the top of the extension ladder they brought. "Tweeter assured me there is no freakin' way this thing will fail. And with the camo body he put on it, blends in with all this natural shit."

"So, Frank de-uah…" Frank's head jerked up at the falsetto female voice.

Frank hollered, "Stop playing and get it installed and make sure it's working right."

Still in his high voice, Al said, "Stop nagging, dear. I can do two things at once, dear. By the way, Frank dee-ahh, did you evah resheduall the luncheon with you-know-who?"

"No."

"What's taking you so long?"

"Only been four days."

"Ah, yes," said Al in a psychologist's voice. "Spoken like a man who has no clue about women."

"What in the hell does that mean?"

"Okay, let me 'splain it sose you unnahstan' me, my bruthah," this in his come-be-saved preacher intonation. "You know how one year in a dawg's li-i-i-ife equals seven in a human li-i-i-ife?"

"Yes."

Al finished the installation. "See it?"

Frank walked all around the tree and if Al's hand hadn't been on the unit, he would not have known it was there. "Nope."

Al climbed down. "Frank, you listen to me and you listen good. One day in a woman's life when she isn't getting attention but she's needing it bad is like three weeks to a man. Carmelita is feeling ignored by you as if you had not heard from her for, oh, let me do the math…"

"I get it. I get it. I'll send her a text right now." Out in the woods as far as they were, though, Frank had no signal. "I'll do it when we get close in."

Al stepped off the ladder. "You better, because let me tell you, this relationship ain't all about you this time and don't you forget it."

"Okay. I won't."

They pulled the ladder down, shortened it, and tramped uphill to the pickup.

Thursday Late PM: Carmelita gets a pleasant surprise

Two long, sad, worrisome days had passed since Carmelita sent a reply to his text and got nothing back. Nothing from him. Nothing. On day one, she understood the job came first. On day two, she stretched her understanding a bit further though worry crept in and hope died. She would never have a man who was enthralled with her and couldn't stay away. Carmelita made up her mind:

She had been a fool to hope.

She'd never allow love's hope to again climb high in her heart. Not for him, not for the life she needed, not for no one. Instead all her hopes would go into her job, something she could control, something she could quantify, something she knew something about.

You're a fool, girl.

She was on her way home from her last call of the afternoon when she heard a quiet ding. She couldn't look at her cellphone, she was driving, but figured it was a friend. It certainly wasn't Martin and by now she knew it wasn't Frank. She thought about her customers — *her* customers; that made her proud — and that it was they who held the key to her future prospects. Yes, customers would come and go, but at least with them it was all business and her heart wouldn't break if they didn't call.

Hopeful fool no more, that's me.

She watched sadly as the garage door rose. She pulled in, put the car in park, and shut it off. She pushed the button to close it and it slowly came back down, shutting out the afternoon sun. She felt as if she was inside a coffin lowered into the ground, and the first clods of dirt were hitting the lid, forever shutting her into a darkness from which there was no escape.

She fought that feeling by checking her phone to see who the message was from. Her right hand, pulling the keys from the ignition, stopped. The text was from Frank. She stared. This was not what she expected. It had been ages — ages! — since he texted and now this? Was this the big kiss-off? She was afraid to read it.

She looked up at the headliner in her car. Closed her eyes. Took a deep breath, opened her eyes, told herself to suck it up, opened the message, and read it.

I'm sorry, baby. Been busy on your murder case. Sushi tomorrow, 12?

She replied *yes*.
Life back on.
Keep the faith, girl.

* * * * *

"Now, was that so hard? You just made a woman very happy." Frank agreed Al was right. Especially when the return text came fifteen minutes later. "What did she say?"

"She'll be there."

Frank was happy for the reply and he smiled. Al stirred Frank's pot and asked, "Want me to meet you two there?"

For the second time that day, Frank's head whipped around to Al. When he saw Al smiling he knew he was kidding.

"I guess that would be a noooo," Al said with mock disappointment.

But turnabout is fair play. Innocently as he could, Frank let Al have it right between the eyes. "How's it going with your lady?"

It was Al's turn to look uncomfortable.

Frank rubbed it in. "Uh, huh. I see. And when was the last time you communicated with your dahlin' love?"

Al stared straight ahead and said nothing. The drive into the city continued.

Twenty minutes later, Frank said, "Oh, hey, I meant to tell you about this very interesting fact I heard not too long ago. It's right up your alley, too." Al loved interesting facts and Frank had his attention. Anything to change the subject from women.

"Yeah? What?"

"You know how one year in a dog's life is equal to —"

"Shut up. I get it."

"Seven in a human's?"

"Got it. Thank you."

Twenty minutes later they pulled into HQ's parking lot. As if he just remembered another important fact, Frank said, "Oh, by the way —"

Al was all attention again. "Yeah?"

"I meant to tell you that it's obvious to me you know nothing about women."

"Damn you."

But Al was smiling. And he took the hint.

* * * * *

"Thanks, man. It worked great." Frank tossed the truck keys through the air.

"Hey, anything to catch the bad guy," Tweeter said, catching the throw. "Couldn't see it in the tree unless you was looking for it, huh?"

"You're right. In fact, I knew exactly where it was and both Al and I debated if in fact that was it. You're a genius."

"Yeah. I know. Too bad my pay doesn't reflect my intelligence quotient."

"Well, you know what they say? 'Crime doesn't pay.'"

Tweeter reminded Frank, "Now, remember what I told you about retrieving the pictures. I have it set up so all you have to do is be within fifty yards and you can download the pictures to your computer through the short-range Wi-Fi I set up. But you need to go out in at least once a week because if there is a lot of animal activity, it will eat up the hard drive space."

"I may want you to go out there with me and handle it."

"Sure. Be happy to. As long as you can figure out a way to explain my absence from The Lab."

Frank nodded. "Hell, yeah. I can figure that out. Or we could do it on a Saturday or Sunday."

"Nope, that won't work. I got mud-bogging those days."

"Of course. How could I have forgotten?"

* * * * *

Frank got home, took a long hot shower, put three large slices of pepperoni pizza on a paper plate and threw them in the microwave. While he waited, he debated whether to have beer or wine with his pizza. He chose wine and half-filled a large wine glass. He leaned against the counter while he waited, and watched the timer on the machine. His hand was already on the handle when the machine screamed. He opened the door, pulled out the plate, and yanked a few paper towels off the roll. Then he, the plate, the pizza, the paper, and the wine plunked down in front of the television for some serious mind-numbing vegging-out.

But Frank could not get out of his mind what Al told him. This relationship isn't all about you this time, Al had said. This time? Had his other relationships always been about him and his career and damn everything else? Not all the women he dated were party animals. He had known some good women. He thought back to the goodbyes they gave him and realized all said pretty much the same thing with the same sad look on their faces.

Frank, they said, you're a great guy. Call me when you're ready to be in my life.

He never understood and never called any of them again. Except for that one, once, when he was feeling sorry for himself. She had gotten over him and married. Surprised the hell out of him. He was drunk, didn't realize it was her husband who answered the phone, and said something a husband doesn't want to hear another man say to his wife. The next day when he was sober, she sweetly forgave the call, but firmly explained to him the facts of life and would he pretty please erase her number from his phone and never call it again, thank you.

After his first slice was gone, he refilled his glass and sat down again, determined this time to watch the damn television and stop this damn introspective thinking. It was bringing him down. But the next commercial was for diamond engagement rings and before the next slice was gone, he couldn't get his mind off those goddamned rings.

They sure were pretty. He finished the slice and refilled the glass. *What was the name of that store again?* Damn. The wine was going to his head.

He better eat some more to soak up the alcohol. But the third slice needed something to wash it down and he filled the glass after he finished the slice. He plopped down loosely in the seat and flipped channels, a happy little smile on his face. There were those rings again.

Aahhhh. Those rings are so pretty. Ah. Lovetts. Name of the store. Must remember. Where's my paper and pen? Damn, they sure are nice. How much those things are anyway?

He had never priced rings before but had heard tales of how high the prices could go. He never understood why anyone would pay that much for a piece of bling to put on a heifer's finger.

He laughed out loud at heifer.

The things you pick up from bad guys. I better not drink any more wine until I eat some more. I'm sounding more and more Southern every day.

But he never got to the eating. He fell asleep in his chair, television blaring, visions of diamond rings dancing in his head, and slept like a drunk baby.

Friday: Info on cotton and Frank and Carmelita do a late lunch

When Al arrived the next morning at work, he swung by Frank's office. It was locked. He knocked and got no reply. By ten o'clock, when Frank still had not arrived, Al called.

Frank answered. "I know. I know. I woke up a half-hour ago. I'm walking out the door now."

"You better hurry or you're gonna be late for lunch." Al laughed and hung up without saying goodbye.

Frank hated to be late and today of all days. He texted Carmelita. *Hey. Running late. Can we do 1:00?*

She could, thank goodness. Frank got to work, checked a few emails and made some calls. Al came by to fill him in on the results from the cotton mills.

"Basically, the only time anything changes for the fibers is when the cotton goes into the dyeing process and chemicals are applied. Yeah, the fibers are different from when they get carded and spun, but fibers fly all over the place, so, unless we can measure the quantity of fiber type, it's a dead end. Other than that, the machines to process the raw cotton are the same. Also, these seven mills buy their cotton from the same sources and the lots get mixed, so, cotton is cotton is cotton until —"

"Until somebody changes the color. Right."

"However, we still have that connection, and Tommy and Otter both work in a cotton mill near Elberton."

"I thought Otter delivered machinery."

Al checked his notes. "Yes, he does, but that's his second job. He works six days a week on second shift at the mill and three days a week on day shift for machinery."

"Geez, when does he have time to kill anybody?"

"Good question. We can't check his attendance records until we know approximately what dates we're looking for and we can't cross-check those with Tommy's until we know the same thing."

"Dead in the water for now." Frank drummed fingers on the desktop.

"Yeah, but we will be checking the camera in six days. Maybe by then…" Al and Frank both left the thought hanging. It didn't need to be said out loud. But they both wondered if the camera would show animal activity of the human type.

Frank stopped drumming. "I hope that camera is quiet."

"It is."

Frank drummed again for a couple of minutes. "I hope that camera works."

Al nodded. "It will. It does."

Frank slapped the desk. "I got to go."

"Say hi."

"Okay."

* * * * *

Carmelita wanted to make the sale. The shop owner was taking her sweet time deciding which size ad to run for six months. She kept a discreet eye on the time. From this store it would take her twenty five minutes to get to Eddie's Money Pit. It was already twenty minutes to one. She was going to be late.

"Melissa? Would you like me to come back tomorrow? You can give it a bit more thought. Maybe a larger ad or even a smaller one will work. Or a mixture of sizes over a period of time on different pages."

Melissa, the owner of Candy Candles, agreed. "Would you mind? I can't seem to make up my mind."

"Not even a problem. I will see you tomorrow then, say around ten?"

"Perfect. I'm sorry I can't make up my mind today."

"Understandable. Talk to you tomorrow." Carmelita made a swift exit, jumped in her car, sent a quick text — *Running 15 minutes late* — and put the car into the wind.

Her cell rang. "Hello?" Carmelita did not look at the Caller ID, she was driving.

"Where are you?" It was Martin.

"I'm on Peachtree Industrial, just getting on 285."

"Oh. What are you doing?"

"I'm working, Martin."

"Oh. When will you be home?"

"Same time I always am, around three-thirty or four. What's up?"

"Nothing. Okay. Well. Whatever. See you later then. I may be late tonight. "

Carmelita did not understand the purpose for this call. "Okay. How late? Where are you?"

"At work where *I'm* supposed to be."

"Are you okay?"

"Sure. Why wouldn't I be?"

"I don't know. This conversation is weird, that's all."

"Well, lots of things are weird now that you aren't home where you belong."

"Oh. That. Okay. See you later."

Carmelita hung up and shook her head. She didn't feel like trying to understand her husband anymore. She set her mind to the man she was heading for. She arrived at quarter after one. He was on the phone, facing the door. She walked over to the table. Frank, still talking, stood to let her slide in beside him.

"Okay, Al. Thanks. Yes, she just got here. I haven't forgotten." Frank hung up. "Al says hey."

"Tell him I said hey."

Frank leaned over and gave her a kiss full on the mouth. When he leaned back, Carmelita was a puddle in the corner of the booth. They simply stared at each other until they were interrupted by the server, a young college student, pierced here and there. Frank thought she was probably a psych major and, if so, God help us all.

Her tongue stud flashed silver and she said, "Ott ood oo ike to rink day, thirs?"

"Unsweet tea."

"Diet Coke."

More flashing. "Eeeddy oo oduh?"

Frank raised an eyebrow to Carmelita. She nodded.

"Yeah, we'll have two sashimi lunch specials."

Flash, flash, flash. "Ank oo. Ee ite up." Then psych major was gone.

Carmelita said, "Eeeww. How do they do that?"

"Do what?"

"Pierce themselves. It has to hurt."

"I'm sure it does."

Then Flash Psych Major ceased to be as they returned to their stares, this time with added smiles.

Carmelita broke the silence first. "Hey."

"Hey."

Frank leaned over and kissed her again, this time lingering over the kiss. And again Carmelita became a puddle, but an active one. Her leg, formerly under control, now took it upon itself to throw itself over his leg as the kiss finished. It took her a minute to get her eyes to refocus and when they did, their drinks sat on the table in front of them and Flash Psych Major was waiting on their attention to come to her.

"Ur oduh ill be out in a ewe."

Frank managed to croak a reply. "Okay." Flash went away, still frowning. For someone so young and pierced, her frown was very disapproving of public displays of affection.

Carmelita's leg remained in place and now Frank's hand was on it. Carmelita wanted to say *remove your hand!* But she could only mutter. "Okay… Okayokay…*Okay*."

"Yeah. It is okay." Frank knew what she was trying to say, but he kept his hand right where he wanted it, holding her leg firmly over his. Their food arrived.

Carmelita sighed. "Thank goodness."

They rearranged themselves in front of their plates and slowly began their meal. After a few minutes, their blood no longer boiling, they were able to talk.

"What's this about some news you wanted to tell me?"

"Oh! That's right." Carmelita told him all about the job, making chore lists, and Martin's unhappiness with the whole situation. Frank enjoyed watching her tell her story. She was so full of life and he caught the hope of better days coming in her voice. When she finished, Frank hated Martin even more.

"Martin can go fffff…" Frank caught himself in time.

"Martin can do what?"

"He can go fly a kite," Frank said. "Don't worry about him. Just don't."

"That's easy for you to say. You haven't been married."

"True. But it's obvious to me he does not understand marriage, either. He takes you for granted. He…well, don't get me started about how stupid he is. Let me ask you a question. I want an honest answer, too. If he was to start paying attention to you, right now, and doing right by you in other ways, would you stay married?"

"Sure."

Not the answer he wanted to hear. "Well, I said I wanted an honest answer, guess I can't complain. I didn't think it would be that."

"Frank, you are missing the point. People like Martin don't change."

"Why not?"

"Because they don't think the problem is them."

Frank sat back in the booth, pushed his plate away, and folded his arms across his chest. "Al told me something yesterday. It sort of threw me. He said all my past relationships have always been about me and my life and what fits into my schedule. He said I couldn't act like that with you. But I'm not sure how to do it differently. What if I'm just another Martin but in a different package and you get hurt all over again?"

Carmelita's eyes softened. She put her palm against his cheek. "I know you aren't another Martin."

"How can you be so sure?"

She stroked his cheek. "It's very easy. The Martins of this world never ask if they are a Martin. Nor do they worry if their actions will hurt anyone. As far as they're concerned, they are the aggrieved party and their feelings are of prime importance. You, Frank Smith," she held his hand, "*you* are worried you will disappoint *me*. Do you know how sweet and sexy *that* is?"

Frank blinked several times. "Sexy?"

Carmelita didn't blink. "Oh. Hell yeah. And sweet."

"Did I hear you cuss?"

"Uh-huh."

On Frank's drive back to the office, he thought of nothing but diamond rings, cost be damned, and he smiled.

On Carmelita's drive home, she thought of nothing but making love with Frank — and puddled up all over again.

Week Six

Wednesday: Boom-Phut-Pop and downloading video

In the fifth week of the investigation, Al and Frank kept themselves busy working on a few other open cases on their desks. Al asked for the report from the cotton agency and got the promise it would be delivered via emailed PDF attachment to him within a week. Frank took a deeper look at both Tommy and Otter's criminal histories and ran down known associates. The case file was getting thicker and they still hadn't been invited in on the case by any jurisdiction.

Of course, they couldn't get — yet — an invitation because there was no body definitively linked to the recording and so no jurisdiction. They waited and the week crawled by even though they were busy. Frank, Al, and Tweeter loaded up their hunting gear in Tweeter's truck and took off south on I-75. Maybe this would provide the break they needed to connect their recorded evidence to the body found near Jackson in Butts County.

Tweeter decided not to make a big deal of getting out of The Lab and took a personal day. The Human Resources Department was always after him to use up his personal days so their accounting wouldn't get too far out of balance. What the heck, he took one. He was getting paid and he was never gonna use them all up anyway. Besides, a day tramping through the woods was a day tramping through the woods even if he was carrying a backpack with a computer next to the rifle slung over his shoulder.

Al and Frank brought orange paper targets. They may as well get in some shooting time if there was no body.

Al worried about the technology. "What if the hard drive got full before they came?"

Tweeter calmed him down. "Nah. I mean, if that was to happen, you'd have to have non-stop movement going 24/7. I mean, you'd have to have a raging storm whipping everything back and forth going on for days. Or a bunch of animals having an orgy every freakin' day or something. I don't think you have anything to worry about."

Frank, bringing up the rear, tried to keep his mind on the reason for the trek, but Carmelita wearing the ring he was going to pick out kept popping into his head.

Tweeter and Al stopped at the top of a rise and waited on him. Tweeter asked, "What's making Frank smile?"

Al knew, but wasn't going to say. "I bet he's thinking about what's on the hard drive and we're about to catch us some goddamned killer, that's what I think he's thinking."

The explanation worked for Tweeter. Frank caught up; the hike was all downhill after that. But the closer he got to the would-be grave, his smile got smaller until it was gone entirely and diamond rings were no longer on his mind.

Frank didn't want the bad guys to see them near the hole with their gear. The plan was to set up their shooting range far enough away not to look suspicious, but within line of transmission of the camera's Wi-Fi network. "You don't have to pull the computer out of the bag, do you?"

"Nope. I have to unzip it. Nobody's gonna be able to see the computer. I'll close it up once I get the transfer going."

"How long for the transfer?"

"Oh, depending on how much is on there, it could be a couple of hours, maybe three. The Wi-Fi isn't high-speed."

Al said, "Well, I'm gonna set up targets. At least we'll have time to practice." He measured approximate distances at fifty, one hundred, and three hundred yards, placing three targets at each. Al would fire at the left target, Frank at the center, and Tweeter at the right. Results compared to see who would have bragging rights.

The computer picked up the signal and the transfer began. The men unpacked their ammunition, set up their tripods for their long-distance shots, and carefully calibrated their scopes. They knew they had plenty of time and plenty of ammo, but they didn't blast away at their targets, instead taking their time to sharpen the skill sets all shooters need. In between shots, they talked shooting strategy, best ammunition type to weapon and the results of those, and told stories about their bad-ass upbringings.

Pop. "I can top that, Tweeter. Once," Al told them, "when I was four, my uncle put me on the back of a half-grown bull and told me to hold on."

"Four?" Tweeter pulled his trigger slow and smooth. *Phut.*

Al sighted. "Truth. God's honest. I lasted about two seconds and off I went. Landed in the dirt flat on my goddamned back. Couldn't breathe. And that damn bull was still bucking as hard as if I was still on it. Uncle Richard ran in, grabbed me up, and said" — *Pop* — "'Get back on the horse that threw ya and before I knew what was happening, I was on the back of the bull again. Man, I lasted about four seconds that time. I was screaming and holding on for dear life. Hit the ground again. Daddy came out and, holy shit, I thought he was gonna kill him." Al rolled onto his back.

"Damn. I didn't ride a bull until I was seven." *Phut.*

"You ever ride a bull, Frank?"

Boom. "Nope. Don't plan to, neither."

Phut.

Al, still on his back, asked, "Tweeter, when did you lose it?"

"Oh, man. I was barely fifteen." Tweeter sighed and reached for his ammo.

Boom. "You remember the girl?"

"Yeah. She was older than me. Almost seventeen. Man, jeez, God Almighty. We neither one knew what the hell we was doing, but had a fine old time figuring it out. Couldn't get enough of getting our freak on. How about you, Al?"

"Who? Me?" *Pop.*

Phut. "Yeah. You. Anybody else out here called Al?"

Al took his time sighting down his rifle at the farthest target. *Pop.* "Twenty four."

Frank laughed out loud. Tweeter stopped loading and his mouth dropped. "Stop lying, man." He finished loading.

"I'm not lying."

"Okay. So you were 'technically a virgin' or a for-real virgin until you were twenty four?" Tweeter couldn't understand what he was hearing.

"What do you mean 'technically'?" It was Al's turn to not understand.

"You know, man, you done everything there was to be done except the deed itself."

Al thought for a second. "I guess you could say I was a for-real virgin."

Phut. "Ah. Now you're just lying."

Frank was on his back, rifle clutched to his chest, laughing so hard tears rolled into his ears. He rolled back over slowly, wiped his eyes, and sighted.

Pop. "I'm proud of that, you know."

Boom. "I'm sure you are and I'm proud for you. Who was the lucky girl?"

Pop. "Somebody I was engaged to."

Phut. "Was she a virgin?"

Pop. "Uh, that would be a big fat no."

Tweeter slowly beat his forehead against his rifle's stock and Frank slapped the ground in front of him.

Pop. Pop. Pop.

Phut. "You feel better now, Al?"

Pop. Pop. Pop. "I do now." Al smiled at Frank. "So, Frank. How about you?"

Boom. "Oh, you don't want to hear about that."

Phut. Pop. "Oh, hell yeah, we do."

Boom. "It was business."

Pop. Phut. Pop. Boom. "What?"

Boom. "Seventeen. Me and two buddies decided to pay a pro and we all took turns losing it in the backseat of my car. No romance. No love. Not even fun."

Phut. "Well, that's just sad. Do you remember what she looked like?"

"Nope."

"Her name?"

"Are you kidding?"

"Anything about her?"

Boom. "Yeah. She cost me twenty."

Pop. "Explains a lot." *Pop.*

Boom. "Yeah. I guess it does."

Boom. Pop. Phut.

Boom. Phut. Pop.

Pop-pop. Boom. Phut.

* * * * *

The Case of the Snuff Tape Killers

The day the Butts County coroner saw the washed-out grave next to the river, he knew it was murder, but he wasn't about to sign off on the death certificate until he proved his opinion was fact. He did so by asking if the wounds could have been made in any other fashion.

Did she get caught in a combine?

Did she get trampled by a herd of goats?

Had she been in a baseball game and got hit on the head with a bat, then trampled by a herd of goats, run over by a combine, and then somehow or another become part of a show as the assistant to a knife-throwing artist whose aim was off?

Yeah. It was murder. But Gerry (pronounced Gary, thank you) Alton Pennyman (Gap to his friends), Southern by birth, Irish by nature, was not about to let some hot shot big-city forensics expert from New York City or The Left Coast shoot down his conclusions due to sloppy work on his part. He ruled out every possible reason for the wounds on the body and documented the entire process.

Yeah. It was definitely murder, and not a fast or pretty one. This girl was barely seventeen, with a beautiful complexion and delicate hands that never knew hard work and probably had taken piano lessons, and perfect teeth that cost Mama and Daddy a pile of money and drove the boys crazy in high school when she flashed that smile — yeah, Gap had a hard time working this body. Her last hours had to have made death a welcome, blessed relief, and one she prayed, and screamed, for.

The body had been in the ground for at least two years but was well preserved comparatively speaking, having been wrapped in four layers of three mil plastic sheeting and then sealed with three-inch silver duct tape and buried deep enough animals and the weather couldn't get at her. Getting her fingerprints had not been difficult. But where to start the identity search was the question.

He circulated an accurate description of her along with a color sketch of what she looked like before the torture.

He asked his wife to do the sketch. She taught art at Griffin High School but was also an accomplished portrait artist whose work was well known. The school was very fortunate to have her remain on staff. This was not the first time Gay Andrews Pennyman (their friends called them Mr. and Mrs. Gap) had done this for her husband, but it was the first time she got so upset. They had a sixteen-year-old daughter and it took her a couple of hours to finish the sketch because she kept crying as she thought about how this girl's mother and father must be hurting.

It was from this circulation that calls came from both White and Floyd counties. White County is directly north of Atlanta in the Appalachian foothills. Floyd is in the northwest corner of the state. But it was the White County parents, living in Cleveland, home of the Cabbage Patch Doll hospital and a stone's throw from Helen, the original Georgia Alpine Village, who identified the girl as theirs.

She had worked in Helen at a candy shop. Five weeks after her body was found, Gap called Frank and left a message officially requesting the GBI's presence in Butts County.

* * * * *

Tweeter checked the download's progress. "We got about five more minutes." Frank and Al sat on either side to watch the footage when it finished.

Al, sitting on the ammo case, asked, "How long do you think this thing is?"

"Not sure. But we can watch it in fast-forward. I mean, if your guys are on it, they haven't buried a body yet because, well, there's the hole over there, but if they're scoping it out, then at least we have that. But it depends on how much they move and how long they stay, so look sharp."

Al was hungry. "I have a suggestion. Let's go get something to eat and then we can watch this more comfortably sitting somewhere else."

Frank said, "But I want to know now."

"I agree with Al. Besides, the battery life on the laptop is running low and we need to plug it in to watch."

They repacked gear, hiked back to the truck, and hit the highway. They stopped at Mama's for lunch and electricity. Tweeter was Mama's next big fan and promised to bring all his friends there very early Saturday on their way to mud-bogging.

Mama set them up in a secluded corner where they could watch their footage privately. Mama heard two hot-damns and one there's-the-little-fuckers-excuse-me. Tweeter paused the footage to get a good look at Tommy, Otter, and another guy they didn't know, as they inspected the hole. Too bad there was no sound.

"More than two killers?" Al wondered out loud.

Frank had a brainstorm. "Tweeter, who do you know can read lips?"

At that, Tweeter and Al smiled. He worked as a sound tech for the GBI. They would see Twitless tomorrow.

Wednesday PM: Creating a new communication channel

Carmelita knew Frank was busy working on the very case she brought him, but she was feeling the need for more attention. She didn't want to constantly text him; that was for kids. She didn't want to email him at work, because that would be stupid. She decided to call him later in the day when he would be at home and have a quick chat about another methodology for communication. She waited until after supper. She grabbed her keys and hollered to anybody who cared to listen that she was going to the grocery store. Her son grunted. It was his night to clean the kitchen after supper and his male ego was feeling assaulted. Martin pitched a fit about his son doing dishes. But Carmelita laid down the law and there was no backing down on any of these points. Martin gave a disgusted grunt but that didn't stop the boy's kitchen rotation.

After she left the subdivision, she called Frank's phone. She could tell he was smiling and happy to hear from her.

"Hey. This is a great surprise. What are you doing?"

"On the way to do a little bit of grocery shopping. How about you?"

"Oh, I'm on my way home, too. Been a long day."

"Oh, yeah? What's going on?"

"Making some headway and had some interesting things happen with your case. It looks like this is a big deal. Got an invite from Butts County to help them with what Al and I think is a related case. That'll give us a chance to go full bore on your case."

"Great. Hey, listen, I may as well tell you what's on my mind —"

"Is something wrong?"

"No! No, no, no. It's just that...I'm getting some nice attention. I sure would like to get more from you but I don't want to send personal messages to your work email and I'm wondering if you have a personal email address that you check in the evenings so that, you know, we can communicate privately...."

"No. I don't."

"Oh."

"Doesn't mean I can't get one. Not sure how to do it, but I'll crank up the computer this evening and figure it out. I'll let you know what it is."

"Okay. I'd like that."

"Yeah. Me, too. Glad you thought of it."

"Yeah. Well, I'm at the store. Gotta go."

"Good night, baby."

"Good night to you, too."

Carmelita liked being called baby.

* * * * *

Frank put down the phone and returned his attention to the call he and Al made earlier that day to Butts County. An appointment was made for two days later where he, Al, the Butts County coroner, and two detectives would sit down and tell their sides of what they now believed could be the same story. Tweeter took the download to Twitless and threatened destruction of his precious iPhone if he didn't get his full attention onto the three men in the video.

"No more sexting to your fancy dancer. You better tell her you're working on some-thing life and death to impress upon her the reason for your lack of response until I get a full transcript. Do you understand?"

"Oh, my God. What the…" Twitless started his famous New Jersey whine.

Tweeter wasn't scared of the whining of anybody, especially anyone from north of the Mason-Dixon Line, and he shut Twitless down cold. "Let me explain to you very clearly. I promise that phone will disappear and you will never see it again if I don't get the transcript from this video by tomorrow. Am I clear? You reading me, bro? Have I put the fear of the Lord in ya yet?"

Painful as it was, Twitless turned off his phone after sending one last text to Darlene about this most very important case and that it was his help that was requested pronto to possibly save a life. *I'll be in touch and hang tough, baby* he closed out before sending and shutting it down.

Frank laughed out loud when Tweeter told him about it, but he was glad he would have the transcript before he went to Butts County.

Once he read it, he would know if the third man was an accomplice or a guy with no clue. He pulled into his drive, shut down the car, and thought of the call from Carmelita as he walked into the house.

Al was right. Frank was always about the job and his career and let the personal chips fall where they may. It had never really hurt him. Women came and went; there was always another. But now he was feeling the blame, call it guilt, for wasting the time of several women who had invested their emotion into him because he had acted like there could be a future.

And they could have had a future with him, if only they hadn't wanted him to have a future with them. This sharing thing he never could get into and never understood. Didn't they understand he was doing important work and didn't have time?

Their faces and names passed through his mind. He mentally apologized to each one, but it didn't make him feel any better. He vowed he wouldn't do that to Carmelita. This was probably his one chance and he wasn't going to blow it. He would eat dinner, then go online and figure out a way to get a personal email address.

He would send it to her first thing in the morning and start her day with something that would make her happy.

It felt good to think about somebody else for a change. His personal life was shaping up into something he never thought it would be and he liked that.

Thursday AM: 1967GBIFrank

At nine the next morning, Carmelita received a text. It was an email address with a gmail.com extension.

She laughed when she saw the full address. Now she knew the year he was born. Unless he was simply the one thousand nine hundred and sixty seventh GBIFrank in the gmail system, which she doubted. Frank Smith was too common, so that had already been taken.

She set up an online email account her husband and children would know nothing about. She didn't want to have to worry about the kids seeing anything and she already knew Martin sometimes used the family email account to send pictures to relatives. Why tempt fate?

Carmelita still couldn't believe she was doing this. There was a time when she would have said it was wrong for anyone who was married and fell in love with someone else to carry on a relationship with thoughts of a future.

But she now knew these were not all cookie-cutter situations and sometimes survival was at stake.

A couple of years before, Carmelita was brutally honest with Martin when she said he needed to be proud of her and happy to see her and want to do things with her that she enjoyed. But after being actively ignored, having her head patted like she was a simple little child pitching a fit for a piece of candy, and then shut down cold several times after that, well, at what point did beating your head against a brick wall still make sense?

Martin was a big boy. Let him reap what he sowed and deal with the fallout. The only thing she worried about was her children. But she wasn't doing them any favors by showing them how to live in an unhappy home and by acting like a doormat willing to take whatever emotional mud somebody decided to scrape off their feet on their way to living their chosen life.

It was difficult choosing a name for herself. Finally she tried her full name at gmail and, wonder of wonders, it was available. She sent him an email from the account then texted she had done so. His one word reply — *great!* — made her happy. She left home to go sell.

Friday: Butts County boys

Frank and Al drove back to Butts County two days after their trip with Tweeter and, as Tweeter promised he would, Frank had the transcript of the video from Twitless. In this, the sexting maniac was a genius. He and Al went over it late Thursday afternoon. Tweeter said he thought Twitless got his ability to read lips because his girlfriend was always sending him video of herself with poor sound and he practiced with those so much he could do it for anybody. The transcript was interesting.

```
Subject1: Unintelligible this damn hole will
        work fine.
Subject2: Where'd you learn unintelligible
Subject1: I saw a movie unintelligible
        Hidalgo. Unintelligible racing and had
        to unintelligible but thought it would
        work.
Subject3: So whatcha think? Can it be done?
Subject1: Sure. But here's the thing. People
        tramp through unintelligible you don't
        want somebody unintelligible and hurt
        themselves. You're gonna have to put
        unintelligible to warn off people.
        But, yeah. It can be done. Course, I
        think there's unintelligible but it's
        your project.
Subject3: Okay. Alrighty unintelligible.
Subject2: Guess we better get started on
        unintelligible.
Subject1: Anything else? You know, I put on
        hunting trips to all sorts of
        unintelligible.
```

```
From this point forward please note subjects
        are moving away and mostly their backs
        are turned. The individual words I was
        able to get are meaningless in the
        conversational context, but are listed
        here for your use. Game. Weight. Deer.
        Bear. Raccoon. Protect. Pull.
End of report.
```

"At least we know the other guy is not part of the killing team," Al concluded after reading. "But who is he?"

"Did you bring the printouts of the faces of these individuals?"

Al patted his briefcase. "Yep. Got them all here."

"And you have copies of the original?"

Al patted his briefcase again. "Frank. Copies of everything are in here. Sound files. Written transcripts. Case notes. Pictures. Video. Everything. Relax."

Frank drummed his fingers on the dash behind the steering wheel. "I want to solve this thing."

"I know. I do, too."

Frank shut up. Within thirty minutes they were at the Coroner's Office where their meeting would take place.

Gap welcomed them in. Two detectives were there, pictures spread out on a table. Coffee and a dozen doughnuts from Krispy Kreme, already sampled, welcomed them. Detectives Alvarez Sanchez and Donald Williams shook hands and made introductions. Business cards were swapped all around.

Sanchez, who looked Mexican, was a fourth-generation American citizen, born and raised in Butts County, who couldn't speak a word of Spanish except for *si* and *no* and a couple of choice invectives. He had been a constant source of disappointment to his now-sainted great-grandmother. She thought it a sin that within four generations nobody cared whether or not they could speak the mother tongue. But Rez didn't see the need to cultivate the language nor the accent. It had nothing to do with him. He was American through and through.

On the other hand, Williams, who looked like a white Bubba from Main Street Redneckville, was fluent in Spanish, both Mexican and Castilian, understood dialects from several pockets of indigenous peoples in South American countries, and spoke enough Portuguese that, if he wanted to, he could start a rip-roaring bar fight in any port of call.

In his previous life Don had been in the Marines, but nobody really knew where he called home nor anything else about his background. One day he was just here and somebody up top said to hire him and he stayed. He never talked about his past.

Rez and Don made a good team. Frank and Al liked and trusted them immediately. Gap got the meeting started officially.

"Agent Smith..."

"Frank."

"Frank, when we talked yesterday you said you had some things you wanted us to hear and see. But what I would like to do is start with what we have here and then, as we listen to your evidence, this might very well shed some light on your stuff. Okay?"

Everybody nodded agreement and for the next hour, Gap walked them through the evidence: finding the body, eliminating and finally identifying how wounds were made, and when in the torture/death sequence they occurred,

length of time in the ground, and the identification of the
body, drugs in her system and, finally but not lastly, her
parents formally identifying the girl and claiming her body.

"The funeral was last weekend."

"You get everything you needed from the body?"

Gap nodded vigorously. "I documented everything.
Took samples. Cuttings of anything I needed. When I got
her, she was not in much of a condition they'd have an open
casket funeral anyway. She was beaten badly and buried for
two years. They aren't gonna notice any parts missing."

"Yeah. Okay." After listening to Gap, and knowing what
he knew about the recording, Frank was feeling more
confident the two cases were connected.

Rez and Don filled in the girl's story.

"Hellen Stephanie Williams was almost eighteen,
lacking nine weeks. She was not a runaway. Never gave her
parents a bit of grief. Straight-A student. Teachers loved her.
She was a cheerleader —"

"Cheer captain," Rez piped in.

"Cheer captain. Did not smoke or use drugs. Wasn't on
birth control. Did her chores when she was supposed to.
Was an only child. They had her late in life. She was a big
surprise to them after giving up hope. Gorgeous girl."

Don handed a picture over to Al.

"Wow." He shook his head in sorrow and handed it to
Frank with all the reverence one gives a dead innocent.

Rez continued, "When she disappeared from Cleveland,
Georgia, everybody knew she had to have been kidnapped.
There was no other explanation for her disappearance that
made sense. They called in the police. They searched the
area several times. Candlelight prayer vigils. Rewards
offered. Newspaper articles. But she was gone. Pure and

simple: gone. No trace of anything. No clues. Her parents hired a P.I., but all he found out was she was a good girl doing good things and being kind and nice."

Frank asked, "No hidden wrong-side-of-the-tracks boyfriend?"

"Nope. Her steady boyfriend was still a virgin, for Godssake, just like her. They held hands. Kissed. That's it."

"She was a for-real virgin, then, not a technical virgin?"

Don added rather sadly, "For real. Well, for real — until she met the two killers."

"She was raped?"

"Yes." Rez spat out the word.

Frank asked, "That bad, huh?"

"Yeah. That bad."

"DNA from the swab?"

"Too degraded."

Gap continued with the forensics. "You know, these guys know enough about DNA and trace evidence to clean her up to where they thought they got everything. But I have a feeling when some of the hairs get back we're gonna find out some were theirs. If that is the case, we will get DNA."

"No prints on the plastic she was wrapped in?"

"Nothing usable."

Everybody paused for a few seconds to let that information settle. Then Don looked at Frank. "Okay. Whatcha got?"

Frank began outlining their case. "A citizen brought in what she thought was an audiobook. She bought it at Tuesday Morning, a chain discount store. Upon listening to it, though, she heard this and brought it to us."

Frank clicked the mouse button and started the sound.

Even though Frank and Al had heard it several times,

every man in the room was hurting when the audio ended. No one spoke for a few moments.

Gap said, "Play it again."

Frank said, "I brought a packet for each of you to read and listen to."

"Great," each said in unison, but Gap added, "Still, right now, play it again."

This time Gap's pen was at the ready, paper in front of him, and he shut his eyes. Every now and then he'd reach over to pause the playback, make furious notes, and start it again. It took thirty minutes to do what he wanted.

"Sorry. I had some initial impressions that weren't fully formed and I didn't want to lose them."

"Anything you need, man. So, the citizen —" Frank stopped when Al choked. "You okay, Al?"

"Yeah," he croaked. "Doughnut must have gone down the wrong pipe."

Frank continued, "Right. The *citizen* brought in all the packaging and the bag it was put in and set it on my desk. Inside the packaging were two things. Fingerprint from a guy by the name of Chip Jason Johnson. Street name Boggle. We don't think he's one of the killers, but he does know who they are even if he doesn't know what they've done. Fibers from raw cotton."

"What do you mean *raw?*" Don asked.

"Cotton that's come off the plant in the field and has not been processed with chemicals yet."

"Gotcha."

"We found out that of the cotton mills in Georgia, none of them have an exclusive source of cotton and all farms feed their crops into all the mills."

Frank looked at Al to take up the rest of the story. "We started with what we knew for certain: Boggle. We ran him down. We met with him and —"

Frank interrupted with a chuckle. "I'm sorry. Al, I'm just now really appreciating the act you put on." Then he laughed out loud.

Al smiled at the memory as he explained to Gap, Rez, and Don. "I put on my Angry Black Man act coupled with Bad Cop. It was priceless. Boggle was scared. I even slapped an onion ring out of his hand when he was slow to answer Frank." Frank and Al couldn't hold back any longer and they roared.

Don was laughing hard. "Been there. Done that. But I bet my Angry Redneck is better than your Angry Black Man." The humor was a welcome relief from death.

They settled down and Frank continued. "Okay. He gave us several names of people he knew who worked in a cotton mill. Two of the names, Tommy and Otter — all their details are in the packet — were two good friends of his whose names he failed to give us. We sweated those out of him. Then we chit-chatted a bit and he brought up hunting. Guess where Tommy and Otter like to hunt?"

"Butts County," Rez said.

Don added, "Where the grave is, right?"

"Yep. Me and Al went back to the grave and took a long hike around the area. Guess what we found?"

"Another grave?" Rez said.

"Yes and no. We found another hole, machine dug, like the first grave, but it is still empty."

"Okay, so…" Rez continued.

Frank held up a finger. "Wait. It gets better. Al here had a brilliant idea about seeing who might visit the grave and

Tweeter, this genius who works in our lab, set up a camera hunters use, only better."

The Butts County boys nodded.

"He covered it in camo and put in short-range Wi-Fi. We installed it in a tree where you can't see it unless you really know what you're looking for. We waited a week and then yesterday went out there to download the footage. Here's the footage."

Al clicked a button and the video began. Frank pointed out Tommy and Otter.

Al pointed out the date/time stamp in the corner. "As you can see, this shows they visited four days ago."

Don pointed to the third man. "Who's he? Accomplice?"

"No, I don't think so. He is a hunting expert from what we can tell from the transcript of the conversation."

Rez said, "Conversation? I didn't hear any sound."

"There wasn't any," explained Frank. "But we have a sound tech that can read lips and he put it together for us. You have a copy of the transcript. From what we could understand from the bits and pieces of conversation he could see, it looks like this guy is well schooled in the art of trapping and killing big game via the use of pits. He also leads hunting expeditions."

"Weird."

"Yeah, we don't know what sort of game these two told the guy they're after or what they're playing at, but for sure they're up to something and it ain't no good."

Gap said, "Camera still out there?"

Frank and Al nodded in unison.

"When are you gonna check it next?"

"We'll do it once a week until we get something."

Butts County nodded their understanding.

"Now what?"

"I wish I could go get these sick fuckers." Frank's frustration showed. "But, we've got nothing concrete yet."

Gap continued, "The connections are just too good. We all know there is rarely coincidence this clear. I spent a lot of time with our victim and I don't want to have to do that again. These are the guys, though you didn't hear me say it. But after hearing our victim's body talk to me and then listening to what was done to the other victim on the recording, they could have been one and the same."

"Do you think this recording could be of Hellen's torture and murder?"

"Sure it could. I know her wounds. I know the order in which they took place. Your stuff sure matched up awfully close to what I saw."

"There are more women on the other recordings. Listen to those sound files and see if you still think that's the case. Because, gentlemen, if we've got a body we can match up to evidence…"

Friday PM: Pouring out a soul

Carmelita's Friday went beautifully. She made a few sales, set up a bank account, and made her first deposit into it of the first paycheck she earned since her daughter was born. She sat at her computer later in the evening, writing her first email to Frank. She didn't quite know what to say and lightly drummed her fingers against the keyboard as she thought about it.

Thirty minutes later she hit send before she second-guessed herself to death about what she wrote. She went downstairs and crawled into bed. Even in his sleep, Martin didn't want to be close to her; she felt the movement of his body as he slid to the edge of his side of the bed.

She shouldn't have been hurt, but she was; his rejection wasn't new. Sleep would have been welcomed, but it was not forthcoming. She tore the bed up trying to get comfortable enough to go to sleep, but Frank's kisses kept sleep at bay and her body wide awake. The last time she looked, the alarm would go off in three hours.

Saturday AM: "I think...life with you"

By the time he got home Friday evening, Frank was worn out and felt like an old man. Hell, he was not far from being an old man. He undressed and went into the bathroom. He stood in front of the mirror and looked at his naked body, something he hadn't done in quite a while. He winced. He wasn't in bad shape, but — he sucked his stomach in — there was a time he didn't have to. He held it in another moment, then let it go. He winced again.

He turned on the water and got in the shower. Adjusted the sprayer to pulsating massage and let it beat the heat into his muscles. Fully intending to reheat leftover pizza for dinner then check his new email account, he lay down on his bed, naked, for only a minute, to rest, collect his....

He woke at two in the morning, pulled the covers down, fell in, and promptly went back to sleep.

The Case of the Snuff Tape Killers

When the alarm went off at seven, he woke with a headache. If he hadn't been positive he hadn't gotten drunk last night, he would have sworn he had a hangover. He went into the bathroom, found a Goody's, dumped it into the back of his throat, and washed it down with several handfuls of water. He shuffled into the living room and cranked up his laptop. He checked his new email.

He logged on and, sure enough, there was a message from her. He clicked on it and began to read.

Dear Frank,

Now that I can write you, I'm having a difficult time with what to say. But here's the thing. I know I told you I wanted to go slow. And I do, in my mind! I know that's the smartest thing what with the kids and all. But, now that I'm getting such nice attention, well, I find I like it and I've missed knowing it. When I come home to what I've got, what I've got now seems worse because of the good that I do have. And am enjoying, by the way.

I know. I know. I know how you feel, but it is easy to feel those things and say those things when you know nothing is going to happen anytime soon. I think about making love with you ALL THE TIME!!!! I think about living with you. I think about sleeping with you. I think about day to day life with you. Yes. That's the word. LIFE. I don't want to go slow. I want to do something dramatic and make my life better. I want to feel good.

I want a man to love me. I need a man to love.

I know I'm rambling. But the depth of what I feel is hard to deal with so I must tell you these things. Please. I beg you to do me a favor. If you have changed your mind about me. If you are having second thoughts about anything you have said to me or your intentions toward me.

Let me know NOW before my hopes get too high so I can brace my heart and mind for the rest of my life with Martin. I need attention and if I have to live without it I must take steps so I don't die.

I reread what I wrote and I know it sounds like a melodramatic teenage girl in love gushing away DRAMATICALLY. But you bring that out in me and I've never had that brought out before. I feel silly. But if I don't say these things then I won't be honest. And I must be honest. Otherwise it's all a game and I hate games.

So. Now I've dumped this emotion on you. Let me know.

Dare I continue to hope?

Carmelita

Frank's headache was now forgotten. His body buzzed. God this woman made him feel alive and good and useful and — he laughed out loud at the thought — like a manly man. He read the message three times, clicked reply, and answered simply.

Yes, you may dare to hope. I have not changed my mind. We shall go at the pace you set. Not a second faster. Not a second slower. I am here for the duration.

The duration — he liked the sound. It implied patient sacrifice for something much loved. And he would be patient and he would, for the first time in his life, make the sacrifice. He hit send, shut down his computer, and stepped lively to the bedroom. Life was good. He was finally living.

The Case of the Snuff Tape Killers

* * * * *

Frank called Al at seven-thirty. He said he was starving and ready for a big breakfast. Al joined him at Rise-N-Dine, a favorite of the nearby university crowd and law enforcement types. Frank was already ensconced in a booth by the window.

"Hey, partner. They should be bringing coffee in a minute."

Al slid into the booth and simply stared.

Frank said, "What?"

"You're lit up like a Christmas tree. What's up?"

"I got an email from Carmelita."

"Well, if I'd known all it took to put you in a good mood was to send you an email, I would have started a couple of years ago."

"Ha. Ha. You couldn't have written what she wrote."

Al leaned forward and whispered. "What? She write something dirty?"

Frank indignantly replied, "Hell, no. What's the matter with you? You think sex talk would get me lit up like this?"

Al didn't say anything. Frank leaned forward and asked again, "What's the matter with you?"

"It wasn't about what she's gonna do to you or what she wants you to do to her?"

"No!" Frank sat back, disgusted.

Al was thoroughly perplexed. "What else can you say in an email then?"

"You're ruining my good mood. You are a cretin, you know that? You know nothing about women. Nothing. Let me tell you, just so you know, I told you I was gonna marry that woman, you mark my words, it's gonna happen sooner than either of us thought because she can't take this anymore and I can't take this anymore and...*what?*"

Al smiled. "Frank's sure enough in serious love. I'll be Suwannee."

"You'll be what?"

"Suwannee. It's a Southern saying. Polite way of saying 'I'll be damned' for the non-cussing crowd."

Their waitress brought coffee. "Ott ull ooo ave, thirs?"

Frank's head snapped up. It was Flash Psych Major working her second job, still with the same disapproving frown, and he and Al weren't even making out. He pitied her future patients.

Weeks
Seven and
Eight

An idiot and two invitations

Al and Frank stayed busy the next two weeks on their other open cases. They started an official file — one they could charge expenses to — for the Snuff Tape Case, and documented Butts County's invitation for assistance.

Gap spent every spare moment listening to the recording of the torture and killing. Because he makes his living dealing with the raw aspects of death, it didn't take him as long to get used to hearing it, and he was able to delineate the process. He made notes. He rechecked them often. Did his conclusions reached on Monday still hold true on Tuesday? If so, he moved forward. If not, he started all over again on that point. He sent Agent Smith an email:

Expect a report in another week.

Rez and Don cleaned their rifles and went hiking regularly. They didn't want to wait a week at a time to find out if there had been any activity at the new grave. They never did find the camera and they knew it was there. Tweeter was good, or else they were getting old and their eyesight was failing. Nah. Tweeter was that good, they concluded, and went away with their desired youthful potency intact.

Al took some to give his girlfriend much-needed attention and called her one evening. They met for coffee. LaVonne liked the attention even if she was mad at him for not staying in touch for almost two months. She called him a few days later and invited him over for a home-cooked meal. Al, an excellent judge of food and very particular about it, suggested he take her out instead. He heard silence and realized his mistake. But what was it? He didn't know.

"You don't like Sugo's?"

LaVonne let another long silence leak through the line to Al's ears. "I like it fine," she finally said with extreme politeness then said nothing more.

"Okay." Al wracked his brain for the reason for the silence. "So...you've eaten there before?"

Long pause, then a curtly delivered reply. "Yes."

"Okay." Al paced his living room. "So...you've eaten there but don't want to go again?"

Long pause. "Did I say I *never* wanted to eat there again? Did I say that?"

"Noooo. No, you didn't." Al stopped pacing and bent over, one hand holding the phone to his ear, the other silently punching the floor in frustration.

"That's right. I didn't." LaVonne didn't want to act this mean, but this man brought it out in her. Within two months — two months! — he called once — one time! — and didn't leave a message. Then he buys her a coffee and she gets to feeling warm and fuzzy and she invites him for dinner — dinner! A home-cooked meal — and he sloughs off the invitation like so much dead skin. He deserved this torture.

Al made up his mind: Sacrifice was the better part of valor. He threw in his ego like a sweat-soaked old towel in the boxing ring — it wasn't pretty but it got the job done. He gave up and threw himself at her mercy.

"LaVonne, baby...obviously I said something wrong and..."

"Don't *baby* me."

"Okay. Okay. Still, I don't know what I've done. I'm swallowing my pride here. Okay? Enlighten me, *please*. Tell me what I said wrong?"

LaVonne lit into him with all the frustration a woman feels after being ignored for two solid months. "Do you realize you didn't call for two months? Do you realize that?"

"Not really…"

"Did I ask you to speak? No. I did not. And yes, it was two months. Thought we were having some fun and you were a good guy. I was enjoying doing stuff together…"

"Yeah, me too, baby."

"Don't. You. *Baby*. Me. And did I ask you to speak? No. I did not. And I was looking forward to doing some more stuff with you. Hey, two months go by and you finally call and I swallowed my pride…"

"And I appreciate that, baby."

"I told you not to *baby* me. And did I ask you to speak? Again, for the record, I did not. I swallowed my pride. I said to myself, 'Hey, he's been busy catching bad guys. Let me do something nice for him. Yes,' I said to myself, 'yes, let me invite this poor bachelor man who don't get no homemade cooking, yes, let me invite him for a home-cooked meal.' And what do I get?"

Al didn't say a word. He was afraid to.

"I asked a question. What did I get for my troubles?"

"You got…I don't know. Why don't you tell me?"

"I'll tell you what I got. I got my invitation thrown in my face, that's what I got. 'Let's go out!'"

"Oh, baby…"

"Don't you *baby* me. You have not earned that right, let me tell you."

"I didn't realize cooking meant so much to you."

LaVonne was silent again, and for a very long time. But this silence was different and Al sensed it.

He ventured, "Baby? You still there?"

LaVonne let that slide. "Yes."

Al shut up and waited. He might be ignorant but he wasn't dense.

He heard LaVonne sigh. "You make me crazy, you know that?"

"I'm sorry, baby."

"Hang up and call me back and let's start this conversation all over again."

Ah. Action, and a definitive one. "I can do that," he said. And he did.

LaVonne answered the phone sweetly. "Hello. How are you this evening?"

"I'm fine. I sure did enjoy having coffee with you the other evening."

"Yes, that was nice. Hey, I was wondering something."

Al knew his role now. "Yes, baby? What wuz you wonderin'?"

"I feel like cooking and I was wondering if you would like to have a home-cooked meal this Saturday night?"

"Oh, baby, wonderful. Tell you what, let me bring the wine, okay?"

"Lovely. Can you be here at seven?"

Al could.

Dinner was set for the following Saturday evening. He would bring three different wines so they would have something nice to drink with whatever she cooked. He made up his mind to eat appreciatively — no matter how it tasted.

* * * * *

Frank, not a true Luddite but not comfortable with using technology in his personal life, was surprised to find he was enjoying this emailing thing. He couldn't wait to get home in the evening to check it.

He was already convinced of Martin's idiocy, but after two weeks reading the outpourings of Carmelita's heart and mind, he was astounded Martin could live in the same house and not be supremely happy he was the man she chose.

Nor could he not understand how Martin wasn't worshipping at her feet.

Frank's replies were often very short. He didn't know what to write about his own heart and mind. He knew the story there and assumed she did, too. He was a selfish jackass who now saw the light because of her. What else was there to say about himself? Nothing. But she said stuff he didn't know existed in a woman, things that made him know it was good being in love and how sharing a life could be great.

Things that made him want to be unselfish and make sacrifices. Things that made him become ever more impatient for their lives together to begin.

Even though she was ready in her heart to move this along, they both knew, for the sake of the kids, they must go slow; and go slow they would. Then he got an email testing his resolve.

Dear Frank,

Aaahhh. All her emails began like that. He liked being called *dear*.

Dear Frank,

    I have debated about whether or not to tell you this and then decided to throw caution to the wind. So here goes.

    Martin is taking the kids for their annual Daddy/Kids trip. They will be gone for four days. They leave in two weeks, Friday morning, and will return Monday.

    Carmelita

Frank's thought was short: Huh. Well. How about that.

* * * * *

Gap was not a profiler and didn't pretend to be one. But he saw the results of sick minds on bodies and made his own conclusions; often those conclusions coincided with the profilers', even if he did get to those conclusions from the other side of the mind. He was confident the report he was sending to Rez, Don, Al, and Frank was, if not spot on, at least pretty darned close. But he didn't dwell on the why so much as the what. He felt the details of what was done and the order in which the acts were done could do as much to tie cases together as anything else.

Gap didn't like to dwell on what motivated criminals, serial killers specifically. To his mind, they were simple people. They wanted what they wanted when they wanted it, then went out and got it no matter the cost to anyone else. They were also lazy opportunists, even if they sometimes did what they did in an elaborate fashion. They also had great self-control. Nobody ever heard of a serial killer who couldn't stop killing when he was in prison. Gap never could understand people who wanted to know them and wrote them letters while in prison.

It wasn't for him to understand the perp, but to document what they did. In that process he was a master. He printed the document to PDF, attached it to an email, and blasted it out to the four.

* * * * *

Al walked to Frank's office. "Seen Gap's report?"

Frank had not. Al handed him the second copy he printed. They sat in silence as they read the four pages. The report was simplicity itself. Formatted in two columns, header one was entitled Wound Order Tape, the second Wound Order Body. Gap simply listed wound type in the order in which it happened for both the audio and the body.

Frank asked, "How did he know what was done to the woman on the recording?"

Al, faster than Frank, replied, "Read the last page."

Frank flipped to the last page.

```
Gentlemen,
    Of course, while some of the wounds
listed on the tape column could be
incorrect, I believe though, knowing what
I know about the body's response to such
treatment and comparing to the transcript
of the recording the GBI produced, I'm
probably correct in these.
    It is my opinion we are looking at a
taping of this girl's murder. I
questioned my conclusions repeatedly and
would appreciate getting us all together
again and letting you rip this apart
before we move forward.
```

They reached the same conclusion as Rez and Don in their office in the Butts County courthouse complex.

"Geez, Don, I can't believe this. Can you believe this?"

"Sure would make our lives simpler."

"Let's set up a meet."

Don logged onto his email and sent out possible dates to pick from. Within an hour, everyone weighed in and a date was set for them to go over Gap's report. Though truth be told, Rez and Don knew Gap well enough to know that no amount of ripping, tearing, or questioning would change the conclusions, but that Gap needed the critique so when this got to court, he would have already addressed any and all obstacles to the accuracy of his findings. Not for Gap to be caught with his forensic pants down and his professional privates flapping in the cold breeze of cross-examination.

Frank had suggested they come to Atlanta for the meeting. He even said he would buy lunch at Mary Mac's Tea Room, whatever in the heck that was, they wondered. They only hoped it wasn't a sissified eating joint and their fingers would fit through cup handles.

Rez pretended to be flustered about his wardrobe for the event and fluttered his hands like his teenage daughter did. "Don, what should we wear? A tux? A bowtie? Oh, my. I don't know if I have anything that will do. I'm gonna have to brush up on my tea room etiquette, too." He held out his pinky, just so.

"I'm wearing camo and muddy boots. That oughta throw 'em."

"Yeah, but it'll be you that gets throwed: throwed out."

Both men shook their heads in wonder: crime fighting, hard driving, manly cussing, how's it hanging, balls-all-in

GBI agents eating at a tea room and inviting other men to go with them. What was the world coming to?

* * * * *

"Guess what?"

Frank hated to guess. "What?"

"You gotta guess."

"Let me see. You won the lottery."

"No. Be serious. I would already have resigned. Guess?"

"Al, I don't like to guess. Tell me."

"Ah, you're no damn fun."

"Al, guessing is all I do for a living. I'd prefer not to do it when I don't have to."

"LaVonne is cooking Saturday night."

"Do you know if she's a good cook?"

"Nope. Scares the bejeezus out of me. I mean, what if she cooks up this pile of total crap and I can't eat it? My tongue is used to the good stuff, man. I don't think I could hide my true feelings and then she would get her feelings hurt and it wouldn't be pretty. But, what's worse is, let's just say, okay, somehow, *somehow,* I manage to hide how bad it is and I manage to croak out 'Oowee baby, yummy' in such a way she believes it. And let's just say that, we fall in love and get married and she cooks that meal the *rest of my life* on every anniversary because she's gonna think that I *lurrv* it. How can I eat that crap for the next fifty years and pretend it's good? Please, tell me if you know."

"Are you taking wine?"

"Yes! Of course. You think I'm stupid? I gotta have something good to at least wash down every bite. It's gonna be bland. It's gonna be burnt. Or else, it's gonna be boring."

Al sat up quickly. "What if she makes salad, spaghetti, and garlic bread? Everybody makes salad, spaghetti, and garlic bread. Won't inspire me in the least and you know this as a fact."

"Sure. Homemade salad, spaghetti, and garlic bread cannot inspire you like a mass-produced chili dog and onion rings from The Varsity. I see your dilemma."

"You laugh. But that's a classic meal with tastes finely honed to work together in ways obviously your mouth is too uneducated to appreciate. I mean, a nekkid dog? Really? What do you know about mixing flavors?"

Silence for the next few minutes.

"And I bet the salad will come out of a damn bag, too. Bottled Eye-Tail-Yun dressing. Margarine instead of butter on the bread. And garlic *salt*."

Al's depression was now complete and he flopped his head against the headrest and stared out the window.

Frank simply grinned and drove on to their next appointment. He took the quiet time to ponder the meaning behind Carmelita's email. She would have several days in a row where she wouldn't have to heed a schedule dictated by family responsibilities. Those days would come on a weekend when he might be free, too. But what did she mean? Did she want to have a picnic at Stone Mountain? Did she want to go to dinner and dancing at 57th Fighter Group? Did she want to spend the night? Or all of the above?

When he got home Friday evening, he slowly unpacked his Mexican dinner, poured a shot of Tequila into a glass of Coke, sat in front of the TV, and very slowly contemplated his reply. He knew what he wanted to say. He wanted to say *baby, put a toothbrush in your purse and come on.*

The Case of the Snuff Tape Killers

But the situation wasn't as romantic as he would have liked it to be for her. There were things to think about. Like birth control.

He said those words out loud: Birth. Control.

Only the Tequila heard him.

Condoms had never failed him, so no little GBI agents running around, as far as he knew anyway. But this was different. This was the last woman he was ever gonna be with. This was his future wife.Could she even have any more kids? Did she want any more? What if she did? He didn't want to use a condom with her. So…unromantic. But he didn't want any kids, yet.

Yet! Where'd that come from? I don't want any at all! I'm too old for kids. Or don't you remember seeing your gut hanging out in the mirror the other day?

Frank saw his Tequila and Coke was gone. He set down his chimis and chips and refried beans with cheese, and floated to the kitchen in his reverie to pour more of both.

What was he gonna reply? Two hours and three Tequila and Cokes later he had the whole thing figured out. He cranked up his computer, logged onto email, found her message, and hit reply.

Dear Carmelita,

Ahhh, he sure did like the sound of that and proceeded to write it again.

Dear Carmelita, Dear, dear Carmelita,
 Did I ever tell you you are a dear? You are a dear. So your bastard husband is, scratch that, so the father of your children is gonna be out of town with the kids for a few days

and you were scared of telling me. That is so sweet. And you are HOT!!!! Do you want to bring the condoms or should I? Forget that. I didn't mean that. What I meant to say was...you know what? I think I will not send this message.

Frank shut down the browser. Somehow his big head managed to get a message through the Tequila fog and stopped his little head from dictating the reply. He made up his mind to answer when no alcohol was in his system. He floated to his bed and fell across it like a log in the fog.

When he woke Saturday morning, he saw two things. One, he could have sworn he had almost a full bottle of Tequila. He must have been pouring with a loose grip. Two, his computer was still on and, now he was almost clearheaded and somewhat rested, he logged on again.

Dear Carmelita,
*   I would like to take you to dinner and then dancing on Saturday evening. Then maybe Sunday we can go to Stone Mountain for a picnic or something. How does that sound to you?*
Frank

More fretting for Carmelita

It had been two days since she sent the message to Frank about Martin's trip with the kids. And nothing. No text. No phone call. No email from Frank. She lay in the bed early Saturday morning, regretting the message. He probably felt pushed to do something and was feeling cornered. Like a drowning rat. A disgusted sigh escaped her lips as she turned over. She punched her pillow into a different shape, but she enjoyed the punching.

That woke up Martin.

Her tossing joggled something in his body and he decided he was horny and slid over to her. He snaked a hand over her side, grabbed a breast, and gave it a squeeze. He waited to see what reaction he would get.

Carmelita did her best to relax as if she was completely asleep. She did not respond to the squeeze nor to his insistent little thrusts against her backside. She let out an unappetizing snore and mumbled as if talking in her sleep, enough to cool his mono-jet, and he rolled over and out of bed. She heard the shower start up and then she promptly fell asleep, for real this time.

She woke four hours later. The extra sleep made her feel drugged. She crawled out of bed. Dragging on a robe, she slid feet into slippers and slapped her way down the hall into the kitchen. The bright light hurt her eyes. She squinted against it, identified the coffee pot, managed to pour herself a cup, then sat in the dark living room to let her body acclimate itself to the novelty of sleeping in.

No one was home. Martin must have taken the kids to their practices. He was going to be mad his Saturday morning rest was interrupted. Oh well, too bad, so sad. By the time her cup was empty she was awake and feeling better. She poured herself another one and thought about checking her email. But what was the point? Frank was feeling completely hounded and she was being a needy woman who dared to make a suggestion. She got busy with things she needed to do around the house and the yard.

This was her life now. She was an unloved woman with nothing to look forward to. She may as well make the most of whatever she could. Her new email account would lie dormant, like her heart.

The yard was well on its way to beautiful by the time everyone returned home and she was well on her way to a nervous breakdown.

Week Nine

Monday: Women!

Frank had checked his email Saturday. He checked it Sunday morning and before he went to bed. Nothing from Carmelita. Though he did receive several email messages about male enhancement products. *How in the hell do those things find their way into every inbox in the world?*

He checked his email again Monday morning before he went to work. Still nothing. He hoped she was okay. He hoped the message he sent her was not too much for her to deal with.

He made a mental note to call her at lunch and see if she got the message. He arrived at work and was promptly waylaid by Tweeter.

"Hey, when we going out next?"

"I was thinking this Thursday. That good for you? And now we have a case to charge it to, you don't have to take off any more personal days."

Tweeter shrugged. "Okay. So early then? Thursday?"

"Yeah. I'll tell Al."

"Okay." Tweeter breezed on down the stairs to his lab.

Frank got on the elevator, pushed four, leaned back, and waited for the doors to close. He thought of the first time he saw Carmelita and the times they were in the elevator together.

Why hadn't she answered his email? He was not going to wait until lunch to call. By the time he unlocked his office door, her phone was ringing.

"This is Carmelita Oliveira."

Carmelita knew who called; his number, programmed into her phone, showed up when he rang. But she was not going to act needy.

"Hey. This is GBI Man." Frank thought he said it teasingly. But he obviously was wrong.

"Ah. Yes. How are you?"

Frank caught the businesslike manner of her voice. He figured it out in a second. She must be with someone and she can't talk freely.

"Is this a bad time? Should I call later?"

"No. This is a perfectly fine time."

"Okay. I sent you an email message Saturday morning. Did you get it?"

Frank heard a small *oh!*, then silence.

"Carmelita? Are you still there?"

She managed to choke out a yes. Ah, shit. He heard crying. What'd he say?

"Are you okay, baby?"

He heard snuffling and blowing her nose and she laughed a little.

"I'm sorry. I'm sorry." Then crying started again.

"Did I say something wrong, baby?"

She cried harder. Al walked in Frank's office in time to hear him say *something wrong, baby?* He smiled big. He was gonna enjoy this. Frank shrugged his shoulders.

Al mouthed, "Is she crying?"

Frank nodded yes.

Al mouthed, "Hormones."

Frank immediately understood and felt better. "Carmelita?"

More snuffling and blowing and hiccupping. Finally he heard her speak.

"You…you sent me a message Saturday morning?"

"Yes, baby. Didn't it come through?"

She cried harder and he could barely make out, "I don't know — *hiccup* — I didn't check my email — *sniffle and blow* — I thought you were mad about me making a suggestion about us doing something and was feeling corrrrrr… nerrrrrred and…" then more sobbing.

Frank covered the phone's mouthpiece and whispered, "I hate that son of a bitch husband of hers."

Then to Carmelita he said, "Baby. Check your email. I fell asleep Friday and didn't get around to sending you the message until Saturday morning. I've made some plans for this weekend. Let me know what you think about them? Love you, baby."

He barely heard her reply through the crying and then they were disconnected. Women. You were damned if you did and damned if you didn't, but damn, just damn. Frank and Al smiled at each other. Life was getting interesting.

"Frank?"

"Yep?"

"Guess what?"

* * * * *

Carmelita hung up. It was a good thing she was still in her garage when the call came through. Her makeup was ruined. She cried all the way back to the bedroom, where she found tissues.

She didn't redo her face until after she checked her email; what was the point when all she was going to do was cry again? There was his message. She read it. Yep, she cried some more. He wanted to take her to dinner and then go dancing. He wanted to take her on a picnic the next day. She cried harder. But the crying didn't stop her from replying *yes and yes*.

Within thirty minutes she was under control, face repaired, and the garage door was closing as she pulled out of the drive.

* * * * *

"Al, don't make me guess."

"Come on. One guess."

"Okay. Ummm...you won the lottery."

"Man, you're no fun."

"What?"

Al's face got serious and his tone was low and solemn. "Ask me how the dinner went Saturday night."

Expecting the worst, Frank cringed. "How'd the dinner go Saturday night?"

Al pointed at his mouth. "You know this tongue is only used to the best. Only the best."

"That bad, huh?"

"That bad? Oh, no. No. It wasn't bad."

"Worse than bad?"

"Nope. I wouldn't say that either. No. Frank." Al closed his eyes, put his hands in prayer position in front of his chest with fingertips barely touching under his chin. "I pray. I pray that that woman loves me."

"That *good*?"

"Oh my God. I brought wine, but I didn't need it. I mean, we drank it, don't get me wrong, but not one drop was needed. I'm gonna marry that woman...that is, if she'll have me."

"No spaghetti, bagged salad, or garlic salt?"

"We had spaghetti. And a salad she made herself. The dressing was primo, three choices, all made by her *from scratch*. The bread had *real garlic* on it. Chopped fine. Chopped real fine, and the butter, no margarine, the *butter*. Perfectly toasted. The sauce, holy cow, I don't know what she put in it, but I guarantee if it could be bottled, she'd make a fortune. The pasta — cooked perfectly. And the dessert. She made a chocolate cake with some sort of white icing I ain't never tasted before."

"The garlic didn't get in the way of kissing her, did it?"

"We both had garlic. Canceled each other out."

"So you kissed her, huh?"

If you can see a black man blushing, then he's got something to blush about — and Al went deep scarlet.

Frank nodded. "Was that a technical kiss or a —"

Al left abruptly for his office. Frank's commiserating laugh followed him across the hall after he called out, "Fastest way to a man's heart is through his stomach or haven't you heard?"

Tuesday AM: Details and lunch

The next day the Butts County boys showed up at Frank's office. Al snagged a conference room early that morning. He and Tweeter were waiting for them when they got there. Coffee and a dozen Dunkin' returned their favor.

"Hey, Frank, I wanted to let you know, Rez and me've been out to the new hole. We thought we would keep an eye on it, too. It's still empty. Hey, Tweeter, we never did find that camera. That's the best camo job I never didn't see."

"Thanks. Grave's still empty, huh?"

"Yeah. Why do they call you Tweeter? Is it 'cause you do a lot of social networking or something?"

Frank and Al laughed. Tweeter smiled and said, "Nah. It's a childhood nickname. Kinda stuck. Came along before the these here Internets were a thang."

Gap was wound tight. He was ready to get into the meat of the meeting. "Are we ready? Can we get started?"

Everyone took a seat and pulled out the four-page listing of wounds.

"Okay. Has everyone looked over this?"

They all nodded.

"Did you notice, both the recording and the body matched up awfully close?"

Nodding all around was accompanied by slurped coffee. Rez reached for another doughnut as he said, "Gap, like me and Don told ya, we couldn't find anything to disagree with you. Don, how many times we go over this list while listening and looking at the autopsy photos?"

"Ah. Geez. Three times, I think."

Gap swiveled his head to Frank and Al.

Frank leaned back in his chair. "We agree. I hate to have made you three drive this far and not have something to ask, but, dude, it was complete and accurate."

Al nodded. "Frank and me went over it several times, too. I'll have to say the only question really bugging me is this: How'd they get the backhoe down in the woods without leaving a trace?"

"Easy," Don explained. "There's a construction access road still passable from when the bridge was built years ago.

Rez asked me the same question. We logged onto Google Earth and got a good view of the road."

"Huh." Al sat back and thought. "Frank and Tweeter and me are gonna be down there on Thursday to download this week's video. How about we all meet at Mama's early, say 7:30? Then let's take a look at the access and see what we can find out. Sound good to everybody?"

Sure did. Frank may have never heard of Mama's, but Butts County sure had. Big smiles met the happy news.

Frank said, "You guys relax for a bit. Al and I have a few phone calls to make and then we'll head out to Mary Mac's."

Gap, Don, and Rez's smiles froze. After Al and Frank left the room and the door closed, Rez held out his pinky finger. A boom of laughter went down the hall.

The Butts County boys needn't have worried about Mary Mac's Tea Room. After eating a proper man-sized meal of proper man-type foods, they left completely satisfied, their manliness not under attack.

Thursday AM: Hole still empty

The group met at Mama's Thursday morning and, again properly fueled, hiked through the woods loaded with computer, ammo, guns, and cameras.

Tweeter got the download going as Al set up targets for everyone. Random pops, phuts, and booms could be heard. Then Tweeter hid the computer under a few downed branches and they took off, guns over shoulders and cameras in pockets, looking for the access road. It wasn't far from the new hole.

"Looks like this is it," Don said. "You can see the tracks from the backhoe's caterpillars."

They followed tracks toward the bridge. Frank and Rez took pictures along the way.

"This is where they got the truck and trailer to." Rez pointed, "You can see where they unloaded the backhoe."

When they looked back down the hill they could see how lazy their killers were. They were almost within line of sight of the new hole. Anyone going across the bridge, if they had stopped and looked, could see them heading through the woods.

The fivesome tramped down the hill, following the track all the way to the new grave. Even Tweeter couldn't find the camera. He hoped when this case was over he would be able to retrieve it.

As they walked past the hole, every man stopped and examined it. Had anything changed from when they were here the other day? No, it had not. Tweeter pulled out the backpack and checked the download's progress. It was finished. They did a bit more shooting and went out the way they came in, happy the hole wasn't filled — and worried that it wasn't.

* * * * *

Everybody went back to Mama's to take a look at the downloaded footage. Disappointment was thick in the air as their food was delivered.

"Hey, Cuz," Mama, also known as Cousin Rochelle, said to Al when she came to check on their food. "No whooping and hollering today. No good news?"

"Nope. Nothing."

"Wait just one damned minute," Don said. "Mama is your cousin?"

Rez looked at Mama. "You poor thing."

Mama laughed as she patted Al on the shoulder. "I know. We love him anyway."

Thursday PM: "The Boys" and more feel plenty of pain

Frank's shower felt nice. After a long and disappointing day, he lingered longer than usual, allowing hot streams of water to massage his shoulders, scalp, and back, steaming the mirror top to bottom. He gave no conscious thought to the water beating his body. He was planning his weekend.

Dinner first.

With wine, of course.

Maybe a little close dancing after that. A couple of drinks.

Sunday take her on a picnic.

How long has it been since I've been on a picnic? It had to have been with Mama, what, ten years ago? Where is there a place around here to have a picnic?

He shut off the water, drew back the shower curtain, and reached for the towel. Distracted by his weekend's itinerary, he didn't put his foot down firmly when stepping out of the tub, and his wet foot slipped. He landed hard astraddle the edge of the tub — and got very sick very fast.

He slid off the edge onto the floor and moaned while clutching mangled manhood. It took him a half-hour to crawl to bed. He fought the nausea, but then his inner thigh started aching, and his ankle felt like it was getting bigger by the second. A peek under the covers and, sure enough, it was swelling fast. He elevated his leg and tucked himself in tight; he'd see what needed to be done later.

He couldn't sleep; the pain was too much. Two hours later the ankle was larger and he knew he would need to ice it. Cussing and hobbling his way around the house, he managed to put on a pair of boxers, make it to the kitchen, swallow three Goody's, dig out an ice pack, and set his laptop on the bed. He might as well send Carmelita an email and let her know about this tragic turn of events.

Tragic? Now who was sounding like a teenager in love?

He would have chuckled except it hurt too much. He got his leg set, slowly adjusted injured man parts so they weren't under stress, logged on, and found an email from Carmelita.

Dear Frank,

Dear Frank. He liked being called dear. He read it again.

Dear Frank,

Tomorrow morning Martin and the kids will be leaving. I am very much looking forward to going out with you Saturday evening and having a picnic on Sunday. What fun! These things have kept me happy all week.

I'm sorry about my emoting all over the phone the other day. Call me tomorrow after 10 AM, okay? No. I'll call you when they leave. I'll leave a message if you can't answer.

Wow. Dancing. What fun. Fun, fun, fun.

Carmelita

The Case of the Snuff Tape Killers

Frank called Al. "Dude. Got two really big problems."

While he waited on his buddy, Frank debated whether or not to tell Carmelita about his injuries or wait to see if he would be alright by Saturday, in which case he could fake his way through any residual pain. His mind was still not made up by the time the doorbell rang. Hobbling, he finally unlocked the door.

"Ouch. Were you in a fight or something?" Al closed the front door and followed Frank back to his bedroom.

"Yeah, had a fight with the shower curtain. I feel so stupid. I slipped getting out of the tub."

"You know people have died like that. You should be thankful you only got a twisted ankle."

He groaned. "It gets worse. I think I pulled a muscle in my thigh and I landed balls-down on the tub edge."

Al cringed and felt himself reflexively draw up in sympathy. "Ouch. What do you want me to do?"

"I have a date Saturday evening and Sunday, too. I can't go dancing if this damn ankle keeps getting bigger."

"Not to mention what else you can't do since your bits and pieces are in triage, too."

"We weren't gonna have sex!"

"Yeah, right. You forget I know you."

"We weren't gonna have sex!"

"Right. Frank Smith was *only* gonna go dancing and then go on a picnic. *Right.*"

"I'm telling you, that's all."

"Okay, sure. I believe ya. Yeah, I believe ya. I do. You're different about her. But ya can't tell me ya haven't thought about it."

"Did I say I ain't never thought about it? *Ow.* No, I didn't. Goddamn, why am I talking to you? I'm in pain."

"What do you want me to do?"

"Drive me to the emergency room. I feel like an old man tripping in the tub."

"Sure, man. Let's go. I'll lock up. If you want, later I can shop for one of those walk-in tub-shower combinations for old people. I'm helpful like that."

Frank tried to laugh, but when he did his man parts hurt. Who knew those were connected to the funny bone...

Ow.

Friday AM: Frank, the patient

They spent most of the night in the emergency room. Smashed balls, a stretched muscle, and a twisted ankle ranked well below a dog attack, a heart attack, a baby turning blue with an acute case of asthma, a sawed-off finger, and three people throwing up all over the place with the flu. The nursed called Frank in at three in the morning.

Al slept draped across two chairs.

Somebody had to go to work.

X-rays revealed nothing broken and, other than painkillers, ice, and elevation, nothing else could be done except laugh at the doctor's joke. He said, "Huh. Blue balls are real."

Frank was sent away with a prescription. Al stopped at the hospital pharmacy to get it filled and they made their way back to Frank's house. Al helped him inside, made sure he was okay, and lay on the sofa to finish his night's sleep.

He brought Frank a cup of coffee in the morning. "Need anything, call, okay?"

"Thanks for taking me to the hospital. Hey, bring me my phone, okay?"

Al left for work; Frank went back to sleep after taking another pill with his coffee. His phone rang but sounded like it was coming from miles away and through a thick fog. The clock was out of focus. How long had he slept?

"'Lo?" he mumbled.

"Frank?" It was Carmelita.

He rubbed his hand over his eyes and tried to wake up. "Mmmm…hey, baby."

"You sound like you're asleep."

"I was. What time is it?"

"Almost noon. You okay?"

"No. I was at the emergency room most of the night."

He heard Carmelita's sharp intake of breath. "Are you okay? What happened?"

"Well…" Frank chuckled, because now, under the influence of meds, it seemed so funny. "…funny thing. I slipped getting out of the tub last night…"

"People can die from that, you know."

He chuckled some more. "Yeah, I know. But I didn't. Anyway, I managed to bruise my — *chuckle* — male ego if you get my drift, rip a thigh muscle, sprain my ankle."

"Oh, dear. Get something for pain? "

"I did. Wait." Frank looked under the covers at his ankle. It wasn't bigger, but it wasn't smaller. "Ankle's still swollen. Not pretty."

"Have you had anything to eat today?"

Frank thought; finally dragged out *nooo*.

Carmelita hesitated. "I'll be happy to, you know, cook you something and bring it over? Or cook something there?"

"I don't keep any food here that needs cooking. But you don't have to…"

"I know I don't have to. Do you *want* me to?"

The meds slowed his response time. "Well…"

She backpedaled. "I don't have to."

"Now, hang on a minute, girl. I didn't say I didn't want you to. Actually, it would be very nice."

"Okay." She got his home address.

Friday Midday: Carmelita, the nurse

Al had fun telling the story of Frank's brush with losing his manhood. All afternoon Frank's phone rang off the hook with well-wishers having a good laugh at his expense. He didn't care. He laughed loud and long. The meds, on an almost twenty-four-hour empty stomach, and the thought of Carmelita cooking for him in his house were enough to make him feel better. The calls finally stopped and he was able to go back to sleep.

Later, he woke to an insistent ringing. He slid the cellphone closer and managed to flip it open.

"Hello?" he mumbled.

"Frank. Do you have a key hidden somewhere so I can get in?"

"Baby! You're here. No key. I'll be there in a min, hon."

Hobbling across the floor, Frank eventually got to the door and turned the locks. He managed a quick *hey* before he was wracked with pain.

"Hey. Ow. Ow. Ow." He felt pain, limped to the bathroom and got a pill. Then staggered to the kitchen for a glass of water. There was a glass and water in the bathroom, but Carmelita was in the kitchen and he had to make an entrance as his old pitiful self. He played up his injuries, though it didn't take much effort to do so.

Carmelita ordered, "Sit. I'll get water."

Hanging on to the edge of the table for support, Frank managed to lower into a chair by the time she returned. She handed it to him, watched him swallow, and made him drink the whole glass of water.

"Back in a minute. I have a few more things in the car."

Unable to turn properly to get the full effect of her walk to the door, he ended up turning too far.

"Ow."

He was laying the pitiful act on thick and he knew it. But it felt nice when she stopped, turned back, and said *You okay?* She was back shortly with the rest of the bags. One of which he heard her drop next to the front door.

Overnight bag? Hmmm…

Frank smiled.

Friday PM: Another girl goes missing

Al got the call late Friday afternoon. The Butts County boys had some news.

"Jones, we tried to reach Smith. He didn't answer. You're the next best thing."

"Guess I'll have to do, Don. What's up?"

"We got us a girl went missing three days ago."

"And…"

"Her parents are just now reporting it because she normally runs away and stays gone overnight, at most. Comes home the next afternoon. She's never stayed two nights away, but she did and Mom and Dad got worried. She's not at any friend's house. The friends are worried, too. Nobody's seen hide nor hair of her. In three days."

"Nothing?"

"Nope. She ain't facebooked, she ain't myspaced, she ain't tweeted, or texted or instagrammed. And according to her friends and her mother, she was constantly doing those things. Her best friend even checked her accounts to see when she'd last used them."

"And?"

"Three days, Al."

"You thinking what I'm thinking, Don?"

"Yeah. I think our hole is about to get filled up."

"I'll meet you down there early in the morning. I'll get Tweeter to come, too."

"Where's Smith?"

Al chuckled. "Frank and his tub got into a fight last night. Tub 1, Frank 0. He can barely walk. He's dead in the water for a few days, but if anything breaks, he'll be there, even if we have to roll him in a wheelchair to the scene."

Al remembered LaVonne and called her. "Hey, baby."

"Hey. How are you?"

"Good, good. Listen, I have to go to Butts County early in the morning. Not sure what we're gonna find or how long it's gonna take. If possible, I'll call you and let you know about tomorrow evening. But if you don't hear from me, it's because I'm hip deep into something and can't."

LaVonne was silent.

"Baby? You there?"

"Yes, I'm here." She paused. Al could hear her breathing. "Is this an excuse not to see me again?"

"No, baby. I really gotta work this thing. Okay? I hope I can make it, but just in case, okay? You understand? I wanna to be there with you. It's what I would rather do."

"Okay. I understand. Work, right? We'll see what tomorrow will bring, huh?"

"Yes, baby."

Friday PM: Tending the injured

Carmelita insisted Frank get back in the bed. She found more pillows and got his leg elevated properly. She propped him up, gave him the TV remote, and tutt-tutted around him until he got settled. He liked being fussed over. Settled against his pillows, lazily thumbing the remote's buttons, he saw nothing on the screen that interested him. He heard her in the kitchen making noises he didn't know his kitchen could make. Domestic sounds filled him with calm.

Carmelita whispered, "Frank?"

His eyes flew open. "Did I go to sleep?"

"Wasn't quite sure. Why I whispered. You must've not been totally asleep. Are you ready for your supper?"

He took a deep breath and savored the scents of the home-cooked meal clinging to her. "Yes, I'm starved."

She smiled. "Let me make you a plate."

He turned television off and pushed himself up a little higher against the pillows. She returned in a couple of minutes. He'd never had that much food in his house at any time, and never served so nicely. She settled him in with food and iced tea and left to make a plate for herself. When she came back she sat on the other side of his king-sized bed. She crossed her legs and watched him eat.

He was hungrier than he realized. Grilled chicken. Lemon. Butter. Broccoli, steamed. And rolls. He thoroughly enjoyed the rarity of a home-cooked meal. He glanced up briefly to say something about the food, but noticed the expression on her face. "What?" he asked.

"*What* what?"

"What are you thinking?"

Carmelita smiled slowly, but her eyes showed the conflict she felt. "This is the first time I've been alone with a man in almost twenty years."

Frank set his plate on his lap. "How're you feeling about that?"

She bowed her head. "Not what I thought I would feel."

"What did you think you should feel?"

She lifted her chin a tiny bit, though her eyes remained downcast. "Guilt. Fear. Lots of guilt."

Frank extended a finger, barely touching her foot. "And what do you feel?"

"Calm. No fear." She raised her eyes to his. "And no guilt. Is that bad?"

"Bad?" He took her foot into his hand and held it. "I wouldn't say it was bad."

"What is it then?"

"Ah, hon. Don't you know?"

Carmelita shook her head. Frank waited while she thought about it. She nodded.

"Yeah. I know."

His hand still caressed her foot. She slid her hand over his. Taking a deep breath, she carefully placed her plate on the opposite nightstand, moved onto her hands and knees, and smiled. Using one hand, she removed his plate from his lap, stretched across his body and moved it to the nightstand on his side of the bed. His eyes followed her every move. She pulled back onto her hands and knees and stared at him, seriously taking his breath away. When her hand brushed across his chest, his eyes closed involuntarily and he couldn't move.

She leaned forward, lightly kissed him, paused a moment, then began the second kiss. The second kiss shut her eyes.

He slid his hand behind her neck, tangled his fingers in her hair, held her mouth against his. Carmelita's passion overwhelmed her. She wanted this man and she wanted him now. Her hand slid down, over his stomach, and —

"Ow. Ow. Ow." Frank grabbed her hand, fighting its natural progression.

Shaking, she shifted away. "What? Do you not —"

"I do, but…" He grinned apologetically. "When I fell last night…" Then shrugged. "I landed in a very awkward position on the edge of the tub…"

Carmelita did not comprehend. "What does that mean?"

"Frank Junior and the Boys are badly bruised. We almost lost them in the accident last night. At least, that's what it feels like."

Carmelita's horror-stricken expression made him laugh. "But everything still works, but even with the meds, oh, hun… they be mighty sore."

It took her a moment, but she giggled. "You look pitifully sorry. Oh, baby." She put her hand on his face, kissed him lightly, leaned over him, grabbed his plate, and said, "Well, I guess I can put all this energy into cleaning."

"Thank you, baby. Sorry, baby."

She backed out through the bedroom door, wagging a finger at him. "Well, I forgive you as long as you tell me everything's intact."

"Intact. For sure."

He heard her vigorously cleaning.

* * * * *

Don and Rez were worried. Worried about the girl. What if she's still alive? Or captive in a hotel room in their county, drugged, being tortured?

Rez shook his head. "Nah, that ain't happening," he concluded after they talked out the possible scenarios.

"And you say that, why?"

"I keep going back to the recording. It was very long and noisy and you know it had to be messy. There ain't no way that's gonna happen in any hotel or motel without them getting found out."

Don sipped his beer. He stared at the game on the screen above Jill's head.

Jill called from across the bar, "You ready for another one, sweetie?"

Don's eyes went from the screen to the glass and up to Amazon Jill, his favorite bartender at Mike's Bar and Grill.

"Yes, ma'am."

"Coming right up, baby."

"You think Al's right about them having a killing trailer in the woods?"

"Yeah. And I think it's very close to the burial sites."

Don's team scored and he yelled, "Hell, yeah. Dat's what I'm talking about."

Jill looked up at the score as she put his beer down in front of him. "You got any money on the game, sugar?"

Don drained his glass and handed it to her. "Who? Me? I don't gamble. I'm an occifer of the law. Don't you know that gambling's illegal?"

Jill smiled indulgently as she took away the empty. "Yeah, right."

"We got to figure out a way to find that trailer and find it fast."

"You think she's still alive?"

Rez shook his head. "I have no idea. I have *no* idea. But, damn, I hope so."

Don sucked the foam off the top of his beer. "I wonder if we could get the traffic chopper from Channel 5?"

"You mean the one sometimes comes further down I-75 than anybody else?"

"Yeah. That one."

"I'd say sure, except for the fact tomorrow is Saturday. There ain't gonna be no traffic jams this far south on Saturday anytime."

"Well, you'd be wrong, or have you done forgot?"

"Forgot what?"

Don yelled again and pounded the bar. "Yeah!" His team scored again.

Rez said, "Forgot what?"

"If you will recall, partner, we got the race in Hampton on Sunday and you know who starts coming in on Thursday and Friday, right?"

"Race fans."

"And who makes a big deal outta reporting where the traffic jams are for those rabid, spoiled-rotten, beer-swilling, RV'ing NASCAR fans?"

"Channel 5."

The detectives grinned. Rez said, "Looks like we be going on a chopper ride in the morning, brutha."

"Let's make a call."

Within 30 minutes, Don had the pilot on the phone; they would meet in the morning. Rez watched in wonder as once again his partner made something happen fast without the aid of red tape or other governmental delay. One day Rez was gonna know Don's whole story.

* * * * *

Sounds of banging and clanging and water running in the kitchen kept Frank company as he lay feeling sorry for himself. He heard her walking his way. He closed his eyes and looked pitiful again.

"Hey, Frank. Where's the detergent to put in the dishwasher? I couldn't find it."

"There's a dishwasher in there?"

"Are you kidding me? You didn't know you had a dishwasher?"

"No. I mean, I noticed a door and I pretty much never opened it."

Carmelita stared at him. "You don't have any detergent for the machine?"

"I don't think so."

"I better get some, then."

"Why?"

"Because the machine is full and you can't wash dishes without detergent."

He heard her dig in her purse for keys. "Hey! Hon. Come here for a sec, okay?"

She came back in, stood at the foot of the bed with a pad and pen. "You need something else while I'm out?"

"No. I need you to come here." He moved over, painfully, so she could sit on the edge next to him. He patted the spot. "Come on."

She clutched her purse tightly in front of her and sat next to him.

Frank asked, "Are you mad at me?"

Carmelita did not speak. She couldn't.

He asked again. "Are you mad at me?"

She tried to speak, still couldn't.

"Why are you crying?"

One by slow one, tears fell to her purse and rolled off. She wiped at her eyes but the wetness wouldn't stop.

Frank continued, "The meds have made me understand profound things tonight. You don't have to answer because it may not be the right question to ask." She nodded. "But know this, I'm gonna make love to you, sooner than later. And tonight?" She nodded. "I want to sleep with you, here, in this bed. Will you sleep with me tonight?"

She nodded hungrily.

He wiped her face dry. "Good. Good." They smiled. "Go get your damn detergent and get back to me."

She flew out the door.

Saturday AM: Hunting clues from a copter and making love

Al and Tweeter met Rez and Don early at Mama's for breakfast Saturday morning.

Don filled them in. "We're going on a chopper ride this morning. Channel 5 is gonna take us up for a lookey-loo."

"And we're looking for what, exactly?" Al asked.

"A killin' trailer. See, me and Rez think the girl that went missing might still be alive —"

"We sure as hell hope so, at least."

Tweeter stared straight ahead. "We worked it out in our mind that maybe they're doing the deed close by where they bury 'em. Moving a body is harder than people think."

They got quiet as their food arrived.

"Gentlemen," the waitress said, "who got the tall stack with country ham?"

Al pointed at Tweeter. Tweeter never batted an eye.

"Dude. Your food is here." Nothing from Tweeter. Al snapped his fingers. "Earth to Tweeter."

Tweeter blinked. "Yeah? Huh?"

"You okay?"

"Okay. Look. I don't need to go up in no whirlybird. Okay? I'll do the download. Okay? I'll wait for ya at the…at the place."

Don had seen it before. "Scared of flying, are ya?"

"Ain't scared of flying. Scared of landing hard."

"Okay, bro. Alright with me."

With that little bit of business taken care of to Tweeter's satisfaction, the shoveling began. Plates were cleaned, coffee siphoned, and within twenty minutes they were on the road.

* * * * *

The bathroom door opening pulled at Frank's consciousness. The early morning light barely shone through the cracks in the blinds. He kept his eyes closed and didn't move. Carmelita slid under the covers, curved her body against his back, and slid a hand against his stomach. She kissed his shoulder and settled her head on the pillow.

"Mmm…mornin', hun," he whispered. In response, he felt her kiss between his shoulder blades. He entwined his fingers in hers, pulled her hand up, and kissed her fingers. His reward was a pressing of her body against his and more small kisses.

She did not stop pressing against him. He rolled onto his back. She cradled her head in his shoulder. Her leg crossed his. She gave a small excited sound and pushed up on her elbow. Her eyes questioned him.

He smiled. "You know what they say."

"No. What do *they* say?"

"Morning wood is the best."

This time when her hand moved, his pain was bearable. She was gentle, though the pillows were kicked to the floor with some force.

* * * * *

"See ya back here in a couple of hours. Shouldn't take long to download. Only been two days." Tweeter took off, happy to leave the flyboys to their adrenaline rush.

Rez, Don, and Al went to their meet-up with the chopper. They watched as it landed, ducked heads, and ran.

Don took co-pilot, shaking hands with the pilot. They put on their headsets.

"Don, how they hanging, brutha?"

"They're hanging fine. Jay, meet Rez, my partner, and Al, GBI."

He shook each hand in turn. "Welcome aboard, gentlemen. Where we going?"

The chopper rose, turned one-eighty and headed toward their search area. Ten minutes later they were over the gravesites. Rez spoke into his headset, "Can't imagine they'd cross the river, so let's stick to this side of the water."

Al added, "And I can't imagine they would cross under the bridge. Let's stay south of the bridge."

Jay, already filled in on what they were looking for, nodded. "South and west it is."

They followed the river south for five miles, turned around, came north, but a bit further west. This pattern was followed until they covered every inch of what could feasibly be considered their prime zone and some beyond it. There were no trailers. And no spots where it looked like one may have been parked.

Don was the first to admit defeat. "Back to square one, gentlemen?"

Al nodded. Rez shrugged and shook his head. Jay pointed the chopper toward the car. When they landed, Tweeter was waiting. From the air, they could see him pacing and waving at them to land.

Once on the ground, Al thanked Jay, Rez waved goodbye, and they jumped down, running low. Don clapped his friend on the shoulder and shook his hand. "Thanks. I owe you one."

Frantic waving continued by Tweeter. He yelled, "You guys gotta see this."

They got into the SUV, Tweeter plugged the computer into a power port. He pulled up the downloaded video and hit play. There were their boys again. Tommy and Otter were in the pit installing sharp spikes. There was some disagreement and forceful conversation, they almost came to blows twice, then a plan was worked out as how best to get the job done.

Tweeter fast-forwarded through the labor, then brought it to a stop where it showed the two men walking away from the pit.

"Do you see what's missing?" His eyes were big, his face angry; he was fuming.

Everybody studied the screen until finally, one by one, they each shook their head *no*. Tweeter pointed to what wasn't there. "Look everywhere and you won't see any warning signs, no human-readable fencing an animal could still get through. Nothing to keep anyone safe."

He looked from one to the other. "We can't let it stay. What we gonna do?"

Don asked, "What time and day was this? Late Thursday after we were there, or Friday?"

"Time-date stamp says yesterday."

"Friday then."

Al made an executive decision. "Get the spikes outta there. We can't leave 'em."

Don suggested, "Let's get pictures, too. Who knows when this bit of evidence may come in handy."

Rez said it for everyone, "What are these sick bastards up to?"

"Did you find the killing trailer?"

The Case of the Snuff Tape Killers

"Nope," Al told Tweeter as he started the truck and beat a path to the pit.

* * * * *

Carmelita, wide awake, lay curled against Frank, her head on his chest feeling its rise and fall. With her fingernails, she lightly and slowly stroked his chest, arms, and belly until she managed to relax. Frank slept with his arm tightly wrapped around her.

She listened to him breathing. She laid her ear on his heart and listened to the beat. Her own heart was a study in contrasts. Racing one minute as memories of three of the most glorious hours of her life flooded her mind and her senses, the next beating calm and steady with the knowledge she was loved. Feeling his breathing change, she whispered, "You awake?"

He stretched and yawned. "Yeah."

They turned toward each other. Carmelita drew her knees up and put them against his belly. He tucked a hand behind her upper knee. They watched each other quietly for a few minutes. She closed her eyes as Frank stroked her hair and face. He noticed tears.

"You okay?"

Carmelita cried silently.

"Are you sorry you did this?"

Carmelita shook her head.

"Then why are you crying, baby?"

It took her some minutes to stop crying enough so she could speak.

"It's not gonna get better. Ever."

Then the crying began again, only this time loud sobs wracked her body. "Sure it will, baby. I'm just injured."

"Not you. Him! My marriage."

As she understood the lack of love she lived with all those years, she cried and grieved its death. It took Carmelita thirty minutes to grieve for her lost dreams. Then she got frantic.

She wailed, "Frank. How am I gonna be able to sleep in the same bed with Martin?"

"Move into another room."

"I don't have another room."

"Then...fall asleep on the sofa every night."

Carmelita thought about it, saw it was doable, and her worry subsided somewhat. She nodded, more determined. "It could work. I could do that."

"Yes, hon. You can do that."

Her worry returned. "But for how long before he makes an issue of it?"

"Listen to me. You listening? Look at me." Carmelita focused on his face and nodded. "Baby..."

Now it was his turn to choke up. He stroked her hair while he controlled his emotions and regained his voice.

"Baby...do you see this house?" He waited for her reply. "Yes."

"This is our home. Ours. Yours and mine. Look, if in a week he's demanding what he views as his rights as a husband and you can't do it, and he's making trouble for you, you can move to our *home*. Here. This place. Do you understand?"

She nodded.

"I am ready for you whenever you want to, or can, come to me."

She nodded. "I'm very sad after this morning."

"Don't you feel good? I feel good."

"Yes. I feel wonderful. I now know what I've been missing all these years and it makes me sad."

"Hun. You're looking at this all wrong, you know."

"How?"

"Instead of feeling sad about what you've missed, think about all the good you're gonna get in the years to come. And you know I'm gonna give it to you good."

Carmelita closed her eyes and thought about what he said. When she opened them, he cocked an eyebrow.

She smiled and said, "Can I start right now getting some more of that good stuff?"

"Hmm…let me think about that for a sec." He took a peek under the covers. "Uh, yeah. I think that is doable. Remember, baby. I'm still on the injured list. Be gentle."

And she was.

To his delight.

Saturday Midday: K.I.S.S. the case

"Occam's Razor," Don said as he stopped pulling at a embedded stake.

Al, Rez, and Tweeter halted their labors, too. "Say whut?" Rez asked.

"Occam's Razor. Always consider the simplest explanation first." Don yanked at the next stake and pitched it over the top into their pile. "I think we should ask ourselves a question."

"And that would be?" Tweeter grunted as he yanked

another stake out.

"Where's the water?"

Al understood immediately. "Damn. You're right."

Tweeter and Rez looked at each other and shrugged.

"'Splain, please," Tweeter said, bening to the next stake.

"We've been saying they're lazy and they aren't gonna transfer a body too far, so therefore, they have to have a killing site close by, right?

Grunt. "Right."

"Yeah." Toss.

"But we forgot one important thing. And Gap told us this at the beginning. At the very, frickin' beginning he told us the girl had been cleaned up, bathed of all evidence, before she was packaged. Remember?"

Rez said, "Yeah. Sure. So what?"

"Well, how many huntin' trailers in the middle of the woods do you know have enough water to do the job properly?"

Rez said, "They could have bathed her in a creek."

"What? Out in front of God and all the possible hunters coming through? No way."

Al said, "And as thorough as Gap is, if she'd been bathed in creek water, he woulda found the evidence."

Rez nodded. "Sho nuff, brutha. Damn. And all this wasted time, too."

Al corrected him. "Not wasted. Now we know what isn't, we can find what is."

Rez threw the last stake into the pile. They rebuilt the bottom of the pit to look like innocent leaves in the bottom of a hole. When the bad guys came back, they would think all was as they had left it.

"I'm not sure what they have planned, but it can't be

good. So, if they're bringing somebody here — alive — and they're gonna throw them in to watch 'em die on the stakes, at least they won't die impaled."

"Yeah," Tweeter said. "They'll just die, but we won't know how that will happen. What're we gonna do about this?"

"We still gotta find the girl." Standing in Don's and Al's hands, Rez was pushed up out of the pit. He gave a steadying hand to Tweeter and Al as they were lifted out. Then he and Al grabbed Don's arms, pulled him up and out.

Standing, Don said, "Occam's Razor, gentlemen. Or to put it another way, we should kiss it."

Rez said, "Kiss it?"

Working for an acronym himself, Al filled Rez in on the meaning. "Yeah. Keep it simple, stupid."

"Boys, let's go back to the beginning and walk it through, shall we?" Three hours after arriving at the death pit, they walked to their truck with their new mandate in mind and their arms full of sharp stakes.

"Okay. We all agree, then? Tommy and Otter must be doing this where they have fresh water and plenty of it."

Rez and Don and Tweeter nodded.

"Apartment? House? Warehouse?"

Tweeter said, "Warehouses with runnin' water are expensive. These guys work in a cotton mill and one has a part-time job on toppa that. Can't see 'em spendin' that kinda money."

Rez said, "True dat."

"Do we know where they live?"

Al answered. "Yeah. Tommy lives with his mother. Otter lives with his sister and her kids."

Don continued with his logic, "Doubtful anything happens at Sis's house. Kids get into everything, right?"

They nodded.

"And it'd be hard to hide that sort of activity and noise from the kids, right?"

More nodding.

"God knows there are some sick women out there who have done worse, but unless the sister is in on this, we can safely assume nothing happens at her house, right?"

Heads bobbled again.

Don paced his logic out. "Mama's house, right? Now, we all know there's some mamas out there that know their precious baby boys can't do no wrong, right? And we know them mamas are notorious for letting their baby boys set parts of their own property off limits, right? Using Occam's Razor, we can safely make a second assumption the logical place for these killings are Mama's house, right? I say we get a good lookey-loo. Agreed?"

Rez said, "How we gonna get inside? No probable cause for her house."

Don was ahead of him. "Don't need to get inside. We need to see if the place can handle that amount of activity in private, like a barn or something."

Al said, "I'm on it."

Don said, "When can you and Frank get out there?"

"I'm calling him now."

Saturday PM: Moving forward with no regrets

Frank's arms were around Carmelita. Her back was to him, tucked in tight to his chest and legs. A few minutes earlier he felt her muscles completely relax and her breathing become even in sleep. This time it was he who could not sleep. He lightly kissed her, buried his nose into her hair and breathed deeply.

As he held her, he couldn't help but think of the other women through the years who shared his bed — including this one. What was different about this woman that he should now give up his fun and accept the responsibility of a real relationship? He couldn't say. But he could say it was the right thing for them both, of that he was sure. He'd never make her regret choosing him and he would never regret loving her. He kissed her hair again, smiled, and fell asleep.

When he woke, it was dark; she was not in the bed. He heard quiet noises in the kitchen. He looked under the covers at his ankle and saw the swelling was down a lot. His thigh muscle had been exercised for several hours and felt much better. Physical therapy was what the doctor ordered after a brief rest and physical therapy is what he got. He didn't need anything else for pain. He stretched, sat up, pulled his legs over the side of the bed, and stood. He stretched again then tested his weight on the ankle. He hobbled, just barely, to the bathroom, brushed his teeth, and went to the kitchen.

Carmelita heard him join her. She turned away from the stove and said brightly, "Hey. You hungry?"

"I'm starved. When was the last time we ate anything?"

"Yesterday about this time."

"Holy cow. No wonder I'm starved."

"Sit. It's almost ready."

"I gotta do something first."

Standing at the stove, she turned toward him while stirring a pot, and said, "Oh, yeah? What's that?"

"I got to plant a big fat one first, that's what."

"Oh —" That's all she got out before he shut her up.

Warmed-up leftovers never tasted so good to Frank. When he finished, there were no more.

"Where did you learn to cook, woman?"

"Mama."

"Your family must be as fat as contented cows."

Carmelita smiled.

A phone rang. Frank said, "Ah. Mine."

Carmelita was already up and brought it back to him before the fourth ring.

Frank saw it was Al. "Dude. Whazzup?"

"You up for a road trip yet?"

"No. Why?"

Carmelita saw his face change from relaxed man in love to GBI man on the job. For the next ten minutes all she heard was the low rumble of Al's voice and Frank giving an occasional *uh-huh*.

"Well, I think it's a plan…Right, she may still be alive and…Hey, do what you gotta do. If you need me to make any calls to the County, lemme know…The ankle is smaller but still swollen. I can walk from the kitchen to the bedroom with no problem, but no surveillance right now…Yes…"

Frank's eyes rose to Carmelita's. He smiled. "Yes, Al… That would be a big ten-four…Ha. Ha. Ha…Yeah, yeah… Hang up and surveille the bad guy."

Frank disconnected and said, "I think I need a shower."

"Okay. I'll do the dishes while you get a shower, then." Carmelita began clearing.

Frank got up, took a plate from her. "Why don't I help with the dishes and then you can help me in the shower?"

Carmelita got a clue, grinned, and said, "Ah-hah. Then, here's another plate. Get busy, big boy."

Saturday, Late PM: A little looky-loo

Al got busy, too, getting directions to Tommy's mother's house. Rez left for home. His babies' mama was a-needing her man and, when she needed him, it behooved him to step lively. Tweeter, fighting the fine law enforcement fight, gladly missed a day mud-bogging with his buddies, but they didn't need him to take a look at a house.

He left to prep for the next day's muddy festivities. Al and Don were now alone.

Al searched the Internet. "Don, you don't need to get home?"

"Nope. You?"

"Nope. Ah, shit." Al whipped out his cell and sent a text to LaVonne.

Hey, baby. Guess you already figured I won't be back tonight. I got to do a surveillance road trip tonight and tomorrow. Call you when I get back.

Don teased him, "*Girl* trouble?"

Al was back to the computer. "Nope. No trouble. Okay..." He hit print and directions to Tommy's rolled out. "Everything loaded? Then, let's go."

Other than crawling through the NASCAR traffic on the south side of Atlanta, the rest of the trip was a breeze. They headed up I-75, hit the Connector, took the split to I-85, put it into the wind, and flew past Gainesville and Commerce exits to Elberton. When they got to their exit, they stopped at the Waffle House, grabbed some food and coffee, made a pit stop, and headed into Tommy's country. Once off the highway, it took another thirty to reach Tommy's house. Al was flummoxed. "How about that?"

Don nodded. "Guess we won't need camo surveillance gear after all."

Out in the middle of nowhere was a subdivision built on the grounds of an old farm. Mama's house was the biggest and oldest. It was their farm upon which all the other houses had been built and their house was at the very back. The driveway was prominently lit and the house was grand and well kept — and sprawling.

"Well, now. Isn't this interesting? Tommy comes from old money. This gets more and more interesting, don't it?"

Don said, "The lawyers' fees for his trial are gonna eat up that pile."

"I hope Mama has put some aside for her old age cuz she ain't gonna have Tommy to look after her none, that's for damn sure."

"He'll kill her before she becomes a burden. We're gonna need camo after all."

Al raised his eyebrows. "Why?"

"We can see the front of the house alright. But if you'll notice the outbuildings behind and, if this old farmhouse is true to form, I bet there's a cellar with access from outside."

"Let's go find the backside."

Don grinned and they rolled on out of the subdivision at a sedate twenty five miles per hour. After all, even if it was late, it was the country and kiddies might be out chasing bats in the gloaming.

Saturday PM: Frank and Carmelita's last night together?

Wet towels were on the floor beside the bed and pillows were damp from wet hair. Carmelita stared at the ceiling. "I have to go home tomorrow."

Frank growled, "I don't want to hear none of that. Why can't you stay until Monday morning?"

"They're supposed to be home Monday morning."

"So? Wouldn't you be leaving early for work anyway?"

Carmelita thought about it, but said, "I didn't bring my stuff for work. I would have to go get it."

"Then go early-early Monday morning and get it. Please, hon. Please stay? Please?"

"I'll think about it." She rolled over onto her side, put her leg across him, and wrapped an arm across his chest. He laid his hand on hers and they twined fingers.

It's not all about you now, he reminded himself. *Don't give her any grief about when she needs to leave.* For now, he was content with her thinking about it. Easy with each other, they fell asleep.

Week
Ten

Sunday 2 AM — Rescue!

It took Al and Don an hour and a half to find the far side of the woods backing the farmhouse. Night-vision goggles on this moonless night helped them get through the woods without being detected. They stopped well back in the woods behind the clearing around the house.

Don and Al pulled out binoculars. Don grunted, "Yep. Sure enough. There's the cellar door."

They scanned the back of the house, eventually coming to the outbuildings. Al said, "I see electricity run to each. Bet there's water, too."

"Could be. Al, holy shit. This can't be."

"What?"

"Two o'clock. Look what's coming out." Tommy and Otter climbed out of the cellar, but they weren't alone. A girl was with them. "Shit. It's our missing girl. Jennifer Howard. Goddamn. She's alive."

They watched as Tommy and Otter led Jennifer toward one of the outbuildings. Don threw his binoculars into his backpack and slipped the safety off his Browning 12-gauge pump. "Cover me. Once the situation's under control, get back to the truck. I'll call you as soon as I can."

Don turned toward the house. He made loud, clumsy tramping noises through the brush, entered the clearing, and hollered, "Thank the Good Lord I found somebody."

Tommy and Otter whipped around, the girl forgotten as she fell to the ground.

"Ah, geez, dudes. I didn't mean to scare you. Hey, your girlfriend fell."

Otter tried to help the girl up. Tommy didn't like the looks of the weapon the man held, and it was his property. He stepped forward and challenged Don.

"You're trespassing, man."

Don put on his best big-city-boy-lost-in-the-country voice and said, "Geez, I'm sorry. I know it sounds weird, but I came up from Atlanta for some hunting, and I don't know what happened. Next thing I knew I was lost and I couldn't find my way back to my car and I've been out all evening and then I saw the lights of your house..."

To anybody looking, it may seem as if Don's weapon hung casually in his arm. They would have been mistaken, of course.

Tommy demanded, "What the hell you want me to do about that?"

Otter was having a hard time holding up the girl by himself. "Uh, Tommy?"

Tommy turned to Otter. "*Whut?*"

"Can you help me with, uh...*this?*"

Don said, "Damn, your girlfriend looks sick, dude."

What neither Tommy nor Otter knew was the girl mouthed *help me* to Don before she collapsed again in the red clay on her hands and knees. She shook her hair to cover the side of her face toward Otter and raised her eyes to Don and silently screamed *help me*. This time she knew Don understood the urgency of her situation.

Tommy told Don, "My girlfriend ain't your problem. You can walk on to another house. Call a taxi if you want."

"Uh, Tommy..."

"*Whut?*" Tommy spat the word to Otter.

"I need some help with...her." *Her* was, by now, back on the ground.

The Case of the Snuff Tape Killers

"She'll be alright till I get this handled." Tommy turned back around to Don.

Don said, "Geez, dudes. I think she's sick. Why don't we get her inside and call nine-one-one."

"Ain't your problem. You can move on now thatcha found civ-ah-lie-za-shun." Tommy smiled at his little joke. Don smiled, too, and shifted his weapon. Tommy looked down the barrel now pointed directly his heart. He hollered, "Watch where you're pointing that thang."

Don asked innocently, "What? *This?* Oh, I took lessons last week on how to use this. Yes, sir. I got my *sir-tiffy-cut.* I'm an expert. You ain't got nothin' to worry about."

"I'm telling ya, point it somewhere else," Tommy said, still clueless.

Don gave him the clue. His eyes went flat. "I tell you what, you little shits. You two are gonna git that pretty little girl up out of the dirt there. And all of us, well, we gonna just all of us walk into that house right there and I'm gonna dial that nine-one-one and get some help here for this little girl. Comprende?"

Otter immediately bent to help the girl. She violently slapped his hands away and scrambled away from him in the loose dirt. She got to her feet, half-staggered and half-ran to Don. He held out his arm to steady her as she slewed behind him. From behind his back she stared from one to the other of her kidnappers and torturers.

Don waved the weapon at them, authoritative and quick. "Walk. To the house."

Otter didn't have to be told twice. He was already moving. Tommy was slow on the uptake. He demanded, "Who do you think you are?"

"Are you stupid? Follow your friend, Tommy."

Tommy was surprised this man knew his name but he didn't give it another thought because now the weapon had his full attention. Tommy stared at the barrel like he didn't know what would come out of the end of it, then he cocked his head. "You got ID?"

"You are stupid. Yeah, asshole. My ID is on the shell that's gonna blow your guts out so you die nice and slow and painful if you don't move. Now *move*."

Tommy moved. Don followed with Jennifer still hiding behind him. She was shaking but holding it together for now. Otter was already halfway up the back steps. The security light went on, bathing the porch in faded yellow. Don waited while Tommy and Otter finished climbing.

"Now, boys. We gonna do this nice and slow. You will not move until I tell ya. Got that?" They nodded. "Otter, I need you to open the door there…Perfect. Now both of you, put your hands on top of your heads…Excellent. Both of you back up to the rail. Now, get on your knees…Cross your ankles. Sit. Stay until I say otherwise."

Don kept his weapon pointed at them. "Jennifer, I need you to walk up the steps, baby girl. Can you handle that?"

Jennifer slowly took her hands off Don and put them on the rail. She pulled herself up, step by step. Don didn't take his eyes off Tommy and Otter. They didn't take their eyes off the barrel. Don and Jennifer reached the top of the porch. Don could see Jennifer quickly losing control. He wrapped his arm around her waist again.

"Hold on, baby girl. We're almost inside." Jennifer held Don tight, gulping deep breaths to calm down. Don gave them the next set of instructions. "Boys! Keep your hands on your head, idiots. Good. Now, I'm gonna step inside with Jennifer. Do not move, understand me?"

Don crabbed sideways past Tommy and Otter with Jennifer behind him. The barrel never wavered. His come-on-boys-please-do-something-stupid grin continued to invite them to try to get away. The boys declined the invitation. Jennifer and Don backed into the house. Don's next invitation was also delivered by the 12-gauge's barrel. "Come on in, boys...did I tell you to stand? Get back down. Walk in on your knees."

They dropped down immediately, grunting when their knees hit the floor the second time. Otter was first through the French doors followed by Tommy. Tommy fixed his stare on Don, but he wasn't in a position to negotiate.

"Excellent, boys. Otter, close the door. Good boy. Got a phone in the kitchen there, Tommy? Good." Don backed into the kitchen with Jennifer behind him. They watched Otter and Tommy walk on their knees through the sunroom into the kitchen.

When they got into the house, Al walked quietly and watched through the kitchen window as the group went in. He saw the girl throw herself into a chair at the table. He saw her quickly lose her battle to remain in control. She was crying and screaming and shaking. He saw Don point with his weapon and then, one by one, Tommy and Otter assume the positions, spread-eagled flat on the floor, face down. He saw Don check for weapons, find a couple of knives, and put them in his coat pocket. He watched as Don dialed nine-one-one. Al saw Don had the situation under control and took off through the woods for the truck.

Don heard Mama stomp in. "What is going on in here?" she demanded.

Tommy spoke from the floor. "Shut up, Mama. I got this."

"Mother?" Don said. Mama turned toward him. "You best sit down and don't say another word. You understand me, Mother?"

"How dare…"

Tommy interrupted her. "Mama! Sit down or get out. Either way, shut up."

Mama sat, but she wasn't happy about it.

Don had his conversation with nine-one-one, and an ambulance and local detectives were soon on their way.

Sunday 4 AM: Al calls Frank

Frank heard his phone ring. He looked at the clock and saw it was four in the morning. *It had to be Al*. He jumped out of bed, forgot his ankle and almost fell, then hobbled into the kitchen.

He grabbed his phone. "Yeah."

"Sorry to wake you up. Guess what?"

"It's four in the morning, Al. Don't make me guess."

"We got her."

"Who?"

"Missing girl from Butts County."

"Alive?"

"Yeah. She's alive. But I need you make a few phone calls. Local up here is glad we found the girl, but kinda mad we didn't —"

"Yeah. Yeah. I'm on it. She alright?"

"Yeah. Damn blind luck we showed up when we did, man. Just damn blind luck."

"Good job. Who do I need to call?"

Al gave him the number and name. Frank hung up and dialed. Twenty minutes later he stood up from the kitchen table, flexed his shoulders, and stretched his arms. He turned to go back to bed. Carmelita, wrapped in a blanket, watched him from the sofa in the dark living room.

"Hey. How long you been up?" He kissed the top of her head.

"Couple of minutes. Everything okay?"

"Yeah. Great. Found the missing girl we're positive was kidnapped by the same guys who killed another girl and buried her in Butts County. And we believe these guys are the same ones on the recording you found."

"It's over?"

She opened her blanket and he wrapped it around them as he sat next to her. "Over? Hell, no. She can't remember how she got to their house and the men both say they picked her up hitchhiking. They said she was out for a good time. Load of shit. But it'll take time to prove otherwise."

"I can't imagine having a job where life and death is involved. It has to be hard."

"It is. Especially when you can't figure it out or find the solution. Mostly, though, criminals are very stupid and we law enforcement types look good when we apprehend them. We aren't that smart."

Carmelita rearranged herself under the blanket, putting her legs across Frank's lap. He pulled the blanket tighter and tucked it under her feet. They stayed there for quite some time, simply breathing in the calmness each brought the other.

"Frank?"

"Mmmm-hmmm."

"Frank? Is this a one-night stand?"

"Nope."

"What is it then?"

"So far it's going on two nights."

"I'm serious, Frank. If this is an affair, it would kill me."

He kissed the top of her head and held her tighter. "It's not an affair, sweetheart."

"You know I have kids."

"Yes. Don't worry about it."

"I can't have any more."

Ah, well, the birth control question was now answered. "Okay."

"Are you wanting kids? Because if you are, I can't do it."

"I'm not looking for a broodmare, Carmelita."

"But what if you ever want kids and…" She left it hanging.

"I don't. I won't." They sat quietly for a while longer.

"Frank?"

"Mmmm-hmmmm."

"I'm cold. Let's go back to bed."

"Okay."

Sunday AM, Early: Wanda gets her girly-girl on in the interests of law enforcement

Mama was making lots of noises about the unfair treatment of Precious, also known as Tommy; local law enforcement was listening to her with deference. Not because they believed her, but because she still carried clout in the county and could make their lives a living hell if she chose to. As only Southern boys can, they sincerely yes-ma'amed her until they were blue in the face. But to avoid any extra conversation, by the time daylight rolled around they had her convinced they knew this whole thing was one big misunderstanding and she was under the impression they would make sure those idiot State boys came to a proper understanding.

Appeased, she left with her pride intact, though her boy was still at the station. Just routine. Since Precious and Otter were the ones who rescued the girl from her willful and wanton hitchhiking ways, and because she lost her memory, why they were going to be helpful and draw on a map where they found her and get her back to her loving mama and daddy so they could get the proper psychiatric treatment she needed. Mama, ever noble and generous, vowed to help with any costs associated with the poor unfortunate's doctoring.

Mama agreed that Precious, being a fine, upstanding, and prominent member of this community, would do his civic duty gladly. She left, confident in the power of money.

While Al and Don waited to fill in the detectives on how they happened to be behind Mama's house a few hours before, the boys cooled their heels together in an interview room. Detective Carl Glass chose a young female officer to play star-struck with the county's heir apparent to put him at his ease.

Wanda looked forward to the task. She had been two years behind both in high school and remembered Tommy's swaggering ways with the girls and heard too many stories about liberties he took with them. One girl claimed rape and she remembered the hell and torture that girl went through at school. It got so bad, her family moved out of the county.

"You can bet I'll handle this just fine, Carl," Wanda told him. The three detectives watched as she transformed before their eyes from a steely-eyed police officer who would just as soon shoot a bad guy as look at him, into a girly-girl swooning over the visit of a royal and rich heir apparent.

She explained how it was gonna work even as she transformed. "See, Carl, I know him." She took her hair out of the bun, bent over, ran her hands through her hair, and shook it out.

"I know what cranks his engine." She stood, throwing back now-tousled hair.

She unbuttoned the top four buttons on her uniform. "I know what gets him in the superior mindset."

She adjusted her cleavage for greater effect. Carl had never seen this Wanda and he had known her since she was a little girl. She didn't notice the glazed expressions on Al and Don's faces.

"Watch and learn," she said, then turned toward the hall and headed to the interview room.

The detectives couldn't get to the video feed fast enough. They saw Otter and Tommy sitting confidently in the room. They saw the door open and their bodies stiffen as their heads swiveled to see who was entering. They saw them visibly relax when they saw it was a girl. Then Wanda started her act.

She squealed as she peeked her head inside. "Oh, my goodness. Tommy? Is that really you?" Her hand flew to her mouth. "And Otter? Oh, my God."

She stepped fully into the room and turned solicitous. "Are you two okay?"

Neither recognized her, but they tried not to let on. Otter waited for Tommy to speak. "Oh, yeah, we're fine."

"I know you don't remember me, but..." Here she fluttered her hands a tiny bit and giggled. "We were in high school together. I mean, I was behind you two years and I'm sure you don't remember..."

Tommy said, "I think I do. Let me see, it's Gayle, right?"

She sounded a touch disappointed but understanding. "It's Wanda. I was such a, well, a nerdy thing. It's Wanda."

Tommy got up and gave her a hug. "Oh, yeah, that's right. Wanda. Of course. I remember you. How're you doing, honey? Wow. It's been a long time." She pressed herself against him in the hug a shade longer than was required. He smiled engagingly as he sat.

"Yeah. I know." She sounded wistful. "Time sure does fly. It seems like just yesterday we were all in school together. Otter," she squealed again as she bounced her way around Tommy to give him a hug, too. The watching detectives saw Tommy shake his head as Otter looked at him with a *what the hell, who is this* expression. "Otter. You have turned into quite the handsome young man. Why don't I ever see you around town?"

She didn't let him answer. She put on a deeply serious sincere voice. "Okay, guys. *Our* detectives are simply astounded at how you two rescued the girl. I mean, I am just so proud..." She let just the hint of sob escape as she clutched her hands to her heart. Which heart, by the way, was usefully placed below her well-adjusted cleavage she had to push up so she could clutch strategically. "I can't wait to tell Mama and Daddy about our very own hometown heroes. You know, they always liked you two. What with playing football so well on the team and all."

Otter and Tommy's egos swelled so much the detectives thought their heads were gonna bust wide open.

But Wanda wasn't done.

"Holy cow." She bent her knees and, putting her hands on those same knees, leaned forward, stretching button number five's ability to stay clasped. "Where are my manners? I started a fresh pot of coffee and the detectives sent out to Marlin's Donuts for a fresh batch made this morning. Can I get you two some coffee and doughnuts? I know it's been a *tryin'* night for you…"

The two perps nodded.

"Tommy? How you want your coffee? Cream? Sugar?"

Tommy accepted the coffee with style and grace befitting the prince he thought he was. "Yes, Wanda, cream and sugar would be wonderful."

"Alrighty then. Otter? How about you, sweetie?"

"Uh…black."

"No sugar for you?" This line was delivered with a hand to his shoulder and a lowering of her voice. The detectives noticed Tommy was none too pleased Otter was getting the sexy, personal touch.

"Nope," Otter flirted back. "Just hot, sweet mama."

"Oh. You are a bad boy." She slapped his shoulder gently. "Now mind your manners and let me go get coffee and a nice selection of doughnuts. Be but a few secs."

She bounced out and the door closed. Each detective's head swung toward the hall. As soon as the door shut, her steely-eyed gaze was back. They pulled their jaws up from the floor and snapped their mouths shut as she came by with a running diatribe.

"Damn sons-of-bitches." She made it to the coffee machine. "Did I tell you or did I tell you?" She poured two cups prepared to their specs. "Do I know where they live? Oh, yes, I do." She piled a plate high with an assortment.

"Damn sons-of-bitches."

She pushed a pile of napkins into her cleavage.

The detectives watched her readjust back into squeally girl, walk down the hall and, using her toe, knock on the door. As one they turned to the video feed.

They saw Tommy and Otter turn. Tommy said, "Answer it, Otter."

Otter jumped up and opened the door.

"I am so sorry to make you get up, but my hands are full. Thank you." She smiled brightly at Otter as she pushed the plate of doughnuts at him.

Otter took them automatically. "Set them over there?" He walked to the table and hovered the plate over a spot, as he asked helpfully, "Here?"

"Yes. Perfect. Thank you, sugar, uh, I mean, Otter. Sorry. Okay, Tommy you got the cream and sugar, right? And Otter you got the black?"

She handed each their cup, a little smile for Tommy and a wink for Otter. As if she just remembered them, she pulled the napkins out of her cleavage and laid them on the table. "Oops. Almost forgot. Here are some napkins for you."

She put one hand on the table as she bent over the doughnuts, pointed with her other hand, and said, "I hope this is a wide enough assortment for you…"

She left the thought hanging.

Tommy nodded but couldn't speak. Otter winked at her. She smiled from one to the other and straightened up. "Well, I will be checking back in with you boys in a little bit. If you need anything before I get back, just holler. I'm down the hall typing up traffic reports, but I can hear you fine."

This time, she bounced out backward with a shy little wave and a giggle. She mouthed *so proud*. The door closed and squeally girl vanished. She joined the detectives to watch the video feed.

Carl spoke for all. "Well done, Wanda."

Don couldn't take his eyes off Wanda; he was in love. Wanda didn't even know Don was alive and her gaze never wavered from the screen.

Carl leaned over and whispered, "She's a lesbian."

Don's look of love turned to stricken heartache. He noticed Carl chuckling. Don grinned wickedly and held up four fingers. "Know what this is, Carl?"

Carl did not. "It's a whole flock of these," Don told him as he lowered three, leaving an upright middle finger. "Payback's hell."

But his expression of love returned.

Sunday AM: A day is planned

Once they got back into the bed, they wrapped themselves in each other and fell asleep immediately. When Frank woke, the sun was high.

He couldn't take his eyes off Carmelita as she lay sleeping. She was curled into a tight little ball that fit into him beautifully. He stroked her arm and her leg and her back and her hair. Slowly and with wonder. She still had not let him know if she would spend Sunday night or not. He wanted to know and he wanted to know now, but Al's reminder kept echoing in his mind: *It ain't all about you anymore*. So, he didn't say anything and let her make up her mind at her pace and tell him when she was ready.

He felt her wake up. "Morning."

"Morning. What time is it?"

"Eleven-thirty."

"Really?"

"Hungry?"

"Yeah. I am. I think you're all out of food, though."

"I'm taking you out for lunch."

"Ooooh. That's sweet."

"That's me. Sweet."

Carmelita stretched to wake up. "I need a shower. Do you have a blow-dryer?"

"A blow-dryer?"

"Yeah. For hair?"

"No. Never needed one. I wash and go."

She smiled at the image. "Well, I won't get my hair wet then."

He thought of joining her in the shower, but decided against it. He guessed sometimes showers were utilitarian and not about sex, and this was probably one of the former for her. He left her to her privacy as he made the bed and got dressed.

His ankle was almost normal and his thigh muscle twinged only occasionally. His manhood, which took the brunt of the fall, was still sore. He laughed out loud. He didn't know if he was still sore from the fall or from all the activity they engaged in during the past forty hours.

What a great forty hours. He waited for her on the sofa. He listened to her quiet singing and the sounds of her dressing. When she popped out of the bedroom, his breath was taken away. *This woman loves me.* He was astounded at the thought.

"You ready?" she asked as she casually slung her purse over her shoulder and smiled down at him.

He smiled and eventually answered, "Yes. I'm ready."

Sunday, Late AM: Time to write things

Al and Don watched as Carl politely walked Tommy and Otter through the process of going into separate rooms to draw maps for him.

"Gentlemen," he explained with excruciating deference, "it has to do with how a jury believes evidence. If they ever find out you two were in the same room and putting your heads together to write the story of what happened and drawing those maps together, trust me on this, they will be thinking you are the guilty parties, not the other dude sitting in the hot seat, ya know whutta mean?"

Tommy and Otter nodded. They didn't like it, but what were they going to do about it? The jury must be placated.

"You two are men of the world. You understand these simple-minded folks they pick for juries."

Tommy and Otter felt better. Wanda did her squeally-girl act as she led Tommy to the other room. At the door of the room, she turned on the heat and let it slip that, you know, he missed his chance in high school, he could call her if he took a mind to, doncha know...

He allowed maybe he would do just that. She slipped a piece of paper into his pocket. He pulled it out and saw what he thought was her number, but it was the number to a cheap, untraceable cellphone.

Their handwritten accounts and hand-drawn maps were collected and they were allowed to leave — with the effusive thanks of a grateful county and nation, of course. Tommy, as the heir apparent to Mama's fortune, took the thanks in stride as a prince will. Otter nodded and said okay.

Don always operated on the principle it was easier to get forgiveness than to get permission. The rest of the morning, he and Al begged for forgiveness in not letting the locals know they were on the scene. After they explained how quickly the whole thing took off and their excitement in getting a workable plan of action after the disappointments, Detective Carl Glass understood. By lunch all was forgiven and plans were made to eat.

"Say, Carl," Don asked casually as they prepared to leave for lunch, "don't you think Wanda should be rewarded for her excellent work today?"

Never raising his eyes, Carl said, "She's getting a paycheck."

"Of course, I understand," Don went on, "but…oh, hell, I want her to come to lunch with us. Can she?"

Carl laughed and picked up his phone. "Wanda. Where we going for lunch today?"

Within an hour, The BB House was arrived at and Al added another excellent restaurant to his list of places to eat in Georgia. Don found out more about Wanda from Wanda herself. Wanda now knew Don was alive and some of her girly-girl act she did so well back at the station showed up quite naturally in conversation at the end of the table.

Al and Carl were going over the case file Al brought with him. Carl got excited.

"I would like to hear some of those recordings, if I could. See, we have some girls went missing. Haven't heard of them since. But knowing Tommy's history…"

Al asked, "What history is that?"

"One girl claimed rape in high school. She and her family were hounded out of the county. I believed her as did quite a few of my fellow officers. But his family carries weight in the county and you know how those things go."

Of course Al knew. He saw the same thing on a state level, too. "Any other reports or stories like those?"

"No official reports, no. But lots of stories. Wanda and my daughter went to high school at the same time as Tommy and Otter. They were a couple of years or so behind them and, honestly, both Wanda and Marielle were ugly ducklings in high school — thank goodness — so none of the jocks or in-crowd paid any attention to 'em."

"Wanda seems to have blossomed."

"They both did. My daughter is a model, believe it or not. Works in New York for one of the top agencies but she ain't a supermodel — yet. Looks just like her mama. I'm a lucky man, let me tell you. Wow. Now that's a weird crowd up there, though. She tells us stories'd make your hair curl. She seems to have kept her head screwed on straight. Has a steady boyfriend who's a cop, just like her daddy. And she's living cheap, socking away all that money she's making. Smart girl."

Al brought the conversation back around. "The stories from high school?"

"Oh. Yeah. Well. It happened quite often. A father would barrel in, distraught about his daughter who didn't want to tell him what happened but finally would. She would beg him not to ruin her life by reporting it. But in he would come anyway. Then the girl wouldn't verify it and…you know how that goes."

"Yeah."

"I heard there were several abortions quietly paid for without Daddy and Mama knowing. One girl wouldn't have an abortion. She just plain up and disappeared."

"How long have Tommy and Otter known each other?"

"Otter's family moved into the county when he was six. They went to school together."

"College, too?"

"Neither of them went to college."

"I don't understand. If Tommy is rich, why is he working in the cotton mill?"

Carl explained. "His family owns it."

"Ah, he's management, in name only. And I bet nobody messes with Otter because he's Tommy's friend, right?"

"Exactly."

"Also means if neither of them shows up for work, nobody is gonna think twice about it nor question it nor dock their pay, right?"

"You got that right, Al."

"Nice gig if you can get it, huh?"

Carl sat up straight and hit the table with his fist. "I want to get these guys."

Al pulled out copies of the bad guys' maps and accounts of *rescuing* the girl. Grim-faced, he vowed, "We gonna git 'em. No doubt. Let's get busy finding holes in their story."

Sunday: A most pleasant lunch

They took Frank's car, though Carmelita drove because his ankle was still on the injured list. Frank wanted to take a drive, anything to lengthen the time she would be with him. They took Interstate 20 West and ended up in Social Circle at The Blue Willow. The line for lunch was long, but when the owner saw Frank limping, she found a place for them to wait without losing their place in line. The Sunday buffet was legendary and worth the wait. Carmelita made Frank elevate his ankle. They sat for an hour and a half with his leg on her lap. He very simply enjoyed this small thing.

Frank had not heard from Al and, if anyone asked, he would have said that after four in the morning he had not given any thought to Al, serial killers, victims, or his job in any way, shape, or form. He only thought of and wanted Carmelita. He wanted her in his bed. In his shower. In his kitchen. In his living room. In his life. He wanted her waiting for him to come home.

Waiting for him to come to bed. Waiting for him to eat. Waiting for him to make love. He wanted to wait for her to get dressed. Wait for her to wake up. Wait for her to smile at him. Wait for her to become a woman loved well and long. He wanted to be the man she waited for her entire life.

And he wanted to know if she would spend the night. Still no answer. Finally a table was ready and they were called. They no sooner sat down than Carmelita's phone rang. She frowned, but answered sweetly.

"Hey," she said into the phone.

Frank saw her listening. She didn't look at him. He saw her worried expression, and became concerned.

"Uh, huh…*What?…Are the kids okay?…* Okay…You're kidding? What did you do?…Do you need me to come get y'all?…Are you hurt?…Good. You sure?…When will you be home?…Sure…Uh, huh…Right…Let me talk to…"

Frank listened as she talked to each of her children and his love for her grew. Yeah. He was hot for a mom and didn't mind telling the world.

"Well, you all have a big adventure, okay? Be safe. Love you. Bye…Yes, I'll call school and tell them."

Frank raised an eyebrow as she put her phone in her purse and explained. "You are not gonna believe this. Martin was pulling out of the parking lot at the aquarium in Chattanooga when a tour bus hit them broadside. The car is totaled. They're okay. It was a slow collision. Thank goodness it hit on the side with Martin; both the kids were on the passenger side."

In reply to his unasked question, she said, "No. Martin was not hurt. Side air bags totally saved him. If the bus had been going faster, no telling what would have happened. Anyway…they have to stay in Tennessee two more days at the very least so everything can be handled. Martin said the kids are okay. They'll rest and do more sightseeing they wanted to do anyway. They already have a rental car."

Frank watched Carmelita tell the story. He watched as she became the mother hen worried about her brood. He never saw anything like it.

"I love you, Carmelita," he blurted out.

She stopped talking.

Frank reached across the table, took her hand, and shook his head. "You should see yourself right now. I've never seen anything like it. You're worried about your kids. You're even worried about that sonovabitch after all he's done to you. You're absolutely beautiful and I love you."

Frank stared at her hand as he held it. The story of their future life was told by the difference in their skins. His, rough and scarred; hers, soft and smooth — leather and lace, they would be a complement and both be the better for it. Carmelita didn't know what to say, so she said nothing. He looked at her. The excruciating pain of love he felt was evident on his face.

She had never seen such adoration in a man's face and she smiled sweetly. There was much he wanted to say, but every time he thought of what those things were, the only words he could think of were *I love you.* That's what he said.

"I love you. Please stay tonight."

She watched his hand caress hers, and silently nodded.

Their waitress, completely oblivious, broke in. "Buffet's down the hall. What would you like to drink?" At least this waitress didn't have a silver stake through her tongue though you couldn't see her ear lobes for all the multi-colored studs lined up and shining bright.

Sunday PM: The self-serving prevarications of perps

Don and Wanda, in the backseat of the squad car, had silly little grins on their faces and, try as they might, couldn't stop sending cute little glances toward each other. Every time Carl looked in the rearview mirror, he caught glimpses of the unfolding relationship.

Wanda was like his second daughter. Carl's daughter and Wanda had been best friends since they were three years old and lived next to each other until college. Carl saw them go through what seemed like hundreds of puppy love crushes through the years. The non-stop boy drama, even if in their minds, was cute as hell.

Wanda's one serious relationship ended three years ago. It broke her heart so badly she threw herself with a vengeance into her police work. It was all about the career with her; good for Carl, but not so good for Wanda. Men could go to hell and leave her alone for all she cared. There were no more dates, though many tried.

But this man was different. It made Carl happy to see the spark in her eyes again.

The Law returned to local's HQ, and they tore into Tommy's and Otter's narratives.

Tommy's account read as follows:

```
    Jimmy Stonecypher and I, Tommy
Higgenbotham, were driving south along
Georgia State Road 441 heading to
Gainesville, Georgia. We were near Lula.
It was Thursday evening. The time was
about 9:30 PM. I was driving. The car I
was driving is mine. It is an Audi TT,
two seater, red, two years old. Jimmy
Stonecypher yelled at me to watch out for
this lady walking in the road. I barely
managed to throw on my brakes and swerve
to miss her. I was afraid she would get
hurt so before any other cars could come
along and hit her, I pulled over and
Jimmy jumped out to bring her into the
car. She was wild. She must have been
```

high on something. She was hitting Jimmy
and I got out to help him because we
didn't want her running into the path of
any other car. We managed to get her into
the car and we were heading to the
hospital when she got all calm like and
she said she thought we were cute and she
sure would like to show us a good time.
Jimmy and I told her no thank you and
that we wanted to take her to the
hospital because we thought she might be
sick or something. She got upset when we
said that and she grabbed the steering
wheel. She was sitting in Jimmy's lap
because there was no other room in the
car. Jimmy pulled her back and together
we managed to get her hand off the
steering wheel and he held her tight
like. She begged us not to take her to
the hospital because she said if she went
her mom and dad would get real mad and
then she would be in a whole lot of
trouble. I told her I wouldn't take her
to the hospital if she would calm down
and promise not to grab the steering
wheel no more. She agreed. Then she
started kissing Jimmy and told him she
would like to thank us properly for
helping her out. She said we could take
her to our place and she would show us a
good time. Jimmy made her stop kissing
him and she got mad and I said we really
needed to get her home because it was
obvious she was high. She said she was a
big girl, and she said she wasn't jail
bait, neither. But she didn't want to go
home to mama and daddy and could she
crash at our place until she felt better.

Jimmy and I were kind of not sure what to do. But after a while I told her she could come to my house, but that she had to stay in the basement where I had a room fixed up and she had to be real quiet so that my mama wouldn't hear her because my mama does not tolerate loose women in her house. She promised to be real quiet and then she fell asleep on Jimmy's shoulder and she snored all the way to the house. We barely could get her awake and keep her quiet when we got to my house, but we managed to get her into the basement room I have fixed up without Mama hearing anything. She slept for two days and we got her some food and stuff and then when Mama was gone one day, I let her in the house so she could take a shower and get cleaned up a little bit as best she could. I ain't gonna lie. She tempted me and Jimmy and we both had sex with her but only because she made us. And she said she liked it and she wanted more, so we did. I know that wasn't right because we weren't married but she was really insistent that she wanted to ~~fuck us~~ I mean do us and she sure did turn on the heat and we just kinda lost our heads. She was getting all kinky on us and said she wanted to do it out in the woods at night. And by that time she had us under her spell and I couldn't say no and so we were on our way out into the woods to, you know, give her what she came for, and that's when that man showed up and acted like we was hurting her. Then when we went inside, she started putting on an act like she was a victim

```
or something, because her mama and daddy
were gonna find out and she didn't want
them thinking she was a whore or nothing
like that. This is the end of my
recollection of the events concerning
that girl.
     Signed,
     Tommy Higgenbotham
```

Don shook his head after reading the self-serving account. "You know he thinks if there's any difference between his and Otter's story, his will be believed, doncha?"

Al said, "Oh, yeah. The perks of the privileged. But he isn't so privileged he'll be able to put this all on Otter."

Carl handed them another sheaf of papers. "Yeah. Wait until you read this one." Otter's statement read as follows:

```
     My name is Jimmy Stonecypher. People
call me Otter. My friend is Tommy
Higgenbotham. We been best friends since
4 grade. We was driving down the road.
The road we was on was 115. We was in
Habersham County on our way to Helen for
a party at this girls house we know. Her
name is Mary Lynn Harbuck and she lives,
I dont know the address, you go through
town and take a right like your going to
Anna Ruby Falls and then you turn left on
this other road and turn right and go up
a long driveway. I can take you there,
but I don't know the number or street.
She lives with her daddy and mama but
they was out of town and they was gonna
be a big party so we was going. So
anyways, we saw this girl, the one that
dude saw us with in Tommy's backyard, and
```

we saw this girl on the road and she was
hitchhiking and I said to Tommy I thought
she sure did look cute and couldn't we
give her a ride. Tommy said we could but
where would she sit. I said she could sit
on my lap seeing as how she was cute and
I didn't mind having some of that sitting
on my lap. So by that time we was past
her and so Tommy turned around and we
went back and she was still there and we
stopped and asked her if she needed a
ride and didn't she feel worried being
out in the dark on the side of the road
hitchhiking and stuff all by herself and
she said she didn't feel worried at all
since two fine gentlemen like us had
stopped she felt even better and so she
climbed in and I apologized that there
was no place to sit except on my lap and
I told her I had on my seatbelt so that
at least my body wouldn't crush her if we
was in an accident and she allowed that I
sure was a nice fellow to think of her
safety and all and then she ask us where
we was going and we told her about this
party and she said she would rather party
with us private like and couldn't we go
somewheres nice and quet and so we did.
We drove to a motel in Clarkesville and I
don't remember the name of it and Tommy
rented a room and we had a party. By
party I mean we drank some beer that we
was gonna bring to the party and then she
got all sexy and started dancing like
those pole dancing women and taking her
clothes off and then she made us take our
clothes off and then we did her. Tommy
went first and then I went next and then

The Case of the Snuff Tape Killers

we just kept on doing her because she kept begging for it and she said we were the best she ever had but she whispered in my ear that I was better than Tommy. The next morning Tommy and me was getting dressed and we thought we would just leave her there but she came out of the shower and said she had such a fun time and didn't we want some more of this and she pointed to her ~~cunt~~ pussy and we both said sure we wasn't gonna turn down no free pussy and so we took her to Tommy's house. Tommy has a room he fixed up in the basement and she stayed there and stayed drunk the whole time on Tequila and she liked doing shots and we had a good old party for a couple of days more and the day we picked her up was Wednesday night. We took her to Tommy's house on Thursday morning and then that dude showed up out of the woods on Saturday night when we was getting ready to take her back to Clarkesville where we found her because that's what she asked us to do. We said you gonna start hitchhiking again? And she said yeah because that's what she does and she was wanting some new cocks to do her because she had enough of us because she was bored. Me and Tommy didn't care cuz we had enough of her too and she was a skank anyway, so then that guy with the gun showed up and all we was doing was helping a girl out and showing her a good time to and he made like we was hurting her or something and we wernt.

```
    That is the whole story, and I swear
to god it is the truth.
    Signed, Jimmy Stonecypher
```

Al laughed. "Sounds like ol' Jimmy here has a little bit of penis envy going on, doesn't it?"

Don shook his head in disbelief. "You know, I've heard all kinds of tales but, jeez, these guys' stories don't match up in any way. Except for the two-seater vehicle and the basement. And the lap sitting. You would've thought while they were in the room together, they'd at least get their stories straight."

"You should've been in the rooms as I got 'em to write their stories," Carl said. "Tommy had lots of questions about details. He kept asking if this, that, and the other was written correctly. He marked out bits and pieces and rewrote. See on your copies the rewrites and strike-throughs? Otter had a stream-of-consciousness thing going on. Never asked any questions, never said a word. Just started and went with the story as it popped into his head. And you can see that clearly, too."

Al pointed out another interesting aspect to Tommy's tale. "What I notice in Tommy's version is it seems he's trying to explain away some of the DNA he may have left behind. And maybe she damaged the car inside, too, because she was fighting them when they abducted her."

Carl took a sip of his coffee. "An Audi TT is an awfully small car to use for a two-man team to abduct a girl."

Don scratched his stubble. "Bundy used a VW Bug."

"Yeah, but it was only Ted, it wasn't crowded. This girl had to sit on one of them. Sheesh."

Don kept scratching. "I hope her memory comes back so we can hear firsthand how she was abducted. Sure would solve our problem."

"Don, didn't you say Rez is following up with the girl?"

"Yeah. He's at Butts County Hospital with her and the parents. She wanted to go home. I can't blame her. I wouldn't want to be in the same county as those boys, either. Her parents wanted her checked out by doctors they know. They're gonna do a kit on her."

Al said, "Okay, all we can do is wait on her to make a statement and the results of the kit. That'd be good if we could get the DNA of those guys from her. They've already admitted to sex with her, you know, trying to explain away their DNA. Let's bring in Otter for a little sitdown. I say let's play to his jealousy of Tommy's position in the community and his obvious envy of Tommy's aptitude with the girls. I tell you what. Why don't you tell him we have a problem with his story because it doesn't match Tommy's. Let's see what else comes out."

"Should we let him know we wanna see him again and ask him to come in voluntarily? If we do, he may have time to call Tommy and then that'd make things more complicated," Carl said.

"Let's find out when he'll be home, sleeping of course, and just show up and talk to him, man to man," Don said. "Like we're getting the story straight for the jury."

"I like it," Al said. "But give 'em a couple of days to think all is well."

Carl worried about waiting. "What if they get all itchy to get their kill back on? I sure would hate it if they abducted another girl because we're waiting."

Don had an idea. "Here's where Wanda will come in handy. She has a disposable cellphone and she slipped Tommy the number. What if she was to call him first?"

Carl was horrified. "She gave him *what?* She should not have done that without getting permission. Now you want me to put her in harm's way? I thought you liked her."

Don explained, "Oh, I like her a lot. She won't be in harm's way. She could call and say she was gonna be at whatever bar and grill you guys have around here, maybe string him along for a couple of days or so. He may not think about her as his next victim, but his ego will think he might get a little *sumpin' sumpin'.* It could keep his mind occupied."

He added hastily, "Al could probably get a couple of State boys to be in the bar along with some of your guys to follow her discreetly as she went to her mom and dad's house to spend those nights. She could also have a girlfriend with her, a fellow cop, right?"

"It could work." And Carl would make sure everything would work fine. Just long enough to get Otter to open his big fat mouth and spill the beans, whether he knew that was what he was doing or not. After all, Wanda was like a daughter to Carl, even if she was a fellow officer.

Al clarified their plan. "In the meantime, gentlemen, let's go through their stories again. Make a list of all points of similarity and differences. I have a feeling we're gonna find some interesting stuff."

Carl added, "I'm gonna make a copy and take it to a man we use occasionally. He analyzes handwriting. One of the foremost in the field internationally and lives right here. He does this for us at no charge because he has a subspecialty in criminal minds. It is research for him."

Al asked, "How will that help?"

"Bascomb will tell us about their personalities. We get confirmation of what we know…or clarification. If we find out how their minds think, it will help us maybe know better how to talk to them, what questions to ask, stuff like that."

"Cool."

Sunday PM: Carmelita clarifies her truth

Frank was hurting. He set his coffee cup down and touched Carmelita's hand. "I'm ready to get back to the house. My leg and ankle are hurting worse."

"Maybe you overdid it today."

He grinned wickedly, but not for long because he was in pain. "Only today? How about this whole weekend? Not that I'm complaining, mind you. I need some of my meds." He yawned. "And I need a nap. You mind if we go?"

"I don't mind. Come on. Let's go." He stood and took her hand. They walked to the front of the restaurant. Frank paid the check while Carmelita brought the car to the front door and waited on him as he hobbled out. He held onto the door and lowered himself into the seat, slowly got his legs inside, pushed the seat back so he could stretch his legs, and tilted the back to recline a bit. He buckled his seatbelt and rolled up his jacket to put under his neck. They were no sooner on Interstate 20 heading into the city than Carmelita heard Frank snoring and smiled and laughed quietly. She put a hand on his arm and headed home.

Home.

The word sounded right. It sounded good. But the reality was she was still married and the reality was her children's lives would change. How would this change affect them? How could she explain it to them without insulting their father? Would they ever understand? Could they ever forgive her? Would they ever forgive?

Carmelita also wondered about Martin. What was wrong with him? Why couldn't he love her? Was he incapable of love? He had no trouble being polite to everyone except her — and lately, she noticed, the children got some of what she always received from him.

Or was she unlovable? She came to believe that, but two things kept nagging at her, saying she shouldn't believe it. One was her parents. They had not changed toward her. Even when she moved away, they called and sent pictures and it was always calm and relaxing and friendly when they visited. Mom and Dad always hugged her and said they loved her.

When she went to visit them without Martin, they laughed and joked and talked and they loved her and all was well.

The other thing was Frank. Parents loving you — isn't that what parents are supposed to do? She did not give their love the same weight as the love of a man, a husband. But here was this man beside her. True, she hadn't known him very long, but there was something about him that told her she could trust him with the worst there was about her and his love would never waver.

Hadn't she already dumped a lot on him through her email letters and had he turned his back? Until Frank, she didn't know what it was like to be accepted and loved by another man, including Martin.

The first few years of their marriage, she confided her worries and her woes to her husband. Isn't that what a mate is for? To share the good times and the tough times and help each other through? She recalled a passage from the Bible she had heard over and over as a child when the preacher gave his sermon on marriage.

If one falls, the other will pick him up.

Even as a small child, she had liked the idea. It was what her parents did. She saw it in action in their house and thereby knew it was possible. She wanted that for herself. If Martin was down, she wanted to help him up. When she was down, she wanted to be helped up. But Martin always got mad when she tried to encourage him and didn't like being asked to help her.

Her mother once asked what was wrong with Martin. Carmelita did a beautiful verbal tap dance around the whole subject, explaining that he was very busy and had a lot of important projects on his mind. She assured her mother all was well and Martin was a good man.

Her mother's face came into mind as she remembered her reaction upon hearing the big long excuse. She did not understand the reaction then, or pretended not to. But she got the full force of it now.

Her mother's eyes went cold and flat. She did not nod her head in understanding. She did not buy the story. She quite simply began to hate Martin for what he was doing to her daughter. Carmelita knew Mom would never forgive Martin for not loving her daughter the way she deserved.

Mama would understand about the choice she was making. Daddy would too. Frank certainly did. But how to explain to the children? More importantly, when?

The accident in Chattanooga gave her a couple of days' grace in facing the prospect of Martin's bed. Still, what was wrong with Martin? His parents didn't act like that. In fact, she got along with them better than Martin did. When he wasn't around, family members were relaxed and happy and joked. As soon as he showed up, everybody got nervous, watched what they said. Easy camaraderie, gone.

Then there was the time when their son was four and daughter seven. She was grocery shopping and had let the kids look at the toys at the end of the aisle she was on. She kept a sharp eye on them and soon noticed a woman — at first she thought a store employee — talking to them. But it soon became apparent the conversation was lasting too long and the kids were answering questions a store employee would never ask.

The woman was hugging them.

She quickly pushed her loaded cart toward the children and said hello to the woman. She asked, and not friendly, "Can I help you?"

The woman stood up and boldly looked at Carmelita. "Are these your children?"

"Yes, they are. How can I help you?"

The woman's physical stance seemed to challenge her. Carmelita waited on the woman's answer.

"I was just wondering because, you know, they don't look a thing like you."

"Again, can I help you?"

The woman looked lovingly at the children. "They take after Daddy, right?"

"Let's go, kids."

But the woman wasn't finished and she put her hands on the grocery cart. "I'm sorry. I must seem rude. Let me buy the children a toy to say I'm sorry."

"They have plenty of toys."

The woman was indignant that her gift was turned down. "It's no money out of your pocket. What does it matter to you?"

"Let's go, kids," she said again; then to the woman, "I'm calling security."

The woman left the store. When Carmelita told Martin about it, Martin asked for a description of the woman. She gave it to him, though what it mattered she didn't know. He told her not to worry about it, put it out of her mind, she wouldn't ever have to worry about that happening again. *That* never happened again.

But there was this other time, a couple of years later at the coffee shop and a woman asked to sit with her and chat. At first she thought it was fun to meet someone new and have a nice chat over a cup of coffee. But the conversation soon turned. She couldn't put her finger on the purpose of the chat, but it became clear the woman seemed to be digging, of all things, for information about Martin.

She did not tell Martin about her. But not long after, Martin brought home condoms in all sorts of colors with knobby things on them that, he said, were guaranteed to please her. She assured him his natural attribute was perfectly great for her. She didn't say she would like it if he could prolong the time he used what he had, but he insisted they use the condoms and she thought what the heck? So she gave it a go, hoping it would be all he said it was. His condom fetish lasted only about four months.

She remembered three other instances. Women who would show up out of the blue and something weird would happen. She saw one woman at her son's Little League games cheering wildly for her son. At first she thought she must be the mother of a teammate and was supporting a fellow team member's efforts. But she didn't cheer on anyone else. She saw Martin talking to her at the refreshment stand. They seemed to be arguing. The woman left and she never saw her again.

Frank kept snoring. Each snore punctuated her thoughts. *Idiot.* Snore. *Under your nose all this time...* Snore. *...and you just had to have those blinders on, didn't you?*

Big snore. *That damn little shit. It isn't me. It's him.* Snore.

She thought of Frank's house, our home, she corrected herself. There were three bedrooms. The kids could live there with her. They would have to change schools. But if they didn't want to change schools, could she leave them with Martin? They were of an age she couldn't legally force them to come with her. But would he want the responsibility for them? It wasn't like she would be moving across the state or anything. What if one child wanted to stay with Martin and the other come with her?

She stopped thinking about the details of it all. It was making her head hurt. Besides, the kids were in high school and already their lives were separating from hers. They would be in college before too long. She was a very good mom. True, she coddled them more than she should, but that was changing and they were learning to carry their own weight. She would always love them and would always be a support to them. They could always count on her to do right by them.

They may not understand at the time what *right* meant. But, eventually, they would. Especially when they saw what it was like to have a man treat their mother lovingly. Yes, that was the next lesson she would teach them — and teach them before it was too late.

She would sleep on the sofa and she would do it every night and make no excuses for it. If Martin made a big deal out of it, well, he better be ready to see that conversation through. Carmelita's head stopped hurting. Her course was set and she was happy with it.

She gently nudged Frank. "Baby? Wake up. We're home."

Week
Eleven

Sunday PM: Wanda enjoys hatching her plan

Wanda loved the plan. She couldn't wait to mess with Tommy's mind just like he messed with so many others through the years. He was a very bad guy, but didn't scare her at all. She would never be alone with him, that's for sure, but she would have her gun and if push came to shove she'd shove it right up his...well, ladies weren't supposed to say things like that and she was a lady. Of course, as all Southern men know, a real Southern lady has a core of steel only a stupid man would cross.

Tommy might be evil, but he wasn't stupid. He might want to play with the line, but he would definitely toe it when he saw the lay of the land.

On the other hand, Otter was stupid. Wanda wondered how they had graduated to being partners in killing women. One day somebody would interview these two in prison and write their story. It was a sure bet she wouldn't buy the book. She already understood them.

Sitting on the other side of Carl's office earlier in the afternoon, Don — whose philosophy was to beg for forgiveness instead of permission — watched in fascination as his soon-to-be third and very last wife put that philosophy into motion. He had never seen such a beautiful job of begging for forgiveness after Carl raked her over the coals for giving Tommy the burner cell number.

Once forgiveness was granted — as Wanda knew it would be — they got on with the plan to keep Tommy's attention from another victim until they could talk further with Otter and hang those sons-of-bitches.

Monday AM: Reviewing the statements of two perps

Al and Don had been in their clothes almost forty eight hours. Even they could smell how ripe they were. In the woods, ripe had a place to blow. In conference rooms and cars, Wanda was wrinkling her nose ever so politely, but the point was made. They found a Wal-Mart, bought jeans and shirts and socks and drawers, rented hotel rooms for the night, showered, and hit the sack. Next morning would come early.

And it did. When their room phones rang revelry, they each grabbed their phone, picked it up and, without answering or opening their eyes, attempted to cradle the handset. They both missed it and the phones slammed everywhere but where they needed to go. That necessitated each man moving from warm, comfortable spots, opening eyes, and attempting to focus. Each showered to wake up, peeled labels, ripped price tags, and dressed. They grabbed coffees in the hotel lobby and were on their way to Carl's office.

Carl greeted them as they arrived. "Good morning, gentlemen. Breakfast?"

Al threw his empty cup in the trash. "Does bad coffee from a hotel lobby count?"

"I don't think it qualifies. Let's walk. We can talk there while we eat."

They followed Carl across the street into Mel's Diner. As he made his way through the crowd to a back corner table, he shook hands with some, clapped others on the back. Called out to a couple on the other side who nodded hello.

Raised a hand to others as he passed.

"Carl, honey. Your usual?"

"Yes, Mel. Thank you. And the same for these two."

Melanie — Mel — didn't ask, just poured coffee into cups, and walked away. Forks, knives, and spoons were in tall containers on the table next to a stack of paper napkins. Al's nose was in the air and he knew he found a place to rival Mama's. Good thing Mama's and Mel's were a fifty miles apart.

Carl began the dissection of Tommy and Otter's statements. "They both have great imaginations. After you left yesterday evening, I went through their statements. The only similarities were these. One: They both say they met the girl on the road. Two: They both say they had sex with the girl. Three: They both say the sex was the girl's idea because she either tempted or begged or commanded them to do it. Four: She sat in Jimmy's lap. Five: They took her to the basement. Six: Don showed up with a gun.

"Now, we all know the stories they're telling are completely fabricated. So, besides ignoring all that, I concentrated only on what they mentioned with elements in common. One: The road. Two: The towns. Three: And the day they picked her up."

Al said, "Tommy said they found her Thursday night and Otter said Wednesday night, right?"

"Right."

Don set his cup down. "But isn't Lula in Habersham the same as Clarkesville?"

Carl answered, "It's right on the edge. Sits in both Hall and Habersham counties. Why?"

Don sipped. "This might be another point of similarity: the county. Just saying."

"Okay, I'll check and add it to the list. Not sure how it will matter, though."

"I don't know either, but document and question. That's all we can do."

Al asked, "Have you heard from Rez yet on the girl?"

"No. Damn. Let me call him and see what's up."

It was too loud in the restaurant to hear; Don took his phone outside. Through the plate glass window, Al and Carl watched him pacing. His breakfast was delivered and by the time he got back, it had cooled. He didn't notice and dug in. Carl and Al raised eyebrows at him, but let him get fuel in first. He ate half his food, sighed deeply, slurped newly freshened coffee, and began.

He shook his head. "She still doesn't know where she met them or how. But the last thing she does remember is walking down the highway near her house, like she always does, to get a pack of gum from the convenience store."

Al mumbled through biscuit, "She did not run away?"

"Nope. She was on car restriction, like she seemed to be every other week, thus the walking."

"So…" Carl began, chomping country ham biscuit.

"Already on it. Rez is on his way now to the convenience store to see if there are any recordings showing our two sadistic Romeos near the place."

Carl slurped, swallowed. "Let's hope it is a remote digital recording they keep for more than twenty four hours."

"We should get so lucky."

Al said, "It's a start." He barely formed the thought when one of Mel's girls was there with a pot and filling his coffee cup.

Carl continued, "Wanda is already calling Tommy to tell him she's gonna be at The Flyaway Bar and Grill tonight at eight o'clock. She's gonna get there around nine. Make him cool his heels a bit."

Don, already feeling protective of his future fiancée, confirmed her safety. "Who's gonna be there?"

Al said, "I've got a couple of our people gonna be there."

"And," Carl interrupted, "it is a community place, and law enforcement is always there on their nights off, so it will be quite natural to have a few of ours there without anything looking out of place."

Don continued checking the details. "Now, you're sure she's staying at her mama and daddy's house, right? And somebody's gonna follow her home, right?"

Carl nodded. "Yes, Don. Between us we got it covered."

"Don't worry, dude," Al assured him.

Don couldn't stop worrying.

Carl reminded him, "That little girl's got steel at her core and don't you forget it. Trust me on this. You'll need to remember that in years to come."

Don's big smile lit up in anticipation.

Carl and Al looked at each other and shook their heads before sipping.

Monday AM: Carmelita makes a house a home

Monday morning was fun for Frank and Carmelita. They got up together. Ate breakfast together. Cleaned up together. Dressed together. Planned their evening together. Walked outside together. Kissed each other goodbye and drove off together but separately. She went to her house and got her stuff for work. He hobbled into the office. They couldn't have been happier, even if it was a temporary fix.

Frank called Al mid-morning for an update on the case. He was happy to hear how it was going and the details of the plan. They were working it. There was forward movement and it was positive. The girl was found alive. Now if only her memory would come back. It probably would, unless it was chemically induced amnesia. Frank hated he said/she said cases. Often there were two versions of truth. But in this case, it was clear she was a true victim.

Granted, she may have been a stupid teenage girl who was always running wild on her emotions, but that was no reason to be tortured and maybe killed.

"Hey, Frank, you remember Don, right? Yeah…well, he has found true love. Wanda. She's police. I mean, man, you never saw a guy fall so hard…Yeah, love must be in the air…Because three of us longtime bachelors seem to have fallen head over heels just in the last few weeks…Don said Wanda's gonna be his third *but last* wife… Hahaha… Yeah, she doesn't yet know that little fact, but Don says he's sure of it…I sent LaVonne a text…*Duty called*. She said she understood…Yeah, I remember the dog-to-human lifespan rule…Okay…I said okay, I'll call her *just to check in*…Now you're giving me words to say, too? Did ya learn anything new this weekend in that department you might wanna pass along?… No. Really. Recommendations of sweet nothings I can whisper to make a girlfriend happy are always welcome...Oh, you don't think I can handle the stuff the big boys say? It got that good, huh…You mind your business and I'll mind mine, lover boy."

Frank laughed as Al hung up with no goodbye. His day flew by even as the minutes crawled, but soon Frank was on his way home.

Home.

It was no longer a house, but a home. A home for him and Carmelita — and maybe one or both of the kids. They were teens. They could take care of themselves. How much trouble could they be, being almost grown and all? Besides, they wouldn't be there for too many years. College was coming up and they would have jobs, too. Either way, he was going home to something definite this evening, at least — and he liked it. He liked it very much.

After work, he and Carmelita met at the store and bought a few groceries. He pushed the cart and followed her around. He watched as she efficiently plucked fresh vegetables from their bins. He watched as she compared two cuts of meat and placed one in the cart. They didn't need much. She wouldn't be there but another day or so and he couldn't cook. She turned to him and asked if he needed anything else. He said wine. They got two bottles.

Stood in line, together.

They drove home — *home* — and prepared a meal together. Cleaned the kitchen together. Closed and started the dishwasher together. Sat together on the sofa with wine while watching television. Held hands and walked into the bedroom together. Undressed and showered together. Made love and then slept wrapped tightly together.

They ended their fourth day together at home. *Home.* And in a few hours they would start their fifth, but not last, day together.

Carmelita had talked to her kids during the day and they were fine; thought it was all just one big adventure.

Monday, 8 PM: Wanda makes it look so easy to keep a perp occupied

Eight o'clock Monday evening, Wanda's phone rang. She answered. Listened to the voice on the other end.

"K." She hung up.

Don said, "What?"

"He's there. At the bar. Right on time. Already hitting on some chick."

Don noticed the disgusted tone she used. "You better be careful, Wanda. Don't let him catch on how much you hate his guts."

Don insisted he sit in the car with Wanda until it was time for her to go in. Officers in the bar called every few minutes to give her an update on how Tommy was acting and whether he was mad about her being late. If she had to go in earlier than nine o'clock, she would. Otherwise, she was going to make him stew in his own juices.

"I'm careful. We've got two State boys in there, several of my fellow officers, and…" She stopped abruptly, smiled.

Don encouraged her to finish her sentence. "And what?"

"And you out here worrying about me."

The Case of the Snuff Tape Killers

They smiled at each other. Don couldn't stand it anymore and leaned over to kiss her. No sooner were they in a nice lip lock, her phone rang.

Don pulled away. "Damn."

She dropped her phone, but found it in the dark car. It took a few seconds of groping to find it. Don couldn't say he didn't enjoy her search because he did.

She finally answered. "Yeah." She listened to the voice. "He's hitting it off pretty good with the chick. I better get in there. Carl doesn't like the looks of it."

"K." Don kissed her. "Be. Careful."

"I will. Besides, you got my back."

Don got out of her car and leaned in. "Yeah. And I hope your front, too, one day." He shut the door, slapped the roof once, waved as he watched her drive away, and got into the truck with Al and Carl.

Al said, "Frank says love's in the air."

Don said, "And it ain't even spring yet."

Carl pulled their attention back. "Minds on the job at hand, gentlemen. That's my Wanda in there."

In unison they said, "Yes, sir." Al turned up the heat and they waited.

* * * * *

Carl knew about the service revolver in her purse. He didn't know about Wanda's throwaway pistol strapped to her ankle under long, boot-cut jeans. He did not know about the knife taped to her thigh. Don helped her fix all that earlier in the evening.

Strapping on the knife when they were alone, Don told her, "Listen. Get forgiveness later. If you have to, shoot his ass dead. He knows you're a cop so if he tries something then he's just asking for it. Use your service revolver first. Go for the ankle next. If that fails, you have the knife. All you have to do is reach down your pants. He'll wonder what you're doing and he'll stop for a few seconds. Rip it hard and make it fast. But somebody should be there by then. Hell, honey, I'll be there by then. I got your back, okay?"

Wanda knew all this. But she simply watched him as he positioned the knife, told her to hold it, and taped it on. She had smiled as she pulled up her pants and they checked for the outline of the knife.

"If he tries to cop a feel, and you know he will, be on your toes and slap his hands before he feels the knife."

Wanda smiled.

Don looked at her sharply. "Well?"

She nodded and said gently as she patted his cheek, "Sir, yes, sir."

She drove into the parking lot, found a spot, and locked the car. By the time she opened the front door, girly-girl was in high evidence. By the time she paid the cover charge for the band, squeally girl was bopping to the beat and looking high and low for her date. She saw him pawing on, and fast-talking, a young hottie who was caving fast. She was going to have to remedy the situation.

"Tommy!" Wanda squealed above the band. His head whipped around. The girl was not happy to see Wanda.

Tommy's expression changed from startled to aggravation to relief that he had a sure thing.

After all, serial killers are lazy; to get hottie's goodies he didn't want to have to work as hard as that girl was making him. Wanda saw him say something to the girl, who flounced away in a huff.

The Case of the Snuff Tape Killers

"Wanda." Tommy slid over to her. He bent at the knees and slid an arm around her, pulling her into the bar with him, careful not to spill his beer.

"Tommy. Who was that?"

"Who was who? Her? Oh, nobody. Somebody I was killing time with waiting on you, baby." He looked at her in mock severity, checked the clock on his cellphone. "Baby, where you been? You're late."

"You wouldn't begrudge a girl a few extra minutes to get dolled up, now would ya?"

Tommy stood back and looked her up and down admiringly. "Well, if it took that little bit of time to get you looking like that, baby, then I guess it was worth it."

"Well? Gonna buy me a beer or what?"

The next hour and a half was a well-orchestrated, freestyle surveillance Tommy never saw happening. Carl, sitting in the car, received text messages from cops inside. Al got texts from his agents. They knew when they were dancing. They knew when he was canoodling with Wanda. Don was furious but knew she was undercover. Still didn't like it. When it looked like Tommy was getting friskier than they wanted, Carl or Al would send in someone to ask her to dance or say hello.

Three times Wanda introduced fellow officers who had been instructed to act sincerely impressed that they were introduced to, and got to shake the hand of, the hero, the man of the hour, the crown prince of the county. Wanda talked him up big time and batted her eyes at him plenty. He thought he had a sure thing.

Then Carl said it was time to shut him down for the evening. In front of the bandstand, a fight broke out. It was a male State agent and a friend of one of the cops fighting over a female State agent, but Tommy didn't know that. Several cops broke it up and the girl came running over to Wanda.

Wanda explained to Tommy the girl was new in town, they'd met at church and she was a good girl. The girl was screaming and having a meltdown over the fight.

"Wanda. Please, take me home. Get me out of here," the female agent cried and begged. Her tears made her mascara streak down her face. The cops were still holding the agent and friend until she got out.

"Tommy. I got to help her. You understand, right? I am *so* sorry," she apologized as she got her friend's purse and put her into her coat.

What could he say? "Sure. Whatever."

"Hey, listen. I'll make it up to you. Okay? Meet me out here tomorrow evening. I promise I won't be late. I *promise*."

Tommy smiled and nodded okay.

Wanda gave Tommy the *call me* hand sign, made it out the door to her car, and was on the road before the agent sat up, dry-eyed. They high-fived each other. The agent said, "*That* was fun." They headed to Wanda's parents' house. No one followed. Cops stayed in the bar and kept Tommy occupied until closing with sycophant worship.

Tommy didn't leave with any girl.

Tuesday AM: Jennifer remembers everything

Rez was back out at Jennifer Howard's house on Tuesday morning. He came because he got a frantic call from her parents, arrived twenty minutes after he hung up.

Dad said, "Quick, follow me."

Mom grabbed Rez by the hand and pulled him through the door, slammed it, dragged him down the hall toward the bathroom where Jennifer sat in the tub fully clothed as cold water streamed over her from the shower head.

Dad filled in Rez. "She keeps rocking and sucking her thumb. And every now and then, she sobs real loud. We can't get her out of the shower —"

Mom said, "And we've been trying for two hours!"

He could hear the shower running full force. Mute and completely bewildered, her parents simply pointed to the bathroom.

Jennifer heard the door open again. She popped her thumb out of her mouth and, with dead calmness and deliberate coldness, said, "Leave. Me. Alone." And then she went back to her rocking, sucking, and sobbing.

Rez went into a bedroom and stripped a blanket off a bed. "Do you have an electric blanket?" he asked. They did. "Good, get her bed warm."

He opened the bathroom door again. The girl never turned her head. Rez turned off the shower.

She screamed at him, "Turn it back on. Turn it back on."

"Why?"

She screamed again. Nothing intelligible, but she scrambled to get to the faucet. He let her turn it on. He left it on for two minutes, then quietly turned it off.

She screamed and turned it on. They went back and forth like that for an hour. Rez could hear Jennifer's father pacing in the hall, the anxiety in her mother's voice as she questioned her husband, and his insistence that everything would be fine.

Each time Rez turned the water off, her scream was shorter and not as loud until finally she didn't turn it on again and was silent. Jennifer was freezing. Rez took a towel and dried her hair and face. He gripped her shoulders and stood her up, wrapped her in the blanket, helped her step out of the tub, supported her as he took her to her room. Daddy pulled down the covers. Mama fluffed the pillow.

Rez lay her down in the warm bed, still wrapped in the blanket. Parents covered her with the warm electric blanket.

Daddy and Mama left the room and stood in the hall, still confused. It killed them to see their little girl like this and they couldn't handle it. Yet they realized she needed someone who was emotionally distant and could give her the strength she needed to draw on.

Rez had that distance and strength. They let him do what was best for their daughter.

Eyes wide, Jennifer never blinked. She began to shiver until the shivering got so hard the bed shook and the headboard bounced against the wall. Rez sat next to her, watched, and said nothing. She finally blinked and when she did, her mouth opened wide in a silent wailing scream followed by loud body-wracking sobs.

Daddy and Mama peeked in every few minutes. They saw Rez calmly helping their daughter. He caught their eyes a couple of times and nodded *all is well*. They believed him and retreated to the safety of the hall to wait it out.

"I'm hot! I'm hot!" she screamed after a while, and threw off the covers. But when she threw the covers her fists followed and she blindly began to beat at Rez. He said nothing, held her arms, and directed her fists to the softness of the bed. He helped her as she continued to cry and strike until she wore herself out, and eventually lay on the bed, exhausted. Rez covered her again.

She whispered, "Thank you."

Rez said, "You're welcome."

And he waited by her side as she slept. When she finally awoke, she looked him straight in the eye, blinked once, and said, "I remember everything."

"Good. You ready to make them sumbitches pay?"

She nodded solemnly. "Oh, yes."

She cried out, "Mommy? Daddy?"

"Yes, baby." They were there in one second flat and Rez let them comfort her — now that they could.

Tuesday PM: Where in the world is Otter?

Al got the call. The girl remembered everything, but she hadn't made an official statement yet. Still in shock, she needed time to gather her thoughts. It could be another day or two. But it was good news all 'round and the celebration ran up and down Interstates 75 and 85, from Butts County to Atlanta and on to Elberton.

"Occam's Razor," Don said. "Can't get all caught up in the complexity of catching these guys. Now that we have the girl's memory back, we got 'em. I say we go visit Otter. Move this thing along."

Like Don, Wanda was ready for action. But honestly, it was because she didn't know if she could stomach putting on the squeally-girl act again. Working undercover against Tommy, she already heard every line he had to deliver and none of them were inspiring.

She was afraid she was gonna smack him silly and put the beat-down on him out of pure boredom. Give her a manly man like Don any day. One who knew how to tape a knife on her thigh.

One who worried her ankle strap might be too tight. One who —

She brought her attention back to the room when she heard her name. Carl was saying, "Wanda can meet up with Tommy again tonight…"

Her hopes sank.

"…and we can have a little meeting with Otter this evening, too. Al, when do you think we might get the girl's statement?"

Al nodded. "Frank's coordinating. He talked to Rez earlier and the girl is already writing the thing down. Rez said she's furious. Thank God they never got around to the torture and killing. So far, it looks like they kept her drugged up and had their way with her. They were going in for the hard stuff when me and Don showed up. So, yeah, it coulda been a whole lot worse. Coulda been a whole lotta dead."

Carl closed the meeting. "Okay, let's get a late lunch, everybody. Then get to your places and put on your show. Al, you and I'll have the chat with Otter. Okay? Wanda, how you gettin' out tonight, honey?"

Wanda mimed her game plan. "I'm gonna get food poisoning and threaten to vomit." The men laughed.

God, Don loved that woman. He smiled. "That should shut him down — cold."

"Hell, yeah."

She smiled.

* * * * *

Otter's sister's house was a study in contrasts. They pulled up in the driveway as far as it was possible. A 1968 Chevy Super Sport, sitting on cement blocks and rusting fast, took up the left-hand side. It was full of car parts and looked like somebody's restoration project got put on hold. Kudzu vines peeked out of the engine compartment, curling over the side to join their brethren.

Next to the car was a neat pile of firewood, cut to lengths and split. It had been there so long it was rotting.

In the carport was a new and very clean SUV tricked out with the latest in DVD players and headsets for the kiddies. God forbid Mom should hear her children speak while they were confined together.

The yard was strewn with new bicycles, and the outline of a Harley could be seen under a vinyl cover. Al took a peek; also new. The paint was peeling from the house and only part of the grass was cut. Two windows were broken and pieces of scrap plywood filled the holes. A fence surrounding the backyard was stout. Carl and Al soon found out why. Two Pit Bulls and one Chihuahua rushed it. But the fence was for the Chihuahua, who was trying to tear it down to get to the men; the Pits wondered who was visiting and wagged their tails in hello.

Carl knocked. The door opened and there stood Otter's sister. Sheila was a study in contrasts, too. Her clothes were low-end tramp. But her hair and nails must have cost her one week's salary. She smoked unfiltered cigarettes but spoke as if she had been educated at a finishing school.

She threw the door open as if she expected someone else and was aggravated it wasn't him.

Hardly a trace of a Southern accent could be heard from her as she inquired, "Yes?"

Carl showed his badge, but before he could say anything, she said, "I knew you were The Law as soon as I opened the door. You didn't have to show me your badge. How can I help you?"

It was Carl's patch, he took lead. "Yes. We're here to see Jimmy. Is he home?"

Sheila barely glanced at Al, but leaned against the doorjamb and looked Carl up and down before answering. "No, sugar. He is not home. In fact, ever since that thing Sunday, I have not seen him, nor have I heard from him. Have you checked with the idiot, Tommy?"

"No. We'll check there next. Is it normal for you to go several days without hearing from him?"

"It's not like we do a lot together, because we don't. But, yeah, I usually see some signs of his being around and his bike is still here and his car is still here, too, and neither of 'em have moved."

"His car?"

"Yeah. It's dark right now and you can't see it, but there's another driveway and he usually parks there. All I can figure is he and Tommy must be on one of their famous road trips again and he forgot to tell me."

"Road trips, ma'am?" This from Al.

She didn't look at Al and directed her answer to Carl. "Yeah. Two or three times a year they take road trips. At least, that's what they call them. Jimmy says they have grand adventures, whatever that means. He's usually in a good mood when he gets back. I suppose it could only mean he's getting… well, you know."

Carl and Al nodded. "Well, ma'am, let me leave you my card and when he gets home, will you tell him, please ma'am, to call either me or the detective here."

She took Al's proffered card without looking at him and put Carl's on top. She slid them real slow into her jeans pocket. "Sure. Whatever. He in trouble?"

Both men said nothing and stared at her. She said, "Oh. It's like that, is it? Big trouble."

Carl said, "It's in his best interests to get in touch as soon as possible. Okay?"

Sheila didn't say anything. She suddenly looked very old and very tired. She nodded, pushed herself away from the door frame, stepped back into the house, took a long drag on her cigarette as she slowly closed the door.

In the car, Al said, "That went good."

"You wouldn't know it, but she was homecoming queen and made top grades. Was always a very good girl growing up. Not sure what happened, but something went way off track with Sheila. I hate it."

"I wonder where Jimmy is."

Carl turned the key and backed out of the drive. They both turned their heads toward the other drive and, sure enough, there was Otter's car.

"She said it and his bike, I'm guessing the Harley, haven't moved since Sunday and she said that's very unusual. We got to find him."

They would find him alright, but not how they expected.

Tuesday PM: A most excellent long weekend ends

Carmelita got the call late Tuesday evening: Martin and the kids were coming home tomorrow. They would arrive sometime after lunch. Her kids asked if she had called the school. She assured them she had. She asked if they were doing okay. No bumps or bruises causing them any pain? *No, we're fine, Mom* came back. Martin said he would be glad to get home.

Carmelita didn't know what to say, so she made a noncommittal noise and he seemed to be okay with it.

She curled up on the sofa with Frank as she talked to them. To comfort her, he stroked her hair and patted her arm and shoulder and hand. She didn't look at him while she was on the phone, but snuggled in closer as soon as she hung up.

"I guess you heard then, huh?"

He kissed the top of her head. "Yep."

"This is our last night."

"No, it isn't."

"You know what I mean."

He hugged her tighter. "Yep."

Thirty quiet minutes later, Frank said, "Come on. Let's go to bed." He pushed her to a sitting position, stood, put her feet on the floor for her, took her hands and lifted her. He hugged her tight, wrapped an arm around her waist, and led her into the kitchen where she turned off the light.

They went back into the living room. She turned off another light. They walked into the bedroom. She turned on a small lamp next to the bed. They brushed their teeth. They washed their faces. They took off their clothes. They each pulled down the covers on opposite sides of the bed and crawled in. The sheets were cold, but Frank gasped at how much colder she was.

He spent the next two hours warming her up. When they eventually went to sleep, the sheets were warm and their bodies relaxed. They slept soundly. When the alarm went off Wednesday morning, they didn't want to leave. Saying goodbye at the car was tough. They drove off. Her phone rang. It was Frank.

"Baby?"

"Yes?"

"I love you, you know that, right?"

"Yes."

"Okay. Don't forget it. Don't doubt it, either. Believe it."

"Okay."

Wednesday AM: Don is jealous

"You shoulda seen her."

Don listened to one of the locals tell about Wanda's descent into sickness the night before. "It was crazy. Don't know how she did it, but when she came out of the bathroom and told him she had been throwing up and felt feverish, I swear she was white as a sheet; her nose was red, like she'd been barfin'."

Everyone was laughing. The man asked, "How'd you do that, Wanda?"

"Easy. I brought real light makeup powder. When I went to the bathroom, I put powder all over my face, then I put heavy blush on my nose and on my eyelids."

Local continued, "You shoulda seen Tommy's face when he thought she was getting ready to yak on him. Did ya see how fast he jumped, Wanda? That was funny. Couldn't get away from you fast enough."

"Yeah. It was great."

Carl laughed. "Good thinking, Wanda. Let's hope he's a hypochondriac and thinks he's coming down with the flu or something."

"Yeah. Too bad I couldn't slip something in his drink, make him throw up, too, you know?"

Don thought the story was good and he was proud of her. He didn't like the local boy's telling of the story; it made him mad as hell. With a start, Don realized the Green-Eyed Monster was rearing its ugly head. Yeah, Don was jealous.

Wednesday PM: Otter is found

Carl got the call. He was sitting in his office, alone, when it came in. Surprised, he stood straight up and yelled, "*What?*" He got the details, said they'd be right there, and stormed out of his office.

"Al! Don! Lee! Let's roll. Got a body."

Lee took his own car. Carl drove Al and Don, and explained on the way. "Guess who's dead?"

Al said, "Carl, don't make me guess."

"Otter." Now it was Don and Al's turn to be shocked.

Carl continued, "Two hikers near the quarry saw a body

floating in the lake at the bottom of the quarry and called it in. He's already been fished out."

Don asked, "For sure it's him?"

"Yep. Face on the body matches the face on the driver's license in his pants pocket."

Al asked, "Accident?"

"Don't know. Guess we might be able to find out when we get there. We'll see."

"How long?"

"Hard to tell. Water's cold this time of year. Preserved it, you know."

Don opined. "Huh. I know when he died. Betcha five dollars he died Sunday sometime. I double-gara-damn-tee it. And I further gare-ohn-tee Tommy did the deed."

No one took the bet.

Carl said, "Crap. Got to tell his sister."

Don said, "Why can't you let Wanda do it? She might be able to, you know, bond like a girl or something, and you know, in her grief the sister might say something important she might not tell you."

"Not a bad idea. I'll confirm it's him and then we'll notify next of kin."

"His parents still alive?"

"No. Daddy shot Mama, then shot himself when the kids were, well…let me see, Otter was fourteen thereabouts and Sheila was nineteen or so? Yeah, I think that's right."

"In front of the kids?"

"No, no. Hell no. He was a nice man. Really was. She was a nice lady. They wouldn't have done anything to hurt the kids. Great family. The note he left was very specific. But it made no sense, and we never really figured it out.

"So, unless he had some sort of mental illness nobody ever knew about, we don't know."

Al asked, "You sure the husband killed his wife and then himself?"

"What do you mean?"

"Think. What have Otter and his best friend since fourth grade been doing the last couple of years or so but killing people? What if, just what if, their first human kills were Otter's mom and dad?"

Carl hit the steering wheel. "Aaahhh, sheeee-itt. I never thought about that."

"And they got away with it better than their wildest dreams. Emboldened them more. What if, just what if, they've been killing longer than we realize? Don't you remember Otter's sister — Sheila, right? — yeah, Sheila said they've been going on road trips for years and he's always happy when he comes back."

Don said, "We need to get Wanda to ask Sheila if she knows where those road trips have been taken. Might find more bodies."

* * * * *

"Yep. It's ol' Jimmy, alright." Don stared at Otter's face and felt nothing but frustration. "Damn. He would've been the one to crack, too."

Al agreed. "Too late now."

They turned to listen to the rescue team lead's narration.

"We got the call around eight this morning. Got out here and realized we were gonna have to go scuba on the retrieval. It took us another hour or so for it to arrive. We got to the bottom of the quarry and took the boat over there. His body was wedged up nice and tight. He was cold and bloated. Took us about an hour to get him free. We floated him to the landing and there we bagged him before we took him out. Damn, the water was cold. I'm still shivering."

"Any idea how he got to that spot?"

"See, that's the thing. He didn't fall. He couldn't have fallen from up there; even if he bounced all whichaways, there's no way he coulda landed there. Ain't no way. And there really ain't a current that would push his body up into that spot. I mean, it's almost like he had to have taken a boat over there, got out, walked to the spot, fell in the pool of water, and died."

Carl nodded. "Okay. Where's the coroner?"

Rescue pointed to the wagon. They walked over and Carl introduced Al and Don. "What we got, Jack?"

"It's too cold to stand out here and do this. Let me get him back to my place and I'll get right on him. But, his head ain't bashed in and his body ain't broke open, so I can definitively state it wasn't a fall from a great height and he didn't get bonked."

"Okay. Call me when you know."

Jack nodded. "Always do."

Carl kicked at a stone as he made his way back to the car. "Sheee-it." He pulled his keys out of his pocket and got in. He sat for a couple of minutes as he thought of Otter. "Well, boys," he smiled grimly, starting the car. "One down. One to go. Let's git him."

* * * * *

The Case of the Snuff Tape Killers

Late that evening, Wanda and Lee rode together to Sheila's house. Wanda called earlier to make sure she was at home. Sheila said, "It's bad news, isn't it?" She was prepared, though for what she didn't know.

Lee knocked and stepped back behind Wanda. He may have rank, but she was lead on this call and he knew she would handle it well. He'd sit back and notice everything. They'd compare notes later.

Sheila opened her door, waved them in, walked to her sofa, and slowly lowered herself into the cushions. Wanda sat on the other end of the sofa. Lee found a chair in the kitchen and brought it in.

Sheila repeated herself. "It's bad news."

Wanda nodded.

"He's dead?"

Wanda nodded again.

"What happened?"

"Found at the bottom of the quarry…"

"He fell?"

"No. He didn't fall."

Sheila shook her head. "Then, what?"

"He was found in the water."

"He *drowned*? In the winter?"

Wanda shook her head. "No. He didn't drown. He was found down there."

"I don't understand. Y'all don't know how he died?"

Wanda explained, "He's at the coroner's now. We should know something soon. We know it's him. The body matched ID in the wallet. Besides, everybody knew him. But if you want to come and formally identify him, you can."

Sheila nodded. There were no tears. Maybe there never would be. She loved her baby brother, but there was something not right about him. He had never been sad about their parents' deaths. He'd never been aggressive with her or the kids. If that had ever happened, she would have kicked him out on his butt and never let him darken her door again. He was always good to them and kept his dark ways out of her home. Still, she heard the stories. She would identify him — then bury the cause of the troubles she was sure would eventually come back to haunt her.

Wanda waited until Sheila took it all in before she continued, "Sheila, when was the last time you saw Otter?"

"Sunday, around one o'clock. After he got back from the police station."

"Did he say anything in particular? Act out of sorts?"

Sheila thought about it. "Now you mention it, he was… different. He was mad at Tommy. He's never been mad at Tommy, not that I've seen at least. Tommy dropped him off here and I heard the car door slam. He had to have given it a big shove for me to hear the slam all the way in here from the end of the driveway. Then he came in and he didn't say hello. Went back to his room. He came out about an hour later. I heard his phone ring and then he came out. He seemed to be…sort of…under tight control. But he said hello to me and the kids. Smiled. Got something from the fridge."

"What'd he eat?"

"Leftover pizza. He grabbed a couple of slices. Then he said Tommy was outside and they had some things to do and he would see me later."

The living room got quiet. Sheila stared at the floor. Wanda waited. Lee watched.

Sheila asked quietly, "Do you think Tommy killed him?"

Wanda hesitated a beat, and asked, "Why do you ask?"

"Tommy's a sick fucker. He might have money and manners and a nice car and house and looks. But he's one sick dude. Always has been. Even as a kid, Mom and Dad didn't like him, but they couldn't figure out why. I remember them sitting at the table. We'd be eating and Jimmy would be telling some story about Tommy he thought was great, but…"

Here she paused and closed her eyes, picturing the scene. "But me and Mom and Dad, we were horrified."

"Like what?"

"Let me think." Sheila rubbed her face with both hands. "It's been so long since I thought about it all. Okay. There was this one time, Jimmy said Tommy and him skinned a cat. Mom said *did you find a dead cat?* Jimmy said no, Tommy had already killed it before he got there. Now, that's not good. We heard stuff like that all the time."

Sheila got quiet for a few seconds while she thought.

"Of course, then Mom and Dad died — that was a weird time, let me tell you — and honestly, I didn't give Tommy much thought for a while and Jimmy stayed over there with him and his mom a lot. I thought it was a nice thing they were doing. That was naïve, wasn't it?"

"Well, you know —"

"Yeah."

"Can you think of anything else?"

"About what?"

"Jimmy's last few days? Last few months? Anything about Tommy recently?"

"Oh, I don't know. Not right now. I'm kind of…numb."

Wanda and Lee stood and each handed Sheila their business cards. "Well…look…I know this is a rough time for you. But if you think of anything, call me or call Lee," she nodded at Lee, "and we'll be happy to talk to you. Okay?"

"Yes. I will. Thank you, Wanda."

Sheila stood and they rose with her. She walked them to the door. Lee shook her hand. Wanda gave her a hug. They heard the door quietly close and lock as they returned to their car.

Five minutes down the road, Wanda said, "Lee, I think she told us a whole bunch of stuff that fits right in with what we suspect —"

"Suspect, hell. We *know*," Lee exploded.

"Yeah, we know. We definitely know."

"Wanda, I'm gonna recommend to Carl you don't do any more meet-ups with Tommy, I don't care how many people are around. He just killed his best friend, his best *from-childhood* friend, mind you. He's not in a good place right now."

"Now, Lee, we have to do what we have to do. I can handle myself."

"Don't you *now Lee* me. Spoken like an inexperienced idiot. Carl will agree with me. You wait and see."

"You're probably right."

Wanda called Carl and told him everything Sheila said.

* * * * *

Martin and the children arrived home late Wednesday. Carmelita ran out the front door as she saw their car coming down the street. She waved and smiled. She even laughed a little bit as Will and Anne got out of the car.

Had Will grown three inches? He sure seemed taller. And Anne. Ah, she's a woman, a beautiful woman.

She wiped tears away and ran over to hug them. She missed her kids terribly and was so happy to see them come home she even smiled at Martin when he got out of the car. The kids brought their bags inside. Then Mom inspected them for bumps and bruises and made sure they were okay. They pretended they didn't need to be checked out and rolled their eyes, but they enjoyed the attention as only Mom could give it and were glad to be home.

Tonight would not be pretty when Carmelita slept on the sofa. It was one thing to make up your mind about your path when the man you love is next to you. It was quite another to take the path without him there for support.

Bags were unpacked and Carmelita made hot chocolate. They sat around the kitchen table, enjoyed their cups, and talked about the accident and the trip. Carmelita took pleasure in watching the adults she could see her children becoming and knew they would be okay with the changes heading their way. Soon the kids were in bed and Martin was showering. Carmelita quickly changed into pajamas and got out of the bedroom before he could suggest sex.

Earlier in the day she put a pillow, blankets, and the alarm clock next to the sofa. Martin was sure to notice them when he came out to watch television. She sat on the sofa, pulled out a book, and was busy reading when he came out to the living room. He sat in his favorite chair, grabbed the remote, and started flipping channels.

He flipped for an hour, never leaving anything on for over two minutes. She felt the tension in the room change.

"What's the alarm clock doing out here?" Martin asked.

She didn't raise her eyes from the book. "So I can wake up in the morning."

"Yeah. I know. Why is it out *here?*"

This time when she answered, she looked straight at him. "So I can wake up in the morning."

"I don't understand. Why do you need it out here?"

She did not turn away from him when she answered, "I'm gonna be sleeping on the sofa for awhile."

"How long?"

"Not sure."

He went back to his flipping, she went back to her book, and that was the end of the conversation — that evening.

Wednesday PM: Who did in Otter?

Carl hung up from Wanda's call. Then he, Al, and Don drove to Tommy's house. This time when they entered the house, they would do it after politely ringing the doorbell in front, instead of coming in the back door with Tommy at gunpoint. They wanted to see what he would do or say when he found out his best friend was dead. Al thought he could probably write the script for this conversation. He would soon find out if he was right.

Mama opened the door, none too politely either. She stood in the doorway with her hand on the knob. "Yes?"

If they had been in the Middle Ages, Al swore Carl would be touching his forelock he was so deferential. "Good evening, Mrs. Higgenbotham. How are you?"

Manners were house rules with Mama and she ruled the house. Still, she was icily formal. "I am fine, Detective. Thank you for asking. And you?"

"I'm fine, ma'am."

She accepted the deference as a queen would, then graciously condescended to ask, "How can I help you today?"

"We'd like to see Tommy. We have some bad news for him and wanted to deliver it personally."

"Bad news? What bad news?"

"Prefer to tell Tommy in person."

Mama stood in the doorway, staring them down. They stared back. She finally said, "Well, Tommy's sick. He's in bed. He can't eat. He can hardly sleep. Frankly, I don't think he's up to talking to you now."

They knew his tale of sickness was untrue and continued silently staring at her. Carl shifted his weight from one foot to the other, dipped his head deferentially again, but still looked her in the eye.

"You need to go get him."

"Well!" She indignantly stamped her little foot. "I have no choice in the matter?"

"No, ma'am. No choice."

"It's cold out. Come in. Will you have coffee? I can get my girl to bring some in."

"No thank you, ma'am. No coffee."

Mama led them into the formal living room, the better to intimidate them. They each picked the stoutest chair they could find, lowering themselves slowly as she watched them try to get comfortable without breaking her vintage, that is to say, expensive furniture.

Mama gave an aggravated shake to her head and said, "I'll be right back."

They heard her heels rat-a-tat-tatting on the wooden foyer floor and each sharp stomp as she hit each stair. They listened. Her steps were muffled by the carpet runner as she made her way down the overhead hall to, what they presumed, was Precious' room. They heard a quiet knock. They heard muffled voices, but could not make out the words. Mama repeated her path downstairs but on her return trip she was followed closely by heavier footsteps.

Mama and Precious entered the room. Tommy didn't look good. The officers stood as one when he entered.

Tommy flinched as they stood, his bravado and king of the castle attitude nowhere in evidence.

Mama took a seat.

Carl said, "Ma'am, it might be in your best interests to leave the room, close the door. Have a cup of coffee in the kitchen, okay?"

Mama began to protest, but quickly backed down when Tommy shot her a look showing he agreed with Carl. She stood, and meekly left, quietly closing the door.

Carl softly walked to the door and opened it. Mama stared up at him guiltily. "Ma'am, you really don't want to hear this conversation."

Tommy spoke his first words since entering. "Go on, Mama. I'll handle this."

Mama saw she couldn't impose her will on these men; Precious was telling her to go, so…she went, reluctantly.

Carl watched her walk away. He closed the door and they all sat down.

Al took the lead. "Tommy, we have some bad news for you. We don't want to shock you or anything, and we know you are sick, but these things never happen at a good time, do they?"

Tommy leaned back. "What things?"

"Otter's been found dead."

Tommy looked as if he was going to throw up.

Don said, "Dude. You need a trashcan or something?"

Tommy fought to get himself under control. They waited. "No. I'm fine."

No one spoke. Tommy wasn't stupid and knew they were waiting on him to speak. "You say he's been found dead — what does that mean?"

Don spoke up. "As in ain't breathing anymore dead. Never gonna contribute to his retirement fund anymore dead. Won't collect Social Security dead, you…"

Don would have continued, but Carl held up a hand shutting him up. Tommy was clearly scared of Don.

Tommy found the courage to squeak out, "Where?"

Al answered. "At the quarry. When was the last time you saw him?"

"Sunday."

"Sunday, when?"

It was painfully obvious Tommy had known this conversation was going to happen. It was also obvious he had not quite figured out how to answer to best serve himself. They saw his wheels turning.

Don prompted him. "*When* Sunday?"

"Sunday afternoon. I picked him up from Sheila's house and we went…you know, driving?"

"Did you go driving or did you not?"

"Huh?"

"What time, Tommy? What time did you pick him up?"

His head swiveled from Don to Carl to Al. "Huh?"

Al said, "Tommy, what's wrong?"

Tommy had an angle and he played it. "I just found out my best friend's dead. I've been sick all week. And now I'm having to remember my schedule?"

The Law stared at him.

Finally, Al spoke. "You're right, Tommy. I tell you what, let's give you a little bit of time to figure out, umm, I mean remember your schedule. I mean, you have been under stress in the last few hours —"

"What does that mean?" Tommy demanded.

"You've been sick and rescuing the girl and now you're finding out your best friend is dead — you know...stress."

"Oh." Tommy missed Al's sarcasm.

"Here's what's gonna happen. We need your input to figure out his last few hours. We know you want to help him, right?"

"Yeah. Right. Sure, of course."

"You take your Vitamin C and drink your hot tea with lemon and honey and get some rest. You should feel better by tomorrow morning, right?"

"Yeah, I think so."

"Come to Carl's office and finish telling him about Otter's last few hours; you know, what you know of them, of course. We can schedule it for...say...tomorrow morning?"

Tommy could do nothing but nod and agree when GBI made the suggestion. He thanked them for their kindness, though it took all of his self-control not to scream at them when they walked out Mama's front door. But he kept his cool and assumed they never suspected his hatred and fear.

He knew he had to play this game out to its end, hoping the few hours would give him the time to figure out a cohesive story. At first he was frightened of the interview; it was an interview, no mistake. Tommy knew they suspected he and Otter had kidnapped the girl, and knew who they suspected of killing Otter.

His best friend since fourth grade, and he had killed him! He hadn't wanted to, but Otter was cracking. He couldn't take the chance he would blurt out everything.

Killing Otter — his best friend who understood him better than anyone — was the hardest thing he'd ever done in his life.

It had been hard and hurt him badly; he got sick from it, for a time anyway. He didn't feel like going in to work and told Mama he had a fever. Mama worried, though she didn't understand how it was his fever went away each evening in time for him to go out. Yeah, killing Otter was the best thing Tommy ever did for his friend. Otter would not have been able to handle prison. Tommy knew this because Otter told him of his fears.

Tommy made the great sacrifice and killed his friend, even if it broke his own heart to do it. Now he needed to get his own story straight. Poor Otter. By the time he got through telling it, Otter will have been accused of doing things he would never dream of doing on his own. But, what the hell? What did Otter have to lose now?

Feeling much better, Tommy went into the kitchen to get the maid, Rosario, to fix him a fat sandwich. And to reward himself, he'd have an ice cold beer with it, too.

Thursday AM: Jennifer makes a powerful statement

The next morning after arriving back home and not sleeping with Carmelita, Martin woke up in a foul mood. He left for work early, saying goodbye to no one.

"Mom? What's up with Dad?" Will, always astute, picked up that something wasn't right. "He acts like he's mad or something."

"Yeah. We had a disagreement. He'll get over it."

Anna shrugged and finished her breakfast. Carmelita knew her son, and knew Will was deep in thought even as he got on the bus. She cleaned the kitchen, dressed, and went out to sell ads. She got a call. It was Martin.

"I want to know what the hell this sleeping on the sofa thing is all about."

"I know you do." She didn't want to talk about it over the phone.

"Well?" he demanded.

"Martin, why don't we meet for lunch today and talk about it?"

He hesitated. "I can't. I have…other plans for lunch."

"Okay. Then why don't we go out to dinner tonight and talk about it?"

"I can't do it tonight, either."

Carmelita sighed. "When would it be convenient for you then?"

"Why do we have to go out to eat for you to tell me?" he asked. "Why can't you tell me right now?"

"Let's go out. Talk there. Okay? Please?"

"What's the matter with you?"

Carmelita didn't answer. "Listen. When and where would be best for you to have dinner with your wife?"

Martin's silence stretched until she wondered if he was still there. "Okay. Tomorrow evening, I guess."

"Okay. Where?"

"It doesn't matter."

As usual, Carmelita made the decision. "Then I'll meet you at Serafino's at six tomorrow evening. Okay? The kids can order pizza tomorrow night."

"I don't see what the big deal is."

"Six o'clock, Martin. Serafino's. Tomorrow evening." He disconnected with no goodbye.

Her workday ended, she met the kids at home, Martin arrived for dinner, and his bad mood continued. To escape the tension, Anne and Will spent the evening in their bedrooms after they finished their chores. Carmelita read a magazine. Martin turned off the television, threw down the remote, said he had something to do, and left the house. When he finally arrived home, she woke but pretended not to hear him.

He locked the door. She heard his footsteps go down the hall, stop, and very quietly come back into the living room. He stood still, watching her, for a few minutes. Satisfied she was asleep, he turned and walked back to the bedroom.

Only when he left could she relax her guard and get back to sleep.

* * * * *

Jennifer Howard may have been a yo-yo as far as her emotional responses were concerned. She may have gotten mad at Mama and Daddy and hated their guts because she thought they hated her and didn't want her to have any fun. She may have thought she could handle whatever came her way. But she didn't know what Mama and Daddy knew for sure and tried hard to protect her from:

There really were evil people who didn't want what was best for her and who would hurt her for the sheer fun of it.

She always thought her smile, quick wit, and sparkling personality could bend everyone to her will. She was secure in that knowledge...until a few days ago. Finding out she was wrong was her first big eye-opener. It was one she would never forget. Mama and Daddy were very smart and she told them she loved them. And then she asked for paper and pen.

Within two days her written account of her ordeal was complete and she asked Daddy to call Rez.

"Detective? This is Mr. Howard. Jennifer's daddy. Jennifer says she has her statement all ready."

"I'm on my way."

When Rez arrived, Mama met him at the door again. This time she hugged him when he came in, then led him to the kitchen. He saw Daddy sitting at the table with Jennifer. She held several sheets of paper against her chest. She looked up at Rez. He understood what she needed.

"Darlene and Jim, I know this is hard, but I don't think Jennifer is ready for you to read or hear this yet. Am I right, Jennifer?"

She nodded, her wide eyes pleading for understanding from Mom and Dad.

"Can you go somewhere else and not listen in? I know it will be hard, but right now it would be best for everyone."

Again, Jennifer's parents felt powerless. But they obeyed because their baby needed them to be out of the room. They shut the kitchen door, went to the living room, sat on the sofa, and held hands.

Jennifer handed the paper to Rez. Her expression did not change. She was resolute, though it took all she had not to break down.

"I'm gonna read it here and I'm gonna read it out loud to you. Okay?"

"Why?"

"What's gonna happen is that, as I read it aloud, you may realize you forgot something and will need to add to it. Or you may say something needs clarifying. I will then hand the sheet to you and you can make your notes in the margins, okay?"

"Sure. Okay."

"If at any time you need me to take a break from reading, let me know and I'll stop until you're ready."

"Sure. Okay."

Rez began reading:

```
     My name is Jennifer Howard. I am
seventeen years old. I live with my
mother and father in Jackson, Georgia.
On Tuesday I was walking to the
convenience store to get gum. I bought
gum. I saw my friend, Renee, and we
talked for a while inside the store. It
was cold out but I wanted to walk home
so I did not take Renee's offer of a
ride. She left and I walked out the door
a few minutes later. I wanted to use the
bathroom because I was afraid I couldn't
hold it until I got home so that is why
I left later.
```

When I came out of the store, there were these two nice looking young men just getting out of their car. They said hello to me and I said hello back. They asked for directions to some street, I forget which one, but I didn't know where it was and I hadn't heard of it either. They thanked me and went inside. I started to walk home.

About five minutes later that car drove by me going pretty fast. It was starting to get dark and I saw their brake lights light up when they slowed down real fast. Then their backup lights went on and they started backing toward me. I didn't think nothing of it, but they kept coming, real fast, and I had to jump the ditch to keep from getting hit.

The car stopped next to me and the guy who wasn't driving, Otter, or Jimmy, jumped out and ran toward me. I started running but I started running too late because he caught me. I hit him with my purse and he hit me with his fist in my face. He dragged me to the car and he pulled me in on top of him so that I was sitting in his lap.

They took off real fast. I was screaming and trying to hit them but the car was small and I couldn't really hit them hard enough. So I thought I would grab the steering wheel and I did but they were very strong and got me off it and then the driver, Tommy, hit me in my chest with his elbow really hard and I couldn't catch my breath. Then the other one put duct tape over my mouth and

```
around my wrists and then I felt a hand
around my throat.
    The driver told me to be quiet or
they would kill me. The other one said
he would choke me to death if I didn't
stop wiggling. We weren't around any
people and I didn't know what to do so I
got quiet and I got still.
```

Rez paused and looked at Jennifer. She nodded for him to continue.

```
    The duct tape was over my mouth but
was partially over my nose, too, and I
had a hard time breathing. Jimmy, the
one whose lap I was sitting in,
unbuttoned my coat and put his hands
under my blouse. He squeezed my breasts
and was licking my face and then he put
his hands between my legs and felt my
crotch and tried to get my pants off but
the space was so tight he couldn't get
my pants off.
    Jimmy started talking about all the
things he was going to do to me. The
driver, Tommy, unzipped his pants and
pulled his penis out and started —
```

"Stop!" Jennifer put her hands over her face and breathed deeply. "Okay. Go on." Rez continued as Jennifer kept her face covered.

```
    "...and started masturbating himself
while Jimmy talked. I could feel Jimmy
under me and he was aroused, too, but he
couldn't reach himself so he just kept
```

pushing up against me over and over until finally both of them started grunting real loud and I could see Tommy's penis and there was all that semen all over his hand. He wiped it on my face and they both laughed. I was crying and I tried to move my face away so he couldn't get it on me but the car was small and I couldn't go anywhere and Jimmy held my face so I couldn't really move it either. Tommy smeared it in my hair, too, and they said something about this being like in the movies, but I didn't understand that.

They drove up the interstate really fast for a long time. I kept trying to think of ways to get away, but Jimmy was too strong and I was tied up and I'm sorry, I never saw any people and we never slowed down and I couldn't unroll the window so I could jump or something. I could see signs and we were moving north and finally we were on Interstate 85. I saw some signs for Elberton, I think that was the exit, but I've never been there before. They got off at that exit.

We drove for a while down a back road and then we got to this really big house and they drove around back. Tommy hit me in the face with his elbow and almost knocked me out. I barely remember getting out of the car or into the basement. I was still woozy from the elbow to the face when Jimmy ripped off the duct tape from my mouth. I tried to scream but Tommy held my mouth open and was pouring something down my throat. It tasted like whiskey or something like that, alcohol for sure.

I choked and tried to spit it out. Tommy said I was to swallow what he gave me and then him and Jimmy laughed and said that wouldn't be the last thing I would swallow for them and then they forced me to drink this huge glass of alcohol.

I must have passed out. When I woke up I was tied to a bed at all four corners. I was naked and my mouth was covered with duct tape again. Jimmy was raping me. When he finished, he patted my face and said good girl. Then he got up and Tommy raped me.

When Tommy was finished, Jimmy brought a needle and held it in front of my face. He said he was going to give me some drug that would make me a whole lot more cooperative. They gave me the shot in my leg.

I don't know what they gave me, but I couldn't move and I couldn't speak. They took off the duct tape from my mouth. I'm not sure how much longer it was but then Jimmy put his penis in my mouth. I tried to bite it but I was too drugged and they laughed and talked about how the drug was working real nice. Then Tommy put his penis in my mouth later.

I'm not sure how long I was there, but the whole time I was there they kept me drugged and I think I remember them pouring more alcohol in me. I know they kept raping me and putting their penises in my mouth. They also showed me a knife

```
and said if I was a real good girl I
wouldn't get cut with it. They laughed
when they said that.
     One time I thought I heard a woman's
voice and I thought I heard Tommy say
something like, "Okay, Mama, I'll be up
in a few minutes" or something like
that. I heard a phone ringing a couple
of times, too.
     Then they put my clothes on late one
night and took me outside and that's
when that man with the gun was standing
there.
     I pretended to faint and then when
Jimmy and Tommy weren't looking I
mouthed the words Help Me! to that man.
He pointed his gun at Tommy and made
them take me inside and he called nine-
one-one.
Signed,
Jennifer Howard
```

By now Jennifer's head was up and her eyes were full upon Rez. The eyes looking at him would never be a little girl's again, but she was strong. She was a fighter. Rez laid the statement on the tabletop. He laid his hands upon it as if sealing the fate of the men who did this. He smiled as he tilted his head toward her.

"Jennifer. I know it was hard to hear. You did an excellent job writing it and listening, too. Is there anything else you thought of while I read it?"

"No."

"If you do, you call me and we'll update this, okay? More details may come later. You call me."

"Yes, sir. I will."

"This should help us a lot to convict Tommy."

"What about Jimmy? He's just as bad."

"We'll make sure the court knows his part in this, but Jimmy is dead."

"How? When?"

"Sunday, actually, is when we believe he died. How exactly, we'll have to find out, but you don't have to worry about him no more...ever."

"Good."

"Well done, girl. We're gonna get Tommy and you're gonna help."

She looked at Rez with a horrified expression.

"What's wrong?" Rez asked.

The words tore out of her. "I want to kill him. I *want* to kill him. I've never wanted to kill anything before ever. Not an ant. Not even a spider. But *I want to kill him.*"

Rez's hard and determined expression was as one professional soldier to another: soldiers together in the war on crime. He said slow and clear, "Understood."

She sat up straighter, squared her shoulders, and lifted her chin. "We'll get him. We'll get him."

They stood. She walked him to the front door. Her parents stood behind her as they said goodbye. Jennifer held out her fist and Rez bumped it with his.

Solidarity.

Strength.

Tommy's fate was sealed.

Thursday AM: Psychological advantages

Carl took a drive farther out into the county. He was going to see James Bascomb with the original copies of the handwritten statements from Tommy and Otter. James lived on a farm at the far edge of the county. A gentleman farmer, he employed several locals and a couple of undocumented aliens, country of origin unknown, who somehow showed up five years before, had never left the property, and never ever spoke a word in the presence of any visitor. The Bascomb farm grew hay, corn, and okra, and made a profit from the sale of the crops.

But Bascomb had not always lived in the county. Going on eighty years old, he owned the farm for past ten years. He paid cash for it and completely modernized the operations within one year.

Carl heard of him when he moved to the county, but had no reason to get to know him. Then one day nine years earlier, James Bascomb walked into Carl's office like it was his and sat easily, crossing his long legs. Feeling almost like an interloper in his own office, Carl stopped himself from asking permission to sit in his chair behind his desk.

He took an immediate dislike to the man. That dislike didn't last long, though, after Bascomb tossed the local paper onto his desk, and asked, "You saw this?"

Carl glanced at the headline. "I haven't seen the article. But I know what it's about. I arrested the guy."

Bascomb merely grunted at the response, and stared at the ceiling.

Carl tapped the paper. "Who are you exactly and why does this matter to you?"

"My name is Bascomb, James. I bought the farm last
year out on —"

"Okay. Heard of you. Know where you live. Again, why
are you here?"

"Let's just say I know things. And I know about this
situation. This guy didn't do the crime."

Carl worried an old geezer with dementia, or worse, was
on his hands. "And you know this how?"

He waved a hand. "Doesn't matter. Easy enough to find
out."

Then he laid out for Carl who he needed to question and
what he should be asking. Bascomb was right and an
innocent man went free. Carl's memory of that long-ago day
brought a smile as he knocked on Bascomb's door. One of
the mutes opened it and silently disappeared to the back of
the house. Carl knew where to go.

"Carl, good to see you. Single malt like always or are
you on duty?"

"On duty, but I'll take it if you promise to keep the
secret."

Then with mock seriousness, Bascomb said, "Cross my
heart and hope to die."

This was the way they began every conversation when
Carl came. Carl took the glass thrust at him, though today he
noticed more feebleness than he had ever seen before.

Bascomb noticed Carl's worry. "Don't worry about me.
I'm feeling a little tired today, that's all. Was out helping
with the birth of a foal during the night. Not that I did much,
but still —"

Carl sipped slowly, laughing while James finished his
story. He finally got quiet and said, "How can I help, son?"

"I brought the handwriting sample of two — "

"Ah, yes. Precious and the late Otter."

"Goddamn, is there nothing you don't know?"

"I keep my ear to the ground, boy. Sure, give them to me and I'll have a report back to you in a couple of days. Is that good for you or need it quicker?"

"Yes, great. Thank you very much."

Then Carl, like he always did, settled in to hear stories from a distant past. If he didn't know better, he would have sworn these couldn't be true. Only fake operational names mentioned, of course. Dates and places changed, too. The better to protect those still alive. The Cold War may be officially over, but that didn't mean the tentacles of past operations and alliances couldn't reach into the present. Carl knew how to keep his mouth shut, and James knew it. After all, James stayed alive this long because he knew how to judge people accurately and fast.

* * * * *

After Rez left Jennifer, he got a call from the home office of the convenience store. Thank goodness it was a regional chain whose president loved technology and understood the value of having the best to protect his employees and customers from bad guys. The high-definition, date-stamped, three-second-stop-action recording from the evening of Jennifer's abduction was not on tape, but was stored digitally offsite for one month before being overwritten. The company burned the footage to DVD and had it hand-delivered. It was waiting on him at his office.

Thursday PM: Tommy is oh so very, very helpful

Don's phone rang. Tommy stared at Don as he slowly reached in his pocket to pull it out. Everything in the interview room stopped while Don looked at the screen to see who it was. It was Rez. Staring at Tommy as he took the call, Don never blinked.

"Hello."

"Don, this is Rez."

"Yeah, man. What's up?"

"I just got word the footage from the convenience store is at the office. I'm on my way there now. I'll call with something definitive. What's going on up there?"

"I'm in the middle of a meeting. Can you give me the update on the outstanding items we've been waiting on?"

"Jennifer gave a thorough account of Tommy and Otter. They're sick bastards, but you knew that. She was one lucky girl for you and Al to have shown up when you did. The footage is waiting at the office. I'm on my way. I'll fill you in as soon I can."

"So forward movement then?"

"Yes. Definitive."

"K. Thanks."

Don flipped his phone shut and slid it back in his pocket. "Sorry, gentlemen. Getting updated on a case."

Carl and Al knew it had to have been Rez who called, and from Don's smile the news must have been good for them — and bad for Tommy.

But Carl played the mind game for Tommy's benefit, giving Don a look that said don't let it happen again. Don acted repentant, thus establishing Carl's rank in Tommy's mind. Carl turned back to Tommy. "Sorry about the interruption. You were saying?"

"I picked Otter up around two or three Sunday afternoon. Honestly, I don't exactly remember the time. Anyway, we went for a ride, like we always do, just a ride to enjoy the scenery. On our way back, he asked me to pull over when we got to Rock Quarry Road. He's my friend, you know? I pulled over. He got out. I said, 'Dude?' He said he wanted to take a hike. Otter liked to hike. He was a hiking fool. He walked part of the Appalachian Trail one time —"

Al said, "Really? The Appalachian Trail? Which part?"

"It was somewhere in Virginia."

"Really? Wow. I have a girlfriend who is into hiking and I think she would love to go for a few days. What time of year did Otter go hiking? Do you remember?"

"Yeah." Tommy sat back and got comfortable. He crossed his arms as he recollected the event. "Yeah, it was in... June? Yeah, that's right, June. I think it was a couple of years ago or so."

Al acted surprised. "You didn't go?"

"Hell, no. Hiking? You kidding? Working up a sweat and blisters on my feet? Nah, Otter went by himself."

"He wasn't scared?"

"Otter? Ah, hell no. Otter and the woods are like this." Tommy crossed his index and middle fingers and held them up. "Hiking out in the woods at night going by the light of the moon was his favorite time ever. He knew all the county roads blindfolded."

Al sat back, relaxed with the conversation. "Sounds like it was a lot of fun. I'm gonna have to look into the trail for my girlfriend and such."

"Well, she shouldn't go alone, you know. I've heard the trail is dangerous unless you're with a crowd or something, or know how to take care of yourself."

Tommy said that with a straight face and a sincerity that would have made a nun proud.

Al nodded. "Yeah. I'll go with her, I'm sure. Carry my service revolver, too. The things you do for love, huh, gentlemen?"

Tommy laughed just as loud and long as Don, Al, and Carl. The interview was over — for that day.

Friday AM: Handwriting analysis points the way and a suggested interview strategy

When the wake-up call came, it was too early for Don. He was always one to burn the candle at both ends, but he wasn't getting younger and worrying about Wanda wore him out. He picked up the phone and tried to cradle it but kept missing until he opened his eyes against his will. He rolled over onto his back and lay there thinking of Wanda. He was fifteen to twenty years older than her.

Age never bothered him before. Why should it? After Marge, relationships had never been permanent, so it isn't like age mattered. But this was the first one that made him wonder.

He did not want children, of that he was sure. Wanda said she didn't want any either, but he'd been around long enough to know that women, focused on careers, almost always change their minds.

He sensed she'd make a great mother, a wonderful mother. Could he deny her the opportunity when she did change her mind as he suspected she would? Don had some serious thinking to do. In the meantime, he would take it slow. Rushing into this would only get him in trouble and make her miserable.

What would Marge say if she was still alive?

Marge, you know I love you, girl. But you've been gone now for fourteen years and, well...I'll always love you, but, baby, I think I've found the one who can hold a candle to you, hun. Yeah. Yeah. I'll go slow. I'll go slow.

I'll go slow, babe. I promise.

He whistled in the shower, dressed, and met Al in the lobby for another quick yet noxious cup of coffee.

* * * * *

Al had called LaVonne the night before and had a chat with her. She seemed distant and snippy and cold, and he thought, you know, enough of this. *If I can't speak straight with this woman, then she's not the one for me.*

And he did speak straight with her. He explained to her the nature of his job. And he told her he was a real man, in case she hadn't noticed, and real men were different from women. If she was looking for a husband she was going to make responsible for her happiness, one that was politically correct, one that could read her mind, then she may as well keep on looking because he was not it.

He was almost forty years old. He loved women, he had played those games plenty, and he was tired of being told he was a creep if he did one little thing wrong according to a woman. Give it some thought, LaVonne, he told her. Figure out what it is you want: a man or a frickin' mouse. And get back with me when you have your answer.

When Al's wake-up call blared at him, he didn't hear it. He was feeling invigorated and fine and was already in the shower, singing a tune he woke up with.

Al sprang from the elevator, big smile, and gave a jaunty salute to Don. "Mornin'!"

Don grunted. "You can't be happy, cuz you didn't get some last night. You didn't get some last night, did ya?"

"Nope. But I did tell a woman what was on my mind and it felt good, let me tell you, brutha, it felt good. What's the matter with you, Don? I thought you had a date with Wanda. You'd think I should be asking you whether or not you got laid."

Don shrugged and gave a sad smile. "Let's go. Carl's expecting us for breakfast."

The two handwriting analyses were waiting on Carl in his inbox when he came in. Carl opened the PDF and hit print. He slid the pages off the laser printer and read:

```
Begin Report
Subject #1, Tommy Higgenbotham
Timmy Higgenbotham (hereinafter referred to
    as TH), like his friend Jimmy
    Stonecypher (hereinafter referred to
    as JS), approaches life
    pessimistically. Both subjects have a
    fatalistic attitude toward life's
    experiences. As a vertically slanted
    writing strokes writer, TH has a me-
    first, self-interest attitude that
    rules his decisions.
As an objective type thinker TH would have
    limited empathy for or
```

responsiveness to others. While his material side shows his capacity to have many friends, his cliquish trait limits his acquiring friends. Again, being very objective about who can help him meet his needs, he would be able to charm others into thinking he cared about them.

His personal pronoun "I" indicates he doesn't have a significant father figure. Again, like his buddy JS, TH is very concerned with acquiring, or hanging onto, material assets.

Both have a very strong acquisitive nature that means they will act to get what it takes to enjoy the pleasures in the lifestyle they seek. The rich enjoyment and appreciation of nature, foods, and music would take lots of money. Good organization, planning ahead, and keen comprehension support TH's talents. Add great manual dexterity and space appreciation and he would make a very good artist.

I would expect that with his strong sense of pride and perfectionist nature, TH would want to dress well. His goals are practical. His signature tells me that generally you would expect him to act as he represents he will. He would try to please others and avoid open conflict. He has a secretive self-protection approach toward others.

TH's emotional feelings run deep; and, they do not fade soon. Not being talkative, he would likely express these accumulated unexpressed feelings in a physical outburst. If he perceived

others may have hurt or slighted him,
he would not soon forget, or
forgive. Compounding the difficulty
that TH has expressing his feelings
toward others is his
suppression/repression of his own
feelings. Expect a physical action
outburst when there is an overload of
unexpressed feelings. He has many
shorter range goals. A good sense of
rhythm, willpower, organization, and
planning ahead could aid him achieving
all of them.

Subject #2, Jimmy Stonecypher

Jimmy Stonecypher (JS) is pessimistic and
fatalistic about life. He is
emotionally withdrawn from
others. Emotionally, JS wouldn't be
responsive to others or express his
feelings; therefore I'd expect, as he
isn't talkative, that when there is an
overload of accumulated unexpressed
feelings, he'd explode physically. He,
like his friend TH, has great concerns
about accumulating and keeping as many
assets as possible (see the very
narrow left margin). Me-first, self
interest, the same trait as TH, though
it's more intense than TH's. Lower
case f's single ample loop below
baseline is an indicator of his many
urges for sensual satisfactions and
accumulation of material assets.
Achieving full gratification of his needs
is mixed, at best. JS's extra long,
forward leaning, deep-descender y-

strokes below the baseline may be interpreted as fending off others. Combine this with his very independent personal behavior (short stem d's) and we know that he'll not care about whether or not others think his personal behavior is right or wrong, but he is sensitive to criticism in other matters.

Contrary to personal behavior sensitivity, he's confident and proud of what he's capable of doing in his work. JS would not soon forget or forgive any perceived hurts or slights from others. Good at remembering and planning ahead, he'd find the time and place for retribution. His need for variety and change can be found in his concave (bent upward t-bars). While his self-esteem is high, he's capable of self deceit and hiding the truth and lying. He's not inclined to express his true feelings to others. JS has issues unresolved from the past with his mother. Sensual satisfactions are very important to him. He would appreciate good foods, sights, and sounds.

While JS has many strong urges he is not generally experiencing gratification. His frequent irregular up and down writing strokes signal difficulty coping with life's challenges. There is clear evidence throughout his writing of his hesitancy in moving ahead in situations; TH has the same trait. JS may frequently assume a snobbish attitude signaled in his

behavior as he's not talkative. Both
are cliquish. JS's talents are
supported by a number of traits, such
as keen and quick comprehension of
people and situations about him.
Excellent manual dexterity, rich color
sense, and a fine sense of rhythm. He
is mostly open and broad-
minded. People generally like and
trust him immediately.
Sexual hang-ups appear evident in his o-
letters. Generally JS seems to have
more deep-seated hang-ups and issues
than TH, though they both have many of
the same traits. JS seems to be more
unstable, flaky, and less serious
about life, even though he has a
number of short term practical
goals. Both have so many traits in
common that they understand each other
well.

Summation:
Our boys here are a pair; two sides of the
same coin. It is my opinion at a very
young age they almost certainly
started criminal behavior. In the
past, look for small animal deaths by
torturous means, some of which might
include fire, knife, guttings and/or
skinnings while alive.
Are there any unsolved disappearances in
the county that go back to when the
boys were in their early and late
teens? Look for prostitutes of any
age, and feeble older men and women to
start, and other unexplained or
mysterious deaths. It is my

understanding that Otter's parents
died under unusual circumstances that
no one saw coming. Might these have
been their first human kills?

Interview Strategy:
It is a sure bet TH believes he did JS a
favor by killing him. I believe, even
though TH looks like the leader, it is
JS who was the psychological driving
force behind the team. I believe he
had a power over TH that neither of
them understood but that was dominant
and strong. Therefore, I believe TH
will go through the following
emotional pattern.

TH will first feel troubled that he killed
JS. That will be short lived. It will
be followed by a euphoric period
during which he will feel bulletproof,
not only during interviews, but
everywhere else. He could begin
driving more recklessly than his
normal pattern. He might sit
comfortably and seem quite at ease
during the interview, almost as if he
is in control. But when the interview
becomes more pointed he will quickly
break up. At that point he will begin
to wish mightily that JS was there and
will feel the weight of the enormity
of the shaky position he feels himself
in, now truly all alone for the first
time in years. The reality is that the
absence of JS is better logically; but
psychologically and emotionally, TH
will be vulnerable and won't know what
to do because he is not getting cues

```
from his partner, his better half.
Play to what TH believes are his strengths,
    give him enough rope, keep him
    guessing, then throw him a curve or
    two. He should hang himself soon
    enough.
Yours, JB
```
End Report

Carl finished reading the report, printed out copies for Al and Don. He picked up the phone to let them know what he had.

* * * * *

Rez had overnighted the DVD to Carl, who turned on the television in his office, powered up the DVD player, and put in the footage from the convenience store. The time stamp began twenty minutes before Jennifer said she arrived and ended one hour after she said Tommy and Otter kidnapped her. Rez watched every second of the ninety five minutes. The footage showed Jennifer told the truth.

He sent a text to Don to let him know.

Don felt his phone vibrate.

"Al, Rez texted. The footage shows Tommy and Otter showing up and leaving the convenience store just like Jennifer said they did."

"Doncha just love technology? Can you have Rez burn me a copy and FedEx it to me at HQ?"

"No problem. What happens now?"

Carl answered, "Well, now we play with Tommy's mind a little bit more, don't you think, Al?"

"I agree. I've got a plan. It will take a couple of days to put it into effect, though."

Carl nodded. "Should work fine. I have the handwriting analysis back. I'll forward it to you, but here's printed copies, too. We should be able to gain insight into how best to talk to Tommy. What is it you want to do, Al? I mean, we have two different cases, maybe more, and at least two different jurisdictions."

"Let's start with Jennifer's case. Here's what I think is going to happen. We're gonna bring Tommy back in. We're gonna tell him what Jennifer said. He's gonna try to put this whole thing on Otter. He's gonna say he had errands to run and all the kinky stuff happened while he was gone. He won't be able to deny the forensics and he'll have to dance around that for a bit, but he's smart and he'll figure out a way to say Otter gave her drugs that made her act like she wanted it and that, he hopes, will explain it away."

Don agreed. "I tell you what else, too. The boy is gonna get some details from his other crimes into this story. We know what happened to the body in the ground and we know what happened to the lady on the recording. I think one of us should sit in the room like a bump on the log and say nothing, absolutely nothing, and listen for the little things he accidentally throws in."

Carl chimed in. "I think you're both right and you're both wrong. I don't think he's gonna get any cases mixed up, but I believe he thinks Otter is now the perfect fall guy and will let details slip about other crimes but he will tell us Otter told him these things."

Al agreed. "You're right. Carl, I would like you to take lead in the interview. Don, I want you as second. He's scared of you; look for opportunities to shake him up. Tommy thinks us *black folk* are there to stay in the background and bow and scrape to the likes of him. I'm gonna sit in a corner and say nothing. But, if you hear me tapping my pencil, it means it's time to take a break."

Carl said, "Hey, Wanda can bring him some more coffee and doughnuts."

Don's eyes glazed over as he thought of it. "Yeah, I sure would like to see her get her girly-girl back on again."

Carl said, "I thought you had a date tonight with her? She's gonna get her girly on for you, you wait and see."

"Yeah. Tonight."

Carl got the meeting back on track. "Okay, Al, let's get our plan for the interview in place here."

A couple of hours later, Carl was on his way home, Al was on his way to his hotel where he would call LaVonne, and Don, riding shotgun with Al, texted Wanda he was going to call her in an hour and firm up their plans for the coming evening.

Friday, Late PM: Carmelita's showdown with Martin

Martin Oliveira left for work well before anyone else got up. Carmelita wouldn't see him until the evening. The day proved difficult for her. She knew what she wanted to say, but couldn't figure out how. Frank told her if Martin pushed the issue, she had a place with him. But she thought it better to handle everything logically and in small steps than to make sweeping changes.

The question was, would Martin agree with her methods? She got home in time for the kids, ordered pizza and waited until it was delivered, then left to meet Martin. She took care to look her very best.

This was not a conversation she wished to have, and looking like a downtrodden housewife would not help make her point with her husband. When she walked across the parking lot to the restaurant, admiring eyes watched her. For the first time in a very long time, she noticed these glances — some openly staring. She liked them. Entering the restaurant, she looked for Martin and didn't see him.

He arrived late, slammed the car door, and stomped across the parking lot. Carmelita watched him through the window. She was already at a table. The waitstaff knew to look for him and led him to the table.

"Hello, Martin."

Martin said nothing as he sat. Menus were placed in front of them. Red wine was in front of her, untouched. He ordered a Zombie. Their waiter recited a long list of daily specials. Martin stared at his menu. Carmelita listened politely and said thank you when the waiter finished.

"Do you need a few minutes to make your selection?" the waiter asked.

"Yes, please. If you could come back in a few minutes?"

"Of course." The waiter disappeared.

Martin continued to stare at the menu.

"Well?" he asked without looking up.

"Well, what?"

"Well, why you sleeping on the sofa?"

"Because I don't want to sleep with you anymore, Martin. Ever."

"Why not? You should be in my bed."

"Yes. I should. And I have been. For many, many years,
as you well know. But the thought of sharing a bed with you
in any way is beyond anything I can handle now. I can't do
it anymore."

"What? Why?"

"Honestly, Martin, do you really have to ask? I
mean…really?"

"What's that supposed to mean?"

His drink arrived; before they continued he gulped half.
Her wine was untouched.

She asked, "You want me to speak freely?"

"Of course. Yes!" He sat back and crossed his arms over
his chest as if defying her to speak her mind.

"Then I will."

She took a slow sip and let the wine warm her as it went
down. She carefully placed the glass down in front of her.
She folded her hands around the stem and looked at the
wine. Her lipstick left a print on the glass. She carefully
wiped it off with her thumb.

Still looking at her wine, she began, "I have to confess
I've been an idiot. A blind, silly doormat who waited for her
man to love her and want her. Who put up with being
treated badly and cheated on —"

"I never cheated on you."

She raised her eyes to him. "Yes, you have and you
know it. Don't sit there and lie to me."

Martin said nothing. She continued.

"I put up with all of that in the mistaken notion that
somehow I was letting you down. And if only I could
become this…this thing you wanted, whatever it was, then
maybe you would love me." She took another sip for
courage. "But that will never be and I know it now."

The Case of the Snuff Tape Killers

Even though the gentleman was mad as a hornet, the waiter approached the table with a smile and kept it on as if he noticed nothing out of the ordinary.

The lady, dressed to kill and clearly in control, must have been delivering bad news. He didn't like to break into emotionally charged discussions, but people want their food no matter what else is happening. Still, he wished they would have their breakups somewhere else instead of at his tables. He hated drama. Besides, it was bad for the digestion and how could anyone enjoy delicious food when their attention was somewhere else?

"Have you decided on your choices for dinner?" He smiled at the lady.

Carmelita said, "Yes. I'll have the chicken parmigiana and —" she glanced at Martin, who nodded — "he'll have the lasagna."

"Salads and bread, yes?"

"Yes, please. Thank you."

"And the dressing choice?"

"House, please."

"Thank you." The waiter got away from this about-to-explode emotional bomb as fast as he could.

She took another sip of wine and continued, "I can't live like this anymore. I won't live like this anymore."

"Are you saying you want a divorce?"

There it was, and a whole lot faster than she anticipated. "That's what will eventually happen, yes."

"What does that mean, *eventually?*"

"Sooner or later. No need being stupid about it. If we plan this transition properly, then the kids won't be affected as much and the finances will be handled better. I'm thinking logically, not emotionally."

She took a sip of wine. Salads and bread arrived. Surprisingly, she was hungry, and began her salad. She ate as if the load of the world was off her shoulders.

Martin began to eat, too, but he picked at it. She watched him openly, though he didn't notice. She saw thoughts and emotions race across his face — and felt sorry for him, much to her surprise. That emotion didn't remain long, though, when he opened his mouth.

"I'll make your life miserable if you try to divorce me. I'll make sure you don't get the kids and I'll make sure you don't get any financial support."

Her reaction was not what he expected. She finished chewing, swallowed, sipped her wine, and smiled at him. But he didn't like that smile; it wasn't friendly.

"Are you threatening me, Martin?" He didn't answer. "Sounded like threats to me. Were those threats?"

She waited.

It took a moment, but he got cocky again and leaned forward. "No threats. Promises."

"Ah. Promises." She leaned back in her chair and smiled up at the ceiling. After a few seconds she took a deep breath and looked him square in the face. "Martin."

He felt confident in his position and stared boldly at her as she spoke.

"This is very sad. Of all the things you could have said to me now...of all the things...you had to threaten."

She leaned forward, placed her hands flat on the table beside her salad and paused to keep herself from crying. When she spoke, she was calm, friendly, but matter-of-fact.

"You do whatever it is you have to do. You're a big boy who can make his own decisions. But you just remember this, *big boy* — what goes around, comes around. I advise you to think long and hard about turning me into an enemy. It wouldn't be smart. And if you drag the kids into a nasty game, you'll see a side of me you've never seen before."

Martin blinked.

"Is that clear?"

Their food arrived. Carmelita said, "Yes, thank you, but we need to leave. Could you box it up for us? Thank you. And give him the check."

Carmelita left the restaurant, and headed home. She called Frank on the way.

"Hey, baby," Frank answered.

Carmelita lost it; cried and shook so hard she couldn't drive. She pulled into a gas station and tried to get control. Frank, not knowing what was going on, was so worried he paced his office as he kept saying *Baby? Are you hurt?* and *Baby? What's wrong?* but got no answer. She finally stopped crying and told him the whole story. It was difficult keeping her mind on the details because she was hungry and the food was driving her crazy.

The aroma filled the car and she kept thinking about eating. Of all things she should be thinking about now, food should have been the least of it. She eventually got the story out and was much calmer by the end of it.

"Ah, baby. You knew that coulda happened. Home is waiting on you, okay? Whenever you need it. Or whenever you want, okay? You know that, don't you? Kids, too."

"Yes."

"I'm proud of you for standing up to him. He better not mess with you if he knows what's best, huh?"

She laughed, shakily. "Yeah. That's right. Yes."

"You okay, babe?"

"Yes. I am. Thank you."

"Love you. Call me whenever you need to, okay?"

"K."

She drove home dry-eyed. Martin was not there. She was still hungry. The food was still warm. She opened the container, found a fork and knife, and ate.

* * * * *

Tommy lay in bed with three trains of thought running through his mind.

First was the interview. Mama didn't know it, but he called a criminal attorney in Atlanta who told him it would be stupid to go into any interview without an attorney looking after his best interests. He knew that, but he thought the attorney was jumping the gun and no amount of explaining made the attorney change his advice. Tommy could handle civil servants. If they had any brains they wouldn't be cops. He felt confident going into the interview with the local yokels.

Second was Mama and the help. Mama kept nagging him about explaining to her what in the hell the cops said to him in the formal living room. Every time he told her to hush up, she wouldn't. He finally got up in disgust and went to his room and slammed the door shut. That hint worked and the rest of his evening was quieter.

The help, Rosario, still smiled when she saw him, but the smile didn't go to her eyes like it used to. He could tell she watched him closely and got out of the room as quickly as she could. Rosario started working for Mama ten years ago and Mama couldn't get along without her, thought the sun rose and fell with Rosario, but Tommy considered her part of the Wetback invasion that seemed to be taking over his county and, besides, she was a woman and a servant, two strikes against her. She shouldn't be treating him like she was better than him. That attitude of hers needed to change. He may have to say something to Mama.

Third was the thing that got him in this mess in the first place: women. Specifically the sluts and whores who couldn't seem to understand their place in the natural order of things. Man is the head of woman. Woman is there to serve man's needs. Why they had to fight him on this point he never could figure out. They should do this graciously. Mama could teach them about manners: She was a real lady.

He felt needs growing. They had been deprived when that cop showed up.

Tommy sat up in bed. How did the cop know about him anyway? Shit. Now he had a fourth thing to think about. Maybe the interview was going to be more complicated than he thought. Was it too late to have the attorney show up?

Tommy pulled out his cellphone and made a call. Damn! He got voicemail and threw his phone across the room.

Monday AM: Tommy favors The Law with his presence

Mel's Diner was packed for breakfast, but Carl had already staked out his corner booth and when Don and Al arrived they didn't have to wait. Wanda and Lee joined them a few minutes later.

"Today's the day, gentlemen." Wanda raised her coffee cup in a toast. Four other cups rose in agreement.

"Lee, is the room ready?"

Lee nodded to Carl. "Yes, sir. Wanda and I took care of that bright and early."

Don was sure Wanda put the props in place as he instructed. The handwriting analyses proved to be of great help in preparing the room. "Great. This is gonna be fun. I'm gonna love messin' with that little boy's mind."

Wanda's fork stopped mid-bite. She asked the question on everyone's mind. "What if he brings an attorney?"

"Then he brings an attorney," Al said. "We work the same, we just have to dance around him, that's all. But somehow, I don't think Tommy is smart enough to bring representation."

"Or he thinks we're too stupid for him and he doesn't need one." Everyone nodded at Lee's comment.

"That's it, alright. Still doesn't change a thing for us," Carl said as he stood. They finished eating and everybody threw money on the table to cover their meal and a generous tip, and walked across the street. Tommy would be their guest in a couple of hours and they wanted to make sure they were ready to receive him.

* * * * *

Tommy woke to a light knock on his door. "Come in."

Rosario's instructions the night before had been to wake him up with a breakfast tray promptly at eight. Tommy's clock showed she was right on time.

"I have your breakfast, sir." Rosario entered but didn't look at Tommy. She placed his tray on the table at the side of the room and left as quickly as possible, quietly closing the door behind her.

Tommy lay still in the bed, only his eyes moving as he watched this insolent woman walk across the room and back out the door. He hadn't noticed before, but she looked like she could have one hot body under her uniform. He contemplated that little fact, then remembered his breakfast. Better eat it all. He'd need it for his interview.

He saw his cellphone on the floor and bent to pick it up. He turned it on. No messages. Damn high-priced attorney hadn't called him back yet. Damn it. He forgot he didn't leave a message.

As he ate, Tommy thought one day his temper was gonna get him in trouble. He called again and left a message.

* * * * *

Don surveyed the interview room. Wanda and Lee did a fine job. The room was cluttered and disorganized. Stakes from the pit in Butts County were in a corner. Some standing, some placed to look as if they had fallen. Case files stacked on top of a rolling cart threatened to fall. A table in the middle of the room was covered with old doughnut crumbs and splatters of coffee. Mismatched chairs ringed the table, another was against the wall.

Don said, "This should shake up his little obsessive-compulsive brain. You look ready for His Worship."

"Hell, yeah. You know it," Wanda said.

Physically, she was in character. Her uniform top unbuttoned four-down strategically showed off her assets — with a minor assist from a push-up bra. Long bangs pulled back and clipped at her crown — in classic party-girl style — framed her face. Curling product and a blow-dryer diffuser helped curls run riot.

Psychologically she was ready to do whatever she needed to reel in the bad guy. She smiled at Don, who was beaming his pleasure of her, both smiles and beamings completely professional, of course.

Carl called it, "One hour and counting. Let's go over strategy. My office."

When everybody turned to follow Carl, Don glanced at Wanda. She batted eyes. He winked. They followed the crowd.

* * * * *

It was time to leave for the interview and Tommy had not yet heard back from the frickin' attorney. By the time he got to the station, though, he convinced himself that the story he was going to tell about his dear, departed, lifelong friend would be believed hook, line, and sinker. He still didn't know how he and Otter had come to The Law's attention, and that worried him some, but he knew that whatever so-called evidence they had was nothing. And the girl they picked up, it was totally her word against his now that Otter was gone and who would believe a whore over him? Nobody, that's who. Besides, the cocky little slut was just begging for it.

Those State boys had better watch their backs, too, because if he had to, he'd get Mama to call in a couple of favors and they would all be unemployed before they knew what was happening to them.

He reached the station and sat in his car for a minute. Well, boy, he thought, this is it. Put your game face on and go for the touchdown. Words from his high school football coach flashed in his mind.

"Do you want the ball?" Coach screamed.

"Yes, sir. We want the ball," Team screamed back.

"Do. You. Want. THE BALL?" Coach screamed louder.

"We WANT THE BALL!"

"Then go get that fuckin' ball and bring in the fuckin' touchdowns and make your school PROUD!"

"Yessir!"

Yeah. Great words to live by. Coach was awesome.

Tommy stepped out of his car. When he closed the car door, he felt he was walking to victory over those stupid civil servants.

* * * * *

Tommy heard Wanda's worshipping voice down the hall and her moving fast his way. As she careened around the corner toward him he thought it sure was weird how their two dates ended — he had been looking forward to getting a piece of that. How he missed her in high school he couldn't figure out, but it wasn't like he didn't have his pick of any pussy he wanted. Of course, Wanda may not have blossomed quite yet, so no wonder he didn't notice her. But boy, oh boy, had she blossomed now and here she came around the corner.

"Tommy!" Wanda threw her hands up and then, as if reminding herself about professional demeanor, stopped short of throwing herself on him and held out a hand for him to shake.

"Wanda. Good to see you, girl."

She smiled widely; lowered her voice. "Coffee, yes?"

"You know it, girl."

"I remember how you like it. Come on, I'll show you to the room and bring the coffee — I just made it nice and fresh. Got doughnuts, too?"

"Sure, baby. Sounds good. Where do they want me?"

Oh, God help me, Wanda thought, Tommy's too damn cocky for his own good. It was all she could do to not slap the hellfire and damnation out of him and holler hallelujah. But for the sake of catching the bad guy, she reined in her inner church lady and smiled.

"Follow me, sweetie."

She turned on her heel, her hips leading Tommy by the nose to his fate. She got to the door and winked. "Here we are. I'll be right back."

On the monitors, Carl, Al, Lee, and Don watched Tommy step into the room and Wanda close the door, stomp up the hall, and mutter her contempt of the man she left. Don met her at the coffee machine. Solemnly, they prepared coffee and doughnuts. Wanda picked them up. Don arranged napkins in her cleavage. Wanda looked down at the paper sticking out of her bra. She looked up at a smiling Don.

"Aren't you artistic," she said.

"You like the fan shape there, do ya?"

Looking up at Don, Wanda transformed back into girly-girl, gave a little curtsy, turned on her heel for the second time and, also for the second time, led a man to his fate — this one knowingly and willingly. Don joined the others at the monitors and watched Wanda enter the room.

"Tommy! Here you are, sweetie," she gushed. "Sorry it took so long."

"No problem."

"Carl's making a cup of coffee and said for you not to worry, he would be right on down. Anything else before I go work on my traffic reports?"

"No. I'm fine."

But he wasn't. Tommy was having a minor meltdown; that much was clear to everybody watching. He paced the room like a caged lion, stopping in front of the stakes from the pit, fingering the case files, straightening the chairs. He used the napkins from Wanda's cleavage to clean a chair and a spot on the table to put his coffee and doughnuts.

Carl shrugged. "Well, boys, guess I better make my coffee and get on in there. You ready?"

Al flexed his shoulders. Lee adjusted the badge on his belt. Don slapped his hip and cussed; he would miss his gun during the interview. The boys nodded at Carl. Wanda confirmed the recorder was working and watched monitors.

Tommy heard footsteps stop in front of his door. His head turned to the knob. From the monitor, Wanda watched him get into a relaxed position when the knob turned. He sat back in his chair, crossed his legs as if he was getting ready to interview the next candidate for a job on his plantation, picked up his coffee and sipped. Setting the tone for who was in charge, Tommy didn't look up right away when they entered, only acknowledging them when Carl spoke.

"Good morning, gentlemen." Tommy stood and held his hand out to Carl. Carl shook it. Each man filed by him and stuck out his hand to Tommy, who shook their hands. All except Don, that is.

Don turned his back on Tommy and grabbed the back of a metal folding chair. With the feet of the chair bumping on the floor, Don casually strolled to the opposite end of the table, took his time positioning the chair, slapped a pad and pen down, and slowly, deliberately sat. Only when he was settled did he raise his eyes to Tommy's. He blinked slowly and barely nodded his head.

Tommy couldn't take his eyes off Don, but when he finally did drag his eyes away, he saw the others had already sat around him in a wide circle.

He would have preferred all to sit across from him in a straight line so all he had to do was turn his eyes to keep them in sight. He let them know his wishes. "Gentlemen, I need you move where I can see all of you at the same time."

Nobody heard him seeing as how they were all busy adjusting chairs and pads and pens. Tommy asked again. "Before we get started, can you guys move closer together?"

"No." That was Don.

Tommy shut up, pulled out his phone. Damn lawyer still hadn't called.

Carl started the party. "Tommy, as you know, we're attempting to find out what happened to Otter. If you don't mind, we're gonna go over the day as we know it thus far. Let us know if we missed something."

"Yes, sir. Anything I can do to help."

"We're not sure where Otter went when he left our place on Sunday. Do you know?"

"Uh. Yeah. I took him home."

Carl, Al, and Lee made notes. Don just stared.

"Okay. How long did that take?"

Tommy thought. "Oh, I would say maybe a couple of hours or so."

Al said, "Did you stop somewhere? Meet anybody?"

"Got some lunch. Stopped for gas."

"Where?"

"Uh. Let me think. We got a hamburger at Wendy's. Got some gas at the QT on the interstate."

"The Wendy's? Which exit for the QT?"

"Why do you need to know that?"

Don chimed in. "Because you little…because, Tommy, Otter may have met someone who may have taken a dislike to him and…"

"Oh. I-85 North. The Wendy's right over the state line. Same exit for the QT."

Carl took over again. He made notes. "Great. Thank you. Did you see Otter talking to anybody? Was it anybody you knew?" Carl looked up, waited.

Tommy took his time with his memory. He acted like he was surprised at the memory. "Come to think of it, Otter went to the bathroom and when he came out I heard him saying something to somebody. I asked him who it was and he said it wasn't anybody I knew."

"Did that surprise you?"

"Did what surprise me?"

"That Otter knew somebody you didn't?"

"Hell, no. Otter was always friendly. He made friends easier than he could breathe."

"After gas, that when you dropped him at his sister's?"

"Yeah?"

Don threw his pen down. "Well, did ya or didn't ya?"

"Yeah. I took him home."

"Thank you, Tommy," Carl noted. "Now, from his sister we know he came home, went to his room, came out, ate some pizza. Then a couple of hours after that, she thinks it was around three or so, he left again. But he didn't take his car or his motorcycle. She thought she heard a car pull up. Was that you?"

"Uh. Yeah. That was me."

"Then what?"

Tommy shifted in his chair. "Well, like I told ya, we went for a drive —"

"You *boys* sure do like to *drive*." That was Don again.

Tommy didn't like Don's implication. "What the hell does that mean? I took him home the long way."

"I mean you two must like to drive seeing as how you took two drives on Sunday. That's all."

"Please continue, Tommy." Carl waited for the rest of the story.

"*This* drive, we drove over to Helen and back. Then, *like I told ya...*" He looked over at Don and back to Carl. "Otter asked me to drop him off at Rock Quarry Road. I did. I don't know nothin' after that."

Tommy sat back, picked up his coffee, and took a nervous sip. As Carl, Al, and Lee made their notes, Don stared. Tommy reached for a doughnut, changed his mind, and wrapped both hands around his cup. Al walked over to Carl. He bent down and pointed to something in his notes and then pointed to Carl's notes.

Carl stared from one to the other and nodded. "Yeah. Okay. Wow. Well, there's got to be an explanation for that. You want to go check?"

"Explanation for what?" Tommy asked.

Carl looked up. "Nothin' you need to worry about. We've got another witness whose story disagrees with yours. We got to find out why they're lyin'. "

"I'm on it." Al walked out the door.

"Oh. Okay." It's a good thing Tommy's cup was ceramic or it would have crushed he was holding it so tight.

The Case of the Snuff Tape Killers

"After you dropped Otter off at Rock Quarry Road, what happened?"

"What do you mean?"

"Where'd you go, you idiot?" Don again, getting Tommy's engine all fired up.

"Hey! I'm —"

"Tommy!" Carl's voice got his attention. "Mind your manners, Don. Where'd you go after you dropped off Otter at Rock Quarry Road?"

Tommy steadied his nerves with a sip of coffee. "Home. Just home."

Silence followed broken only by pens scratching paper. Tommy's curiosity got the better of him and, on cue, he piped up.

"So, uh, what's all this stuff in here for?"

Carl looked up. "What stuff?"

"Them stakes over there."

"Oh, you don't have to worry about that. It's a murder case we're working on. Nothing to do with you."

"Murder case?"

"Yeah. Fascinating case."

"What's fascinating about it?"

For the first time since he entered the room, Lee spoke up. "Can't tell you. Ongoing."

But Tommy couldn't shut up. "Them files over there with the case, too?"

Don looked over at the stacks and back at Tommy. He pointed. "You talking 'bout these files? Whaddaya care? You know something about it you wanna add to the record?"

Lee shook his head and rolled his eyes: Don and his wit; there was no stopping it.

Tommy shook his head.

The Case of the Snuff Tape Killers

"You know something and don't want to add it? Or you don't know something?"

"Uh…uhh…" Tommy was thinking fast.

Don was faster. "*Uh* don't look good on you, boy."

That fired up Tommy again. He shot off his big mouth. "No. I don't know nothing. Got nothing to add, you damn sonuva—"

"You want to finish that statement?"

Tommy, breathing hard, clinched his fist around his cup and slammed it down, adding more slop to the tabletop.

"Hey, watch out there now. This table cost the county a pile of —"

"Don!" Carl shut him down and closed out the interview. "Okay, Tommy. Thank you. Appreciate your help to firm up the timeline."

Tommy stood with the rest of them. He shook hands with Lee and Carl, Al wasn't back yet, and he ignored Don. Wanda was nowhere to be found when he exited.

As Tommy drove home his cellphone rang. *Now the damn attorney calls.*

"Hello?"

"This is Burton Sutton's office calling for Mister Tommy Higgenbotham."

"Speaking."

"Hold for Mr. Sutton, please." A few seconds later the attorney was on the line.

"Mr. Higgenbotham. Didn't get your message until a few minutes ago. Trust you haven't done the interview yet. Can you postpone it until tomorrow? I can join you then."

"I just left."

Sutton replied, "Please tell me you didn't say that. Did I or did I not advise you about having an attorney?"

"Yes, you did. But listen, this was a small interview to get the timeline straight for my friend's last day. Easily handled."

"Easily handled? Really?" The sarcasm drip was heavy. "Then why did you call me in the first place, Mr. Higgenbotham? Huh? Tell me. Why, if it was, as you say, so easily handled?"

Tommy started to answer, but Sutton shut him down. "Shut up. Just shut up and let me think. Okay. Tell me about the room you were in."

"It was a room. What's to tell?"

"What was in the room?"

"Oh...*that*. There were some stakes and case files."

Sutton had a bad feeling about this boy. "What do you mean 'stakes' and 'case files'?" Tommy started to answer again but Sutton interrupted. "You know what? Don't, don't, *don't* tell me until you pay me and we have a contract. Otherwise, this won't turn out well for you."

The attorney ended the conversation with this advice, "When you are ready to be represented, you call down here and make an appointment with my secretary. Don't forget to bring a check that will cover a big fat retainer, and be ready to sign a very binding contract. Then and only then will I listen. Until then, keep your mouth shut to everybody. That advice is free. From this point, my advice will cost you."

Tommy had a feeling about Burton Sutton. He felt he was going to need him — and badly. Time to talk to Mama and get those purse strings loosened up.

While Tommy was having his Come-to-Jesus talk with Burton Sutton, Carl and his boys sat in the interview room, reviewing.

"Thoughts?" Al asked.

Lee had one. "He's never once asked how Otter died."

"He knows how," Don drawled as he leaned back on two chair legs and spoke to the ceiling. "Why belabor the obvious?"

"The stakes shook him up." Carl stared at the pile in the corner. "I can't believe he hasn't retained an attorney."

"That's coming, guaranteed." Everyone nodded agreement with Al.

Week Twelve

Monday PM: Tommy has a long-overdue talk with Mama

Martin was furious with Carmelita. How dare she break up the marriage? She was the mother of his children. Besides, who would he have to look after them and the house when she left? And she was good at giving dinner parties for his bosses and high-profile customers. What in the hell was he going to do?

He thought of all the times he had cheated on her. He wondered how she found out. He had been careful; though some of the women made contact with his wife, they had told him they hadn't spilled the beans. Did she have proof or only suspicions? She had never talked to him like this tonight. *I advise you to think long and hard about turning me into an enemy*, she'd said. What ammunition did she have? None, that's what. Nothing but empty threats. Ha. He could play that game better.

Martin was going to show her what playing hardball was all about. She better watch her back. When he got through with her, nobody was going to want her. Nobody. Not her kids. Not her parents. Not even that idiot company she was working for. He would ruin her. And it was what she deserved because she was ruining his life.

His plan of attack in place, Martin's last three miles before arriving at Patricia's apartment found him in a better mood. He knew Patricia would make him feel even better, too. He wouldn't mention the divorce to her, though; wouldn't be prudent. More trouble he didn't need.

Besides, Patricia's skills did not translate well to hostess duties for a business dinner.

* * * * *

Tommy thought all day about Burton Sutton, Criminal Attorney, and all day he tried to figure out how to get Mama to pay for his very high-priced and out-of-town services. Mama, being true to her county roots, will insist they retain the services of her longtime friend from childhood, Charles Johnston. The worst case "The Chipster", as Mama called him, had ever been involved in was a drunk driving hit-and-run and everything else was local fluff-and-stuff cases, never anything like murder.

Mama will insist her boy is innocent and that Chip has known him since he was a baby and surely to goodness can speak eloquently on that innocence. Certainly better than some high-priced lawyer from the big city with an ego to match and who knew nothing of her precious son.

He had to convince her this matter was bigger than The Chipster could handle yet not let on it could blow up for real. He decided the best thing would be to have a nice sit-down dinner with Mama and listen to her talk about her day. Yeah. Butter up the old lady and she'll do what her one and only child — and a son to boot — wanted her to do. He skipped down the stairs.

"Hello, Mama." He kissed her on the cheek. "Smell's good. What's for dinner?"

Rosario kept her eyes on the growing pile of peeled potatoes and chopped onions.

"Are we to expect you for dinner, Son?" Mama smiled up at Precious.

"Of course." Tommy put his arm around her shoulder as she rubbed spices over a whole chicken, but his eyes took in the gorgeous figure Rosario was hiding. She had the curves. Damn, he'd been blind. "I'm sorry, what, Mama?"

"Do you want roasted or creamed potatoes with dinner?"

Tommy poured on the charm. "Creamed, Mama. You always make the best creamed potatoes, better than everybody. Daddy always said so."

Mama's eyes got misty at mention of Tommy's father, not because she missed him because she didn't. That no-account slug's only job seemed to be draining her family fortune. She was glad he was dead, though how he fell off that cliff was a mystery nobody ever figured out. But she knew he and Tommy had been close and she was sorry Precious had to grow up without his daddy. Not that she hadn't done her best to try to find another for him, but nobody was good enough for her boy.

She wiped a tear. "Then creamed it is, Son. I'll call when it's ready."

Two hours later she let him know dinner was served where Tommy began his campaign. "Rosario, could you bring out a bottle of wine to go with this chicken? Mama, you'd like some wine, wouldn't you?"

She shook her head. "Son, the wine is for special occasions."

"Now, Mama. What's life for if you can't live it? Rosario? Thank you, dahlin'."

Rosario returned to the dining room with stemware and an opened bottle of Zinfandel.

"Bring it to me, Rosario. I'll pour. You need anything else, Mama? No? You can leave now, Rosario."

Tommy poured and handed Mama her glass. He raised it in a toast. "Here's to the best mother a good Southern boy can have." Mama smiled as she accepted the toast.

"Mama, what with me being so busy and all, I haven't had a chance to have a nice chat with you. What have you been up to lately?"

The question began an hour and a half recitation of garden clubs and good works and grocery shopping and other crap that turned Tommy's brain into mush. He never worked so hard in his life to maintain a smile and feign interest, even with some of the imbecilic women he and Otter met on the road. Mama finally shut up, and with the serving of dessert, Tommy got around to his reason for being there. It was Mama herself who created the opening that Tommy, barely tuning in, almost missed.

"Anyway, I was telling Charlotte — you remember Charlotte from church? — I was telling Charlotte I was gonna have to get The Chipster to look into the legalities of the operation of the GBI. What those State boys have done is wrong and must be illegal."

"Speaking of attorneys, Mama. You know Otter died. I've been helping local law enforcement with his last hours."

"Really? How is it going?"

"Not so good. It seems his manner of death is a big mystery to the police. They can't seem to figure out how he died, why he was at the quarry — you know how much he loved to hike, they know nothing. But the only thing they have to hang their hat on is…" Tommy paused for effect.

Mama nodded and then looked at her son. She knew what was coming.

"…me." Tommy didn't have to fake this worry. "They seem to think that because I was the last one to see Otter that somehow I'm the one that done him in. It seems they have some witnesses that can attest to us being together —"

"But you've never hidden that fact, Son!" Mama was indignant. "You've cooperated with them from the first second. It's those State boys that are causing all this trouble. I'm calling Charles right now."

Tommy put a hand on her arm as she rose from her chair. "Mama, I think this is much bigger than The Chipster can handle."

"Now, Son, you know he's —"

"Mama. Now, Mama, you need to listen to me. You're used to dealing with stuff in the county and so is he. This thing coming at us is from outside. We need someone from the outside who is used to dealing with these State boys. Somebody who knows how to play hardball on a bigger playing field. Now, Mama, I like The Chipster just as much as anybody. But Mama, you gotta be honest and admit —"

"Son. His feelings will be hurt if we don't call him."

"I know, Mama. But he don't have to know right now and besides, you know how to handle him. You'll make it right with him, won't you, Mama?" He patted Mama's hand.

She reluctantly agreed and clutched his hand. "Yes, Son. I will. But I don't know anybody to call."

Tommy sheepishly glanced at his mother. "I do. I've already spoken to him and he's agreed to help out. I'll call him first thing in the morning and make an appointment, okay, Mama?"

"Okay, Son."

"I love you, Mama."

"I love you, too, Son."

Tommy pulled her chair out and, like the perfect gentlemen he was raised to be, took her arm in his and escorted her to the front porch, placed her on the swing, kissed her cheek, gave a slight bow, and said goodnight. He didn't go directly to his room, though. He thought he would get to know Rosario a little bit better.

Monday PM: Tommy makes nice with Rosario

Rosario heard Tommy come into the kitchen after he finished with Mama. She never did like Tommy, but he was the son of her employer, so as long as he stayed out of her way she could smile and be pleasant. The recent turn of events, though, did not make her happy. Nor was her family happy, as they vehemently told her. Her husband, Trinidad, wanted her to quit.

Mama, in Mexico, begged her to leave the house of the crazy gringo. Papa told her if she insisted on staying, to remember that a knee to the nuts was a good way to stop a man. The money was good, she had been there a long time, Mrs. Higgenbotham was a good employer. Where else was she going to work and have it as good?

Trini did not agree. The safety of his wife came first. But on this she would not change her mind. She thought Tommy would not do anything on his home turf to an employee. He might be crazy, but he wasn't stupid. Still, she had not liked the way he had been eyeing her the last few days and now, here he was, in the kitchen, starting a conversation.

This was new.

She didn't like it.

Leaning against the refrigerator door, Tommy said, "Rosario. Have I told you lately I appreciate the good job you do for Mama and me?"

"No, Mr. Tommy. You haven't." Rosario kept moving from the stove to the sink to the dishwasher.

"Let me remedy that right now." Still feeling his Southern gentleman persona he put on for Mama, Tommy stood straight and tall. "Rosario, you have done us a fine, fine job. Why, I remember when you came to work for us. Couldn't hardly speak a word of English and now, here you are able to read and write it almost as good as any real American."

"I *am* a real American, Mr. Tommy. My husband and I became citizens four years ago. You remember."

"Oh, yeah. I seem to remember something about that. Well, good for you and…your husband, too. You'll always have a place here with us, on that you can depend, ma'am. Yes, ma'am. Always have a place with us."

"Thank you, Mr. Tommy. Is there anything else I can do for you this evening before I leave?"

"Naw. Naw. Don't think so. You have a good evening, Rosario-ma'am."

"Of course, Mr. Tommy. You, too."

Tommy stared at her a few more seconds before he took his time leaving the kitchen. Rosario was beginning to think Trini might be right. She'd watch and see. If things got worse, she would go.

Tommy's head was on his pillow and he was thinking. Call the attorney in the morning and make an appointment. Drive to Atlanta with one of Mama's checks. Tell Mr. Burton Sutton what he was going to be defending against. Tommy smiled. He couldn't wait to see his face.

Old Burton might be from the big city, but he'd learn a thing or two from this country boy.

Soon Tommy's thoughts turned from business to pleasure and there was Rosario's face. Tommy pulled his arms up and tucked his hands under his head. What he could do with her and who would care? Citizen or not, she wasn't nothing but a Wetback putting on airs. Did she have kids? Tommy had to think about that. Nope. He never remembered her mentioning any; never saw her pregnant either. Her husband might squawk a bit if something happened to her, but who was going to listen to him or take him seriously?

Nobody, that's who.

Tommy had been deprived of his previous game and he cursed Don out loud. His itch was getting worse. He couldn't take a road trip right now. That would bring out the dogs in force. The only thing he could do was pluck somebody close by that didn't have much standing and whom he could get to easily. Rosario fit the bill.

Tommy's physical response to his plans for Rosario kept him occupied for a few minutes. Then, tired from his efforts at pleasing himself and his long trying day of dealing with The Law, he went to sleep. His dreams kept him happy and relaxed.

Tuesday AM: They're all alike

When Tommy woke up early the next morning, he made the call and left a voicemail that he was on his way, got the signed check from Mama, and by eleven was in a high-rise office complex in Buckhead. He took his parking ticket and gave it to the secretary for validating. No sir, he wasn't paying Burton Sutton this much money and paying for parking, too. Tommy was escorted into Sutton's office.

"Mr. Higgenbotham. Good to meet you. Have a seat, please." Sutton sat behind his desk. "Coffee? Soda?"

"Nothing right now, thank you." Tommy took in the view of Atlanta from this height. He liked it, but he wouldn't want to live there. "Maybe later."

"Sure. You have the check? Excellent. Please read this contract. If you have any questions, you may ask me or you may take it to another attorney and come back with it later. Your choice?"

"You got a pen?"

"Yes." Sutton handed one across the desk. "I suggest you read it first, Mr. Higgenbotham."

"I trust you. Let's get this show on the road." Tommy signed with a flourish and handed it back to Burton.

"Of course." He punched a button. "Teresa?"

The door opened. "Teresa, please make two copies of this signed contract. Thank you. Here is the check. Deposit it in the working capital account."

"Yes, sir. Anything to drink, sir?"

"Coke. When you come back."

"Yes, sir."

Burton waited until Teresa closed the door behind her before he spoke again. "Mr. Higgenbotham —"

"Tommy will be fine."

"Tommy. From this point I represent your interests in what is obviously a criminal case. I cannot represent them to the best of my ability if I don't know what's going on. Therefore, please be candid. I assure you there is nothing you can say that will shock me."

Tommy smiled. "Sure 'bout that?"

Burton sighed. "Yes, quite sure. We can do this one of two ways. I can ask questions and you can answer, or you can start talking and let me clarify as we go along. I would prefer we stick to what is happening with The Law and why they believe you are a suspect."

Tommy chose to tell his story. Burton leaned back in his chair and listened. He found that simply watching and listening to a client told him more than they ever thought they had revealed. At the end of their narratives, he would know how long the case would take, whether or not it would go to court, if it did go to court what the verdict most likely would be, and how much money he was going to make on it.

Five minutes after Tommy started, he finished. Burton tapped a pen on his teeth then threw it on the desk and sat forward abruptly.

"You're lying to me."

"How dare you —"

"Shut up. You're lying to me. You think I'm an idiot? I told you I had to know the facts, Tommy. The facts."

"I've told you the truth —"

"No, you didn't. Look, I can go with what you told me and you have agreed that if you lie to me, you cannot complain about my performance. Oh, you want to read the contract now? Yeah. See. Already not listening to advice that you paid good money for." Sutton waited for Tommy to digest that before he continued, "I make recommendations to you based upon what you tell me or you can start the story over and tell me what I really need to know. Your choice. Your money."

Sutton sat back and waited. Tommy began again. When he finished an hour later, Sutton sighed. Serial killers are all the same. They want what they want, when they want, and how they want, and they don't care who they hurt to satisfy their want — and they all think they're something special and smarter than anyone else. Sheesh.

But now Sutton had the facts, or at least a better version of Tommy's. He began his advisement.

* * * * *

About the same time Tommy was getting ready to head south, Frank decided he needed a road trip. He needed directions to the Elberton station. He picked up his cell.

"Al. You awake?"

"I am now."

"Guess you're not in front of your computer?"

"Nope. Whatcha need?"

"I'm heading your way and need directions."

"Okay. I'll email them to you in a few. Hey, bring my mail that's on my desk and can you drop by the house and get that mail, too?"

"Sure. Need me to pick up your dry cleaning, too?"

"Thanks for the generous offer, man. But, no laundry."

"You're picking up some bad habits, dude. Sleeping late. Expecting to be waited on hand and foot. I'm gonna have to see these attitude changes are mentioned in your next annual employee assessment. Gonna have to document the slide to mediocrity."

"And you're just now noticing these things? Where you been, man? Besides, I already sent a memo about you; it's tit for tat, brutha."

Frank laughed. "Benny Hill lives!"

Al yawned. "Who?"

"Benny Hill. He perfected the tit for tat joke? English comedian? Dead now? Ah, go back to sleep. Wait. Send directions first."

But Al had already hung up. Ten minutes after mail was retrieved Frank was hitting I-20. A few minutes after that he was crawling on I-285 heading toward Spaghetti Junction. But once he got to I-85, the north-bound trip was against the traffic and he made good time.

The solitary drive gave him time to think. The case against Tommy seemed to be coming together, though they were betting on his arrogance. Frank knew most cases solved usually involved the good guy seeing the opening the bad guy provided because he couldn't keep his mouth shut. It wasn't for nothing criminal attorneys always advised to have them present during an interview. Tommy, if he had gotten such advice, ignored it and walked right on in of his own free will.

Of course, what he didn't say was as important as what he did and told them a lot about what they already knew. Not that they could prove it yet. The county coroner came back with an official cause of death. It had been up close and personal, though Otter never saw it coming. Tommy brought a bottle of whiskey and shared it until Otter was fall-down drunk. With a blood-alcohol level that high, Otter probably fell asleep sitting against a rock soaking up the sun and the booze, though where he was sitting was pure speculation. What did in poor old trusting Otter was good old-fashioned suffocation.

Tommy didn't have to drag Otter's body far to place it in what he thought was a hidden pool of water, though not hidden enough, obviously. Tommy had to know the net was getting tighter. He knew the victim gave her statement and he knew what was in it. His stress level had to be high. Frank wondered when he'd pop.

Frank thought of the long weekend with Carmelita. The sex was great and he couldn't wait for more. He was still surprised at his willingness to take on a woman with children. Granted, the children were almost grown, but there was still at least six years of living with kids. He always avoided that scene and never wanted it. Here he was, almost mid-fifties, a time when most people already have grown children, hell, and grandkids too, and they're ready to enjoy freedom, and he's stepping into being tied down.

Could he put up with the noise? Was he becoming an old man who would scream at kids for ruining his precious quiet? Hell, no. At least he hoped he wasn't. This would be the acid test. What if they wanted or needed Carmelita at the same time as he did? Wasn't it about time he learned to share and sacrifice? Hell, yeah. Was he ready to settle down into the previously despised category of domestic bliss?

Was he now the marrying kind? He smiled. Why yes, yes he was.

Northbound Frank passed southbound Tommy and was soon at his exit. He pulled over for a pit stop and checked his email for final directions. Al did not go back to sleep and they were waiting for him in his inbox. He called Al to let him know his ETA, filled up with gas, got a cup of fresh coffee, and bagged a couple of doughnuts. By the time he got to the car, he remembered he needed to watch his figure because he had a younger woman watching it with him. One doughnut went in the trash.

Eighty minutes later he pulled into the police station and went inside. He was escorted to Carl's office. Don and Al were waiting on him.

"Hey, man." Don stood to shake his hand. "How they hanging?"

"Hanging fine."

"We were worried there for a minute, what with the accident and all. It's tough when the boys take a fall like that. I know."

"Yeah, it was bad. But stretching and warm showers and such as that made recuperation faster, though I'm not completely healed up yet."

"Yeah. Physical therapy always helps." Don, the comedian, winked at Al.

"Doncha know it. Hello, I'm Frank, and you must be Carl, right? What we got? Anything new?"

"Our boy Tommy headed south this morning. Probably getting himself a fancy attorney."

Frank nodded. "My guess is he's gonna retain Burton Sutton, but that's a guess."

"Who's he?" Don asked.

"The attorney of choice for serial killers," Al told them.

"You're kidding, right?"

"Wish I was," Frank continued. "Still, we won't know until we hear something. Tommy could be heading out for another road trip, but would he be that stupid?"

Al laughed. "Hey, never underestimate the arrogant stupidity of a psychopathic criminal Mama's Boy with a burnin' need."

"Okay. Let me see if I understand this." Don held up a finger. "Serial killers have a favorite attorney?" Frank and Al nodded. "Okay. How do these guys find out about him?

Google search? Recommendation from the Association for Serial Killers? Article in the *Serial Killer Times*? Does he give talks at their annual conferences? I mean, how? And does Burton only service serial killers in the Southeast region?"

Frank shook his head. "He travels. But how they come to choose him, I can't say. Been meaning to ask him. Maybe I'll get my chance in the next few days if Tommy's hired him."

"Has he ever turned one of them down? Would he be scared to? Now that's worth knowing." Don walked out of the room still thinking about that.

Carl picked up his keys. "Frank, let's you and me and Al take a drive so you can see where we found Otter."

"Okay, but before we go, I'd like to see the famous interview room."

"Sure thing. Then we'll get lunch and go to the quarry."

"Sounds like a plan. All I had for breakfast was a doughnut."

"One? Watching that figure now, are ya?" Al smiled.

"Somebody's got to."

"Somebody is."

Frank smiled. "Smartass."

Tuesday PM: A high-priced lawyer makes a list of don'ts

By the time Frank was at the top of the quarry looking down at the crime scene, Tommy was on his way home after receiving his first dose of advisement from Burton Sutton. It was full of don'ts.

Don't get a speeding ticket.

Don't drive erratically, drunk or sober.

Don't go on any road trips.

Don't miss work.

Don't talk to the cops without your attorney present.

Don't kill anybody else.

Okay. Burton hadn't actually said that last one, but he may as well have. He said not to have anything to do with women in any way, shape, or form. Didn't he know how bad his itch was? Didn't he care?

Tommy missed Otter more than he had ever missed anybody, including Daddy. He could talk over these things with his best buddy. Maybe he had been a little bit premature in silencing Otter, but what was done was done and Tommy would have to live with it. Still, what would Otter do? Several times Otter took trips without Tommy. Tommy was sure he had some fun without him, though Otter never told him outright. Maybe Otter had itches he couldn't control, too. Itches Tommy didn't have. Tommy had never scratched his itch without Otter there because he had needed his friend beside him. They were a team and wasn't that what friends were for? Otter had proved he could act alone. But could Tommy? He would soon find out if he was capable of scratching his itch by himself.

Tommy wondered when Otter's funeral would be. He knew they hadn't released the body to his sister for burial. Had they figured out how he died? Tommy thought he had been very kind to kill Otter the way he did. Get him very drunk so his mind was clouded and his body so weak he couldn't fight back too much and hurt himself while he was forced to stop breathing.

It had only taken a minute for Otter to loosen his grip on Tommy's arms, another minute before he stopped trying to buck under Tommy. Another minute until all twitching was over. And another two minutes to confirm he wasn't faking.

That was the longest five minutes of Tommy's life, and he had cried when it was over. Yes, he, Tommy, shed tears for his friend, his friend who he could have killed painfully but didn't. If Otter was here, he would thank him for being kind as to do this thing painlessly, saving him from living in a tiny prison cell for the rest of his life.

It took Tommy all of twenty minutes for his inner reverie to conclude. He turned on the radio and cranked up the volume. Maybe he would go out and do some karaoke tonight. Yeah, that's what he'd do. Old Burton didn't say anything about singing in public. Maybe performing in front of a crowd would scratch his growing itch. He practiced singing all the way home.

Tuesday PM: Al grows a pair

"Thanks for bringing my mail." Al sat alone in an interview room with Frank, busily ripping into envelopes.

"Give me a few minutes and I'll have this finished."

"Sure. Take your time. Don't want to leave now anyway. Get stuck in traffic."

Don knocked on the door and stuck his head in. "Frank, you want to go out to eat tonight before you leave?"

"Sure."

"Okay." Don shut the door.

"Here, you need to see this, too." Al handed over a piece of paper.

Frank read it. "Yeah. Okay. I'll handle this tomorrow."

"So…" Al opened another envelope.

"So, what?"

"So what's up with Carmelita? Have a nice weekend?"

"Yeah. Very nice weekend. Very nice long weekend. Ended up she could stay another couple of days."

"Nice."

"She's gonna divorce the sumbitch and I'm gonna marry her."

Al opened another envelope and nodded. "I knew it was serious."

"Oh, yeah? How'd you know?"

"Because you've never bought clothes that look GQ and never cared how many doughnuts you scarf. Until now."

"That obvious, huh?"

"To me? Yeah. To you? Not so much. I bet you're having second thoughts, aren't you? Wishing you hadn't met her? Am I right or am I right?"

"You're wrong. No second thoughts."

When Al looked up from his shrinking pile of letters, he saw a happy man.

"What's up with you and LaVonne? She mad you've been out of town?"

"Yeah. Right. LaVonne."

"Trouble in Paradise Kitchen?"

"The job is hard enough without having a woman sniping atcha about it."

"Ten-four."

"The last time we talked, she was sniping. And you know what? I realized right then and there what it is about all my past relationships that's drove me crazy. I don't like being fussed at for catching the bad guys."

"Yeah. And…"

"I've kept my mouth shut and walked away the other times. And this time, I said nope. She's a good woman, but she needs to understand some things upfront. So I told her."

"What'd you tell her?"

"I said, 'LaVonne, baby, honey, I really like you a lot and I would like to continue to see you. But baby, you gotta stop that fussing and sniping and all that negativity. I can't handle it. I won't handle it. I will not live like that. Baby, honey, when you are ready to stop trying to run this show'" — Al sat up straight and pointed to himself — "'then you give me a call, little girl. Ball's in your court.' Yessir, that's what I told her."

"Hey, sounds like you grew a big ol' pair this past week. She call back?"

Al deflated. "No."

Frank sighed. "Women."

"God help us." Al slit another envelope.

Wednesday AM: An employee evaluation at the cotton mill

While Tommy sang karaoke, Frank leisurely drove the eighty five miles home. The night was cool enough; he turned off the air conditioning and radio, and rolled down the windows. He enjoyed the sound of the tires on the road from the passing cars and the rumble of the engines from the big rigs with their sharp rattles of jake brakes. He felt the wind beating him up and breathed deeply of the scents that only existed at night. He could almost feel himself back on the chopper, weapon in hand, getting last-minute instructions for the mission he and the soldiers beside him were on their way to.

And he thought of that first night with Carmelita, and the second and the third nights as well as the mornings and the afternoons. She was a soldier fighting a war of her own, her weapons wit and grit, her first critical mission a success. She was doing what all true soldiers do: fighting not for the hatred of what was in front, but for the love of what was behind. In this case, her children.

Her children, soon his by proxy. Frank a stepfather. He laughed out loud at the thought and poured on the gas. He needed to get some sleep.

* * * * *

Karaoke Tommy put on a show for the patrons of Willie's Cantina over the county line. Had there been a contest, he would have won. But there wasn't and the only people who didn't like that he was outperforming them were the six people who came out regularly, sat together, and who each sang their own song set each time, dressed in what they thought was Country Star attire, of course. The rest of the crowd screamed for more and Tommy ate it up.

The more he drank the better he got, and he shut the place down. A couple of girls tried to hit on him and he enjoyed flirting a bit, but even with the Patrón in him, he didn't forget Sutton's advice: Stay away from the women. He got in his car and drove home.

Being good was hard work. And hard work awaited him in the morning. He had already missed a few days at the mill, but Sutton's advice was clear: Show up for work. When he slapped the alarm in the morning, though, his itch was back in full force. He dressed then went down the stairs into the kitchen — and there she was. Rosario.

"Good morning, Mr. Tommy. Coffee?"

"Yes." Tommy lowered himself to a seat at the table. She placed the coffee in front of him along with the cream and sugar and a spoon. Tommy did not say thank you. He stared at Rosario while Sutton's advice ground on and on in his brain: Stay away from the women.

Rosario wouldn't stop flaunting that body at him and he had to get out of there before he lost control. Tommy slammed the coffee cup on the table, stomped out the door, and left for work. He didn't say goodbye.

He may have been the crown prince of the county, and he may have job security, but that didn't mean people at work were happy to see him. Since what he was given to do he hadn't been doing and now other people were behind, it was a sure bet he had not endeared himself to his co-workers. Barely mumbled hellos were all he received when he arrived.

He made his second cup of coffee that morning, grabbed a danish, stomped down the hall, slammed his office door, slammed his cup and food on the desktop, threw himself in his seat — and stewed. He didn't see the papers piled on his desk. He stared at the door, thinking of how he could scratch his ever-growing itch, feed his need, and — knock!

He focused on the door. "Come in."

"Tommy. Good to see you back." It was Doug. President. Head honcho. Big muckety-muck. Head Shit. "Got a minute?"

"Sure." Tommy smiled, barely.

Doug closed the door and sat across from Tommy. "I'm gonna come right to the point. I'm having this conversation with you privately at this point, but will call Mama if I need to. You understand?"

Tommy stared.

"I'm gonna take that as a yes. I know your family owns this business and I know you are assured a job here. But it is a job. It does have duties. When you don't perform those duties..." Doug pointed at the stack on Tommy's desk. "...people can't do their jobs and the whole thing starts grinding to a halt. How do you want to handle this?"

Tommy stared.

"I'm gonna take that as my cue to provide a choice of action plans for you. One: Show up and do the work. Two: Let me mail a check to you and don't show up again. You have a preference?"

Tommy stared. Oh, yeah. He had a preference. But Sutton's voice came through the fog of hate: Don't kill anybody else. That's not exactly what he said, but his advice was understood. Tommy stood up, walked ahead of Doug, opened the door, and left.

"I guess that would be Action Plan Twooooo." Doug sighed in relief, picked up the stack of papers, and left to inform Tommy's soon-to-be-relieved co-workers of their vice president's exit strategy.

Tommy was finding it awfully hard to be good.

Wednesday, Lunch: Justice is served

Two hours after Tommy walked out of work, Lee, Al, and Don heard Carl even though his office door was closed.

"What the hell?" Lee said as he saw Carl waving at them with one hand and gripping the phone with the other.

"We're on our way. Twenty minutes!" He slammed the phone down. "You are not gonna believe this."

Don put his hands together in prayer and looked heavenward. "Please tell me somebody saved the taxpayers a lot of money."

"They did. Tommy's dead. Let's go."

"What the fuck!" Lee said.

Don grinned from ear to ear. "Hey, we gonna bring Wanda? Can we bring Wanda? Wanda needs to see this. You want me to get Wanda?"

Carl waved at him. "Yeah, yeah. Bring Wanda. We'll meet you there." Al, Carl, and Lee headed out the door. Don peeled off formation and headed to Wanda's office. "Wanna, Reekie gots beeg supreyes for ewe."

"What?"

"I'm about to make your day, baby. Come on. I'll tell you on the way."

"But I got —"

"Carl said for you to come. We'll take your car and meet them there."

She followed him out the door. "Meet them where?"

"Mama's house."

Wanda looked at Don and she knew. Her grin matched his. She couldn't get to her car fast enough.

Frank answered his phone. "Yep."

"Guess what?"

"Al, don't make me guess."

"The second half of our favorite serial killer team is dead. You wanna come on back up?"

"On my way."

"I'll text directions to the body."

"Ten-four." Frank was already out the door.

EMTs were already on the scene when Carl, Lee, and Al arrived. Wanda and Don followed one minute behind them.

Carl asked, "What's going on?"

"Victim One: D.R.T. Victim Two: Alive but covered in blood, not sure if it's only Victim One's or hers, too. Perp: Making hot tea for Victim Two."

The five new arrivals walked into the kitchen.

"Yep. There's Tommy. Dead Right There." Don smiled grimly at the hole through Tommy's head, or rather what was left of it. He looked at Wanda. This wasn't her first dead body but it was her first with spilled blood and splattered brains. Don noticed she was pale. "You gonna be sick?"

Wanda shook her head. "Nope." Her face may have been pale, but her eyes were taking in all the details; she learned fast.

A Latina sat in a chair, EMTs checking her for wounds. Mama was at the stove, waiting for water to boil, putting tea bags in cups. Carl walked over to her, turned off the stove, gently took her by the hand, and led her to the front porch swing. Wanda went with him and the three of them sat in the swing. Wanda patted one of Mama's hands and Carl held the other, or rather, Mama gripped his tightly.

Mama pushed the swing lightly and together they moved back and forth. She looked out at the neighborhood. Finally she spoke. "Such a nice day, isn't it, Carl?"

"Yes, ma'am, it is."

She was quiet again for a minute. Then she asked, "Has anyone called Trini?"

"Who's Trini, ma'am?"

"Rosario's husband. He should be called. I should call him. He needs to —"

"The EMTs will make the call for you, ma'am."

"Yes. Of course." Mama kept staring.

Carl and Wanda felt her body relax. Looking up at Carl, she smiled sadly, "Good help is so very hard to find."

"I know, ma'am. You sit here with Wanda and relax, okay? Don't you never your mind about the trouble."

"Yes. Thank you."

Carl went inside. He sent out an EMT to check on Mama, then turned to the scene.

Lee stepped to the other side of the kitchen with Carl, Don, and Al and quietly filled them in. "Victim Two is Rosario. She's been with Mrs. Higgenbotham for over ten years. Tommy left early, but was back in a couple of hours. She said he left in a weird mood, and came back in a foul one. She was alone in the kitchen and didn't know where her employer was when Tommy came in."

He checked his notes before continuing.

"She said he started talking to her, trying to make conversation, but he was having a real hard time of it. She noticed his eyes kept looking her over and she didn't like it. She went to the fridge to get something out and that's when he came up behind her and put his arms around her in a hug and said something he must have thought would turn her on. She stood still. Turned her head back toward him and asked him what he was doing. She said he started feeling her up and she slapped his hands away and attempted to move out of his reach. He took exception to that and slapped her across the face, grabbed at her, ripping her shirt."

The men turned to see Rosario, shivering, encircled by EMTs, ripped blouse now covered with a blanket.

"She said the slap knocked her to where she couldn't see for a few seconds, but she was slapping at his hands and face. He escalated the attack, ripping at her clothes as she was knocked to the floor. She was screaming and hitting him and the next thing she knew, Mrs. H. came running in with a pistol. When she saw it was Tommy attacking her, she told him to stop right that instant. Rosario said it was like he didn't even hear her.

"Mrs. H. yelled at him one more time to stop. He didn't. She fired a warning shot over his head. That got his attention but made him madder. He got up and came at Mama and she fired again."

"Okay. Has anybody called her husband yet?" Carl asked, looking at the EMTs.

"No."

Al said, "You got his number yet? Ma'am. Give me her husband's number. I'll call him."

"Any of that blood hers?"

"Nope. She was still on the floor. The shot knocked him back and he landed on her, so that's the blood on her."

"Good. Okay. Get this documented. Get her out of here."

"Coroner's on his way, too."

They listened to Al call Trini and tell him what happened. He hung up. "Her husband will be here in about twenty minutes. He'll bring her some clean clothes."

"I'll let them know outside he's on his way. Bring her," Carl told Lee, nodding at Rosario, "to the front porch now."

Lee walked over to Rosario. "You okay to walk, ma'am?" At her nod, Lee helped her stand and supported her while he took her to the front porch. He sat her on the swing next to Mama.

Mama held her hand. "I am so sorry, Rosario. I am so sorry."

"It's okay, Mrs. H. It's okay. Shhhh…"

"I never suspected Tommy could… could…"

She began crying.

"I know, Mrs. H., I know. Shhhh…"

Week
Thirteen

Wednesday A.M.: Loose ends

One week later, Al fell into a chair in Frank's office.

"Guess what?" Al smiled.

Frank didn't look up from his screen. "Don't make me. I done told you this."

"Yeah. I know. But, guess what?"

"Oh, for crying out loud." Frank thought a moment. "LaVonne called?"

"Now why'd you gotta go and bring that up? I was feeling good. Guess again."

"I don't have time for this, Al. Speak?"

"Okay. Looks like we may have some good possibilities of solving a few murders and disappearances along the Appalachian Trail and in three other states so far."

"Great. How?"

"Gonna love it. Otter liked to keep a diary and souvenirs. So, his sister was cleaning out his room and found the stash, started reading, and knew what she had. Called Carl."

"Wow. You talk to Carl yet about Tommy's mother?"

"Yeah. The deposit Tommy gave Burton Sutton will go toward Mama's defense. The way this is going, she should get a refund. I mean, who's gonna put her in prison?"

"Right. She did the world a favor, not to mention the taxpayers. Got to be tough though, killing her only child."

"It's been rough. Carl sends Wanda 'round each day to check on her until this settles down."

"Did the victim quit working for her?"

"No. She's staying. Seems she agrees with Mama."

"How's that?"

"Mama said 'good help is hard to find'. Seems the lady thinks good employers are hard to find, too."

"Ain't that the truth. Have you heard from Rez or Don about the girl in Jackson?"

Al slapped his forehead. "Oh, yeah. I wanted to tell you about that. Her dad still doesn't know all the details about what happened. He can guess. And, honestly, I don't think I would wanna know all that about my daughter's attack either. But the girl told her mom. The mom called Rez and met with him one day to find out what they could do to help her when she has another meltdown. He said the mom is a lot stronger than he would have thought. And she's realistic, too. The dad is kinda like *that's my baby girl* and he's having a hard time dealing with his emotions. So Rez had a good talk with Mom. Mom'll make sure she gets what she needs. The girl called Rez and told her that some girls at school have come up to her and told her about getting raped by their mothers' boyfriends and others, too. She didn't know what to do; now she gives them Rez's number."

"Geez. Man. That's great." Frank finished paperwork. "You wanna go to lunch with me and Carmelita today."

"Uh, no. I got plans."

"Plans? Want me to guess at them?"

As he got up, Al said, "No."

Frank laughed, checked his watch. "I got to go. Long drive." It took him forty minutes to get to her. She was just pulling up, and smiled and waved.

"Hey, baby." Frank hugged her.

"Hey to you, too." She put her arm around his waist and they walked in together.

The waitress took their drink order and left menus on the table. "I've got some news for ya."

Carmelita looked up from her menu. "Yeah? What?"

"The Snuff Tape Case is officially over."

She slowly sat back, menu forgotten. "You found him?"

"Them, actually. Two. Serial killer team. Both dead. One killed the other and then he was killed by his mother."

"What? Are you kiddin' me?"

"Can you believe it? We're almost positive the body that washed up when a dam broke in Butts County is the same one on the recording you found."

"How did the snuff tape get into the store?"

"We never did get to ask, so we're not sure. We know it wasn't the guy whose fingerprint was on it. He just happened to know them. Randomly touched the packaging for some reason or another."

"Lucky break. What's your idea about how the taping might have happened?"

Frank thought for a second and said, "I think it was Otter who did it without Tommy knowing. Serial killer teams are a team because there is something each of them bring to the table and when those things get mixed together they're like diesel fuel and fertilizer. By themselves each can hurt you somewhat, but when combined they will explode exponentially larger than the sum of their parts.

"Tommy may have seemed liked the leader, but it was Otter who was the driving force. The thing about it is that Otter, for all he was evil, had a good heart. He really didn't want to be doing this and, my opinion only of course because I have no proof, I think he wanted them to get caught. If it hadn't been for Boggle's fingerprint, they wouldn't have been caught so soon."

He continued, "Of course, you know, the fingerprint would never have been found without your quick thinking. You kept all the pieces of the evidence together and brought them to us."

Carmelita watched Frank, remembering the day she first heard the recording of torture and murder, neither of them knowing how many lives would be affected. "If I had not gone shopping that day. If I had not wanted an audiobook. If I had taken it to the police station. If you —"

"Hadn't been in the office or answered the phone —"

She smiled. "Yeah. If, if, if."

Carmelita stopped smiling. "I'm glad the bad guys are dead. I'm sorry the other woman died. And I'm sorry my marriage turned out like it did. But, Frank, I'm happy because now I can live."

She nodded her head as if to cement the thought, picked up her menu, and began to read again.

Frank watched her slowly reading and turning the pages. He saw the excitement in her eyes — eyes no longer as sad as the day he met her.

"Carmelita?"

"Yes?" She didn't look up.

"Carmelita."

She heard the tone of his voice change and looked up at him. "Are you okay?"

He nodded. She waited for him to speak. "You will marry me, right? You're not gonna change your mind?"

"Yes, baby, I will marry you. No, baby, I'm not gonna change my mind." She smiled at him. "Are you worried? Oh. That's so sweet."

She kicked off a shoe and put her foot in his lap. Frank reached down and caressed her foot. He smiled.

Week
Sixteen

Wednesday PM:
A body at Six Flags

Three weeks after the end of the Case of the Snuff Tape Killers, the phone rang in Al's office. He listened for a few minutes. Asked a couple of questions. Took notes. He pressed the button disconnecting the call and punched another. Frank's phone rang.

Al said, "Our presence has been requested."

"K. When?"

"Now. I'll drive."

"K. Where?"

"Six Flags over Georgia."

"Inside the park?"

"Yep."

"What we got?"

"Dead body. Female."

"Why do they want us?"

"They said we would have to see it to believe it."

"She fall off the Superman ride or something?"

"They wouldn't say. Just that she was dead and we would have to see it."

"K." But Al didn't hear Frank because Al had hung up.

It took them an hour and a half to get to the park. The evening's rush hour traffic going out I-20 West was never easy. The setting sun boring into drivers' eyes only made it worse. Al showed his badge to the parking attendant, who had been advised more Law was on its way. They drove to the back gate, parked, walked to the back entrance and showed their badges for the second time. They were waved through.

They heard a young woman ask, "GBI?"

A young executive type with a two-way radio was fast bearing down on them. They nodded. She said into the mouthpiece, "They're here. On our way." Then to Frank and Al she said, "Follow me."

She walked quickly. "Must be bad," Al said.

"Usually is when we're called."

The young woman stopped and waited for them to catch up to her. She pointed to what they thought was a bush but was actually a well-concealed path park personnel used to get to the business end of the rides' machinery. When they stepped through, a paved path led them to the activity. No wonder the park had not been closed. The public couldn't see this at all; the trees hid the view from above.

Local LEOs shook hands with them silently then simply stepped back so Frank and Al could get their first view.

Sitting on the ground against a tree was a woman. Not a particularly interesting woman in the looks department. She had once been gorgeous but a little too much cosmetic surgery turned her features to plastic. Now those features were gnawed by rats and other night creatures. She had been there for less than twenty four hours because park records showed the last time personnel had been back there.

"What the hell?" Al said. He whistled low.

Frank said, "Damn."

The local detective said, "Exactly."

Frank said, "You don't understand. We just finished with a case that…Al, what are the odds?"

Al shook his head and shrugged his shoulders.

No, the woman against the tree wasn't that interesting. But what was written in red lipstick across her face was very interesting. It said *Only a bitch.*

The Case of the Snuff Tape Killers

[the end]

Provided the handwriting analysis report language based on the characters is **Josh Batchelder**.

Certified Graphoanalyst® and member of International Graphoanalysis Society (IGAS); Southeastern Handwriting Analysts (SEHA); Southern Handwriting Analysts (SCIGAS); American Handwriting Analysis Foundation/American Association of Handwriting Analysts (AHAF/AAHA). Author of over ten books, guest lecturer, Harvard University AB graduate, and U.S. Air Force Lt. Colonel, retired. 5000+ flying hours including worldwide missions; and chief wing navigator. Civil Air Patrol, PDK SR SQDN; instrument rated pilot.

joshbatchelder.com

FINAL THOUGHTS

I started this story just as I was getting ready to divorce my husband...and yes, he needed divorcing. To maintain my sanity during those last few dark days I had started a file on my laptop computer labeled "Vignettes". This story was originally entitled "Bitch 3" because I had three stories that featured the use of the word bitch: one for a dog (wonderful love story and a true one, too), one for the book you just read, and one for a private investigator overhearing a neighbor call his wife the name and she ends up dead.

I worked on this story steadily until life took me on various twists and turns and I didn't quite finish it. But Smith and Jones kept hollering at me, "When are you going to get us off the computer and onto readers' shelves, huh?"

Finally, after reworking it several times and editing it over and over for plot continuity, story arcs, and taking out anything in there that smacked of my ex, I got it done.

Well, some more of life smacked me across the face and other twists and turns arose, but here I am in 2021 finally getting the book published, and the next one in this series almost done, and a third planned.

Therefore, I would like to thank Smith and Jones for their dogged insistence to let them live in the real world. Also, I would like to thank my writing critique group who, upon reading "Bitch 3", wanted to know the rest of the story and encouraged me to tell it. They are — among others later who were vastly encouraging in very practical ways — in no particular order:

- Chuck Clark (Atlanta architect)
- Charles Olaf Johnson (now deceased) author of *Rainbow in a Lemon Fizz Tin"*, the most brilliant political-religious satire I've ever read
- Jedwin Smith (JedwinSmith.com) retired journalist and author of several books including *Our Brother's Keeper* and the leader of the group I named The Jedwinistas
- Jim Butorac
- Jennie Helderman
- Carolyn Graham
- Ron Aiken
- Fred Whitson
- Greta Reed
- Brad Cameron
- Cathy McCabe
- Candis Stephens
- and others too numerous to name

Thanks also to Eagle Eye Book Store in Decatur, Georgia. The owner, Doug Robinson, very much supports authors and we thank him. I have worked his store into this novel; maybe you caught that? Bob, here's a shoutout to you.

I have learned from every single author I've ever read, well-known or not. Often what I've learned is how to improve. Other times it is what not to do.

My children get an honorable mention for staying out of their mother's way. My son finds it remarkable that his mother has bloomed. My daughter merely tolerates her mother's "interests"…yes, the quote marks are ironic. In any case, I am a mystery to both of them and happy to be so.

Under my real name — Angela K. Durden — I've written other books, written many songs, recorded an album, run a songwriters club in Atlanta, have been censored by Big Tech for daring to come up with a solution to a problem, sing at Jazz jams, put on shows, and have started another imprint where I am now publishing OPB, other people's books.

But I can tell you that I could not have done all this without Tom Whitfield, my editor, who has questioned everything, demanded rewrites, stoically pushed me to the nth degree until I was sitting at the computer with him next to me as I screamed and cried in fury, in sadness, in despair, and in hope. Tom and Jedwin worked together in the newspaper game for over 30 years. It was through Jedwin I was introduced to Tom.

I have learned a massive amount from Tom and have been benefited (or benefitted, for those who are freaking out at the sing t) from our collaboration as he now is Editor in Chief at my publishing company.

Thank you for reading. Thank you for recommending this and other books of mine to your friends. Word of mouth is the best advertising ever.

OTHER BOOKS BY Durden Kell
Whitfield, Nebraska
A Benjamin Turner Novel
(2015)

Death In E minor 9[mm]
(2020)

Death on the Downbeat
(2021)

BOOKS BY Angela K. Durden
Eloise Forgets How to Laugh
(2004)

A Mike and His Grandpa Story: Series
Heroes Need Practice, Too!
(2006, hardback)
(2012, paperback)

A Mike and His Grandpa Story:
The Balloon That Would Not Pop!
(2012)

Opportunity Meets Motivation:
Lessons From Four Women Who Built
Passion Into Their Lives and Careers
(2010, out of print)

Men! K.I.S.S. Your Resume and Say Hello to a Better Job
(2013, Audible.com)

Men! K.I.S.S. Your Resume and Say Hello to a Better Job
(2013)

9 Stupid Things People Do to Mess Up Their Resumes
(2000, out of print)

First Time For Everything (2018)

Do Not Mistake This Smile (2018)
Music Business Survival Manual (2018)

Navigating the New Music Business as a DIY and Indie (2015)

Conversations in Hyperreality —
and Other Thoughts Umberto Eco and
Dave Barry Never Had
(2019)

Dancing at the Waffle House (2018)

Nagging Women and Clueless Men (2017)

From Blue Room Books
blueroombooks.com | blueroombooks@outlook.com

Jedwin Smith
I AM ISRAEL: Lions and Lambs of the Land
(2018)

A Marine and a Journalist Walk Into a Bar
(2021)

Alan Ray White
Rock Around The Block
(2019)

1960s Pop Music Legend Len Barry
Prose and Cons

Mike Shaw
The Musician

W.F. Whitson
The Librarian: Intrigue at RAF Greenham

Coming in 2022

Joey Huffman
East to the Sun:
Memories From the Life of an Accidental Rock Star